A Maiden's Voyage

Rosie Goodwin is the *Sunday Times* bestselling author of over thirty novels. She is the first author in the world to be allowed to follow three of Catherine Cookson's trilogies with her own sequels. Having worked in the social services sector for many years, then fostered a number of children, she is now a full-time novelist. Rosie lives in Nuneaton, the setting for many of her books, with her husband and their beloved dogs.

🐦@RosieGoodwin
f/RosieGoodwinAuthor

Rosie
GOODWIN
A Maiden's Voyage

ZAFFRE

MIX
Paper from
responsible sources
FSC® C018072

Zaffre is an imprint of Bonnier Books UK
www.bonnierbooks.co.uk

This book is in loving memory of
Philip Howells 20th January 1933 – 17th July 2018
A dear uncle and a very brave man.
Rest in peace.

Thursday's child has far to go

Prologue

'Oh, *do* hurry up. Father will be home soon. He took his dinner suit to the office with him so he could get changed there and you know he'll be impatient to be off.'

'Yes, miss.' Eighteen-year-old Flora was suddenly all fingers and thumbs as she tried to pile her young mistress's hair on top of her head in loose curls, but the faster she tried to do it the more the curls escaped. Constance's – or Connie as she preferred to be known – wild tresses seemed to have developed a life of their own. Connie had only recently adopted this style, saying that it was more sophisticated and made her look older but Flora hadn't mastered the art of getting it quite right yet. 'It's just that you have so much hair,' she muttered through a mouthful of pins.

Connie grinned at her in the mirror of her dressing table. 'You're a fine one to talk,' she said, and she was right, for Flora's hair was just as long and thick as her own although not quite so curly. In fact, the girls were very similar in looks in many ways. They were both of much the same height and build with long dark hair, but where Connie had deep-blue eyes, Flora's were a warm brown colour. They were very close in age too. Connie had just celebrated her eighteenth birthday, while Flora would be nineteen the following March. Connie supposed that was why she had managed

1

to persuade her father to let Flora be promoted from general maid to her own personal maid, and she had never regretted it. It was nice to have someone her own age to help with her dressing and act as her companion. Since Flora had taken on the role, it had afforded Connie a lot more freedom. Her father didn't mind her going out so much if Flora escorted her, whereas before he had always worried if she were to go out on her own.

'There! I think that's it,' Flora breathed suddenly as she jammed yet another hair clip into the mass of springy curls. 'What do you think, miss?'

'Hmm . . .' Connie turned her head this way and that then smiled. 'I suppose that will do nicely. I think you're getting the hang of it. But come along. I need to get dressed.'

She rose from the dressing table and moved across to the armoire that stood against the far wall of her bedroom, where the gown she'd had specially made for the occasion was hanging. She fingered the smooth, cream silk and asked, 'Do you think Father will approve?'

'I don't see 'ow he couldn't, miss,' Flora said enviously.

'*How* he couldn't, not *'ow*,' Connie absently corrected her and Flora sighed. Connie had been giving her elocution lessons ever since the day she had appointed her as her maid but she still tended to forget herself from time to time.

While Connie stood in front of the mirror, Flora began the difficult job of lacing up her corset.

'Pull it *tighter*,' Connie instructed. 'I want my waist to look *really* tiny.'

'If I pull it any tighter you won't be able to breathe,' Flora pointed out.

Connie supposed she was right, so she stood quietly while Flora lowered the gown over her head, careful not to mess her hair, and fastened the buttons at the back. Finally, Flora helped her slip her feet into dainty satin shoes. It was to be Connie's first trip to the

2

opera with her father and she had gone to endless trouble to make sure that her outfit was just right, although Flora was a little concerned how the shoes would fare outside. It had been snowing steadily all day, but then she supposed that Connie couldn't wear boots beneath such an elegant gown and she did only have to go down the steps and straight into her father's gleaming new Rolls-Royce after all.

At last the girl was ready and turning to Flora in a swish of silken skirts she asked, 'So how do I look?'

'*Beautiful*,' Flora answered truthfully, wondering what Connie's father would think of the plunging neckline on her dress. She did indeed look very grown-up.

'Right, then I'll go downstairs and wait for Father.' Connie snatched up a dainty satin evening purse and a fur-lined cape and headed for the door where she paused to say, 'Do take the night off if you want to, Flora. You've more than enough time to go and see your family if you don't mind braving the weather. I doubt we'll be back before eleven o'clock at the earliest.'

'Thank you, miss.' Flora bobbed her knee and set about tidying the room. There were clothes and underwear strewn about all over the place but she was used to it by now. Connie liked to be waited on and was not the tidiest of people.

Downstairs she heard the general maid opening the front door and she rightly guessed that it was Mr Ogilvie, Connie's father, returning home after a day at his office. He owned a number of warehouses in Whitechapel as well as a fleet of boats that imported goods from abroad and it was rumoured that he was one of the richest men in London. Flora had never had any reason to doubt it, for his town house was situated in one of the richest areas of Mayfair and Connie had had every advantage a young woman could possibly have – private tutors, a nanny and beautiful clothes. She had never known what it was like to be cold and hungry as Flora had, but for all that she didn't envy her.

3

Her family lived in a poor part of Whitechapel and her father was reliant on getting work daily on the docks unloading the boats that came in. If he didn't get work one day they didn't eat, it was as simple as that, yet for all that they were happy, unlike Connie who, Flora had realised within a very short time of working there, was desperately lonely. The girl's mother had died while she was still very young, but before she'd died, she had coldly informed the child that she was adopted and that she had never really wanted her. Poor Connie had been heartbroken and had never really recovered from these cruel words. Thankfully, though, her father doted on her and spoiled her shamelessly, but he had a busy job so after her adoptive mother's death Connie had been left in the care of a number of tutors and nannies who came and went.

Flora hurriedly finished tidying the room. It wasn't often she was given some unexpected time off and she intended to make the most of the next few hours. Once everything was neatly put away she threw some coal onto the fire so that the room would still be warm when Connie returned then hurried away to fetch her hat and coat. Much to her delight, she now slept in the room next to Connie's, which was not only much nicer but was also warmer than the chilly room she had slept in up in the servants' quarters in the attic when she had first started there.

In no time at all she was wrapped up warmly and once down in the hall she smiled at Gertie, the little general maid who was flitting in and out of the dining room laying the table in readiness for Connie and her father's breakfast the next morning.

'Off out, are you?' Gertie raised an eyebrow.

'Yes, Miss Connie said I could 'ave . . . sorry, *have* a few hours off seeing as she was going out.'

Gertie shuddered. 'Well, ravver you than me. It's enuff to freeze the 'airs off a brass monkey out there.'

Flora laughed as she stepped out into the snow, then gasped as the cold almost took her breath away. Gertie was right but there

4

was no way she was going to waste the chance of a few precious hours at home. Hopefully she would be able to take a tram most of the way there if she got her skates on. That's if the snow hadn't stopped them running!

Thankfully, as yet it hadn't and half an hour later she stepped off the tram close to the workhouse in Whitechapel. Averting her eyes from the grim building, she made for the backstreets that would lead to Pleasant Row where her family lived. The name always made her smile for the rows of tiny, damp, soot-blackened terraced houses were anything but pleasant. They were all exactly the same with front doors that opened directly on to the street. In the winter the houses were bitterly cold and in the summer stiflingly hot. Tonight black icicles hung from the window frames and the eaves.

Even so it was the only place she had ever called home and soon she walked into the tiny kitchen. Flora's eyes swept around the familiar room. Gas mantles sputtered on the walls and an oil lamp spread a warm glow across the table that stood in the centre of the room. On the wall next to the table stood an old oak dresser displaying her mother's mismatched but much-loved china, and brightly coloured rugs, which her mother had spent countless hours making, were scattered across the floor.

Her mother, Emily, turned from the stove where she was stirring a pot of stew for the family, and swiped a lock of hair from her eyes, looking surprised but pleased to see her. 'What are you doing here, luvvie?' Then the smile faded as she whispered fearfully, 'You ain't got the sack 'ave you?' She'd come to rely on the wages that Flora gave her each month.

Flora giggled as she removed her bonnet and crossed to warm her hands by the fire. 'No, Ma, I haven't got the sack. Connie has gone to the opera with her father tonight so she gave me a few hours off and I thought I'd pop home to see you all.'

'Hmm, well lovely as it is to see you I reckon you'd have been better stayin' in the warm.' Emily glanced towards the window, through which she could see the snow still steadily falling, and shuddered. 'But now you are 'ere pull up a chair an' come an' 'ave somethin' to eat.'

Flora shook her head as she bent to plant a kiss on Timmy's head. At five years old he was the baby of the family and Flora adored him.

'Thanks, but I've already eaten,' she assured her mother. She knew that any stew that was left over from this evening would have more vegetables added to it and be served up again the next day and she didn't want to deprive them of it.

Emily smiled. 'Eeh, you don't 'alf talk posh now since you went to work for that young lady,' she commented proudly.

'I try to.' Then glancing about, Flora asked, 'Where's Dad?'

'Still at work unloadin' a big cargo ship that docked this morning.' As Emily served herself a small portion of stew and carried it to the table, Flora noticed how tired she looked. People often told her that she looked just like her mother had at her age but worry and overwork had prematurely aged her and now she looked like a woman in her fifties rather than one who was only in her early forties. There were streaks of grey in her hair and her face was lined, but for all that she was still attractive and Flora loved her unreservedly. Shortly after, Katie, Flora's sixteen-year-old sister, breezed in having just finished her shift in the match factory, she was followed not long after by her brother, Ben, who was seventeen and working with his father on the docks, then came Eunice, the bookworm of the family, who was fifteen and had found herself a job in the city in a small bookshop, which she loved, and finally there was little Timmy. There had been three more children but they had all died in the flu epidemic that had swept through the city a few years ago. Looking back, Flora realised that her mother had never really got over losing them but she had struggled gamely on as most women from hereabouts had to.

'So 'ow come you didn't go to see your young man, then?' Emily asked with a twinkle in her eye.

Flora blushed. 'If you're talking about Jamie, I didn't know that I was going to get any time off until the last minute so there was no time to make arrangements with him.'

She and Jamie had met back in the summer after he'd come to London from Nuneaton, a small market town in the Midlands, to find work. They had hit it off straight away and had been seeing each other every Sunday afternoon ever since. Jamie was such a lovely person and Flora knew that she would only have to say the word and she could be planning her wedding but she wasn't sure she was ready to settle down just yet. Because much as she had come to love him, there was no hurry. She and Jamie had their whole lives ahead of them so why should they rush? She didn't want to be like the other girls from these parts who ended up marrying when they were too young, having a baby every year and becoming old before their time. Oh no! Flora had ambitions. Wasn't she already a lady's maid?

But she wasn't going to tell her mother that, so instead she continued teasingly, 'Why, would you rather I'd have gone to see him than come here to see you?'

'O' course I wouldn't, you daft ha'p'orth.' Her mother grinned. 'But anyone wi' 'alf an eye can see the lad's mad about you! When are you goin' to put 'im out of 'is misery an' agree to court 'im proper?'

Flora grinned, but didn't answer. She loved Jamie and she knew he loved her, but she was only eighteen! Once the meal was over she helped her mother to clear the table and wash the dishes and before she knew it it was time to think of heading home.

'Eeh, but it's blowin' a blizzard out there, luvvie. Wouldn't yer be better to stay 'ere tonight?' her mother suggested worriedly as Flora began to put her coat on.

'No, I shall be fine,' Flora assured her. 'I need to be there when Connie gets home to help her undress.'

'Hmph! I should think she could manage to undress 'erself for one night at 'er age,' Emily grumbled as she tightened the scarf around her daughter's neck. There were kisses all round then and Flora set off again into the cold night.

As she neared the smart town house in Mayfair she frowned when she saw a policeman standing outside the front door. The snow was settling on his helmet and the dark material across his shoulders. She climbed the front steps towards him and asked, 'Is anything wrong, constable?' Close up she noted that he looked barely older than herself and he blushed furiously.

He touched his cap and cleared his throat nervously. 'Er . . . the sergeant's inside, miss,' he told her. 'He'll explain what's happened.'

A sick feeling started to grow in the pit of her stomach and nodding she rushed past him to find a policeman in conversation with Mrs Merry, the housekeeper, who was wringing her hands and looking distraught.

'Ah, here you are Flora.' The woman looked relieved to see her. 'Something dreadful has happened. It's the master and Miss Constance . . . They've been involved in a terrible accident.'

Flora's heart began to thump with panic and she suddenly felt sick. 'Are they all right?' she asked in a wobbly voice.

The woman shook her head. 'I'm afraid not. It seems the master's Silver Ghost skidded and left the road before crashing into a wall. Miss Constance is in the hospital and the master is . . .' She gulped deep in her throat before forcing herself to go on. 'And the master is dead, God rest his soul!'

Chapter One

Connie was discharged from the hospital two days after the tragic accident. Miraculously she had escaped with cuts and bruises and a broken arm, which was now encased in a heavy plaster, much to her disgust. Her father's solicitor, Mr Wainthrop, who had also been a close family friend, collected Connie and drove her home with promises that he would return the next day to read her father's will to her.

Flora, who was waiting at the door for her when she returned home, saw at a glance that her young mistress's eyes were swollen from crying, but then she supposed that this was to be expected. Connie's father had been the only close living relative that the girl had, so far as Flora knew, apart from an aunt who she had not seen for many years who lived in New York.

'Come on, miss,' she said kindly. 'There's a nice hot pot of coffee being made for you. Shall I tell Gertie to bring it to you in the day room?'

'No . . . thank you, Flora, but I'm feeling rather tired. I think I'll have it in my room.'

'Of course. I'll just let Gertie know then I'll help you up the stairs,' Flora offered.

Connie almost bit her head off when she snapped, 'It's my *arm* that's broken not my legs, in case you hadn't noticed!' Then instantly repentant she muttered, 'Sorry, Flora. I . . . I just seem . . .'

'It's all right,' Flora soothed like a mother to a child. 'You're just tired and upset, but hopefully you'll feel a little better when you've had a decent nap. I know you can't sleep properly in hospital. I went in when I was about ten to have my tonsils out and the moans and groans from the other beds kept me awake all night.'

Connie nodded wearily as Flora gently steered her towards the staircase. On the way they passed the coat stand and at the sight of her father's Sunday best coat hanging there, Connie began to sob loudly.

'It's *so* unfair. My father was such a kind man. *Why* did this have to happen?'

'I don't know, miss,' Flora answered gravely as tears pricked at the back of her own eyes.

Connie was quite wobbly on her feet, no doubt because of the shock and her numerous cuts and bruises and Flora walked steadily behind her in case she fell. Once in Connie's room, Flora carefully helped her off with her gown. It was dotted with blood and the nurses at the hospital had been forced to cut the sleeve off it to get it over her plaster cast. But from now on that would be the least of the girl's worries. She had wardrobes full of gowns and this one could easily be replaced. But sadly she could never replace her father and Flora could only imagine how she must be feeling.

Flora had just slipped a nightgown over her head and helped her into bed when Gertie appeared with the coffee tray and some freshly baked shortbread still warm from the oven. Knowing how much she liked it the kindly cook had made it especially for her but today Connie merely shook her head and pushed the plate away.

'I'm not really hungry,' she said listlessly. 'I'll perhaps just have a little coffee.'

Gertie scurried away as Flora poured it but by the time she had added milk and sugar and carried it to the bed, Connie, who was clearly exhausted, was already fast asleep.

Flora hastily threw some more coal onto the fire and closed the curtains to shut out the dismal day before creeping downstairs to the kitchen.

'Ah well, happen sleep is the best cure for 'er in a case like this,' the cook commented as she kneaded some dough for a fresh batch of bread. 'I'll make 'er a nice pan o' fresh chicken soup fer when she wakes up. Meantime, I should get rid o' that if I was you.' She nodded towards the ruined gown across Flora's arm. 'It'll only upset 'er an' bring everything back every time she looks at it.'

Flora agreed and hurried outside, shivering, to dispose of it. When she got back to the warmth of the kitchen the housekeeper was there too and she and the cook were discussing what might become of them all as the cook poured them all a cup of hot, sweet tea.

'I can't see the young mistress bein' allowed to stay 'ere on 'er own,' the cook commented. 'She ain't of age yet.'

'Well, Mr Wainthrop is returning tomorrow with the master's will. Hopefully we'll all know more then,' Mrs Merry answered glumly. 'But if he has left instructions for the house to be sold then we'll all be out of a job.'

At this, Gertie started to cry softly and Flora patted her arm. 'We'll be all right, you'll see,' she told her with a confidence she was far from feeling. 'My ma's a great one for saying everything happens for a reason.'

For now all they could do was sit back and wait to see what fate had in store for them.

On the dot of two o'clock the next afternoon Mr Wainthrop arrived and Gertie showed him into the drawing room where Connie was waiting for him. Flora was with her and she instantly rose to leave, intending to give her mistress some privacy, but Connie caught at her arm. 'No, don't go, Flora,' she implored. 'I want you to stay with me.'

Flora glanced uncomfortably at Mr Wainthrop but when he gave her a kindly smile she sat back down, lowered her eyes and folded her hands primly in her lap as Connie had taught her to do.

'How are you feeling today, m'dear?' he enquired gently although Connie's bloodshot eyes had already given him his answer. He scratched his head then, clearly feeling ill at ease as he took a seat and informed her, 'I have made all the funeral arrangements as you requested. It will be conducted three days before Christmas Day. I'm afraid I couldn't get it any earlier. There's another flu epidemic you see and . . .' His voice trailed away. This was proving to be particularly difficult for him. Connie's father had been a close friend for much of his adult life, added to which he'd had a soft spot for Connie right from the day her parents had adopted her. Even so there were legal things to be addressed so putting aside his feelings as best he could he withdrew a legal-looking document from a leather case and cleared his throat.

'This is your father's last will and testament,' he began in a voice little above a whisper. 'He updated it every year at my office in the presence of a witness. Normally it wouldn't be read until after the funeral but because of the circumstances I thought you would like to know what it contains. Shall I proceed?'

Connie nodded as tears burned at the back of her eyes and so he began. Most of what he was saying went in one ear and out of the other until something suddenly made her glance up with a startled look on her face. 'What did you just say?' she demanded. Surely she had misheard him?

'I told you that your father's wish, should anything happen to him before you reached your majority, was that you should go and reside with your aunt, Alexandra Ward, in New York.'

'But I don't even *know* her,' Connie yelped. 'And . . . New York! But what about the house?'

'Ah, now your father suggested that you might like to close it up with just one person staying here to maintain it until you come of age. Alternatively, if you'd prefer, it could be sold. The choice is entirely yours. As for your aunt, I have sent her a telegram telling her of what has happened but I haven't yet received a reply . . . although I'm sure I will,' he added hastily. Then, after studying the papers in front of him for some minutes he went on, 'It appears that your aunt was your late mother's younger sister.'

'I already *know* that,' Connie said waspishly. 'She has always sent birthday cards, Christmas cards and presents for as long as I can remember. But I don't actually *know* her, do I? What if we don't like each other? How could Father *do* this to me?' She was clearly very upset and Victor Wainthrop almost felt as if it was all his fault.

'I'm sure she will love you,' he muttered ineffectually.

Connie thought on his words for a moment before saying, 'And what if she doesn't even *want* me there?'

'Oh, apparently she and your father have had this arrangement ever since your mother passed away.'

'I see.' Connie chewed on her lip. 'And is there an uncle there?'

Mr Wainthrop hastily turned his attention back to the paper-work balanced on his knee and after a moment he nodded. 'Yes, it appears so.' Then in a softer voice he told her, 'This agreement only stands until you are twenty-one, Connie. And then if you are unhappy you are free to come back and reopen the house. Meanwhile, you are now a very wealthy young woman. The house, business and all his assets are yours. It only remains for you to decide if you wish to keep the businesses running with managers in place and me overseeing them, or if you wish them to be sold. But there's no need to make a decision right away. Let's give you a few days to get over the shock of everything

13

that's happened and then when the funeral is behind us after Christmas you can decide what you wish to do. Whatever it is, I promise that I will assist you in any way I can.'

Her face softened then and she looked at him guiltily. He and her father had always been such close friends that she was sure he must be feeling his loss too. 'I know you will,' she said. 'And I'm sorry for being so difficult. It's just that within such a short time my whole world has turned upside down and I just can't make myself believe that I'll never see my father again . . . I keep expecting him to walk through the door and . . .' She began to cry and Flora hurried across and placed her arm about her shoulder. For now she forgot that this young woman was her mistress. She was just another girl the same age as herself who was grieving for her parent.

Mr Wainthrop meanwhile was gathering his papers together and Flora could have sworn she saw tears sparkling on his lashes too.

'Well, that's about all for now,' he said as he rose from his seat. 'Please don't hesitate to contact me if there's anything you need. And, er . . . should you wish to say your final goodbyes to your father he will be lying in the chapel of rest at Ducalles' Undertakers as from tomorrow morning.'

He pressed a piece of paper with the address into Flora's hand and she nodded. Then after gently squeezing Connie's heaving shoulder he quickly departed.

After a while Connie calmed down a little and Flora hurried away to fetch her a tray of tea, silently scolding herself that she hadn't thought to offer Mr Wainthrop a cup, but then it wasn't really her place to and Connie was clearly far too distressed to think about niceties.

'So what's happenin'?' the rosy-cheeked cook asked the second Flora entered the kitchen.

Gertie and Mrs Merry were also there and they too looked at

14

her expectantly. 'I, er . . . don't really think it's my place to tell you,' Flora muttered.

The cook rolled her eyes in exasperation. 'Why ever *not*? If we're goin' to be hoofed out onto the street don't yer think we 'ave a right to know?'

'Of *course* you do,' Flora agreed hastily. 'And I'm sure Miss Connie will tell you what's happening very soon. In fact, I'll ask her to speak to you as soon as she feels up to it – but I'm in the same boat, you know? If you lose your jobs, I'll lose mine too.' The thought was depressing. She'd enjoyed being Connie's maid. She'd started off doing the job that Gertie did now until Connie had asked her father if she might become her maid and companion. Edward Ogilvie had always found it very hard to deny his daughter anything but in actual fact he had thought it was a very good idea for his daughter to have someone her own age to spend time with now that she was a little older and was no longer receiving schooling. And so Flora had been promoted and her life had changed drastically for the better from that moment on.

Admittedly Connie had been spoiled and could be quite moody at times but, overall, they had got on well together and Flora had never looked back. She had been fortunate enough to accompany her young mistress on shopping trips and now she wore smart but plain dresses instead of the drab maid's outfit she had become accustomed to. Connie had helped her to improve her reading and writing skills and had done her best to rid her of her cockney accent too. But now it looked as if it was all about to come to an end and Flora hated the thought of having to go back to being a general maid again, not that she had much choice. She wasn't trained to be anything else.

Clearly with her nose out of joint, the cook huffed and turned her attention back to the saucepan she was stirring as Flora prepared a tea tray and left the room as soon as she could.

Back in the drawing room, Connie was staring dully into the

fireplace. Glancing up as Flora came in, she asked, 'So what did you think of that then? I'm to be carted off to live with someone I've never even met as if I'm nothing more than a parcel!'

'I'm sure your father was only doing what he thought was best for you,' Flora assured her as she strained tea into two delicate china teacups. 'I suppose he just wanted to make sure you'd be taken care of, and I doubt he would ask someone who he thought you might not like to step in. Your aunt is probably a lovely person.'

Connie sniffed. 'But I still can't see why I can't just stay here!'

After being brought up in Whitechapel, Flora was a lot more worldly wise than her mistress, who had led a sheltered, cossetted life. 'Think about it. You're only just eighteen and if what Mr Wainthrop said is right, you're a very wealthy young woman. You'll have every young blade in London after you now and it might not be for the right reason. They could be just after your money . . . Not that you're not very pretty,' she added hastily, as Connie scowled.

After a while Connie nodded. 'I can see what you mean but I'm not a complete idiot, you know? I'm sure I would recognise the gold-diggers.'

'Well, as Mr Wainthrop said, you have no need to make your mind up about anything just yet. But whatever you decide to do about the house and businesses, the house is going to be shut up for a few years, so perhaps you should give the staff warning? I know they're all worrying about losing their jobs but if you tell them what's happening at least they'll have time to look round for other positions.'

Seeing the sense in what Flora said, Connie nodded glumly. 'I will,' she promised. 'But not tonight . . .' And then once more she broke into a torrent of fresh weeping as Flora looked on helplessly.

Chapter Two

Over the next days, Connie had an endless stream of visitors all wishing to pay their respects and offer their condolences. Somehow Connie greeted each of them with dignity. The tears had dried up for now but she seemed to be a mere shadow of her former self, barely eating and seemingly only existing on endless cups of tea.

'I'm really worried about her,' Flora confided to the cook one evening after she had helped Connie prepare for bed. 'I think even the tears were better than seeing her as she is now. She hardly says a word but just floats about the house like a lost soul.'

'Ah, well that's the thing wi' grief,' Cook nodded, setting her chins wobbling. 'There's different stages you 'ave to go through. I were the same when I lost me 'usband. First there's the tears an' the shock, then it turns into like a dull acceptance. An' the thing is everyone takes losin' someone close to 'em differently. It's worse for that poor girl, cos her father were the only one who ever really showed her any affection. When her mother were alive she just went through the motions to save face. But Connie an' her dad adored each other, see, so she's bound to take it 'ard. The only thing you can do is what you're doin' now. Just be there for 'er. She'll come out of it 'opefully once the funeral's over, but it takes time.'

Flora could only bow to the woman's superior wisdom and hope that she was right, but it didn't stop her worrying all the same. And now there was the funeral to get through tomorrow and Cook had been baking from morning till night to prepare food for any of the mourners who might wish to return to the house after the service. Briefly she wondered whether she ought to decorate the Christmas tree that had arrived the day before. It transpired that Mr Ogilvie had ordered it to be delivered shortly before the accident. Normally Connie and Flora would have spent the whole afternoon giggling as they decorated it with the pretty glass baubles that were packed safely away each year, but today it merely stood propped up against the wall in the hallway. No one even had the heart to stand it in a bucket of earth, let alone decorate it.

'We'll chuck that tree out into the yard in a while. No point leavin' it standing there droppin' its needles all over the place if we ain't goin' to dress it,' said Cook.

Flora nodded absently, wondering if cook was a mind-reader and wishing with all her heart that the next day could just be over.

It dawned grey and overcast. The snow had thawed and what was left of it was slushy and slippery underfoot. The dressmaker had rushed to make Connie a black dress with a wide sleeve that would slide over the plaster on her arm and the girl stood lifelessly as Flora helped her into it. Her bruises had faded from an angry purple to dull yellows and greys that made her look sallow and ill but the doctor had informed her that she would need to keep the cast on for at least another four weeks. Connie didn't seem to care. In fact, Flora was concerned that she didn't seem to care about anything anymore. It was as if she had locked herself away in a little world of her own where no one could reach her, but again Cook promised her that this was normal. 'She'll come out of it eventually,' she had assured her.

Now Flora piled the girl's hair up onto the top of her head and placed a bonnet with a short black veil on her and they were ready to go. At Connie's insistence she too was dressed from head to

18

toe in black and although the gown Connie had bought for her was the best she had ever worn, Flora felt uncomfortable in it.

When they stepped outside the first thing they saw was a glass hearse pulled by four magnificent coal-black stallions with plumes on their heads. Inside the hearse was Mr Ogilvie's coffin, the finest that money could buy: lead-lined and carved from rosewood with solid brass handles. Even the sight of this didn't prompt a reaction from Connie, and she climbed silently into the carriage behind it, closely followed by Flora who she had insisted should accompany her. A fine drizzle had begun to fall and when they reached the church a thick fog obscured some of the gravestones from view.

Throughout the service Flora kept a close eye on her mistress, who stood woodenly, not even attempting to join in the prayers or the singing. Finally it was over and the pall-bearers lifted the coffin and followed the solemn-faced vicar out into the graveyard. The fog gave an eerie feel to the proceedings and Flora thought the mourners looked as if they were floating between the drunkenly leaning gravestones. By this stage, Connie was gripping her hand so tightly that it was all Flora could do to stop herself from crying out. And then at last the coffin was lowered into the gaping grave, the final prayers were conducted and it was all over.

Slowly the mourners drifted away to be swallowed up by the fog but Connie stood staring down at her father's final resting place. Flora wondered what thoughts must be going through her young mistress's head. Was she remembering happy times she had spent with him? But then Connie suddenly turned abruptly and walked away without so much as glancing back. Flora looked back just once from the lychgate and shuddered as she saw the grave-diggers shovelling dirt into the grave, blocking the light of day from the dear man who lay there for all time.

When they arrived back at the house, many of the mourners were already there, wandering about with cups of tea or a glass of spirits in their hand while Mrs Merry had Gertie circulating amongst them with plates of sandwiches and tempting treats that the cook had baked, but the minute she and Connie entered the room a hush fell. The next second, people were vying to offer their condolences and say what a lovely man her father had been. Connie listened, nodding her head when it was required as she walked through them to her father's favourite wing chair by the fire. Flora hovered close by.

'Shall I get you something to eat?' she asked in concern. 'A sandwich, perhaps? Or I could get Gertie to make you something warm? Your hands are frozen through.'

'Thank you . . . but no . . . I'm not hungry at the moment.' Then seeing the concern on Flora's face, she added, 'Perhaps later.'

Flora continued to stand close to her young mistress's side, wishing that the mourners might all disappear in a puff of smoke, but it seemed they were all keen to take advantage of the feast spread out before them and it was almost two hours later when the last of them finally departed, leaving only Mr Wainthrop behind.

He smiled at Flora then pulling up a chair close to Connie he asked, 'How are you feeling, my dear?' The second the words had left his lips he realised how ludicrous they must sound. The poor girl had just buried her father, how could he expect her to feel?

'I'm all right, thank you.'

She managed to raise a weak smile so he rushed on, 'Well, I'm sure that you must be ready for a little time to yourself now so I shall be off too. And may I say that your father would have been very proud of the dignified way you conducted yourself today. I just wanted to let you know that I have written to your aunt in New York and the moment I get a response I shall be round to show it to you. Meanwhile, you have no need to worry about anything. I shall continue to pay the household expenses as your father requested and I shall ensure that you receive your allowance each month. But is there anything else I can do for you? Anything at all?'

'No, thank you, Mr Wainthrop,' she replied woodenly and so with a nod towards the girls he rose and left the room, closing the door softly behind him.

'Flora . . . I think I'd like to be on my own for a while now, if you don't mind,' Connie said and Flora nodded understandingly.

'Of course. Just ring when you need anything.' Flora discreetly hurried away and was soon in the warmth of the kitchen where Cook was sitting with her swollen ankles on a stool by the fire and a cup of tea perched on her ample bosom.

'Eeh, I'm glad that's over. How is the poor lass?' she asked Flora as the girl fetched a cup and lifted the teapot.

Flora shrugged as she poured the stewed tea and added sugar. 'Quiet as a mouse,' she answered. 'I think I'd rather have had the tears but then perhaps she's got none left.'

'Hmm, well soon she needs to decide what's happenin' 'ere,' the cook huffed. 'If she's goin' off to her aunt's in New York an' closin' the 'ouse up we'll all be out on the street wi'out a job.'

'That isn't *her* fault,' Flora said defensively. 'She wouldn't be going by choice. It was her father's express wish that she stayed with her aunt until she comes of age but we just have to wait and see what her aunt says now. Mr Wainthrop has written to her and is waiting on a reply.'

'I dare say yer right.' Cook looked suitably shamefaced. She'd worked for the Ogilvie family for years and just didn't want things to change, but sadly she knew that this was inevitable now and she wondered what the future had in store for them all.

Christmas was a dismal affair as was the New Year with no cele-brations of any kind in the Ogilvie house. The staff crept about

21

like ghosts so as not to disturb Connie who seemed to have locked herself away in a world of grief. The one bright spot for Flora was when she managed to slip away for a few precious hours on Christmas Eve to see her family and spend a little time with Jamie.

'I can't stay long,' she apologised to him breathlessly when they met at their usual meeting place. 'Not with Connie in such a state.'

'I understand,' he answered sympathetically. 'The poor girl must be distraught, but here I have something for you.' He presented her with a little box that contained a small silver locket on a delicate chain and Flora's face lit up.

'Oh, Jamie, it's beautiful,' she breathed as he fastened it about her neck. 'I shall treasure it forever.'

Jamie looked at her tenderly. 'It looks beautiful on you,' he said, kissing her softly on the lips. 'I knew it would.'

Flora stroked his cheek, gazing into his beautiful blue eyes and thanked God that she had him in her life.

And then on a cold and frosty morning early in January Mr Wainthrop arrived with news.

'I've heard from your aunt, m'dear,' he told Connie who had come down to the drawing room to speak to him. It was one of the very rare occasions she had ventured downstairs since the funeral. 'And she enclosed a letter for you.' He handed the young woman an envelope before going on, 'She is quite happy for you to stay with her so now it will be up to you to decide whether you wish to keep this house on or if you would like me to sell it for you.'

Connie looked around at the familiar room, her eyes dull. She knew every stick of furniture, every knick-knack, every corner.

'I want to keep the house on,' she told him listlessly. 'I know my father wanted me to go to my aunt and I shall do as he wished because I have no choice, but as soon as I reach my majority I shall come home.'

Mr Wainthrop nodded understandingly, wishing there were something he could say to ease her pain.

'In that case, with your permission, I shall speak to the staff. Sadly, they won't be needed while you are gone but I shall ask Mrs Merry if she is prepared to stay on as a caretaker. I'm sure she'll agree to it and then at least you can go knowing that your home is being left in safe hands.'

Flora entered the room then, bearing a tray of coffee and biscuits.

'I thought you might like something to warm you up, sir.' She smiled politely and after pouring out the coffee she discreetly left the room.

'So what's going on?' Gertie asked her as she went back to the kitchen.

Flora shrugged. 'I have no idea but I dare say we're about to find out.'

She took a seat at the kitchen table and shortly after there was a tap at the door and Mr Wainthrop entered looking decidedly uncomfortable.

Mrs Merry sidled in behind him and seeing that the staff were all gathered together he coughed to clear his throat before telling them. 'I have come to inform you that Miss Ogilvie's aunt in New York has replied to my letter and she has agreed to her going to stay with her indefinitely. Mrs Merry, Connie has decided that she will keep this house on in case she wishes to return to it so I was wondering if you would consider staying on to take care of it?'

Mrs Merry nodded, a look of relief on her face.

'Good.' The solicitor smiled at her before turning back to the others. 'Unfortunately, this will mean that the rest of you will no longer be needed.' He saw the looks of dismay on their faces and hurried on, 'However, it is going to take me some time to arrange a passage for the young mistress so this should give you all ample time to find another position. A couple of months at least, I should think, and on top of that she has asked me to give you all an extra month's wages when you do leave.'

This statement went a long way to calming them and Gertie

sighed with relief. 'Well, at least we ain't goin' to be chucked out on us arses tomorrow,' she commented drily, which drew a disapproving frown from Cook.

'Ah well, I think we all expected this,' the older woman sighed. 'But thank you, Mr Wainthrop. Under the circumstances the young miss is bein' more than fair. After all, it ain't as if she wants to go, is it?'

'Quite.' Mr Wainthrop shuffled from foot to foot. 'Now, if you will excuse me I should get on but rest assured I shall keep you all informed. Good day, ladies.' And with that he took his leave.

Once the door had closed behind him, Gertie sighed and, tears in her eyes, glanced around the kitchen. 'I've loved workin' here an' I'll be really sorry to go,' she said regretfully.

'We all will,' Cook pointed out. 'But there's no point in cryin' over spilt milk. An' you've got age on yer side, Gertie, an' you have, Flora. I heard yesterday as they're settin' on in the jam factory if yer can't get another live-in position. They earn good money there, by all accounts.'

'I might try there,' Flora said, but her heart was heavy. She had loved her time working as a personal lady's maid but then she supposed any job was better than none, although she would miss Connie and the rest of the staff desperately

'Right, well at least we know where we all stand now so chop chop, let's 'ave you back to work,' Cook ordered bossily. Obediently, they went about their duties, although now they were all wondering what was to become of them.

In the drawing room, Connie was unfolding the letter her aunt had enclosed with Mr Wainthrop's and she began to read.

My dearest girl,

I cannot begin to tell you how distraught your uncle and I were to read of your father's untimely accident. He was a truly wonderful man and will always be remembered fondly. Of

24

course, you must come to us for as long as you need to, forever if necessary. I have instructed Mr Wainthrop to organise your passage here as soon as is possible and to let us know when we might expect you so that someone can be there to meet you off the ship.

Your arrival cannot come quickly enough for me. Until then, know that I am thinking of you and very much looking forward to seeing you,

With much love,
Aunt Alexandra xxx

As soon as Flora joined her again, Connie handed her the letter and urged her to read it.

'She sounds nice, at any rate,' Flora said miserably once she had read it and handed it back.

'Hmm, but I wonder why my mother and she never really kept in touch,' Connie said thoughtfully. 'From what I can remember my mother never had a kind word to say about her. In fact, I can remember she used to get really huffy every time we heard from her. Rather strange considering she was her younger sister, don't you think?'

'I suppose she had her reasons,' Flora said cautiously. 'And she certainly sounds like she's looking forward to having you there, which is the main thing, surely?'

'I suppose so,' Connie sighed, but she didn't sound at all convinced.

Chapter Three

'Cheer up, it ain't the end o' the world,' Flora's mother told her when she visited her home on the following Sunday afternoon. 'Somethin' will turn up, you'll see,' she told her daughter optimistically as she stirred the large pan of stew and dumplings simmering on the range. 'So, when is Connie planning to leave?'

Flora shrugged, looking thoroughly miserable. 'She doesn't know yet. Mr Wainthrop is making all the travelling arrangements for her. He reckons it could be March or April before she goes. But I don't want her to go. I'm going to miss her so much.'

Her mother's face softened and she gently squeezed her daughter's hand. She knew how close Flora and her young mistress had become. 'There you are then,' Emily said. 'That gives you more than enuff time to look round for another position. A clever young lass like you shouldn't 'ave any trouble at all in findin' somethin' else. Now, 'ow about a nice dish o' this stew to warm you up?' she suggested, hoping to cheer her up a little.

Flora shook her head as she reached for her thick shawl. It had been a present from her mother for Christmas. 'No thanks, Ma. I'm meeting Jamie in half an hour.'

'Huh!' Emily tutted as she glanced through the window at the frosted cobblestones. 'Yer must be mad trailin' about in this wevver. It's enuff to freeze yer out there. Still, I dare say I'd 'ave done the same at your age.' She crossed to pull Flora's shawl over her mop of thick dark hair and followed her to the door. 'Now, don't you go frettin'. Things'll come right, you'll see.'

Flora kissed her cheek then hurried off to meet Jamie. He was standing where he always waited for her on the dock and at the sight of his tall figure, Flora's breath caught. He was so good-looking, with his curly fair hair that seemed to have a life of its own and twinkling blue eyes that always seemed to be smiling. Her heart speeded up at the sight of him and the butterflies started fluttering in her stomach, Flora knew she had to accept that no matter how much she tried to deny it, she was in love with him. The thought of seeing him each week was the one thing that was keeping her going at the moment.

His face lit up at the sight of her, and she smiled back. 'It feels like ages since I last saw you. How are you bearing up? How's Connie?' he said as he wrapped his arms around her and gave her a soft kiss. Then hooking his arm possessively about her waist he began to wander along as she told him about what Mr Wainthrop had said.

'But it's not the end of the world,' he pointed out, much as her mother had done.

'I know that,' Flora said miserably. 'But I really enjoyed being a lady's maid to Connie and we've grown close.'

'Well, if it's money you're worrying about, don't,' he told her. 'Because I've got some I could let you have.'

She stared at him curiously and it came to her then that she didn't really know all that much about his background, except that he had been orphaned as a child and then adopted by a couple in the Midlands. She knew that the stevedores and the men who worked on the docks weren't very highly paid and yet whenever she met him on a Sunday he was well turned out in what looked like surprisingly expensive clothes. He was well spoken too and sounded more like a gentleman than a dock worker. She'd not thought about it properly before, and had just assumed he didn't like talking about his childhood, but now she felt able to ask him a bit more.

'So how come you're so flush?' she asked curiously and he grinned.

'Let's just say that my parents aren't short of a bob or two,' he answered.

Flora scowled. 'So why are you working here then?'

He shrugged. 'Because I want to, it's as simple as that. My parents weren't too happy with the idea but I want to see a bit of life.'

'So, who exactly are your parents?' Flora asked, more curious than ever now.

'Hmm.' Jamie scratched his chin. 'Well, as I told you, they're my adoptive parents. I can't really remember much about my natural parents, except I can remember being always cold and hungry but I was lucky because Sunday and Tom Branning took me to live with them then. From then on I had a *wonderful* life. They run a children's home called Treetops in a village called Hartshill near Nuneaton and from that moment on my life changed for the better. It's a great, rambling house surrounded by woods. It used to belong to Sunday's mother who was once married to a lord and they treated all of the children who lived there like their own. They never had children of their own, you see? So we all had the best of everything. The best clothes, the best food, the best educations, but most of all they loved us and made us feel we were wanted.

'But as I got older I started to feel that I wanted to spread my wings a bit, try different jobs and see a bit more of the country, so here I am. To be honest, though, I don't think I would have stayed as long as I have if I hadn't met a certain young lady.'

Flora blushed prettily as he squeezed her arm. 'When and if I decide to settle down I shall probably head back there. Nuneaton is a market town and the pace of life is so much gentler there than it is in the city. I suppose I'd want my children to be brought up somewhere where there's woods and countryside around them, but we'll have to wait and see what happens, won't we?'

Flora nodded as she glanced up at him and her heart did a little cartwheel again. Jamie was truly handsome, but it was more than just his looks that made her heart beat faster, and now that he had opened up a little more about his past, she was beginning to understand what made him stand out to her. He was so different to the people hereabouts: he'd had a very privileged upbringing and all the advantages he could have wished for, and yet he had an independent spirit as well, otherwise why else would he have set out on his own to experience what life had to offer? She hugged his arm closer and for the next hour they strolled about, talking about their hopes and dreams and barely noticing how cold it was. When the light began to fade, Jamie reluctantly walked her back to the house.

'Don't get worrying about your future,' he said softly then gently kissed her lips. 'See you next Sunday.' He walked away whistling merrily, and she stood for a moment watching him, her mind all of a whirl. She had promised herself that she would focus on a career before settling down, but Jamie had wriggled his way into her life, and the thought of him moving back to his home town without her made her heart sink. Shivering suddenly, she hurried inside out of the cold.

It was early in February when Mr Wainthrop called again. The two girls were in the morning room altering a dress that Connie had given to Flora and Connie eyed him nervously when he appeared.

'I think I might have quite an exciting idea to put to you,' he told Connie while Flora hurried away to fetch a tray of coffee and biscuits.

'I've been making enquiries about a ship that might take you to New York and I spotted this article in the paper about a brand-new liner that's to be launched for her maiden voyage in April. She's called the *Titanic* and is said to be unsinkable. She's also supposed to be the most luxurious ship that ever sailed the seas, a veritable floating hotel, in fact. It has everything you could wish for: tennis courts, swimming pools, restaurant, squash court, Turkish baths and even shops aboard. It is quite expensive to travel on her, of course, but they say that the elite of society are booking their passages already. I thought it might be nice for you to travel in style. Now, it is a bit expensive – £870 for a first-class suite of rooms, but luckily you can afford it, and I think you deserve a little treat. What do you think?'

'I suppose it *does* sound lovely, but that's an awful lot of money,' Connie pointed out doubtfully.

He chuckled. 'My dear, that's a drop in the ocean, excuse the pun, to you. At least give it some thought. I shall be calling back in a few days so let me know then. Meanwhile, I'll leave you this newspaper so that you can read all about it. It looks set to be the trip of a lifetime. Just what you need to lift your spirits after . . . Well, anyway, let me know what you think.'

He rose to leave and remembering her manners, Connie asked, 'Won't you stay for coffee? Flora should be back with it any moment now.'

'I won't, if you don't mind,' he demurred. 'I have to be in court with a client this afternoon so I should get on. Good day, m'dear.' He rammed his hat onto his unruly thatch of grey hair and retreated hurriedly, leaving Connie to read about the *Titanic*.

'Oh, has Mr Wainthrop left already?' Flora asked when she appeared with a loaded tray minutes later.

'Mmm.' Connie nodded absently. 'Yes, he has to be in court soon, but he called in to ask if I'd like to make the trip to my aunt's on this ship. Look at the picture of her, she looks absolutely enormous.'

'Blimey.' Flora stared at the picture of the ship in awe, as side by side they began to read about her.

'It says that she's over eight hundred feet long!'

Flora whistled through her teeth, which brought a scowl from Connie but she ignored it. 'So how can anything so huge and obviously heavy even float?' she asked bewildered.

'It's the design, I suppose.' Connie chewed on her nail, a habit she had adopted since her father's death. 'Look, it says the ship contains fifteen watertight bulkheads running across the hull – whatever those are – that's what makes it unsinkable, apparently. And she can travel at twenty-four to twenty-five knots – I suppose that must be fast if they've written about it here, which means we could get to New York really quickly.' Connie read on. 'She has a sister ship called the *Olympic*, and it says here that the *Titanic* is only slightly larger, so you see, a ship that size *can* float.'

'I have to say it sounds wonderful. It will be quite an adventure for you,' Flora said with a touch of envy in her voice, but even so she was pleased to see Connie taking an interest in something again, she had been gravely worried about her.

Connie eyed her thoughtfully as something occurred to her 'So why don't you come with me then?' she suggested.

'*Me*? On the *Titanic*. Going to *New York*!' Flora bleated, dumb-struck.

'Why not?' Connie shrugged. 'I would feel better if I had someone I knew accompanying me. And it's not as if it's forever. I fully intend to come back when I'm twenty-one. Think about it . . . this could be an adventure for you too.'

Flora stared back at her open-mouthed. The idea was prepos-terous . . . and yet . . . as Connie had said it wouldn't be forever and it would be an opportunity that may never come her way again.

'I'd have to see what me ma and dad thought of the idea,' she said. 'And Jamie, of course.'

31

'Mother and Father,' Connie corrected her. 'And yes, *of course* you'd need to speak to them. But do *please* give it some serious thought. I'm dreading going to live with strangers but if I had you there to support me . . .'

- 'I will,' Flora promised, her mind reeling at the prospect. *New York!* Suddenly she had an awful lot of thinking to do.

When she told her mother of Connie's offer on her next afternoon off, Emily stared at her open-mouthed. 'All that way on a big ship,' she croaked fearfully.

'Oh, but it's quite safe. Unsinkable apparently,' Flora assured her. 'And it would only be for less than three years till Connie comes of age. Oh, I know it's still a long time, Ma, but it's not as if I'm planning on going forever, is it?'

'I suppose not,' Emily admitted reluctantly. 'But what about young Jamie? He's clearly very sweet on you. Will he be willing to wait all that while for you? Three years is still an awful long time even at your age.'

'I know.' The thought of leaving Jamie had been preying heavily on Flora's mind too. What was she to do? Was their relationship worth giving up the chance of a lifetime for? She loved him, but she still wasn't sure she was ready to settle down yet. But, if she did go, would he wait for her? She couldn't bear the idea that he wouldn't, but the pull of adventure was strong. She'd never been out of London before, and after what he'd told her about his background and why he'd left home, she was sure he'd understand. Flora chewed her lip nervously, feeling sick at the thought of losing him. But surely, she reasoned to herself, if he really loved her he would be prepared to wait. Well, she'd find out soon enough.

After leaving her mother's, Flora walked to their usual meeting place with butterflies in her stomach and there was Jamie waiting for her with a broad smile on his face.

'Is everything all right?' he queried, noting the preoccupied look on her face as he tucked her hand into his arm and began to stroll along.

Flora licked her lips, which were suddenly dry. 'It all depends what you mean by all right,' she said, then hurried on to tell him what Connie had suggested. 'So . . . the long and the short of it is, Connie wants me to go to New York with her,' she finished breathlessly.

'New York!' Jamie was clearly shocked. 'But . . . but what about us?'

'It would only be for three years or so,' she told him timidly, wondering why she felt so guilty. 'And just think what an opportunity it would be for me to see a bit of the world before I settle down.'

'I could show you as much of the world as you want to see,' he answered grumpily. 'I've told you I'm not short of a bob or two. And . . . well, to be honest I was hoping to speak to your father soon . . . you know? About making our relationship official.'

'Oh, *Jamie.*' Flora's eyes welled with tears as she drew him to a halt and looked up into his handsome face. 'I think the world of you, you know I do but . . . but I don't think I'm ready to get married just yet. We'll both be so much older and wiser when I come back if I go with Connie and perhaps then, if we still feel the same away about each other . . .'

'What you're saying is you expect me to sit about here waiting for you to come home in the hope that you'll have made your mind up on whether you want me or not in three years' time! That's what you're saying, isn't it?' His eyes were flashing fire now and Flora felt devastated.

'No . . . I didn't mean that.' She yanked her hand out of his arm and glared back at him, feeling as if she was being pulled in two directions. On the one hand, how could she abandon her dear friend just when she needed her so badly? Connie was all alone in the world, and when Flora thought about it, she realised that she was Connie's only true friend. But then again, looking into Jamie's furious eyes, she could also see his hurt. And that made her feel terrible. Whichever way she turned, she'd hurt someone she loved. *'Surely* if you love me as you claim to, you'd be happy to wait?' Suddenly the thought of leaving him for all that time was painful but Connie needed her too!

His head wagged from side to side as he took a step back. 'Three years is a long time. I don't think you understand, I love you, Flora. I want to marry you! And if you're happy to leave the minute someone suggests, it seems you don't feel the same. Happen you've got a lot of thinking to do and some difficult decisions to make,' he rasped. 'Should you decide we do have a future together, I'll be here at the same time next Sunday and if you're not . . . then I'll know what my answer is.' With that he turned abruptly and marched away without giving her so much as another glance.

Flora watched him leave, tears pouring down her cheeks. More than ever now she realised how empty her life would be without him but how would Connie cope going all that way alone? As Jamie had pointed out, three years was a very long time, a lifetime in fact, and she realised it was too much to expect from him. As she turned to set off back to the house, her heart broke. Because, much as she loved him, Connie had been so good to her and she loved her too. And then there was a part of her that she hadn't even been aware existed until now: a reckless side that longed for adventure. No matter what the cost.

Chapter Four

Mrs Merry was the first person Flora set eyes on when she entered the house and the kindly housekeeper saw at a glance that something was wrong.

'Come along to my room, dear,' she said, taking Flora's elbow. 'I'll make you a nice hot cup of tea and you can tell me what's bothering you.'

Flora went without argument and sat in Mrs Merry's comfy fireside chair as the woman bustled about preparing the teacups and warming the teapot.

'So, were your parents not keen on the idea of you travelling so far?' she asked eventually when they both sat with steaming cups of tea in front of them.

'It wasn't so much my parents as Jamie.' Flora looked thoroughly miserable.

'Is that your young man?' Mrs Merry asked gently.

Flora nodded, her eyes still bright with unshed tears. 'Yes, we have been walking out together for some time but I never dreamed he'd take the idea so badly.'

'Hmm, you're in a bit of a dilemma then.' Mrs Merry sipped at her tea delicately. 'All I can advise is you must do what *you* want to do, not what someone else wants you to do. I must admit *I* would be far happier if I knew that you were accompanying

35

Miss Constance. It's a very long way for her to travel alone, but as I said, it's up to you.'

Flora nodded in agreement and after draining her cup and thanking Mrs Merry she made her way up to her room. Even though it was still her afternoon off and her time was hers to do with as she pleased, she decided that she needed to speak to Connie. So after taking off her bonnet and her coat she made her way to her young mistress's room and tapped on the door.

She found Connie sitting on the window seat reading a short book of Shakespeare's sonnets.

'I thought you would still be at your parents' or walking with Jamie,' she remarked, looking mildly surprised to see her. 'Has something happened? Have your parents refused to give their permission for you to come with me?'

'Oh no, they haven't,' Flora assured her hastily. 'I don't think they're thrilled with the idea but they won't stop me. It's Jamie that's the problem. He took it quite badly when I told him that I had the chance to go.'

'I see.' Connie looked crestfallen. 'So, have you reached a decision?'

Flora shook her head. 'Not yet,' she admitted. 'I feel as if I'm being pulled in two different directions. I want to come with you, of course I do, but then as you know I'm also very fond of Jamie and he's made it more than obvious that he's not prepared to wait for me.'

Throwing her book aside, Connie hurried across to Flora in a swirl of silken skirts. 'But, Flora, I *need* you to come with me,' she said, her lip trembling. 'I'm closer to you than anyone else on earth now that Daddy is gone. You know everything about me and leaving here won't be half so bad if I know that you are coming too. Oh, *please* think about it, Flora! Surely if Jamie *truly* loved you he would be prepared to wait. Three years isn't such an awful long time after all, is it?'

'I suppose not,' Flora said uncertainly. She was so confused, she didn't know if she was coming or going at that moment. She loved Connie and Jamie in different ways and whatever she decided one of them was going to be hurt. 'I think I ought to sleep on it, so if there's nothing you need, I think I'll go to my room and get some rest.'

'Yes, why don't you do that,' Connie said quickly. She would have done anything to get her way, she usually did, as her father had spoiled her shamelessly, even more so after the death of her mother. And so Flora trudged heavy-hearted back to her room where she lay on her bed as the afternoon shadows lengthened, trying to decide which direction she should take. It was funny, she thought, she'd known she was falling in love with Jamie before. But now there was a chance she might lose him, she realised how strong that love actually was. Could she really risk giving that up?

Downstairs, Mrs Merry was restlessly pacing up and down her sitting room like a caged animal. She had been like a surrogate mother to Constance since long before her adoptive mother had died, for Alicia Ogilvie had never had much time for the child and had been only too happy to leave the little girl in the care of a nanny and the housekeeper. Now the kindly woman looked upon the young girl as her own child, for she had never been blessed with children.

Mr Ogilvie's death had come as a great shock to her but that was nothing compared to the shock she had felt when she'd learned that Constance was to be sent away to live with her aunt. Her only consolation was that Constance had assured her she would return as soon as she possibly could, which would hopefully be in a little under three years. Thankfully she was being allowed to stay in the house to wait for her return, but now how could she ensure that Flora went with her? Constance had led a very sheltered life and Mrs Merry feared what might happen to her if she had to travel alone.

The answer to her concerns presented itself to her the very next morning when a tap came at the door. The young maid was busily cleaning so it was Mrs Merry who answered it to find a very respectable looking young man standing on the doorstep.

He hastily swept his hat off as he said politely, 'I'm so sorry to trouble you and I know that Flora will be working but would it be possible to speak to her . . . just for a moment? I won't keep her, I assure you.'

'May I ask who is calling?'

'Of course. I'm James Branning, a er . . . friend of Flora's.'

So this is Jamie, she thought as she stared steadily back at him. She could see now why the decision Flora was being forced to make was so difficult. Even so, Constance was still her main priority so she answered, 'I'm afraid Flora and her mistress have gone out for a short walk. Flora thought the fresh air might do her mistress good.' She felt sick with guilt but she didn't know what else to do.

'Oh . . . I see.' His shoulders visibly sagged with disappointment.

Softening slightly, she asked, 'Could I perhaps take a message for her?'

'Yes.' He looked a little uncomfortable and shuffled from foot to foot before saying, 'Could you tell her that I have received word that my father has suffered a slight stroke and I have to return home to Nuneaton for a time. I shall write and let her know what's going on but yesterday we er . . . well we parted on bad terms and I wanted to tell her that I was sorry and that I didn't mean what I said.' His cheeks were flaming with colour now.

'I shall tell her,' Mrs Merry answered as she began to close the door on him. 'And I do hope that your father makes a full recovery.'

The door clicked shut just as Flora appeared from the drawing room to ask, 'Who was that, Mrs Merry?'

'Oh, just some pedlar trying to sell rubbish,' the older woman answered, then turning about she headed for the kitchen feeling sick to her stomach.

Flora swallowed her disappointment as she glanced at the door. She had secretly hoped that it might be Jamie calling to tell her that he would wait for her. But then, she consoled herself, there was still time, and if he *didn't* come she would tell him on Sunday just how much he meant to her. Feeling slightly heartened at the thought she went back to join Connie in the drawing room.

The following Sunday when Flora set off for her mother's she was in high spirits. She had reached her decision but before she told Constance she decided she would tell her parents and Jamie first.

'So you're not going, then. Well, I can't say as I'm sorry,' her mother told her as she placed a freshly baked scone on the table in front of her. 'I was worried sick about you going all that way. But what changed your mind? I had a feeling you were intending to go last week.'

'I was,' Flora admitted. 'But then I got to thinking and realised how much I'd miss you all . . . and Jamie.'

'Ah, I *see*.' Emily chuckled. 'Got under your skin, has he? Then I reckon it's time you brought him home to meet the family. I'll lay a nice little tea on for you next week. But now get that drink down you and go and put the poor lad out of his misery.'

Minutes later Flora set off for the docks with her face glowing. She could hardly wait to see Jamie's face when she told him the news, but as she approached the spot where they normally met she was surprised to see that he wasn't there. She began to walk up and down in an effort to keep warm as she waited for him. Once or twice she saw men approaching and her heart leapt as she started to rush towards them, a broad smile on her face as she tried to imagine how happy he would be when she told him of her decision and how much she loved him, but as they drew closer she saw that it wasn't him, and she quickly turned away, feeling foolish and hoping they hadn't noticed her smiling at them. Slowly the minutes ticked away and after what felt like a very long time it dawned on her that he wasn't coming and anger began to build inside her.

He can damned well please himself if he wants to be so petty, she fumed to herself as she turned and headed for her employer's home. *He couldn't have thought much of me if he couldn't even wait to hear whether I intended to go away or not.* She rubbed at her cold face and realised that it was wet with tears. She dashed them away angrily. She refused to allow him to hurt her, not after he'd left her waiting for him. Well, that was the last time she'd trust a man who claimed to love her. She sniffed and tried not to think of the future she had imagined for the two of them, and how it had disappeared like morning mist.

Once back at the house she barged into Connie's room without knocking and before she could change her mind she told her young mistress, 'I've made my decision, miss. I'm coming with you so could you ask Mr Wainthrop to arrange a passage on the *Titanic* for me too, please.'

Delighted, Connie threw her arms about her. 'Oh, that's *wonderful* news,' she exclaimed. 'It won't be half so bad if I have you to keep me company. I'll send word to Mr Wainthrop first thing in the morning.'

And so it was decided and Flora wondered why she didn't feel excited at the prospect anymore. Mrs Merry on the other hand was elated when Flora told her of her decision to go, although she also felt incredibly guilty. She'd noticed Flora wasn't looking her normal cheery self and she knew that this was her fault. Had she informed her of Jamie's visit she had no doubt the girl's decision might have been very different, but it was too late to do anything about it. Now all she had to do was worry about them going all that way on such a big ship.

'It's all right, Merry,' Connie told her. 'We shall be quite safe.'

'Huh!' Mrs Merry huffed. 'I shan't rest till I know you've arrived safely at your aunt's. It feels like you're goin' to the other side of the world!'

Connie and Flora exchanged an amused glance then went to the loft to start bringing down the luggage they would need for their trip.

Five days later when Mrs Merry collected the mail from the doormat one morning she saw a letter with a Nuneaton postmark addressed to Flora and she hastily thrust it into her pocket. She hated being so deceitful but then, she reasoned, it was in Connie's best interests for Flora to go with her to New York and that's what mattered most.

When she finally got an opportunity to be on her own, she opened the letter, and as she read Jamie's words her eyes filled with tears.

My dearest,

I'm so sorry I missed you when I popped round to Connie's house to see you and I'm also sorry that we parted on bad terms. Although I hate the idea of us being apart for three long years I shouldn't have said what I said and I sincerely hope that you will forgive me, for the thought of a life without you is unbearable. Of course you must go to New York if you feel that Connie needs you, safe in the knowledge that I will still

41

*be here waiting for you when you get back, no matter how
long you are gone.*

*My father remains quite poorly so it will be some time before
I am able to be back in London, although thankfully the doctor
hopes that he will eventually make a full recovery.*

*Please write back to me, my love, and tell me that I am
forgiven,*

Until then, all my love

Jamie xxxx

Mrs Merry gulped as she jammed the letter back into the envelope
and pushed it deep into the pocket of her pinny. The deceit was
proving hard to live with but surely she was right to think of
Connie above all others, fond as she was of Flora? All she had to
do now was pray that Jamie didn't return before the girls set off
on their journey.

Over the next few weeks Connie and Flora carefully packed whatever clothes they thought they might need in New York and set
about packing a separate trunk of clothes they would need for the
journey. Connie was still dressing in dark clothes, black, lilac and
purple, as a sign of respect for her father but she did give Flora
a number of things that she no longer wore and Flora was thrilled
with them.

'You look quite the young lady,' Flora's mother commented
when she visited wearing one of Connie's discarded gowns late in
February. 'Though I still can't think what made you change your
mind about goin'! You was quite adamant that you wouldn't not
so long ago.'

Flora flushed. She was too proud to tell her mother that it was
because Jamie had dumped her and merely shrugged. 'A girl can

change her mind, can't she?' she quipped and got on with slicing the cheese they were having for tea.

Disgruntled, Emily didn't make any more comments. She knew her daughter inside out. Flora could be as stubborn as an old mule when she had a mind to be and she also knew her well enough to know that she wouldn't let her young mistress down now that all the travel arrangements had been made. She just wished that she wasn't going because she knew that she would miss her terribly and three years was an awfully long time.

Chapter Five

The next night Elizabeth Merry tossed and turned restlessly in her bed. Constance had received another letter from her aunt and had questioned her about what she was like.

'Does she look anything like my mother? Is she nice?' Constance had asked curiously.

'I suppose there was a similarity in their looks,' Mrs Merry had answered. But she decided that this was as much as she would divulge. In truth, she had never really liked her mistress. Alicia Ogilvie had been beautiful to look at admittedly, but her heart had been made of stone and she had often wondered why the master put up with her. Alicia had never been content and had been even less so after they had adopted Constance, whereas she herself had fallen in love with the baby at first sight and had loved her ever since.

It was she who Connie would run to as a child if she fell and grazed her knee. She was too afraid to go to her mother for fear of getting blood on one of her fine gowns. It was Mrs Merry who would read the child a story each night and tuck her into bed. Alicia had usually been too busy gadding here or there or resting in her room.

On the other hand, her sister, Alexandra, had been a gentle, caring soul from what Mrs Merry could remember of her from the few times she had visited them. She had married a titled gentleman who was many years older than herself when she was still very young and gone to live with him in New York, and from what she

44

had heard the late mistress say it had been the biggest mistake of her life. Alexandra's husband had made a virtual prisoner of her and like Alicia had been, he was as cold and uncaring as a dead fish as well as being insanely jealous, and now Mrs Merry worried about how he would treat Constance. Would he welcome her into his home or would the next three years be unbearable for the girl?

Whatever the outcome, she was uncomfortably aware that there was nothing she could do about it apart from pray that the time would pass quickly until Constance could come home to her again.

The next morning, Mr Wainthrop arrived bright and early as did yet another letter with the Nuneaton postmark, which Mrs Merry hurriedly hid in her skirt pocket before scuttling away to read it in private.

It was from Jamie, as she had guessed, and was just as heart-breaking as the last letter he had written.

My dearest girl,

I am so disappointed that I have not as yet received a reply to my letter. Is it because you have been too busy to write? Or is it because you have not forgiven me? I cannot bear this bad feeling between us, Flora! Please write soon and put me out of my misery, I miss you every single day! I have now given notice on the room I was renting in London but will soon find another when I return.

On a happier note, I am pleased to be able to tell you that my father is making a good recovery and I pray that very soon now I might be able to return to put things right between us. Please, please write to me, my darling!

All my love always

Jamie xxxx

Tears flowed freely down Mrs Merry's cheeks as she slowly made her way to her room and she wavered as the enormity of what she was doing by withholding the letters from Flora came home to her. But then her loyalty and love for Connie made her harden her heart and opening her drawer she added Jamie's letter to the first.

'I have all your tickets here,' Mr Wainthrop told the girls in the drawing room as he placed an envelope on the table. 'I have booked you the finest first-class suite of rooms and adjoining it is a room for you, Flora. I'm sure you will be quite comfortable.'

'I'm sure we shall, Mr Wainthrop,' Constance said politely but her voice was dull as were her eyes. Since losing her father she seemed to have lost all her sparkle, and even the excitement of preparing for their adventure hadn't brought it back.

'I have also taken the liberty of booking you into a hotel in Southampton quite close to where you will sail from for the evening before your departure,' he informed her. 'The first part of the journey to Southampton will be by train the day before you set sail and again the tickets are all there.'

'You have been most helpful.'

He stared at her for a moment wishing that there was something he could say that would ease her pain, but of course he knew there wasn't. Grief was a funny thing, different people grieved in different ways and there was a process to go through before the healing could begin. He knew that better than most after losing his beloved wife some years before. Now he just hoped that a trip on what was being claimed to be the most luxurious ship in the world might help take her mind off things a little.

Could he have known it, Flora was also looking forward to their journey with very mixed feelings. Part of her was excited at the thought of the adventure that lay ahead but the other part was sad at Jamie's abrupt exit from her life. It was only now that he was gone that she realised just how unfair she had been to him. He had often told her how much he cared for her but she had never committed to him so she supposed the way he had reacted to the thought of her leaving served her right.

Days before she had swallowed her pride and visited the lodging house he had been staying in only to be told by his landlady that he had vacated his room some time ago. She supposed that she could have travelled to his home town to try to find him but how did she know if he was even there? He could have gone anywhere. Anyway, now she knew that he had gone, pride forbade her from doing that. What would be the point? He clearly hadn't thought as much of her as she had thought he did, so she had tried to put him from her mind now and focus on the adventure ahead.

'I shall be bringing you a sum of money to travel with a little nearer to the time,' Mr Wainthrop went on. 'And of course, I shall have some transferred into a bank account in New York that you will be able to draw on whenever you wish. But now I really should get on. Good day, ladies.' He gave a little bow and Mrs Merry showed him out as Flora gathered the documents together.

'I'll go and put these with our luggage, shall I?'

Constance nodded so she left the girl alone and hurried away upstairs. Mrs Merry joined her moments later to show her a little bag she had fashioned.

'I've made this for you to carry Constance's jewels in,' she told Flora solemnly. 'You know how careless she can be about leaving them lying about. It fits about your waist on the belt beneath your skirt or dress, look.' She hurriedly attached it around Flora's waist and the girl thought how ingenious it was. It was made of a very thick twill material that Mrs Merry had added many coats of varnish to, to make it as waterproof as it could possibly be.

'You can keep her aunt's address in there as well, in case you forget it, and any other important papers,' the kindly woman told her. 'And I'm making one now for Constance to wear.'

Flora stifled the urge to laugh. She felt there was very little likelihood of them needing waterproof belts. Already she knew the address they were going to by heart and even if she didn't they were being met off the ship, but not wishing to offend the kind soul she gave her a grateful smile.

'That's ingenious, Mrs Merry. And have no fear, I shall make sure we both wear them at all times.'

Mrs Merry looked pleased and once she had left the room Flora wandered to the window and peered out into the garden. Winter was melting away and spring was in the air. It couldn't come quickly enough as far as she was concerned. The last couple of months had been full of doom and gloom but surely when the trees began to come to life again and the flowers began to peep through the hedgerows they would all feel better. Then, with a sigh she went about her duties.

On Sunday afternoon, just as she had every Sunday since they had parted, Flora made her way to her and Jamie's meeting place on the off-chance that he might be there. Her eyes moved up and down the road looking for a glimpse of him as the minutes ticked away but once again she was disappointed and eventually, with a heavy heart, she turned in the direction of her mother's. Soon it would be too late to tell him that she did genuinely care for him, she and Connie would be gone, but what could she do about it?

'What's up with you then?' her mother greeted her when she stepped through the door. 'You've got a face on you like a wet weekend.'

Flora shrugged as Timmy pottered over to her and wrapped his arms about her waist. 'Oh, nothing really . . . I suppose I'm just getting a bit nervous about going so far away from home now that the time to leave is drawing closer,' she murmured. She would miss seeing them all every week. But then, trying to be a little more cheerful she told her mother, 'Gertie has got herself a new job. She's quite excited about it, as it happens, though goodness knows how she'll go on. She's going to work in a café but she's a terrible butterfingers. Mrs Merry is always telling her off about dropping things.'

'I dare say she'll cope,' her mother said stoically as she expertly sawed a freshly baked loaf into thick slices. There were hard-boiled eggs to go with it this week, courtesy of the neighbour whose sister had visited bringing along a basketful from her hens on her small farm on the outskirts of the city. Emily cut the bread slices in half and when fifteen-year-old Eunice daringly pinched one from the bowl she slapped her hand with the back of the carving knife. Eunice merely giggled and skipped away as Flora stared round at the familiar room. Her father was sitting in his chair at the side of the fire snoozing with the newspaper open on his lap. Only Ben and Katie were missing and when Flora commented on it her mother chuckled.

'Well, they're both at the age when they're just discovering the attraction of the opposite sex,' Emily said with a sigh. 'Our Katie is smitten with a young chap who works at the match factory with her and Ben has his eye on one of his mate's sisters. At this rate you'll all be flown the nest before I know it.'

'Now, Ma, you know that's not true,' Flora scolded. 'I shan't be gone forever for a start off. I shall be back before you know it.'

'You might think that now but three years is a long while. A lot can happen in that time. You might meet a handsome young American who sweeps you off your feet and decide to stay there.'

'I think that's rather unlikely.' After the way Jamie had disappeared out of her life so abruptly, Flora secretly thought it would be some long time before she trusted a fellow again, and anyway, she knew that there would never be anyone but Jamie for her.

She stayed a little longer than usual that day, firstly because she no longer had to rush away to meet Jamie and secondly because she was suddenly realising how much she was going to miss them all when she was gone.

One day in March when Connie was sitting reading the newspaper she asked Flora, 'Have you read this? About the suffragettes going on the rampage in West London. Over a hundred and twenty of them have been arrested, including Mrs Pankhurst. They attacked the shops causing thousands of pounds worth of damage and threw stones at number 10 Downing Street. They're awfully brave, aren't they?'

'Stupid more like,' Cook sniffed. She didn't believe in women fighting for their rights at all. As far as she was concerned girls were bred to be wives and mothers. It was perhaps as well that Miss Connie was going to New York after all. She'd always had a mind of her own and had she been staying she wouldn't have been at all surprised to find her getting involved with the movement.

'I'm not so sure they're brave,' Flora answered. 'I mean, I do believe that women should have equal rights to men but surely they could go about getting them in a more peaceful manner?'

'Well said,' Cook agreed and dropping the tray of tea she had brought them onto the table she sniffed disapprovingly and shuffled away. *But at least she's starting to take an interest in things again*, she thought and took it as a good sign.

Before they knew it, April had arrived, and suddenly it was the week before the girls were due to leave. There was a flurry of last minute packing and making sure they had everything they needed before their trunks were collected to go ahead of them onto the ship. As Flora made her way home after saying goodbye to her siblings on her last Sunday afternoon before their departure, her eyes were full of tears and her mind full of doubts as to whether she was doing the right thing, but it was too late to do anything about it now.

Connie was a bundle of nerves and Mrs Merry wasn't much better so by Monday morning they were all slightly irritable.

'I shall be glad when it's time to catch the train tomorrow morning and just get under way now,' Flora commented to Mrs Merry as she helped her prepare the evening meal.

'Yes, I suppose it will be for the best,' the woman answered, and lowering her head to hide the guilty stain that rose in her cheeks as she thought of the letters hidden in her drawer, she sliced the cold beef that was left over from dinner time. She was going to make sandwiches with it as none of them seemed to have much appetite today. Gertie had left to take up her new post at the café the week before and she was already missing her so she dreaded to think how she was going to feel when Connie and Flora were gone too. It was an awfully large house to rattle round in on her own but then she was grateful that she still had a home at least.

Connie had gone to her room to have a rest some time ago so when the tray was prepared Flora nipped upstairs to fetch her while Mrs Merry carried their meal through to the dining room. She had just placed the tray on the table when someone rapped on the front door and sighing she hurried away to answer it. The colour drained from her face when she found Flora's young man standing on the doorstep. He was very smartly dressed and after respectfully removing his hat he asked, 'May I have a word with Flora, please?'

51

Mrs Merry was all of a dither as she stepped out onto the step to join him, closing the door softly to behind her.

'B-but I thought you'd gone home because your father was ill,' she stammered.

'I did, but thankfully he's much recovered now so I felt it was safe to leave him and come and see Flora before she leaves.'

'I-I'm afraid you're too late, young man . . . they've already gone.'

He looked confused. 'But Flora told me they were sailing on the *Titanic* and that doesn't leave until Wednesday,' he said.

'Ah, well . . . there was a change of plan and they sailed on an earlier ship,' she told him, feeling even more guilty as his face crumpled.

'I see.' He fingered the brim of his hat, looking devastated. 'And did she leave no message for me? You did tell her I called, didn't you? Perhaps you could give me the address in New York where she'll be staying? I could write to her there, although she hasn't replied to any of the letters I've written so far.'

Mrs Merry's heart was hammering so loudly now that she feared he must be able to hear it. Should Flora come back downstairs now she would discover her deceit and she didn't know how she would be able to bear the shame.

'I'm very sorry.' Her voice was firm now. 'But Flora made it perfectly clear that she didn't wish to see or hear from you again, young man, so I'm afraid you are wasting your time here. Good day to you.'

'B-but, *please*—'

She turned abruptly, stepped back into the hall and closed the door firmly in his face. For a moment she stood with her back flat to the door as her heartbeat slowed to a steadier rhythm, then as she headed for the dining room she heard Flora's light footsteps on the stairs.

'Was that someone at the door, Merry?' she asked.

'Oh, just someone selling something,' the woman said, keeping her voice steady but guilt was eating away at her as an image of the young man's sad face flashed in front of her eyes.

She saw Flora's devasted expression. She knew the girl had been hoping against hope that Jamie might still come before she and Connie left. But then, she consoled herself, both he and Flora were young with their whole lives in front of them. There would be plenty of time for them both to meet someone else they would care for, surely? Right now, Connie needed Flora to go with her to New York after all she had been through, so she tried to convince herself that she had done the right thing.

Chapter Six

'Now, are you quite sure you've got everything?' Mrs Merry asked on the morning of their departure for at least the tenth time in as many minutes.

'Yes, I'm *quite* sure, Merry,' Connie told her gently as she fastened her hat on with a large, lethal-looking hat pin. It was a fancy concoction in a dark purple, wide-brimmed and trimmed with ostrich feathers. She was wearing a deep-purple two-piece costume in the latest fashion to go with it, which had a short jacket, a straight, ankle-length skirt, and a smart, white ruffled blouse.

'And have you got your belts safely on?'

'Yes, Merry.'

Where did the time go? Mrs Merry wondered as she fussed about the girl. It seemed like only yesterday that Connie had been just a little girl and now here she was a young woman about to embark on the biggest adventure of her life so far. Standing beside her, Flora was also looking very smart in a cloche hat and a long-sleeved, pale green day dress that Connie had given her to travel in. Cook was there as well and was sniffing noisily into a big white handkerchief. Later that day she would be leaving to take up her new position in a big house on the outskirts of the town but she had purposely waited to see her young mistress off.

Outside a horse-drawn cab was waiting to take them to the train station where they would begin the first leg of their journey, the horse restlessly pawing the ground and snickering, so Connie gave Mrs Merry and the cook one last gentle kiss on their cheeks.

'Take care of yourselves,' she said, her eyes full of tears. 'And don't forget, Cook, when I come home you can come back if you want to.'

'I certainly shall, yer needn't worry about that,' Cook assured her as they all stepped outside. On the step, Connie paused and took one last glance back at the house that had been the only home she could remember, then with a sigh she urged Flora towards the cab.

Flora's parents would be waiting for them at the train station and Flora didn't know if she was looking forward to seeing them one last time or dreading it. She knew how hard it was going to be and hoped that she wouldn't break down when the time came for her and Connie to board the train. In no time at all they were settled in the cab and they hung out of the window and waved until Mrs Merry and Cook were gone from sight.

Connie leaned back against the leather squabs and sighed. 'This is it then,' she said quietly and Flora nodded. She had only been on a train once before some years ago when her parents had taken her and her siblings to Southend for the day, and she was looking forward to the journey with a mixture of emotions: sadness, excitement and trepidation.

Just as they had promised, Flora's parents were waiting on the platform when they arrived at the station. She had said her goodbyes to her brothers and sisters the Sunday before and as Connie settled herself into a carriage, Flora placed her arms about them both.

'Look after yourselves, do you hear?' She blinked back tears and forced a smile. 'And just remember to write. Never forget I shall be back before you know it. Three years will pass in no time.'

Her mother sniffed into a big white handkerchief as her father lifted her overnight bag onto the train.

'You just be careful, now,' her mother told her in a wobbly voice as she clutched her daughter to her as if she might never let her go. 'And don't get venturin' out on your own in that strange city!'

The porter blew his whistle then and they heard the large engine chug into life.

'Best climb aboard, love.' Even her father's voice was choked as he pecked her on the cheek and she scrambled aboard closing the door behind her then stood waving through the window as the train chugged out of the station.

The journey from Waterloo Station was uneventful, although Flora did find it somewhat harrowing as she thought of leaving Jamie and all the people she loved far behind her. Would she ever see Jamie again? she wondered. If only he hadn't disappeared like that, she could have told him how much she loved him. She wished he'd given her just one more chance. But now it was too late, and her heart mourned at the thought of her lost love.

Connie was quiet so Flora spent most of the time watching the passing scenery from the window and in the late afternoon the train drew into Southampton. A porter quickly collected their luggage and loaded it onto a trolley for them then led them to the exit where a row of cabs was waiting for fares.

'We're going to the South Western Hotel on the corner of Terminus Terrace and Canute Road,' Connie told the porter as she consulted Mr Wainthrop's list of instructions. He had been very explicit.

'Ah well, that's just down the way, miss,' the kindly porter answered. 'It's hardly worth getting in a cab if you don't mind a short walk. I'll bring this along for you and show you the way if you like.'

'That's very kind. Thank you.' Connie inclined her head then she and Flora set off at a trot trying to keep up with him. At the hotel entrance, which was very impressive indeed, another young porter in a smart uniform rushed outside to lift their bags from the trolley while Connie thanked their guide and gave him a handsome tip.

'Thank you, miss.' He doffed his cap. 'Here for the launch of the *Titanic*, are you?'

'We're sailing on her, actually,' Connie informed him and he whistled through his teeth.

'Then I wish you a good journey, miss.' He gave both girls a beaming smile and went off whistling merrily, trundling his empty trolley behind him.

'Right, let's go and get booked in,' Connie suggested, seeing that Flora was looking a little out of her depth. 'Then I suggest we order some food to be sent up to our room. I could kill for a cup of tea right now. We could go out later on if you feel like it and have a look around.'

'Oh yes, I'd like that.' Flora nodded as side by side they entered the magnificent hotel. The foyer was splendid and full of very wealthy-looking people dressed in the very latest fashions.

'Miss Ogilvie and Miss Butler,' Connie told the receptionist as the woman quickly ran her finger down a list of names in a large register that stood open in front of her on a highly polished desk.

'Ah, yes, Miss Ogilvie, here you are. You have adjoining rooms on the third floor with a view of the docks. I do hope it's to your satisfaction. The porter will deliver your luggage to your rooms immediately and a maid will be up shortly to unpack it for you. Is there anything else I can do for you?'

'Yes, you could have a tray of tea for two sent up and perhaps a selection of cakes,' Connie answered confidently and Flora gulped. This was like walking into another world.

A glittering crystal chandelier hung in the centre of the foyer and beyond it a sweeping staircase with a huge, galleried landing led up to the first floor. The floor was covered in a thick wall-to-wall carpet that Flora's feet seemed to sink into and everywhere she looked were tiny, gilt-legged chairs and leather settees with well-dressed people taking afternoon tea on them.

Connie and Flora followed the young porter to a lift that was set to one side of the foyer and Flora got into it feeling nervous as the porter slammed shut the metal grille on the front of it. The next second, she felt as if she had left her stomach on the ground as it purred into life and began to ascend, but before she could comment on it to Connie it slowed to a stop.

'Third floor, ladies.' The young porter wheeled their trolley ahead of them then, stopping in front of a door, he opened it for them and lifted their luggage into the room before handing the key to Connie who quickly slipped him a tip.

Flora stared about her open-mouthed. '*Wow!*' she squeaked eventually as she ran to the window. 'This is just *beautiful*! And look, Connie. *That* must be the *Titanic* there.' She stabbed her finger towards the most enormous ship she had ever seen. 'But she's *huge*, how will she ever manage to stay afloat?'

Connie joined her at the window and grinned. The *Titanic* really was quite majestic and towered above the docks making the other ships look like little rowing boats. The sailors standing on her decks high against the skyline looked like mere specks. 'That's modern technology for you, but that must be your room through that door there. Do you want to take a peek?'

Flora was off like a shot and once again Connie heard her squeal with delight. There was a pale green carpet on the floor and in the centre of one wall was a four-poster bed. Chintz curtains to match the ones that hung at the window were hung about it and there was a whole suite of matching furniture in a highly polished rosewood.

'It's fit for a princess,' Flora declared as Connie joined her to take a look. 'I never thought the day would ever come when I would stay in a hotel like this. It must have cost a fortune.'

Connie shrugged as she went back to her own room to check

out another door that led to their own private bathroom. 'Mr Wainthrop has certainly done us proud,' she admitted. 'But then I can well afford it so just enjoy your stay. If what they say is true then our cabins aboard the *Titanic* will be just as lovely. They say she's like a floating hotel and she's so big she could house the people of a whole town.'

Flora nodded as she peeped at the enormous ship from her bedroom window again. The docks below her were bustling with activity. Burly seamen were rolling barrels and all manner of things up gangplanks onto her while many finely dressed people strolled by, keen to get a glimpse of what was reputed to be the world's first unsinkable ship.

There was a tap at Connie's door and a young maid appeared in a starched white mobcap and apron trimmed with broderie anglaise, wheeling a tea trolley.

'Shall I pour for you, miss?'

'No, thank you, just take it over to the chairs by the window, please.'

The young maid did as she was asked then bobbed her knee and left as Connie and Flora took a seat each. For a moment, Flora gazed in admiration at the solid silver teapot, sugar bowl and milk jug before remembering her duty and straining the tea into two bone-china cups that were so fine she could almost see through them. As they helped themselves to a selection of tiny cucumber sandwiches and small, bite-sized cream cakes, Flora sighed with delight.

'I swear this tea tastes better than any I've ever had,' she told Connie with a sparkle in her eye. Despite her initial nervousness she was beginning to feel excited now.

As they were finishing another maid appeared and quickly unpacked their night things for them before asking, 'Will you be wishing me to unpack gowns for dinner, ladies? The restaurant is open from seven till ten o'clock each evening.'

Flora flushed. Connie had given her some beautiful dresses but they were mostly day dresses. She didn't even possess an evening gown.

'Yes, you can unpack the blue stain and the lilac chiffon.'

The maid quickly did as she was asked and once the gowns were safely hung away in the armoire she discreetly took her leave.

'You can borrow my blue satin gown this evening,' Connie told her.

Flora shook her head. 'Thank you, but I think I'll stay in my room,' she mumbled. 'I'd feel out of place down there with all those posh people and I might let you down by using the wrong knife or fork or something.'

'Nonsense!' Connie scolded. 'All you have to do is remember to work from the outside of your cutlery in for each course. Just watch me. You have to eat, Flora, and that dress will suit your colouring perfectly. If you don't go down to dinner, then I can't,' she added craftily. 'It would be very unseemly for an unattached young woman to be seen dining alone.'

'Very well,' Flora agreed reluctantly, knowing when she was beaten, and they both decided to rest for a while before going out to take a look at Southampton.

As they strolled along the dock early that evening the air was heavy with anticipation as people clustered in groups to stare at the majestic ship. There was a nip in the air so after a time the girls returned to the hotel to get ready for dinner. Flora would have much preferred to dine alone in her room but knowing that Connie couldn't go down without her she sat patiently while Connie tried to dress her hair, smiling to herself slightly at this reversal of roles. It was usually her dressing Connie's hair.

'It's so thick, it seems to have a life of its own,' Connie complained through a mouthful of pins, but eventually she managed to pile it on top of Flora's head and was clearly pleased with the results.

'It makes you look older and more sophisticated,' Connie commented as she studied her efforts in the dressing table mirror. 'But why can't I do yours for you as quickly as you do mine?'

Flora chuckled. 'Because I have had a lot more practice,' she pointed out as she reached out for the dainty evening bag that Connie had lent to her. In the lovely blue gown, she felt like a princess and quite unlike herself, and it was a feeling she was sure she could get used to it. Suddenly she wished Jamie could see her now. Would he regret running away from her if he could see her looking like this?

The happy feeling continued down in the luxurious dining room as waiters served one delicious course after another. Connie merely picked at her food but Flora ate everything that was put in front of her and enjoyed every mouthful.

'I know you told me it's etiquette to leave a little on your plate and I meant to,' she whispered to Connie between courses. 'But everything is so tasty that I cleared the plates without thinking.'

Connie gave her an indulgent smile. It was nice to see Flora enjoying herself. She had been her rock since she had lost her father and Connie really didn't know how she would have got through things without her. She glanced around, feeling a little uncomfortable, they were both attracting more than a few admiring glances from the gentlemen in the restaurant, although Flora seemed oblivious to it, and Connie was glad when they could escape back to their rooms. After confining herself to the house following her father's death she was finding it hard to be out in company again, although Flora was clearly loving every minute.

Once they were back upstairs, Flora helped Connie prepare for bed then went to her own room where she tossed and turned as she thought of the adventure ahead. It was strange to think that at this time the following day they would be out at sea with their homeland far behind them. Her happy mood evaporated and her eyes filled with tears as she once again thought of her family and,

Chapter Seven

The sound of people on the docks woke Flora early the next morning and hurrying out of bed she crossed to the window and drew aside the curtains. She had thought it was busy the night before but that had been nothing compared to now. Already passengers were pouring up the gangplanks to board the ship and for a moment she panicked and wondered if they had overslept as she raced to the door adjoining Connie's room. She found Connie already up and the girl smiled at her.

'Hello, sleepyhead,' she greeted her. 'I've ordered breakfast to be brought up to us. I was just going to come and wake you.'

'I'm so sorry,' Flora murmured sleepily, knuckling the sleep from her eyes. 'I lay awake for ages then when I did drop off I must have gone into a deep sleep.'

Connie shrugged. 'It doesn't matter. We have plenty of time.' The words had barely left her lips when there was a tap on the door and a young, fresh-faced maid appeared with a trolley.

'Full English and tea for two, miss?' She smiled cheerily as she wheeled the trolley to a small table set in the window. 'Would you like me to pour?'

'No, thank you, I can do that,' Flora assured her and once the maid had gone they began to lift the covers from the dishes. Flora had been sure, after the enormous dinner she'd consumed the evening before, that she wouldn't be able to eat again for at least a week but suddenly she was hungry and did full justice to the meal. There was crispy bacon, fat juicy sausages, devilled kidneys, fried eggs, and mushrooms. There was also toast and a huge pot of tea, and by the time she'd finished she was sure that she was going to burst.

'I'm afraid I've made rather a pig of myself again,' she apologised but Connie waved her hand airily. She herself had merely nibbled at a slice of toast and even that had stuck in her throat.

'That's what it's there for, but now if you've finished we ought to get dressed.'

An hour later they were ready to leave and Connie summoned a porter to go to their room and collect their luggage. In no time at all they were amid the thronging crowds on the dock as Connie rifled through their bags for their tickets. By then a boat train from Waterloo had arrived carrying passengers and they joined the queue to board the ship. The vast majority of these were people emigrating to the United States, lured by the White Star's campaign promising a better life there. There was also a large number of crew who had been boarding the ship since six thirty that morning, although Flora noticed they used a separate gang-plank. Eventually they reached the deck where each passenger was greeted by Captain Smith. Since deciding to sail on her, Connie had read every detail she could about the *Titanic*, so she knew already that he used to be the captain of the *Olympic*, the *Titanic*'s sister ship. It reassured her that he clearly knew how to manage such an enormous ship.

Connie and Flora were shown to their state rooms, which were so magnificent they took their breath away. They had wall-to-wall carpets and beautiful furniture and fittings. They even had their own private promenade deck and Flora ran about inspecting everything, as excited as a child.

'I can't *believe* we're on a ship,' she said, her eyes sparkling as she threw open the wardrobe doors. Their luggage had been sent on ahead and already it had been neatly unpacked and hung.

'That must be the door leading to your room there,' Connie said and sure enough when Flora raced away to check she found herself in another room almost as luxurious as Connie's.

'Oh, everything is just *so* beautiful,' Flora crowed, throwing her arms out and dancing a little jig.

Connie smiled indulgently as she strolled out onto the deck to watch the activity on the dock. It was heaving with people now who had come specially to see the *Titanic* off on her maiden voyage. A band was playing somewhere and the air was buzzing with excitement. Connie and Flora set off, intent on exploring the ship but realised in a very short time that it was going to take a while. It was absolutely enormous and divided into three sections for first-, second- and third-class passengers. In the centre of their section was the most magnificent staircase that Flora had ever seen. She stared in awe at the glass dome that sat above it, then hurried to catch up with Connie who had continued on without her. The staircase ran from the top of the ship down seven decks to the bottom, and the girls decided to go all the way to the bottom and work their way up. They peeped into the Turkish baths and Flora was very taken with the open-air swimming pool. 'Just imagine having a swimming pool aboard a boat!' she gasped.

They walked back up and soon they found themselves in the dining saloon. The room itself was huge and decorated in the Louis XIV period – or so Connie said – but all Flora knew was that she could never have imagined such elegance and magnificence even existed. It was panelled from floor to ceiling in beautifully marked French walnut in a delicate light brown colour and all the mouldings and ornaments were richly carved and gilded. Large electric light brackets, fine-chased in brass and gilt and holding candle bulbs, were fixed along the entire length of the panelling and Flora couldn't help but think of the gas mantles back in her mother's tiny house in Pleasant Row. There were huge bay windows draped in fawn silk curtains with embroidered detail with richly embroidered pelmets and the floor was covered in a beautiful Axminster carpet that stretched from wall to wall. Small tables and chairs were laid out about the room and elegant crystal lamps with rose-coloured shades illuminated each one. A bandstand partly recessed and raised on a platform stood at one end of the room and on either side of it was a carved buffet table.

'It's really hard to remember that we're on a ship, isn't it?' Flora mused as they walked back up to deck.

Throughout the rest of the morning passengers continued to come aboard until finally the gangplanks were hauled away. Then, promptly at twelve noon as Connie and Flora stood on their private deck once more, three loud blasts of the *Titanic*'s powerful whistles heralded her departure. A roar and a cheer went up from the people on the docks. Passengers were leaning over the ship's rails waving wildly to the people they were leaving behind. Some were sobbing and Flora felt tears prick at the back of her own eyes as she thought yet again of Jamie and her family.

Slowly and smoothly the enormous ship began to pull away and very soon the people on the docks were merely dots in the distance. The first stop was to be Cherbourg in France, followed by Queenstown in southern Ireland. From there it would be full steam ahead across the wide-open waters of the Atlantic to New York.

Once their homeland had disappeared from view, they set off to explore further. The movement of the ship was so smooth that Flora remarked that it was hard to believe they weren't on dry land.

There was so much to see that they barely knew where to start. They came across a large and spacious lounge decorated in the Georgian style where friends could meet for a drink before going in to dine – at Connie's explanation, Flora rolled her eyes. At this rate, she'd know far more about furniture than she'd ever really wanted to – with elegant little settees and easy chairs upholstered tastefully in carmine-coloured silk that exactly complemented the carpet and the walls. Next they went to peep into the shops and were shocked to see that there was even a hairdresser. 'Although I would much rather you do mine,' Connie assured Flora.

It was late that afternoon when they returned to their cabin to find that Connie had received an invitation to dine at the captain's table that evening. She knew that it was a great honour but nevertheless she politely declined explaining to the messenger that she was still in mourning for her father and wished to cause no offence.

'I'll be sure to relay your message, miss,' the young steward replied and quietly slipped away.

Flora frowned. She was thoroughly enjoying being in such opulent surroundings and would have loved to dine with the captain, although of course she realised his invitation would not extend to maids and, at the end of the day, that was what she still was.

'You should start to move on with your life again. You can't stay in mourning forever,' she gently pointed out.

Connie shrugged. 'That's easy for you to say, never having lost someone close who you love dearly,' she responded.

Much to Flora's disappointment, after their initial exploration, Connie had stated that she was going to keep to her suite, and not wanting to leave her on her own, Flora stayed with her. But the following day, Flora grew restless from being cooped up. She was pacing on their private deck and listening to the hubbub around them, wishing she could see what was going on, when Connie said, 'Why don't you go and have a wander around? I'm going to curl up with my book.' She had borrowed *The Lost World* written by Arthur Conan Doyle from the ship's library and was quite looking forward to a little peace and quiet so that she could

67

read it. Since boarding the ship Flora had been so excited that she had chattered almost non-stop.

'*Well* . . . if you're quite sure you don't mind and you won't need me,' Flora replied hesitantly.

'I'm *quite* sure!' Connie dropped onto a chair and put her feet up on a stool as if to prove the point so Flora quickly went to find her bonnet and after promising not to be gone too long she set off. First, she went to peep through the window of the splendid first-class dining room, which she still considered was surely one of the most impressive rooms on the whole ship. She then went to watch the people playing squash for a while and took a stroll round the swimming pool. Next, she headed for the shops, swooning with envy as she saw some of the magnificent things for sale. The ship was clearly catering for the very wealthy for most of the things cost more than she could earn in a whole year. Still, it was nice to gaze through the windows. As she was drooling over a ruby ring in the jeweller's shop window she became aware of someone standing close behind her, and thinking that it was Connie come to join her she swung about with a wide smile on her face, 'I say, have you seen . . .' She stopped and blushed furiously as she found herself face to face with a tall, good-looking young gentleman.

'Good afternoon, miss. I'm so sorry if I startled you.' He swept his smart bowler hat off and gave a little bow as Flora's stomach did a little flip.

'It's quite all right . . . I just thought you were someone else.' Her voice came out as a squeak and she blushed an even deeper shade of red.

'Ah.' His smile was infectious and she found herself smiling back at him. 'Are you enjoying the trip?' he asked genially and she nodded.

'Oh yes. The ship is just . . .' She spread her hands as she tried to think of words that could describe it. 'Just beautiful,' she said eventually. She was captivated by his wonderful American accent. It was like nothing she had ever heard before.

He glanced about the deck then before asking, 'Are you travelling alone?'

She was so busy staring at him, taking in his thick dark hair and deep-blue eyes, that she almost forgot to answer. 'Oh n-no,' she stammered eventually. 'I'm travelling with my mistress.'

'I see.' He raised his eyebrow a little. He had assumed that because she was in the first-class area of the ship that she was some rich young woman. But then, he asked himself, did it really matter if she was merely a maid? She was pretty in her own way and could certainly help to pass the time on board. 'Tobias Johnson at your service, ma'am,' he introduced himself with a gallant little bow.

'F-Flora Butler,' she muttered as he gravely shook her hand.

'Would you like to take a turn about the decks, Flora?'

Her heart began to race and, afraid that she might make a fool of herself if she tried to answer, she merely nodded as he crooked his arm for her to thread hers through. She hesitated for a second. It seemed very forward to stroll about with a young man when they had only just met and a picture of Jamie flashed in front of her eyes. But Jamie had left her and not even tried to contact her, she thought with a burst of anger, so what could be the harm in it? she asked herself.

Seconds later they were walking along looking for all the world like a young couple in love. It was still only April and now that they were out on the open sea there was a cruel bite in the air but Flora hardly noticed it as she peeped at her companion from the corner of her eye. He was certainly very handsome, and wealthy too if the way he was dressed was anything to go by.

'So, are you going to holiday in America?' he asked after a time.

Flora shook her head. 'No, Mr Johnson. My mistress is going to stay with her aunt in New York for three years.'

He squeezed her fingers and her heart did a little somersault as he told her, 'You must call me Toby. All my friends do, although my parents will never shorten my name.' He chuckled. 'I'm travelling with them now. My father has a number of businesses in London that he needed to visit and seeing as I had nothing else on I decided I would come with him and my mother.'

'Don't you have a job?' she asked innocently and he chuckled.

'Goodness me, no. Why would *I* work? My father is very wealthy indeed. I have a monthly allowance and that, along with an inheritance from my late grandmother, ensures that I don't need to. Of course, when anything happens to my father I'll probably have to take over the businesses but until then I shall just concentrate on being young and enjoying myself.'

Flora secretly thought that this sounded very selfish, yet it didn't put her off him in the least. Admittedly as she looked at her hand resting on his arm she did feel a little pang of guilt again as she thought of Jamie, but she quickly pushed him from her mind. It was he who had left her after all, so why shouldn't she enjoy herself while she could?

Toby began to tell her of his home and the horses he owned and she hung on his every word. Every now and again she felt she ought to pinch herself just to make sure that this was really happening. Who would ever have thought that a wealthy, well-brought-up young gentleman would ever look at the likes of her? But he had and suddenly she wished that the journey could go on forever, but as it couldn't, she intended to make the most of every single minute of it.

Chapter Eight

'Flora . . . *Flora*! Whatever is the matter with you? It's as if you're in your own little world.'

'Wh-*what*? Oh, sorry, Connie. I was miles away,' Flora apologised. 'What was it you said?'

'I *asked* three times . . . where is my bed jacket?' Connie frowned. 'What's wrong with you? Are you feeling seasick or something?'

'Oh no, no, it's nothing like that,' Flora hastily assured her as she crossed to a chest of drawers and immediately found what Connie wanted. 'It's just . . . Well, if you must know, I've met someone. A really lovely young man, as it happens.'

Connie frowned again as she saw the dreamy look in Flora's eyes. 'Well, I hope you won't forget what you've come for – to keep me company?' she griped.

'Of course I won't!' Flora was indignant now. 'I just met him this afternoon and only then because you wanted some quiet time and sent me off out so you could read your book. Had you needed me I wouldn't even have gone out, you *know* I wouldn't.'

'Sorry,' Connie said, feeling guilty now. 'And of course you need some time to yourself too. But do be careful. I mean . . . this man could be anybody. Is he from the steerage passengers?'

'As it happens he and his parents have a suite of rooms like this in first class.' Flora's chin came up as she gazed at Connie as if daring her to dispute it.

'Oh . . . I see.' Connie gazed back at her solemnly. 'Then just be careful all the same. We are two young women travelling on our own and you know what Mr Wainthrop said, trust no one.'

Flora pursed her lips and started to prepare the table ready for their meal. She desperately longed to go to the sumptuous dining room but Connie was still insisting that their meals were served in their room. Still, she thought, she'd taken to going to bed early since she'd lost her father, so it might be possible to slip out and see Toby later that evening. He had hinted that he might take a stroll along the promenade deck before retiring.

Just as she had hoped, Connie was settled in bed with her book by nine o'clock so Flora hurriedly slipped away to her own room and brushed her hair till it shone. She put her cape and bonnet on and tiptoed out into the cold night air. She could hear music coming from the direction of the dining room and was lured to the sound like a moth to a flame. Through the window she could see elegant women wearing stunning gowns in all the colours of the rainbow, seated next to gentlemen who dressed in formal black dinner suits that made them look like the pictures of penguins she had seen in books. Every woman seemed to be dripping in jewels as if they were trying to outdo each other and they flashed in the lights of the spar-kling crystal chandeliers. Huge vases of exotic-looking flowers were dotted about the edges of the room and although she was outside she could imagine how beautiful they must smell. She was so taken with the sight that when Toby came up behind her and gently placed his hand on her arm she almost jumped out of her skin.

'Sorry, I didn't mean to startle you.' He grinned. 'I thought it was you staring through the window. Why don't you come in?'

He too was wearing a dark evening suit, complemented by a crisp white shirt and a black dicky bow, and he looked very suave and sophisticated.

'Oh, I er . . . I'm not really dressed for it,' she muttered, staring down at her plain day dress. It was one of Connie's old ones and by far the best she had ever owned but she knew that she would stand out like a sore thumb if she were to walk into the dining room in it and felt deeply embarrassed.

'For what it's worth I think you look quite delightful,' he told her smoothly, making hot colour burn in her cheeks. 'But if you don't feel comfortable coming inside why don't we take advantage of the music and have a dance out here?'

'*Here!*' She stared around the deserted deck. It was far too cold for many people to want to venture outside and her breath was hanging in the air in front of her like fine lace. Even so when he placed his arm about her waist, heat flooded through her. The band were playing a waltz and she lowered her eyes as she told him, 'I-I'm not really much good at dancing.'

'Then I'll teach you,' he told her, raising her hand into his. Very gently he began to lead her and as she stared up into his handsome face she did her best to match her steps to his.

'There you are,' he teased. 'You're a natural.' Very soon they were gliding along the deck and Flora felt as if she was floating and wished that it could go on forever. The moon was turning the sea to liquid silver and the night took on a magical air. However, after a time he told her regretfully, 'I suppose I should be getting back in now. My parents will wonder where I've got to. Are you sure you won't come in?'

Flora came back down to earth with a bump as she hastily stepped away from him. Whatever would his parents think of her . . . a maid!

'No, thank you, I ought to get back to make sure that Connie doesn't need anything.'

'Very well, then hopefully I shall see you at some point tomorrow, Flora. Goodnight.' Before she knew what was happening he bent his head and as his lips lightly brushed hers her heart started to hammer so loudly in her chest that she was sure he must be able to hear it.

'Goodnight, Toby.'

He gave her a courteous little bow and she stood as if rooted to the spot until he disappeared back through the doors. When he was gone she raised her hand to touch her lips and just for a second she thought of the kisses she'd shared with Jamie, but she pushed the thought away; he'd made his choice when he ran away. So, smiling to herself, she hurried back to her room where she sat shivering and staring through the cabin window at the stars overhead, reliving every second of the evening in her mind.

The following morning at breakfast Connie remarked, 'You're very quiet today. Are you feeling unwell?'

'Not at all.' Flora helped herself to another fried egg. All this fresh air was giving her an enormous appetite. 'On the contrary, I feel wonderful. Who wouldn't aboard such a lovely ship? Why don't you come for a stroll this morning? You're looking a little pale and the fresh air will do you good.'

'I suppose it wouldn't hurt to take a turn around the deck but we'll have to wrap up warmly, it seems to be getting colder by the minute. The steward who brought my cocoa last night said we could be seeing icebergs in another day or so.'

As Flora laid Connie's clothes out for her she groaned as she saw the belt that Mrs Merry had made for her. 'Do I *have* to wear that again today? It's rubbed all the skin around my middle.'

'Mine has too,' Flora admitted. 'But I have worn it religiously just as I promised her I would.' Connie's jewels and papers were evenly spread between the two belts.

'Let's just hide them in here for today. It's hardly likely that anyone is going to come in and steal them, is it? Merry was so worried that I might forget my aunt's address but I swear it's burned into my brain even if I were to lose it.'

'Mine too,' Flora admitted and promptly pushed both of the belts into the bottom of the wardrobe and covered them with a carpet bag. 'There!' She stood back up and rubbed her hands together with a satisfied sigh. 'It will be nice not to have it digging into me every time I sit down for a while.'

They set off for a brisk walk along the promenade. The first-class deck was decorated in a Tudor style – for once, Flora recognised this – and stretched all along the side of the ship with comfortable padded chairs set down the length of it, where wealthy women in expensive-looking fur coats sat sipping coffee and chatting. The deck was under cover but it was still bitterly cold as the girls stood at the rails looking out at the vast expanse of the ocean. They walked up and down for a little while, until by mid-morning Flora persuaded Connie to go into one of the many salons leading from it. The fragrant aroma of coffee greeted them the second they stepped through the door and they had barely had time to find a seat when a waiter in a snow-white jacket with a little towel folded neatly across his arm hurried over to take their order.

'Yes, ladies, what may I get for you?' he purred respectfully and Connie gave him their order.

'Ah, this is the life,' Flora remarked, her cheeks pink from the cold air outside. 'I could get used to being waited on like this.'

'Instead of you having to wait on me, you mean?' Connie asked with a grin.

'No . . . I didn't mean that at all. I love working for you,' Flora told her. 'But that doesn't mean to say that I can't make the most of it, does it? We've been sailing for two days already. The voyage will be over before we know it so I'm going to make the most of every minute.'

They enjoyed coffee and fresh-baked biscuits and Connie

watched Flora tuck in with amusement. 'You'll be the size of a house by the time we get to New York at this rate,' she teased.

'I know.' Flora managed to spray crumbs all down the front of her dress. 'I really should stop eating so much but everything is so tasty.'

At that moment a heavily made-up, middle-aged woman and a gentleman went by them and leaning towards Connie, Flora whispered, 'Do you suppose that's a real mink coat she's wearing?'

Connie nodded. 'Undoubtedly. There are some very rich people aboard. She's probably got a wardrobe full of them.'

'*Blimey!*' The word slipped out before she could stop it and Flora glanced at Connie apologetically. Soon after they embarked on another tour of the ship, this time to the tennis courts, but as lunchtime approached they made their way back to their rooms.

'I'm not really hungry but get the steward to bring you anything you want,' Connie told her. 'I'm going to lie on my bed and read for a while.'

Flora spent a restless hour pacing up and down. She longed to go and see if she could track Toby down but didn't dare to in case Connie needed anything. She was supposed to be there to cater to her every need after all, although the maids and stewards seemed to be doing a very good job of that. All she was really needed for was to arrange Connie's hair and help her with dressing and undressing.

It wasn't until Connie was settled that evening that she managed to get out again and once more she headed for the dining room to stare through the windows, hoping for a sight of Toby. Once again she was mesmerised as she stared at the women in their beautiful gowns and listened to the sound of the orchestra. The dining room was quite stunning with huge marble pillars that reached right up to the ceiling and with the beautiful sweeping staircase rising up from it, the entire scene looked like it had come straight out of a fairy tale.

'I hope you're looking for me?'

The voice made her spin around and when she saw Toby standing there her face lit up.

'I was hoping you'd come,' he said, and taking her hand he began to lead her away. Soon she was completely lost as they climbed up to the upper decks, but still she followed him trustingly until they came to the lifeboats where he dragged her into the shadows.

'I know what girls like you want,' he said as his arms came tightly about her and the first feelings of panic fluttered to life in her stomach. Where was the knight in shining armour who had held her tenderly in his arms and danced the night away with her the night before? He had her backed up tight to one of the lifeboats and now his hands began to roam up and down her body.

'What are you *doing*?' she snapped indignantly as she tried to thrust him away. 'And what exactly do you mean? Girls like *me*!'

'Now don't be a tease.' His mouth was pressed against her ear and she began to struggle.

'Toby . . . stop it this minute, do you hear me?' she yelped but he appeared to have gone deaf as he thrust his hand into her cape and viciously squeezed her breast.

'I shall scream if you don't stop!' she warned him and when he ignored her and carried on groping she brought her knee up with all the force she could muster, catching him right between the legs. It was a little tip her brother had taught her years ago if ever she found herself in just this position. He instantly doubled over and reeled away from her as she hastily stepped around him and attempted to straighten her hat which was all askew.

'*You* are no gentleman, sir!' she spat as she sailed past him, but inside she was crying. How *could* I have been so foolish as to trust him? she berated herself. Men like him felt that girls from the lower classes like me are just there to be used and abused. Didn't Connie try to warn me? But I was so swept away with him and so flattered at his attention that I wasn't thinking straight. *Well, I certainly won't make that mistake again*, she promised herself, feeling dirty and humiliated as she raced back to her room without once looking back. She couldn't help thinking how different Toby was to Jamie. Not once in all the time she had known him had Jamie ever attempted to abuse her, nor had he ever treated her with anything other than loving respect. But then Jamie was a true gentleman. She realised now that she had only responded to Toby's attentions because she was trying to forget the way Jamie had abandoned her, not that she could blame him, and once again she felt bereft.

'What a difference a day makes,' Connie remarked the next morning as Flora poured the tea. 'You were on top of the world yesterday about your new beau but this morning you look as if the end of the world is nigh. What's wrong?'

'Nothing . . . I just have a slight headache, and I er . . . thought on what you said and decided that I perhaps didn't want to see him again after all,' Flora replied sulkily. She was far too humiliated to tell Connie the truth.

'That must have been the shortest romance in history,' Connie answered, raising an eyebrow inquisitively, but Flora remained stubbornly silent.

But at least I've learned a lesson, Flora told herself silently and tried to go on as if nothing had happened. It had been a very hard lesson indeed.

Chapter Nine

Connie and Flora were strolling along the promenade later that day when to her horror, Flora saw Toby heading towards them with an older couple who she assumed were his parents.

The woman was wearing a long, fur-trimmed coat and the man looked like an older version of Toby. She flushed and averted her eyes but as they drew abreast of them Toby raised his hat and gave Connie a dazzling smile.

'Good morning, ladies.'

'Good morning,' Connie answered and Flora's humiliation was complete. He hadn't even glanced at her.

'He was a very charming, handsome young man,' Connie remarked when they had passed them. Flora didn't reply, she had no intention of telling her that he was the man she'd been sneaking out to meet. She just hoped that she would never have to clap eyes on Tobias Johnson again.

The weather had turned even more bitterly cold now and here and there they could see icebergs towering out of the sea.

'Let's get back into the warm,' Connie suggested a few moments later. 'It's far too cold to be out here.'

Flora was only too happy to oblige. The extreme change in temperature and the towering icebergs that jutted out of the sea were making her feel nervous. That, on top of seeing Toby, made her feel that the whole trip was ruined for her and she could hardly wait for them to dock in New York now.

They spent the rest of the day in their rooms, reading and resting and Flora was glad when it was time for them to retire.

The next day it seemed even colder and they ventured no further than the ship's library but luckily, they didn't bump into Toby again.

'Just a few more days and we'll be in New York,' Flora commented as she brushed Connie's hair for her that night before they retired.

Connie nodded. She too would be glad when the journey was over now. She was bored.

Flora went to bed at about ten thirty after making sure that Connie no longer needed her and for the first time since they had sailed she fell asleep almost instantly.

Suddenly, she was jolted awake. Glancing at the clock she saw that it was eleven forty-five. There was a loud, piercing grinding noise that seemed to go right through her and set her teeth on edge and she felt the ship shudder. She lay for a moment, eyes wide and staring into the darkness, wondering what on earth had happened. Slowly she became aware that the engine noise that had been in the background since the ship had set sail had fallen silent. Had the engines stopped? Throwing back her covers, she jumped out of bed and rushed into Connie's room where she found her awake too.

'Did you hear something?' Connie asked fearfully as she peeped over the top of the bedclothes.

'Yes, it was like a grinding noise and I can't hear the engines. I felt the ship shudder too. What do you think has happened?'

Connie shrugged as she swung her legs out of the bed. 'I have no idea but it can't be anything serious, can it? They have said this ship is unsinkable, haven't they?'

There were noises outside in the corridor then and the girls crept to the door and peeped out to see what was happening. A steward was trying to reassure other passengers who had been awakened and were streaming out into the corridors in their nightclothes.

'There's nothing to worry about whatsoever,' they heard him say. 'We have hit an iceberg but it just means it might take us a few more days to reach New York than planned.'

Flora glanced at Connie and noticed that she had gone terribly pale and she looked terrified.

'Come on now, don't start panicking, you heard what he said,' Flora urged, squeezing her arm reassuringly although her own heart was beating alarmingly hard. 'But let's get dressed, eh? We can go up on deck then and see what's going on.'

'I'll get dressed but I'm not leaving my room,' Connie retaliated in a wobbly voice. An awful feeling of foreboding had come over her and she couldn't seem to control it.

Both of them hurriedly got dressed then sat together holding hands, listening to the sound of footsteps hurrying up and down the passageway outside. People were clearly panicking and they could hear them firing questions at the staff.

'Why have the engines stopped? . . . What's happening?'

At that time the staff were obviously trying to calm them but as the minutes passed the sound of doors slamming and running footsteps intensified until suddenly someone hammered on the door and shouted, 'Get your lifebelts and some warm clothes on and get up on deck immediately.'

'The squash court and the baggage bay is already submerged,' someone screamed and now Connie started to tremble.

'W-we're going to die,' she whimpered but Flora gently shook her.

'No, we are *not*. Now come along – we'd best get the belts on that Mrs Merry made us then we'll get our lifebelts on.' She instantly began to rummage beneath the bags in the wardrobe

81

then slinging the first belt that came to hand at Connie she quickly hoisted her skirt and fastened the second one around her own waist. Connie did the same although it took her longer because her hands were trembling so much, then they grabbed their coats and let themselves out into the hallway where they were immediately swept along by a tide of terrified people. Most of the women were crying and the men were doing their best to comfort them as Connie clung to Flora's hand.

Once up on deck, Flora's hand rose to her throat and she suddenly realised that she had left the little silver locket that Jamie had given her in their cabin, it was the only thing she had to remember him by, and she desperately wanted to go back and get it, but the ceaseless jostling of the passengers behind her made her realise there was no way she could make it. Anyway, she couldn't leave Connie.

As the crowd jostled up the stairs to the lifeboat deck at the top of the ship, they passed the purser's office. Glancing through the door, Flora caught a glimpse of piles of papers and valuables laid out on a desk, and a crowd of people were clamouring to retrieve their valuables. Suddenly, for the first time, she realised that they were indeed in mortal danger, and she grasped Connie's hand, partly to reassure herself, and partly to ensure she wouldn't lose her in the crush of people.

When they finally emerged onto the deck, the cold air hit them like a slap in the face, almost taking their breath away. An officer stepped forward to help them adjust their lifebelts before pushing them none too gently in the direction of the lifeboats, which had already been uncovered. Still holding tight to Connie's hand, Flora looked at them in dismay. *Is this all there is?* she wondered. *Surely there aren't enough boats for everyone on board.* She looked around, hoping to see some other boats hidden somewhere. But there was just the press of screaming, shivering passengers. *Maybe there were some lifeboats stowed on another deck as well,* she thought hopefully. She didn't dare voice her thoughts aloud, though. Connie was in a bad enough panic as it was, and to be honest, for the first time since she had woken up, Flora was beginning to feel that maybe everything wouldn't be all right.

In addition to the screams of the other passengers and Connie's sobbing, now they were at the top of the ship, there was a ceaseless, deafening roar of escaping steam, which they hadn't been aware of while they were inside. It added to the sheer terror of the scene and was too much for Connie, who pulled her hand from Flora's and put both hands over her ears, screaming, 'Make it stop! Make it stop!' Not sure what to do, Flora grabbed her hands and pulled Connie in close, whispering soothingly in her ear. 'Shh, now, we'll be safe soon. Don't you worry, my darling. It's all going to be fine.'

She hoped Connie couldn't hear the trembling in her voice, because right then, Flora was not convinced that anything would be all right again. Gradually, Connie quietened, and the girls stood with their arms wrapped around each other and watched wide-eyed as the seamen worked frantically to prepare the boats to be lowered.

Finally, the first one was ready to be hoisted out on long ropes and dangled beside the ship. People were screaming and wailing all around them and the girls were swept forward in the panic-stricken crowd as the sailors shouted for women and children to come forward. Soon they were hanging on to the rail staring down into a lifeboat that was rocking precariously from side to side.

'I can't get in that,' Connie cried in terror as she gazed down into the black sea far below and before Flora could stop her she was off, racing like a hare back the way they had come. Somehow Flora pushed and shouldered her way through the crowd until eventually she caught up with her just as she was about to launch herself into the passage leading back to their state rooms.

'What the *'ell* do yer think you're doin'?' she cried furiously as

83

she caught Connie roughly by the arm and swung her about. 'If you go back in there an' the ship goes down you'll bloody well go down wi' it, you fool!' Suddenly all the elocution lessons she had had from Connie were forgotten and she was just a young, frightened girl from the docks in Whitechapel.

Connie was fighting her and moaning deep in her throat so Flora brought her hand back and landed a glancing blow on her young mistress's cheek.

Connie was so shocked that she stopped whimpering immediately and now that Flora had her attention she barked, 'We *have* to get off the ship – do you understand? If we don't you may *well* die! Now what are you going to do? Because I'll tell you now I'm going to get into one of those boats while I still can!'

Connie gulped, her terrified eyes huge in her pale face but at least she was calmer now.

'I-I'll come.'

'Good!' Flora grabbed her arm again and dragged her back to the deck but it was clear they had lost their chance. The crowd trying to escape was twice as big as it had been and people were elbowing each other out of the way as they tried to secure places in the lifeboats.

'Stand back now . . . women and children only. D'you hear me!' A seaman's voice yelled.

Once full the other lifeboats were being swung out prior to being lowered but because it was dark it was impossible to see how many people were in them.

'Come on, let's try the deck below,' Flora yelled to make herself heard above the noise of the crowd and grabbing Connie's hand she hauled her along until they came to the steps leading down to B deck below. The same mayhem was happening there as sailors held off the men and pushed and shoved the nearest women and children into the boats. Somehow Connie and Flora found themselves right next to a boat and a sailor quickly grabbed Flora round the waist and unceremoniously threw her inside it. She landed in an undignified heap in the bottom of it and after struggling to her knees she looked round desperately for a sight of Connie. On one of the decks the band had started to play to try to allay the people's panic and Flora thought how brave they were as hands reached out to help her onto the cold plank seat. Then suddenly a young, poorly dressed woman clad only in a thin shawl despite the bitterly cold night, who looked as if she might have come from the steerage section of the boat, threw something into Flora's arms and as Flora glanced down she realised with horror that it was a tiny baby.

'Look out for her for me, miss. God bless you,' the woman shouted as the sailor pushed her back to make way for Connie. Connie also landed awkwardly in the boat but as she stood up another woman was lowered in and, somehow, she lost her balance. The next few seconds would remain engraved in Flora's mind forever, for as she stretched out a hand to help Connie the back of the girl's legs struck the side of the boat and she teetered as she tried desperately to right herself before plunging backwards over the side down into the deep dark sea below.

'*Nooo . . .!*' Flora's scream echoed across the waves but as she made to stand many hands pushed her back down onto her seat again.

'*Sit still* or you'll have us *all* capsize,' someone threatened as tears began to stream down Flora's cheeks and drip onto the baby in her arms. 'There's no help for your friend now, God rest her soul. She stands no chance after a fall like that into the sea!'

'No, let me see. I've got to find her! Oh God, I can't let her go. Take the baby, please, I need to find her!'

The woman beside her put an arm around her and held her firmly. 'For God's sake, don't be such a fool, girl! Think of that poor baby! You'd give up your child to find your friend? Sit down and be quiet before you kill us all!'

Sobbing uncontrollably, Flora knew the woman was speaking sense, but how could she sit here and do nothing? After everything Connie had done for her, it would be a betrayal to just leave her to her fate. And how would she ever live with herself if she didn't try to do something? But what choice did she have? She could hand the baby to someone else, and go after Connie, but she would surely die. She looked down at the baby, then back at the water, hanging over the side of the boat as far as she dared and searching in vain for a sight of Connie in the seething black water below, but there were so may poor souls already thrashing about down there that it was impossible to find her.

At that moment the baby began to wail too and all Flora could do was rock her helplessly as she tried to take in what had happened. Just seconds before, Connie had been there with her and now she could be gone forever, snuffed out like a candle in the wind. It was just too much to take in.

Soon after the boat began to rock dangerously as it was lowered into the waves below and Flora clung to the side with one hand while she gripped the baby with her other, still desperately searching the water for a sight of her friend as tears streamed down her cold face. The boat hit the water with a splash and the oarsmen quickly released the lowering ropes and started to row frantically. Thankfully, once they had managed to steer the boat clear of the thrashing waters around the ship the sea was calm, giving no hint of the freezing treachery that lay beneath the surface.

Above them countless stars shone down onto the icebergs, making them glisten like diamonds to match the ones that the women from the first-class cabins were decked in, and everything began to take on an air of unreality. Flora screamed Connie's name over and over again, making the child in her arms sob even harder, as she continued to look for any sign of her dear friend. She reasoned that if only she could spot her they could somehow pull her aboard the boat but another little voice in her head said that perhaps she had been sucked beneath the sea.

Suddenly an SOS flare flamed up into the sky, illuminating the ship for just long enough for the people on the lifeboat to see that the unsinkable *Titanic* was indeed actually sinking. Vaguely Flora could see other lifeboats around them but it was far too dark to see how many people were aboard them. And still the haunting strains of a waltz floated across the water from the deck making the whole scene seem unreal. *This can't be happening,* Flora thought. *I'm having a nightmare and when I wake up I shall be back in the state rooms with Connie safe and sound.* But she knew all too well that it was real. The baby in her arms was crying harder now but apart from gently rocking her, Flora could do nothing for her. Teeth chattering, she slipped the tiny child inside her coat to try to keep her warm, but she wasn't sure it would work. She was chilled to the bone, and she could see that everyone else in the boat was also shivering.

'God willing a ship will see the flare and come to our rescue,' an elderly lady said and a murmur of agreement rippled through the passengers.

'Well, it had better come soon or it will be too late for the poor souls left aboard, look it's split in two, people are jumping into the water,' someone said and Flora watched in horror as the great ship slowly began to sink beneath the waves. It was as if some great unseen hand had come and cleaved it neatly in two with a gigantic axe. Then the lights went out and they were plunged into darkness. Even from a distance the sound of terrified people screaming could be heard and now wreckage from the ship was beginning to spread across the surface of the sea. People in the water were trying to cling to it to keep afloat but it was painfully obvious that they couldn't survive for long in the freezing water.

'*Turn back* for God's sake!' one woman implored the rowers. 'We could get *at least* six more people aboard this boat.'

Chapter Ten

It was some minutes later when a frail old lady who was sitting next to Flora stood up and sobbed, 'I can't bear it . . . I have to go back. My Arthur was on that boat. I must get to him . . .'

'*Sit down*, or you'll have us all overboard!' the seaman hissed as the boat began to rock precariously but she simply stood there for a moment and gave him the sweetest smile.

'But you don't understand, young man,' she said softly. 'We've been married for nearly fifty years. I have to find him, we're a pair.' And with that she plunged into the water before anyone could stop her.

'*No!*' Flora made a mad grab for the back of the old lady's coat but already the poor soul was moving away from the boat. She had gone no more than a few yards when the weight of her clothes began to pull her under and within seconds there was nothing to be seen of her as she sank into the depths.

Flora bowed her head and offered a silent prayer that a boat might come to rescue them soon. Already dead bodies could be seen floating amongst the wreckage and she shut her eyes again so that she wouldn't have to look anymore and silently willed the distressed baby in her arms to stop crying. Soon after she found that she couldn't open her eyes again even if she had wanted to. Her tears had turned to ice and her eyelids were frozen shut. Strangely she had gone past feeling cold now. In fact, she felt hot and as she drifted off to sleep she sighed and welcomed the darkness and the eerie silence.

'Wake up . . . that's it.'

From far away Flora heard a voice and as she tried to blink her eyes open she became aware that someone was leaning over her.

'Wh-where am I?' she asked blearily and struggled to sit up but gentle hands pushed her back against soft pillows.

'It's all right. You're aboard the *Carpathia*. We got a distress call from the *Titanic* and came as quickly as we could.'

Flora blinked, confused. But where was Connie? And what did he mean a distress call? And then it all came flooding back to her and she began to cry.

'The . . . the baby . . . where's the baby?' She was staring up into the face of a kindly white-haired gentleman with little gold spectacles perched on the end of his nose. He was dressed in a white jacket and she guessed that he must the ship's doctor.

'Ssh . . . we won't talk about that for now,' he soothed but Flora wouldn't be put off.

'But I . . . I *must* know where she is,' she mumbled as her head thrashed from side to side. 'Her mother entrusted her to me.'

'Ah, she wasn't your baby then?'

'Of course not. Now tell me where she is. She was upset, she wouldn't stop crying and then after a time she went very quiet and she didn't wake up again.'

'I'm very sorry, my dear. The baby didn't make it,' he told her gently. 'It was the cold, you see? She was already dead when we took her from your arms. Do you know what her name was?'

'N-no.' Tears spilled out of Flora's eyes. She hadn't made a very good job of taking care of the child, had she? And Connie . . . *Poor* Connie. She wanted to ask more questions but she was so tired and her chest felt as if it was on fire. She was hot and cold all at the same time and then the darkness was rushing towards her again and she gave herself up to it gladly.

It was twenty-four hours before Flora next opened her eyes and when she did she found that she was as weak as a kitten. Turning her head, she saw that they were in a large room with row upon row of people lying on mattresses on the floor and huddled into blankets.

A young nurse hurried up to her. 'Ah, you're awake again then.' She smiled as she took Flora's pulse. 'You gave us quite a scare back there, I don't mind telling you, miss. You've had a raging fever but, luckily, it's broken now so you should start to recover. Come on, have a little drink.' She gently lifted Flora's head from the pillow and as she trickled water between her chapped, dry lips, Flora was sure that nothing had ever tasted sweeter. She was aware then that she was dressed in a long, thick nightgown. As if reading her mind, the nurse told her, 'Don't worry. Your clothes are safe. And so is the belt you were wearing about your waist. From that we were able to identify you, Miss Ogilvie. There was an address inside the belt, presumably of the people you were going to visit and they've been sent word of when we're likely to dock so that they can come and meet you.'

'But I'm not . . . no . . .' Flora clamped her mouth shut. This young nurse thought that she was Connie but . . .

'It's all right, don't get distressed,' the nurse said before Flora could go on. 'You've had a terrible shock but things will get easier.'

Flora lay there for a long time staring at the ceiling as tears coursed down her cheeks. Connie was gone, there was nothing she could have done to save her and she could never come back. But Connie had had someone waiting for her at the end of the journey whereas she had no one. She had merely been Connie's maid so what was to become of her now? Connie's aunt would have no allegiance to her, and she would be in a foreign country with no money, no friends and no way of getting home. It was a terrifying thought but then an idea occurred to her. What if *she* were to become Connie? Her aunt hadn't seen Connie since she was just a babe in arms, to the best of her knowledge, so how would she know if she were to pose as her niece? She dismissed the ludicrous idea almost immediately. It was ridiculous and deceitful and then her eyes became heavy again and she slept once more.

When she next awoke it was morning again and she felt a little better although she was still very weak and she had developed a terrible cough.

'Get some of this into you,' the same young nurse who had tended to her the day before urged as she helped her up onto her pillows and placed a tray with a dish of porridge and a cup of hot, sweet coffee in front of her.

The porridge was heavily laced with sugar but it tasted like grit and it stuck in her sore throat although she did manage to drink some of the coffee.

'Well, at least you managed a little bit,' the nurse said approvingly when she came back a few minutes later to remove the tray and take her temperature. 'And your temperature has gone down slightly as well,' she told her. 'Now, do you feel well enough to get up and sit in a chair for a while?'

'I think so,' Flora croaked. Her chest was still burning and her head and throat ached too. The nurse assisted her to the bathroom first and by the time they got back and Flora had been settled into a chair she was exhausted.

'Feeling better, dear?'

Flora glanced at the lady next to her. She looked quite frail and her eyes were red-rimmed from crying.

'Yes, thank you,' Flora answered politely and the woman promptly burst into tears.

'Forgive me,' she spluttered as she mopped at her streaming eyes with a large white handkerchief. 'I know I should be grateful

92

that we survived but it was all so . . . so . . .' She shook her head as if that would somehow miraculously wipe out the terrible images behind her eyes. 'M-my husband and son and his young family were on the boat with me. It was supposed to be the trip of a lifetime but they all went down with the ship.'

'I'm so sorry.' The words seemed inadequate but Flora could think of nothing else to say.

'And you, dear . . . did you lose anyone?'

'Yes, my . . . my maid,' Flora faltered. The second the lie had left her mouth Flora clamped her lips together. Her heart was beating so loudly that she was sure the lady must be able to hear it. She knew that if she were to embark on this lie there could be no turning back and it terrified her, and yet, she asked herself, wasn't the thought of being all alone thousands of miles from home even more terrifying?

'I'm Mrs Willis,' the old lady chattered on. 'What's your name, dear?'

Flora gulped and licked her lips, which had suddenly gone dry. 'I'm Miss Constance Ogilvie. I was on the way to stay with my aunt in New York when . . .' And so the lie began.

'It's all right, you don't have to talk about it if it's too painful,' the old lady said sympathetically. 'You're still in shock and you've been very poorly but things will get easier, you'll see.'

Flora nodded numbly and closed her eyes, eager to escape any more talk. She had a lot of thinking to do now.

Over the course of that day Flora learned from the nurses that there were only 705 survivors from the *Titanic* aboard the *Carpathia*, the majority of them women and children. Over fifteen hundred people had perished in the icy seas. She shuddered to think of the poor souls and wept when she thought of the poor little baby who had been entrusted to her care. If only she could have saved her! She was told that the offices of the White Star Line in both New York and Southampton had been deluged with terrified friends and relations all waiting to hear a list of the survivors as they prayed that their loved ones were amongst them. It was only then that she suddenly thought of her family and her heart sank. If she was to take on Connie's identity, her parents and siblings would believe she was dead and they would be heartbroken. Her mother had never wanted her to go to New York in the first place and knowing her as she did Flora was sure that she would blame herself for not stopping her. But on the other hand, she reasoned that if she *did* go ahead with her plan she could send them money regularly, which would help their financial position no end.

Later that evening, as she was still wrestling with her conscience, the patients in the ship's makeshift hospital were informed that they should be arriving in New York late the following day. Flora was relieved and sure that if she could only get off the *Carpathia* safely she would never sail again.

The next day, although still weak, Flora dressed in the clothes that had been returned to her and joined the rest of the survivors from around the ship.

At 8.20 p.m. that evening the rescue ship arrived opposite her dock. It was a wild and windy night outside the harbour and as the ship sailed up the channel it was surrounded by a heavy fog. It was raining and at intervals lightning lit up the sky. Crowds had begun to gather in the vicinity of the docks long before it got dark and as time passed it became larger and larger. Over three hundred police had been drafted in to stretch ropes across the streets leading to the pier and the crowd was halted at Eleventh Avenue and allowed to go no further.

Inside the lines were many automobiles and ambulances. Relatives of the survivors were gathered on Pier 54, but it was eerily quiet as they waited apprehensively for a sight of their loved ones. The only sound was the relentless beating of the rain and the surge of the tide. Next to the relatives was a knot of undertakers who would have the unhappy job of removing the dead who had been pulled from the sea to their premises and they were joined by white-uniformed ambulance surgeons who were prepared to minister to those survivors who were still ill or injured and transport them to the nearest hospitals if necessary. Over five hundred black-garbed Sisters of Mercy and a score of priests also stood ready to reunite the survivors with their relatives whenever they could.

There was an air of tense expectancy as everyone was informed that the *Carpathia* had passed Pier 59 where they had dropped off the empty lifeboats, but still no one moved from the places they had been assigned to. It was a very sorrowful assembly. At last at 9.55 p.m. the first three women passengers walked down the gangplank followed by a sailor and a man in a big brown raincoat and a soft hat. Then came other survivors and it was instantly obvious that most of them had lost their own clothes and were wearing whatever the passengers of the *Carpathia* had been able to provide them with. Two poor women who appeared to be violently insane were carried from the ship while others appeared to be in a state of shock and plainly unbalanced.

At this stage the crowd tried to surge forward but the police held them back. The heart-rending cries of some of the hysterical survivors and their relieved relatives rent the air as they sobbed for the loved ones they had lost, and throughout it all the Sisters of Mercy were desperately trying to reunite them with any relatives that were waiting for them, which was no easy job with such a huge crowd. Reporters were baying for news and flashlights regularly lit up the sorry procession of survivors as they made their way down to the pier.

Finally, it was Flora's turn, and as she hesitated at the top of the gangplank, gazing down at the sea of solemn faces below, she took a deep gulp of the foggy night air. It was time to begin living the lie. What would become of her if she didn't?

Chapter Eleven

'Name, child?' a kindly nun asked Flora as she finally stepped onto dry land. There had been times when she was adrift in the lifeboat that she had been convinced she was going to die and now that she was there she felt overcome with emotion as she thought of all the people who had perished in the freezing sea.

'It's . . . Constance Ogilvie.'

Flora's legs had suddenly turned to jelly as the woman put her arm about her waist and led her across the pier. The rain was bouncing off the cobbles and in minutes Flora was chilled to the bone. Each of the people waiting for a loved one had been separated into alphabetical groups to make it a little easier and the nun paused in front of one such group and called, 'Constance Ogilvie!'

Flora kept her eyes on the crowd and watched transfixed as it parted and a woman in a plain but smart outfit accompanied by a man in a dark coat and hat hurried towards her.

'Oh, Constance, my *poor* girl, what you must have gone through!' the woman cried as tears sparkled on her cheeks. 'But come along, we need to get you home and into something warm. Help her, please, Thomas.'

The man instantly stepped forward and before she knew it he had swept Flora up into his arms as if she weighed no more than a feather and was striding back towards a waiting automobile with the woman hurrying along behind him. He settled Flora onto the back seat and tucked a warm blanket about her knees, then nodding to the woman as she climbed in beside her, he asked, 'Straight home, ma'am?'

'Oh, yes please, Thomas,' the woman answered as she tucked the blanket even more tightly about Flora. 'And as fast as you can if you please.'

She turned back to Flora and told her, 'This is not quite the welcome I'd envisaged for you, my dear. It must have been awful. But anyway, as you've probably realised, I am your Aunt Alexandra, although I'm quite happy for you to call me Aunt Alex.'

'M-my father always called me Connie,' Flora muttered and was glad of the darkness that hid the colour that she felt flooding into her cheeks. This wasn't going to be as easy as she had thought and just for a moment she was tempted to tell the truth.

'Then Connie it is,' the woman said gently, taking her hand and squeezing it. 'And I can't tell you how happy I am to have you here. I just thank God that you survived.'

The woman seemed so sincere that the moment for telling the truth was gone and Flora knew then that she would have to go on with the lie. What alternative did she have? The car was moving now and soon they were passing buildings that seemed to stretch right up into the sky. And there were so many lights everywhere she looked, even the sky above the buildings seemed bright. She had thought London was a busy place but it was nothing compared to here. There was so much traffic and so many shops that she hardly knew where to look first, and people, so many people of all nationalities. The cold air had made her start to cough again and she was aware that Alex was watching her with a concerned look on her face, although she said little. When she had the opportunity, Flora peeped at her from the corner of her eye and thought how pretty she was. She looked like a younger version of Connie's mother from what she had seen of her in pictures, but

97

then she supposed she would. They had been sisters. She had the same fair hair and deep-blue eyes and she was tall and slim. Flora estimated she must be somewhere in her late thirties to early forties but she was still a very attractive woman and she seemed to be very kind, which was going to make Flora's deception all the harder. But then, she reasoned, she had been no blood relation to Connie. Connie had always known that she had been adopted at a few days old so surely there could have been no bond between them? And she was sure that Connie had said that she couldn't even remember her, for she hadn't visited them since she was just a baby. Leaning her head back against the seat she closed her eyes. The next thing she knew, someone was gently shaking her arm and she realised, to her surprise, that she must have fallen asleep.

'Wake up, darling. We're home.'

Flora opened her eyes to find Alex leaning over her but then Thomas opened the car door and lifted her out and she was carried into the house. The entrance hall was beautiful but she didn't have long to study it for Thomas was carrying her up a sweeping, carved mahogany staircase that ended in a galleried landing.

She was carried into a room with a four-poster bed standing against one wall where a young maid was waiting for her.

'I've run you a nice hot bath, miss,' she said respectfully. 'And the mistress has laid some nightclothes out for you on the bed. We didn't think you'd have any of your own after . . . Well, anyway, would you like some help?'

'No, I can manage thank you,' Flora croaked as another bout of coughing made her red in the face. Alex had joined them by then and she led her towards a pretty chair with gilt legs.

'Run and fetch some hot chicken soup,' she instructed the maid, then turning her attention back to Flora she told her, 'I have a doctor downstairs waiting to examine you when you've had your bath, dear. I'm sure he'll be able to give you something for that awful cough. And when you're ready the bathroom is through that door there but take your time. Are you quite sure that you can manage on your own? Young Patsy, who you just met, will be your maid from now on so anything at all you need, just ask her. When you're well again we'll take you shopping for some lovely new clothes. That will be nice, won't it? Shopping together, I mean? I'm sure we're going to have so much fun, although . . . I was so sorry to hear about your father's passing, he was a truly lovely man.'

'Yes . . . he was,' Flora croaked, feeling more uncomfortable by the minute. Alex was so nice she felt even worse about deceiving her now. But what alternative do I have? she asked herself as she stretched out in a bath full of warm, soapy water minutes later. Alex was being kind to her because she believed she was her niece, but if she was to discover that she was only a maid, she might turn her out into the street. Flora shuddered at the prospect as she tried to put her confused thoughts into some sort of order. And how would Connie's uncle accept her? She remembered Connie telling her that he was much older than her aunt. But she supposed she would find out soon enough, so for now she gave herself up to the pleasure of a long, leisurely soak as she tried to block the terrible images of Connie tumbling into the sea. Once she was dry and had slipped into the nightclothes that had been laid out for her, the young maid came back carrying a tray with a pot of tea and a dish of hot soup on it.

'The mistress says you're to try and eat this, miss,' she told Flora. 'And when you're done, the doctor will come in to see you.' The girl placed the tray on a table next to the window. The heavy velvet drapes were drawn tight shut against the cold night and Flora sat down and tried to swallow some of the soup. Soon after, the doctor, a bald little man who looked to be almost as round as he was high, appeared and gave her a thorough examination as Alex hovered nervously nearby.

'Hmm, her chest is very tight but then that's to be expected after being out in the freezing cold for so long. She's lucky it hasn't turned to pneumonia. And she's still quite shaky. Again, to be expected after what she's been through, but I'm sure careful nursing, nourishing food and a few days complete bed rest will sort that,' he observed.

Alex breathed a sigh of relief. At least the doctor didn't seem to consider there was any permanent damage done.

The doctor left her a bottle of foul-smelling medicine then took his leave as Alex fussed about her. 'It's into bed for you, miss,' she said kindly as she led Flora to the bed and tucked the covers under her chin. 'And there you'll stay until I'm quite sure you're fully recovered. Now, is there anything I can get for you?'

'Perhaps some newspapers I could read?' Flora said falteringly.

Alex nodded and hurried away and minutes later Patsy reappeared with a pile of different newspapers.

'I'm afraid they're all full of the disaster on the *Titanic*, miss. Are you sure it won't upset you reading them?' she asked worriedly.

Flora shook her head and once Patsy had gone again she began to read down the list of the dead and missing people that had been identified so far. And soon she found what she was looking for, MISS FLORA BUTLER. The name seemed to jump off the page as the enormity of what she was doing came home to her. How would her parents feel when they read this? It would break their hearts. It should be Connie's name there not hers, but already the deception had gone much too far for her to turn back. On the next page she found Connie's name amongst the list of survivors. Toby's name was there too – he must have been on the *Carpathia* as well, and she thanked God they hadn't seen each other – although it appeared the majority of people who had survived were women and children. She thought once more then of the tiny little soul who had frozen to death in her arms and the tears came again. She knew that the memory of that poor dead baby would haunt her for many years to come. Finally, she wiped her eyes and laid the paper aside. What was done was done and from this moment on she would have to become Miss Constance Ogilvie.

Five days later, when Alex considered that Flora was well enough to get up for a while, she was allowed down into the drawing room one morning, and there for the first time she met Connie's uncle and his spinster daughter, Margaret.

Her aunt, which was now how Flora thought of her, had gone out of her way to make her feel welcome, but her husband and his daughter eyed her with contempt.

'So, you're Constance, are you?' Magnus Ward was a tall well-made man with a shock of snow-white hair and grey eyes, and from the moment he set eyes on his guest he made no attempt to make her feel welcome.

His daughter, who looked to be in her mid to late twenties, was like a pale female version of him, and Flora wasn't at all surprised to learn that she was unmarried. She certainly wasn't the prettiest of women. She was very well built and her face was angular. Her mousy brown hair was scraped back into an unbecoming bun on the back of her head, which did nothing to enhance her features, and her grey eyes were cold.

Suddenly, in their presence, Alex became quiet and jittery and Flora found herself feeling sorry for her.

'Should she be allowed downstairs yet?' Margaret questioned her.

'Oh, yes, dear. The doctor called in again yesterday and said that a couple of hours a day out of bed shouldn't hurt her now.' Her aunt was wringing her hands and Flora frowned. Why did she let them talk to her that way? she wondered. They were

101

addressing her as if she was one of the servants. But she said nothing; it wasn't her place.

'So, how long do you reckon you'll be staying?' Magnus asked bluntly and Flora flushed.

'Er . . . until I reach my twenty-first birthday and then I can go home.' Already, even she felt intimidated by the man. He really was extremely rude.

He sniffed. 'Hmm.' Then perching a pair of spectacles on his nose, he shook out the newspaper and began to read as if she wasn't even there while Margaret sailed out of the room without so much as another glance at her.

'Actually . . . I think perhaps I'd like to go back to my room, if you don't mind, Aunt.' Suddenly Flora felt so in the way she couldn't wait to get away from him.

'Of course.' Alex placed her arm about her shoulders and led her away and as they were climbing the stairs she whispered, 'Don't mind your uncle. That's just his way. Margaret is the same. She is his daughter by his first marriage. His first wife died.'

'I see.' Flora could only imagine what a horrible life Alex must have had with him but she kept her thoughts to herself and once she was back in her room she sighed with relief. From now on she would avoid both Magnus and his daughter whenever she could. But he had highlighted one problem that hadn't occurred to her before. He had asked when she would be going home, but how could she now? Merry was there taking care of the house and there was no way she could pass herself off as Constance to her. What was she to do?

Chapter Twelve

Some days later, Alex summoned her dressmaker to the house to measure Flora and to let her look through some dress patterns.

'She'll just make you a couple of outfits to wear for now,' Alex told her. 'And then when you're properly well we'll go on that shopping spree I promised you.'

Flora's terrible cough had hung on persistently and although she was now much better than she had been, she was still not fully recovered and she was suffering from terrible nightmares in which she would hear the screams of the dying and see Connie plunging to her death. She would feel the tiny body of the baby who had died in her arms and would wake up in a cold sweat and a tangle of damp bedclothes. Alex had nursed her devotedly and already Flora was more than a little fond of her. She was such a sweet, gentle woman, it was hard to imagine her married to someone like Magnus who was so stern and cold.

'Would you mind very much if I addressed you as Alex rather than Aunt Alex?' she tentatively asked one day. 'It's just that we don't know each other well and—'

'That would be quite all right,' Alex assured her with a gentle smile. 'Once we get to know each other a little more you'll start to feel better about things. It's bound to take you a while to get over what happened and get used to living with strange people in a strange house.'

'Alex seems to be a very kind person,' Flora remarked to Patsy later that day as the girl was brushing her hair for her. Being waited on was still taking some getting used to.

'She is,' Patsy answered. 'But the master can be, er . . . a little brusque.'

'I know exactly what you mean.' Flora nodded in agreement. 'And I didn't even know he had a daughter by a previous marriage until I got here. She's a little abrupt too, isn't she?'

'Yes, she is.' Patsy piled Flora's hair onto the top of her head and started to secure it with pins. She paused as if she was wondering how much she should say but then she went on, 'She can be a bit of a tartar. She was engaged to be married some years ago, apparently. Rumour had it that he was only marrying her for her money but then he met some other young lady who was just as rich but shall we say . . . a little better-looking? Miss Margaret isn't the prettiest of women, is she? Anyway, he broke off the engagement and they reckon she's been difficult to live with ever since. I feel right sorry for the poor mistress sometimes. Those two rule her with a rod of iron and she can't seem to do a thing right. Between you and me, I don't know why she doesn't just clear off and leave them both to it. Anyone with half an eye can see that she isn't happy but I suppose she must love him. And he is very wealthy. He owns a huge fleet of ships that sail all over the world, both passenger and cargo.' She stopped abruptly then, concerned that she had said too much but Flora smiled at her encouragingly.

'Don't worry. I shan't repeat anything you've told me,' she promised.

Once she was dressed, Patsy left the room to get on with her other duties and Flora stood at the window staring thoughtfully out into the street below. Poor Alex. She had been right in her assumption that she wasn't happy. But why did she stay then? she wondered. She didn't seem like the sort of woman who would stay with a man simply because he was rich. Whatever the reason she had already decided that the couple were completely unsuited. Today she was wearing one of the day dresses that Alex's dressmaker had had delivered to her the day before and so she decided to go downstairs to see if she could find something to read. She was getting rather bored of staying in her bedroom now. Luckily at the bottom of the stairs she bumped into Alex who had been on her way upstairs to check on her.

'Why, I do believe you're looking a little better today, dear,' she said with a relieved smile.

'I do feel better and was wondering if you had any books or anything I might read. I've read all the magazines you sent up to me.' Flora had stopped reading the newspapers. They were still full of the news about the *Titanic* and she found them depressing.

At that moment Margaret appeared from the door of the drawing room and she eyed Flora with open disdain.

'Oh, you're up and about then,' she commented rather unnecessarily.

'Yes, I er . . . was on the hunt for something to read.'

'Come with me,' Alex said quickly before Margaret could say any more and, taking Flora's arm, she led her quickly away to a room just a little further down the hallway. 'This is my own private little sitting room,' she told her as Flora looked around. It was a comfy room with heavy navy-blue velvet curtains at the windows, which complemented the soft, light grey paint of the walls. Antiques were dotted about here and there but there was nothing pretentious about it.

'There's a bookshelf over there.' Alex pointed to a corner of the room. 'Do help yourself to whatever takes your fancy and feel free to use this room whenever you wish. No one else comes in here apart from me and the maid who cleans it.'

Flora found this rather strange. But then, on the few occasions she had been in their company, neither Magnus nor his daughter had even attempted to include Alex in their conversations so it was no wonder that she preferred her own company. Today Alex was dressed in a simple, dove-grey day dress. That was another thing that Flora had noticed about her. She always tended to dress in quite plain, dull-coloured clothes and yet, if her husband was as wealthy as Patsy said he was, surely she could have afforded to dress more fashionably? Crossing to the bookshelves she began to leaf through the books as Alex ordered morning coffee and when they were both seated her aunt asked, 'When do you think you'll feel well enough to go shopping? I'm aware that you must desperately want to get some more clothes of your own but I don't want you to venture out until you're quite sure that you feel up to it.'

'Perhaps we could go tomorrow?' Flora suggested hopefully. 'We could always come back if I get tired.'

Alex's face lit up like a child's at the thought of the shopping trip ahead. 'We'll do that then,' she said excitedly. 'And I think we'll start off in Macy's. We'll probably be able to get almost everything you need there. It's absolutely huge and I'm sure you'll love it. We'll open you an account there. Mr Wainthrop has already deposited quite a large amount of money in a bank for you and he will be paying your allowance into it each month. Speaking of which, I almost forgot, I received a letter from him this morning enquiring after you. He informs me that as well as being your father's solicitor he and his late wife were also close family friends and he's most anxious about you. He enclosed a letter for you too. I'll get it now.'

As she hurried across to a small escritoire in the corner of the room, Flora's heart began to thump as the enormity of the deception she had embarked upon hit her afresh.

Alex handed her an envelope then and Flora opened it with shaking hands and began to read.

My dear Connie,

I cannot begin to tell you how concerned and distressed I was when I received the news of the Titanic *sinking and what relief I felt when I discovered that your name was on the list of survivors. I must offer sincere condolences for the loss of your maid, Flora. I know that you were close and her death must have been a great blow to you, poor girl, especially so soon after the loss of your father. She was a dear girl and will be sadly missed by all that knew her, especially her family who I believe are deeply mourning her.*

Can you begin to imagine how guilty I feel? It was I who booked your passage believing that it would be the trip of a lifetime for you both! I can only extend my heartfelt apologies, but who would have believed what happened after the ship had been declared unsinkable?

Anyway, my dear girl, I have been to see Mrs Merry, who like myself is grateful that you are alive and well. Would it help if I were to come and visit you? It would be no inconvenience whatsoever if seeing a familiar face would help you.

With very best wishes
Victor Wainthrop.

Panic threatened to choke her for a moment but aware that Alex was watching her closely she said shakily, 'I must write to him immediately. Mr Wainthrop was almost like an uncle to me. He and his wife regularly came to dinner with me and my father before she passed away and he and Father used to play golf together. He's known me since I was a baby so he's feeling very bad because it was he that booked the passage on the ship for me and Flora. I just need to let him know as soon as possible that I am well again. I also need to go to the bank and arrange for some money to be sent to Flora's family. She . . . gave them some of her wages each month, you see?' she ended falteringly as tears welled and streamed down her pale cheeks. Only now did it hit home to her how bereft her family must be feeling. And also, she was terrified that Mr Wainthrop might take it into his head to visit. Were he to do that she would be found out in her lie.

'Of course, you must write to him,' Alex told her sympathetically as she saw how distressed she was. 'You'll find everything you need in my desk. Please just help yourself and when you've finished give it to me and I'll get Thomas to post it immediately for you.'

'Th-thank you.'

Alex left her then and Flora hastily sat down to reply to Mr Wainthrop's letter. For a long time she sat staring blankly at the sheet of paper wondering what she should write and eventually she began

Dear Mr Wainthrop,

Thank you for your letter. I am pleased to inform you that I am now much better and I assure you that there is absolutely no need for you to make the long journey here to see me. Of course I am still grieving for Flora and would be grateful if you could pass on my condolences to her family and ensure that some money amounting to Flora's wages could be forwarded to them each month. It seems the least I can do under the circumstances. Please also forward my best wishes to Mrs Merry and assure her that I am recovering and please do not feel any guilt for what has happened. You thought you were doing us a kindness when you booked our passage and you were only following my father's wishes. Who could have foreseen what was going to happen? I shall write again in due course.

Yours sincerely

Constance Ogilvie.

Thankfully she had seen Connie's handwriting dozens of times so it was quite easy to imitate and if it did look a little shaky, hopefully he would think it was because she was still not quite herself following her ordeal. She silently blessed Connie for all the hours she had spent helping her to improve her reading and writing. But then she felt even more guilty. How would Connie feel knowing that her friend was using her lessons to deceive everyone? She'd be disgusted with her, and rightly so.

It was only when she came to put the letter into the envelope that she realised that she had no idea where to send it. Then she spotted the letter he had sent to Alex, which had his address on so she carefully wrote it on the envelope and sealed it.

True to her word, Alex dispatched Thomas immediately to post it and suddenly feeling worn out and emotionally drained, Flora went back to her room to rest until lunchtime.

It had been arranged that Flora and Alex would eat in the dining room that day and when Flora came downstairs she found Margaret and Alex already there. She saw at a glance that Margaret had taken her place at one end of the table, which she thought was rather strange. Magnus sat at the other end when he was there, which she was pleased to see he wasn't, but surely as his wife, Alex should have sat in Margaret's seat?

'You're five minutes late,' Margaret snapped shortly as a maid began to carry the meal in.

'Magnus has gone to see his manager at the shipping office,' Alex cut in hastily before Flora could retort. 'He's quite happy to sit back and let others run the company these days, but he still likes to go in and check the books and that all is running smoothly from time to time.' She smoothed a snow-white linen napkin across her lap as Flora sat down and the maid began to spoon soup into their dishes from a steaming silver tureen. 'As you've probably gathered we like to have a fairly light meal at lunchtime. Soups, cheeses, salads and such and then we have our main meal in the evening.'

'I think she's been here quite long enough to know that,'

Chapter Thirteen

The following morning, Alex insisted that Flora should borrow one of her coats. It was slightly big on her but even so she was in good spirits as they set off in Magnus's gleaming automobile with Alex and herself snugly tucked under blankets in the back seat.

'Take us to Battery Park, would you please, Thomas?' Alex asked. 'I'm sure Flora would love to have a peep at the Statue of Liberty. There's a good view of it from there.'

Flora stared in awe from the windows as the car swept along. It was the first real look at New York City she had had. It had been much too dark to see a lot when she had first arrived and she had been far too upset to take much notice of anything anyway. She was struck by the difference in the areas they passed: some of them were slums with hungry-looking children playing in the gutters outside while other areas appeared to be very prosperous. In these parts, uniformed nannies strolled along the pavements with their noses in the air, pushing expensive-looking perambulators.

'Of course there is so much to do here, if you have a mind to,' Alex told her. 'In the winter people flock to Central Park to skate on the ponds and there are a great many theatres, opera houses and music halls to visit.'

Flora listened avidly and once they arrived at Battery Park she and Alex strolled to the perimeter to gaze out across the harbour to Liberty Island where the huge statue stood in all her glory. In the park behind them squirrels leapt from tree to tree and watching them it was hard to believe that they were in the middle of a city, although they didn't have the best view as it was somewhat foggy. An old bag lady passed by quite close to them bundled up in layers of grubby, ragged clothes and hauling everything she owned behind her in an old, rickety trolley and Flora fished in her purse and handed her some coins.

'One day we'll take a boat trip over to the statue . . . but only when and if you wish to,' she added hastily, realising that Flora might not wish to go on a boat again after what had happened on the *Titanic*.

There were so many things she wanted to show her but she wanted her to be completely better before they did anything too strenuous. They headed back to the car and soon they were once more cruising through the busy streets of the city. When they finally reached the enormous Macy's store, Flora got out of the car and gazed up at its exterior open-mouthed.

'Is this really all just *one* shop?'

Alex grinned and nodded and arm in arm they went inside. The next two hours passed in a blur as they rushed from one department to another. Flora bought shoes, dresses, underwear, nightwear, a new coat, and so many other purchases that her head was spinning. At one point she held up a lovely blue chiffon evening dress in the very latest style, saying to Alex, 'Look, this is just the colour of your eyes. Why don't you try it on?'

Alex shook her head. 'I don't think Magnus would approve of that at all,' she said as she stared at the dress longingly. 'He likes me to wear more subtle colours and not stand out.'

Flora thought it was a shame that Alex always wore such drab colours, but it wasn't her place to comment so they continued shopping.

Alex finally led her to the cafeteria, telling her, 'I think it's time we had a tea break. You're not getting too tired, are you?'

'Oh no,' Flora assured her. She was enjoying herself immensely until suddenly she felt guilty, for she knew deep down that this wasn't really *her* money she was spending. Until she had gone to work for Connie all her clothes had come from a rag stall in Petticoat Lane and now suddenly here she was not even having to check the price of things.

With her tea she had a blueberry muffin, which Alex informed her were very popular with Americans, and she thoroughly enjoyed it. 'Now, what else do you need?' Alex asked as she sipped at her drink.

'I don't think we'll be able to carry any more when we collect everything we've bought already,' Flora responded.

Alex chuckled as she helped herself to a scone and spread it lavishly with butter and jam. 'We don't have to collect anything. Now that you have an account here everything will be delivered to the house later today,' she informed her.

Flora was surprised at the change in her. Back at the house the woman tended to be very quiet and anxious but now that she was away from her husband and stepdaughter she was smiling and relaxed. Even so, as she thought of all the things she had bought, Flora's conscience got the better of her and suddenly she wanted to go before she spent anything else. After all, she had stolen someone else's identity and now she was spending their money like there was no tomorrow. Were she ever to be found out she had no doubt whatsoever she could wind up in prison, and, truthfully, she knew that it would serve her right.

'I, er . . . think I've had enough shopping for one day actually,' Flora muttered and Alex was instantly concerned.

'Oh dear. I fear I've made you overdo things,' she fretted. 'I was having such a nice time I forgot how ill you've been. Come along, I'll get Thomas to drive us home immediately and then you must go straight to your room and rest until dinner.'

Flora felt worse than ever as she followed Alex through the store. She was such a kind person and she really didn't deserve to be deceived.

On the way home Alex told her, 'You might like to wear one of your new dresses this evening. Magnus has invited a business colleague and his wife and son for dinner.'

A mischievous sparkle appeared in her eye as she confided, 'Between you and me I think he's hoping the son will take a shine to Margaret. He's always inviting eligible young men to dinner but none of them have seemed in the least bit interested in her up to now. It's hardly surprising, is it, really? She doesn't even attempt to make the best of herself and she isn't the easiest of people to get on with either. Still, I dare say she'll get lucky one day.'

'I er . . . can't help but notice that she can be quite rude to you,' Flora admitted.

Alex nodded in agreement. 'Yes, she is but she and Magnus are very close so there would be no point in my complaining to him about it. He would simply take her side.'

'Did you and Magnus never want children of your own?' Flora enquired curiously, then instantly wished that she hadn't as colour rose in Alex's cheeks.

'Shortly after Margaret was born, Magnus had an illness that left him infertile,' Alex told her wistfully. 'So, in fairness, I knew even before I married him that I would never have a child. It didn't seem to matter at the time because he was so handsome and so kind that he swept me off my feet. My parents were totally against me marrying a much older widower but I was at the age when I thought I knew best.' She stared out of the window and Flora saw that there were tears glistening on her long lashes as she went on, 'For a while after our marriage I was blissfully happy but right from the start Margaret refused to accept me in her

114

mother's place and eventually it caused a rift between me and Magnus.' Suddenly she stopped talking and forcing a false smile to her face she said, 'Hark at me telling you all my woes. I shouldn't complain, I have a lovely home and now I have you too so I should be counting my blessings instead of feeling sorry for myself. Just take no notice of me.'

It was obvious that Alex wasn't happy, and Flora thought again that she should just leave Magnus and Margaret to it. She was still a very attractive woman. But then, perhaps she was afraid of leaving her husband and the stability he offered?

Nothing is ever straightforward, she thought. She herself was a prime example. Look at the mess she was in now and all because of one lie that had started aboard the *Carpathia* when they had assumed that she was Connie.

Flora stared miserably from the window as she thought of her family and Jamie far away. She now had more money at her disposal than she had ever dreamed of but at what cost? They would all be so disappointed in her if they knew what she had done and the thought drained all the pleasure from the day as she sank back in her seat.

Within minutes of them arriving home the delivery van from Macy's drew up outside and a young man in uniform began to carry all Flora's purchases into the hallway.

'Goodness, did you buy up half the shop?' Patsy asked with a grin as she started to cart all the boxes and packages upstairs to Flora's room. She oohed and aahed as she unpacked them and laid the contents across the bed, stroking the soft materials enviously. And then she felt guilty. The poor young woman had lost everything she owned when the *Titanic* sank and here she was feeling jealous of her.

Flora meanwhile had flopped down into the chair by the window, not showing much interest in her purchases at all.

'Which dress would you like me to lay out for you to wear to dinner this evening, miss?'

Flora shrugged. 'Whichever you think is the most suitable, Patsy.'

'Hmm, then I think this green one. It's such a pretty shade, it will set off your dark hair something lovely!'

Flora nodded without even bothering to look at the dress, so sensing that her new mistress wasn't in the mood for chatting, Patsy efficiently set about putting all the new things away then crept from the room without another word.

That evening Patsy helped Flora to get dressed for dinner but when she eyed herself in the mirror she could feel no thrill at her new finery. It had all been bought with Connie's money and once again the deception she was caught up in weighed on her heavily as she thanked Patsy and followed her down to the dining room.

The family and their guests were already gathered there and Alex rose and hurried across to draw her into the room, saying, 'Why, you look quite beautiful, my dear.' Then turning to her visitors, a middle-aged couple with a spotty-faced son in tow, she introduced her.

'Mr and Mrs Fallows, Levi, this is my niece, Constance.'

The woman, who was dripping in jewels and had a fox fur stole draped across her shoulders, inclined her head, while Levi, the son, gave her a dazzling smile, much to the obvious annoyance of Margaret who up until then had been doing her best to get his attention. He looked to be somewhere in his late twenties. His short, dark hair was caked to his head with Macassar oil and he had a long, beaked nose and buck teeth. Flora didn't take to him

116

at all. Even so, she shook his hand politely and went to sit down, painfully aware that Margaret was openly glaring at her.

'Well, if we're all ready now shall we take a seat?' Margaret said pointedly, looking at Flora as she rang for dinner to be served.

As soon as everyone was seated at the table the maid appeared and began to serve them with the first course. Margaret had made a beeline to ensure that she was seated next to Levi and Flora was grateful for that at least. The way he was staring at her was making her feel distinctly uncomfortable.

The starter was chargrilled mackerel served with sweet-and-sour beetroot and Flora noticed that Margaret cleared her plate in seconds. The main course was mustard-stuffed chicken served with a selection of seasonal vegetables and tiny sweet potatoes followed by poached pears and Poire Williams pudding. Flora had never heard of it before but it turned out to be liqueur-soaked sponge topped with poached pears and cream and was quite delicious. When the dessert had been cleared away, a selection of cheese and biscuits was placed on the table along with a fresh pot of coffee and Flora had to stop herself from groaning aloud as she politely declined any more food. She was so full that she was sure she would burst but she saw that Margaret was still eating and wondered where she managed to put it all.

Throughout the meal, the men had talked mainly of shipping but Alex had said little. Margaret meanwhile had directed all her conversation at Levi who was beginning to look slightly embarrassed. It was a relief for Flora when Magnus suggested that the men should retire to his study for a glass of port and a cigar while the ladies rested in the drawing room with a glass of sherry.

'So, my dear, how are you enjoying New York?' Mrs Fallows asked when they were seated in the next room.

'I um . . . haven't seen too much of it up to now,' Flora answered quietly, desperately wishing she could just escape to her room.

'Ah well, there's plenty of time,' the woman said, taking a dainty

117

sip of her drink. 'Your aunt told me that you were on the *Titanic*.' She tutted. 'It must have been very frightening for you.'

'Y-yes, it was.' Flora gulped as a vision of Connie falling to her death floated in front of her eyes and Alex instantly addressed the woman, keen to change the subject.

'And how is your daughter, Mrs Fallows? I believe she recently gave birth to your first grandchild. They are both well, I hope?'

'Oh *yes*.' Mrs Fallows beamed now. 'She had a little girl, Charlotte Elizabeth, and she is quite delightful. I just need to find a nice young wife for Levi now.' She glanced at Flora meaningfully and Flora felt a cold sweat break out on her brow. Margaret, meanwhile, was glaring at her and suddenly Flora knew that she could stand it no longer.

'I'm so sorry,' she mumbled, rising so abruptly that she almost overbalanced her chair. 'But I'm not feeling too well. Will you please excuse me?' And with that she fled from the room as if old Nick himself were chasing her.

'Do forgive her,' Alex hastily apologised as the door slammed behind her. 'She still hasn't fully recovered from her ordeal.'

'Of course.' Mrs Fallows gave a gracious nod. 'But you must bring her to dinner at our house when she is better. I have a feeling my Levi has taken quite a shine to her.'

From her seat at the side of the fireplace, Margaret pouted and swallowed her sherry in one great gulp.

Chapter Fourteen

For the next two weeks, Flora kept out of Margaret's way as much as she possibly could. Since Levi Fallows's interest in her at the dinner party, Margaret now made no attempt to even be civil to her, and sometimes Alex felt as if she was caught in the middle of a war zone, although Flora's behaviour was exemplary. Magnus wasn't much better and Alex was forever trying to placate them.

'Why *we* should be landed with her I'll never know,' he would growl whenever the opportunity arose. Alex knew better than to argue with him and would quickly try to change the subject but now it was taking a toll on her nerves, which felt as taut as piano wires.

Finally, they were into May and slowly the weather began to improve, so at least Flora could get out and about a little more to explore the area. If she didn't hop on a tram she spent the day walking the streets and window shopping and didn't get back to the house until it was time to get ready for dinner.

Sometimes Alex went with her but not often. Magnus seemed to disapprove of his wife spending too much time with her and so mostly she set off on her jaunts alone. Already she had visited Brooklyn and Manhattan but she particularly liked visiting the dockyards along the Hudson River. They reminded her of home. New York had always sounded like such a glamorous place to her but now that she was venturing out and about she had soon discovered that it had slum areas just as there were in London.

These excursions were the only times she felt truly happy because she was away from the cold atmosphere of the house, and time and time again she wished that she had never begun the deception, but it was far too late now and, somehow, she was just going to have to make the best of things. But she missed her family and Jamie and the simple life they had had.

It was funny when she came to think of it. She had always envied people with money but now that she had access to it she realised that money couldn't buy happiness. Certainly not if Alex was anything to go by. The poor woman seemed to be permanently walking on eggshells trying to keep her husband and stepdaughter happy and Flora thought that if Alex did leave, as she wished she would, they surely wouldn't care if the way they talked to her and treated her was anything to go by. The one bright spot in her life was her maid, Patsy, who always had a cheery word and a smile for her.

'The master's holding another dinner party tonight,' Patsy confided to her one morning as she tidied Flora's room. Flora still found it hard not to do it herself and often when Patsy arrived it was already done.

Flora groaned. There had been two others in the last two weeks, each a family with an eligible son in tow, although thankfully neither of them had shown the slightest interest in her, or Margaret, for that matter.

'Oh no!' Flora plonked herself down heavily on her dressing-table stool. 'That will mean Margaret will be watching me like a hawk again.' She could talk easily to Patsy, just as she once had to Connie, who she still missed terribly, possibly because they were of a similar age and she knew that she could trust her not to repeat anything she said.

Patsy giggled. All the staff were aware that the master was desperate to find a husband for his daughter.

'Per'aps they should find someone with a blind son,' she said with a wicked twinkle in her eye. 'He wouldn't be able to see how plain she is then. Though that wouldn't really matter if she was nice, would it? Trouble is I don't think she's got anything going for her. She's fat, ugly *and* rude and unkind!'

'Well, I wouldn't have put it *quite* that bluntly,' Flora answered, trying not to grin as Patsy plumped up the pillows on her bed before smoothing them out again.

'Why not? It's the truth, ain't it? But anyway, what are you going to do with yourself today?'

'Oh, I thought I'd just go out and have a wander about.' Truthfully Flora was finding having so much time on her hands was becoming boring now.

'Hmm, well judging by the tangle this bed was in you had another bad night,' Patsy said observantly.

Flora flushed. The nightmares were getting worse if anything and she supposed it was down to her guilty conscience. The only comfort she had was knowing that her family in England were receiving a monthly payment from her, which she hoped would make life a little easier for them.

After Patsy had left, Flora gathered her hat and coat together and headed out into the street. After a while she found herself outside a tailor's shop in a gloomy little backstreet. She was admiring the suit displayed in the window when the shop door opened and a tiny man who barely reached up to her shoulders popped his head out.

'*Boker Tov*, young lady,' he said and Flora realised that he was Jewish. 'May I help you?'

'Oh no . . . I was just admiring the suit,' she explained.

He nodded. 'It is good stitching, yes?'

'Very good,' Flora responded with a smile.

'And what brings such a pretty young lady to the backstreets?'

Flora lifted her shoulders. 'I'm staying with my aunt and I was bored so I decided to do a little exploring.'

'Ah!' He shook his head making his tiny skullcap wobble dangerously. 'It is good to walk and exercise but perhaps not in certain areas. There are many bad people hereabouts,' he warned. 'They will pick your pockets without you even knowing they have touched you, or worse still they will drag you into a brothel. Avoid Soho at all costs, my dear. There are many ladies of the night there.'

'Thank you, I'll remember that,' Flora said, casting an anxious glance across her shoulder. She would heed his warning and be careful where she walked in future. The little man disappeared into the shop and Flora made her way back to Alex's house to find Patsy was waiting for her in her room with her clothes laid out across the bed.

As soon as she saw Flora, Patsy whistled through her teeth. 'Oooh, you cut that fine, didn't you, miss?' the girl said. 'You know what a stickler the master is for punctuality. His guests will be arriving within the hour but I've run your bath for you so if you go and pop in it I'll help you get dressed when you've finished.'

Flora sighed and did as she was told. Thanks to Patsy, she was ready on time and as she started down the stairs she heard Alex and Magnus greeting their guests in the hallway. It looked like another dreary night lay ahead. And then as she neared the foot of the stairs she found herself staring into a face that she recognised and she felt the colour drain from her cheeks.

'Ah, Mr and Mrs Johnson, Tobias, this is my niece. You might have met on the *Titanic*?'

Flora's legs seemed to have developed a life of their own as she stared into Toby's eyes.

'I believe we did briefly,' he said with a wicked grin, 'Although I can't remember the name . . .'

'This is Constance,' Alex told him and Flora wished that the floor would open up and swallow her.

'It's very nice to meet you again . . . *Constance*.' He held out his hand and when she placed hers into it he grinned and held on to it a fraction longer than was necessary, much to Margaret's disgust.

'Right, well shall we go and have a drink before we all go into dinner?' Magnus suggested and they all trailed after him into the drawing room where a maid was waiting for them with glasses of wine on a silver tray.

'We were all *so* lucky to survive the sinking of the ship, weren't we, my dear?' Mrs Johnson trilled as she stared at Flora but all the girl could do was nod mutely. Seeing Toby again seemed to have robbed her of her voice, for she knew that just one word from him could end her pretence, and then what would become of her? Would she be carted off to a cell somewhere with no one to help her, or would she be turned out onto the streets? She could see that Alex was watching her closely, as if she could sense her unease and she forced herself to give the woman a little smile.

Thankfully, Alex managed to steer the conversation away from what had happened on the *Titanic* – she knew how much it upset her to talk about it – and for now they began to speak of other things. Eventually they were summoned into dinner and Flora felt faint when Toby offered his arm. She knew it would look rude if she refused to take it so she steeled herself to walk sedately at his side. Once in the dining room, he pulled out a chair for her and when she was seated he sat down right beside her.

'Your niece and my son seem to be getting along remarkably well, don't they?' Mrs Johnson whispered approvingly to Alex, leaning towards her so Alex got the full force of her perfume. 'It would be *so* nice if Tobias could meet a nice girl now,' she continued. 'I'm not entirely happy with the company he's keeping at present. I think it's time for him to settle down.'

Alex smiled. It appeared that Mrs Johnson had her sights set on Flora but what would be would be.

Very soon they were being served with one delicious course after another but the whole meal was torture for Flora, so much so that she found she couldn't eat a thing and afterwards she couldn't even remember what they had been served. Then, once the meal was over, things got even worse, if it were at all possible, when Alex suggested to Flora, 'Why don't you play a piece on the piano for us, my dear? I seem to recall in one of his letters your father telling us what an accomplished pianist you are?'

Flora gulped. 'I er . . . don't really feel up to it this evening, if you don't mind,' she said in a wobbly voice as Toby looked on with amusement. 'I'm feeling rather hot, as it happens.' She began to fan herself with her hand as if to add emphasis to her words.

Connie had been a wonderful player but she herself couldn't play a note if her life depended on it.

'Then why don't you take dear Connie out into the garden for a little fresh air, dear?' Toby's mother simpered, leaping at the opportunity to push the two young people together.

'Of course, it would be my pleasure.' Once more, Toby offered his arm and knowing that she had little choice Flora reluctantly took it and allowed him to lead her away as Margaret glowered at her.

They entered the garden through the French doors in the drawing room and once outside Flora wrapped her arms about herself and shivered; the days were warming up but the evenings still tended to be cold. She stared at Toby warily as he leaned lazily against the wall and grinned at her.

'So . . . *Constance* . . . how are you?' His voice dripped sarcasm and she flinched but remained silent. What could she say? She had been well and truly caught out in her deception and she knew that she deserved all that could be coming to her. One word from Toby and everyone would know what she had done.

His hand snaked forward then and she forced herself to remain still as he trailed a finger down her cheek. 'It must be nice to suddenly become an heiress,' he remarked. 'It's quite a transformation from being a maid, isn't it?'

'I . . . I never intended to do this,' she answered in a shaky voice. 'But I was afraid of what would happen to me. I have no one here, I know no one and . . .' Her voice trailed away. The excuse sounded ridiculous even to her own ears. 'So, what are you intending to do?' she asked then. 'Are you going to tell them?'

'That all depends.'

'On what?' She stared at him.

'Well . . . on a few things actually.' Dusk was falling now but she could still see his face clearly and she could tell that he was enjoying this immensely. She was like a rabbit caught in a trap and it came to her then that there wasn't a single thing she could do about it.

'For a start off I find myself in a bit of a sticky situation at the moment. A gambling debt, you know? And Mother doesn't seem too keen on bailing me out of it at the moment so perhaps if you could be . . . *nice* to me . . .'

'What you *mean* is you're going to blackmail me!' she answered sharply and now the smile slid from his face and he glared at her.

'Don't you come the injured party with *me*,' he growled threateningly. 'A few gambling debts are nothing like as serious as what *you're* doing impersonating a dead girl. I could blow the whistle on you right now and then you'd be out on your ass on the streets and what would become of you then, eh?'

'So how much do you need?' she asked dully. He had her tightly in a corner and she knew it.

'A hundred dollars should do . . . for now!'

'*A hundred dollars!*' Horrified, Flora stared at him.

'*For now*,' he repeated. 'But of course . . . if you'd rather I went back inside and—'

'*No!* I'll get it for you tomorrow,' she told him in a panic.

He smirked with satisfaction. 'That's better. And now . . . how about a little kiss, eh? We could start where we left off aboard the ship.' His eyes were gleaming menacingly, and before she could stop him, his hand suddenly reached towards her and brushed across her breast.

Badly shaken Flora stepped away from him so quickly that she almost lost her balance and gathering together what dignity she could she told him, 'I'll pay you what you ask but if you want me to do more than that then you'd best go in there right now and tell them what you know and get it over with!'

'All right, all right, we'll play it your way . . . for now.' He chuckled but the sound held no mirth. 'I'll be back tomorrow afternoon for my money. I'll tell everyone that I'm calling on you. Just make sure you have it ready!' With that he walked back inside without giving her so much as another glance and once alone again Flora sagged against the wall as her legs threatened to give way beneath her. Her future suddenly looked very bleak indeed.

Chapter Fifteen

In London, Emily was drinking her first cup of tea of the day before starting to clean the bedrooms. Timmy had left for school and all the others were at work so she welcomed these few moments of peace and quiet before she began her chores. She always changed the sheets on all the beds on Mondays, weather permitting. She would then take them to the small washhouse that was shared by the rest of the courtyard and after scrubbing them and feeding them through the mangle she would hang them on the lines stretched across the courtyards to dry. It had always given her a measure of satisfaction to see them looking crisp and clean as they flapped in the breeze but since news had come that her firstborn had perished on the *Titanic* each day now was just another monotonous list of tasks to endure and somehow get through.

Added to her grief for Flora was her concern about her second eldest, Ben. She'd heard it rumoured that he was mixing with a bad crowd lately and she knew for a fact that he'd been skipping work. The Wilkinson's lad in the cottage opposite, who Ben usually teamed up with on the docks, had told his mother, although Ben had strongly denied it when she confronted him about it. An added worry was a rather lovely pearl necklace she had found under his pillow when changing his bed some weeks back. It had been shortly after they'd been informed that Flora was lost and

Ben had taken the news badly. He had always been very close to his big sister.

'Explain *that*, me lad!' She had dropped the necklace onto the table in front of him that evening after finding it when he came home and he had blushed to the roots of his hair. 'I . . . it's only a cheap 'un off the market,' he had blustered as his mother's lips drew back from her teeth.

'Hmm, well I'm no expert when it comes to jewellery, never havin' had any apart from me weddin' ring,' she had admitted. 'But it certainly looks expensive and real enough to me!'

'Then you're *wrong*!' Cheeks flaming, Ben had slammed away from the table to tower over her. He had just turned eighteen and was over six feet and Emily suddenly wondered when he had grown so tall. But then she had been so wrapped up in grieving for her daughter that she was forced to admit she hadn't taken much notice of anyone or anything since learning of Flora's death. His work on the docks had turned his arms and chest into solid muscle and with his shock of dark hair and his lovely eyes, Emily wasn't surprised that girls had started to flock around him like bees to a honey pot. Of all her children he and Flora had been the most alike and now every time she looked at him she felt a pain in her heart as she was reminded of her daughter.

'It's just a cheap trinket I picked up for a lass I'm seein',' he insisted, then reaching into his pocket he withdrew a handful of silver coins which he tossed onto the table for her. 'Here,' he said gruffly. 'You'll be needin' this now that you ain't got part of Flora's wages comin' in every month.'

Emily's mouth had dropped open as she gazed at the amount. 'But where did you get all this?' she gasped. 'I hope it was by fair means? I'll not have any dodgy money comin' into this house even if we were starvin'. I've just turned down Miss Constance's offer of a monthly payment an' all! It was kind of her to offer but we ain't quite charity cases yet!'

the sheets would dry outside. Throughout the winter she had had to string them up on lines stretched across the ceiling from one corner of the room to the other which only added to the damp atmosphere in the cottage. But then she supposed she was lucky compared to some. At least she had her own front door, many thereabouts lived in rented rooms huddled together like flies.

It took her no more than a matter of minutes to strip the sheets from the beds, she had it down to a fine art now, but when she came to Ben's bed she frowned. There was yet another piece of jewellery tucked beneath his pillow and she didn't need to be an expert to see that this was no cheap trinket. It was a gold ring set with blue stones and diamonds that flashed in the light filtering in from the tiny leaded window. She had seen a blue stone like this once before in the window of a posh jeweller's shop in Oxford Street and had remembered it because of the beautiful, vivid, cornflower-blue colour. Now what was it called . . . a sasp . . . no, a sapphire, that was it! This must be one because no piece of glass could ever be cut to sparkle like this, surely? She frowned as she lifted it to examine it. She'd get the truth out of Ben tonight if it killed her, she promised herself as she set the ring on the small chest of drawers at the side of his bed thinking about how the day before, Jess Bromley from across the other side of the court-yard had almost broken her neck to tell her that she'd seen Ben talking to Gus Miller, a criminal who was well known to the police.

'Well, there's no harm in speaking to someone you know, Jess,' Emily had told the woman but inside she was quaking. What would her lad be doing mixing with the likes of him? It was no secret that Gus had gangs of young lads who were only knee high to grass-hoppers out pickpocketing for him. And then there were the older lads who did the more serious crimes like breaking and entering. Gus had taken most of them from the workhouse and the police were always after him but Gus was as wily as an old fox and they could never pin anything on him. *But my Ben wouldn't be daft enough to get mixed up in something like that*, she tried to convince herself as she filled the tin bath in the washhouse with water from the pump and began the tedious job of washing the sheets.

The day passed in a blur and by the time Timmy got home from school the little cottage was as clean as Emily could make it and a tasty stew with fat juicy dumplings floating in it was simmering on the range. Like most women from thereabouts Emily was adept at rustling up a meal from almost nothing.

'There's been a robbery out at one o' the big posh houses in Mayfair,' Timmy informed her innocently as he drank a glass of milk almost in one swallow. He was growing like a weed and Emily teased him that he must have hollow legs, for she never seemed able to fill him up. 'I heard the teachers talkin' about it while I was in the playground when we was havin' us break. The robbers took lots o' jewellery but worse than that someone got hurt real bad. A lady tried to stop 'em an' they pushed her down the stairs. The teachers reckon she might die!'

'How awful,' Emily replied, her stomach churning as she thought of the ring upstairs. At the first chance she got she hurried up there and slipped it into her pocket. But no, she tried to convince herself, Ben would never be so stupid . . . would he? She knew for a fact that he hadn't come in till the early hours of the morning, for she had lain awake listening for him. Then today when she rose he had already gone out again.

I'll have it out with him the second he sets foot through the door, she promised herself. Meanwhile, she tried to concentrate on the family who were arriving home for their dinner.

That night when the rest of the family had gone to bed and the house was quiet, Emily sat downstairs beside the dying fire. Ben would have to come home sometime and when he did she wanted

131

to be there to confront him. Eventually she fell into a doze and her chin drooped to her chest but then suddenly something made her start awake and when her head snapped round she saw Ben creeping down the stairs with his shoes in one hand and a bag in the other.

'And just where do you think you're going?'

Her voice startled him and he almost jumped out of his skin. He came to stand in front of her with his head bowed, shamefaced.

'I . . . I've got to go away for a while, Ma,' he said miserably.

'Oh, and why is that?'

When he raised his chin, she was shocked to see tears glistening in his eyes. 'Would it be anything to do with this?' she asked, taking the ring from her pocket and he gulped deep in his throat making his Adam's apple do a little jig.

'Right then, me lad, I think you've got some explainin' to do,' she said sternly.

For a moment he just stood there but then he started to talk and everything came out in a rush.

'I've been such a *fool*!' he said bitterly. 'An' it started when we lost our Flora, not that that's any excuse for what I've done. You've allus taught us right from wrong but for a time back there I don't think I was thinkin' straight an' I got into a card game wi' Gus Miller. I ended up owin' him a lot o' money an' o' course I had no way o' payin' it, so he agreed that if I did a few . . . little jobs for him he'd forget what I owed him. I didn't want to do it but everyone knows Gus ain't a bloke to mess with so I agreed.' He licked his lips as his head wagged from side to side.

'So . . . he sent you out on the rob?' Emily whispered and he nodded miserably.

'Yes, twice. Last night was supposed to be the last time. He gave us the address of this posh house in Mayfair. He knows the people that live there an' assured us that they'd be out. He even told us where the woman's jewellery box would be, though I ain't

132

got a clue how he knew! Anyway, we got there an' all was going' well. Me an' Nipper found the box and emptied it then went out onto the landin' only to find a woman there brandishin' a candlestick at us. We were desperate to get away but as Nipper tried to push past her she slipped an' ended up goin' from the top to the bottom o' the stairs where she just lay still.' He started to cry then, great gulping sobs that shook his body. 'We never *meant* to 'urt no one, Ma, I *swear* it, an' if the woman dies I don't know how I'll live wi' meself even though it were an accident.' He took a few deep breaths before going on as his mother listened to the story horrified. 'That ring' – he pointed to the one in his mother's hand – 'must have got caught in the lining of me pocket. We went straight to Gus after we left the woman's house and passed everything over to him. I didn't realise I still had that till I got home. But if the woman dies the police will come lookin'. Gus won't take the rap if they catch him, he'll squeal like a stuck pig an' put all the blame on me an' Nipper.'

'Ah, so it was Nipper you were with was it?' Ben and Nipper had been friends since they were barely out of nappies but the lad had gone off the rails since he'd left school. She should have guessed that it would be him Ben was with.

Ben nodded, his face waxen. 'He's disappeared and I need to do the same till things quieten down. We can't risk staying around here, not till we know if the woman is goin' to survive. You do realise that, don't you?' He reached out to squeeze her hand but her throat was too full to answer him so she merely nodded. As much as she hated the thought of him going away, she hated the thought of him dangling at the end of a noose even more and if the woman should die, God forbid . . . She couldn't bear the thought of losing yet another of her offspring.

'So where will you go?' she forced herself to ask shakily.

'We're gettin' on the first boat out of the docks tonight, if we can, but I'll get word to you where we are when I know. Meanwhile, keep that ring. You might be able to pawn it when the heat's died down a bit.'

He rose and lifted his bag again. It was time to go and he didn't want to prolong the goodbye. It was just too painful.

'Be careful, lad, an' may God go with you.' Emily stood and kissed him on the cheek before gently pushing him towards the door. As soon as it had closed behind him, she sat back down in her chair and, rocking back and forth, she finally gave way to tears.

She had no idea how long she sat there but eventually she rose and lifted her shawl from the hook on the door, then, quiet as a mouse, she let herself out into the velvety black night. She knew every inch of the alleys like the back of her hand and soon she came to the docks behind the warehouses. She stood for a moment staring down at the flotsam in the dark water then, raising her hand, she flung the ring as far away from her as she could. She heard a gentle plop and satisfied that it was lost forever, she retraced her steps. It might have been worth a king's ransom for all she knew but should the police come sniffing around and find it, it would prove her lad's guilt and she couldn't risk that. She would rather starve.

Chapter Sixteen

The following morning when she went down to breakfast, Flora found another letter from Mr Wainthorp waiting for her. It still felt strange to open mail that was addressed to Connie and she'd almost ignored it. This living a lie was turning out to be a lot harder than she had thought it would be, especially now Toby had clocked on to what she was doing. The letter informed her that her family had politely declined the offer of a monthly wage and she was bitterly disappointed, although in hindsight she supposed she should have realised that her mother was too proud to accept what she would class as charity.

If she hadn't already have lost her appetite thanks to Toby's threats the night before, this letter would certainly have taken away any desire for food. She felt sick with guilt and she suddenly missed her family unbearably.

'Are you feeling unwell?' Alex glanced at Flora as the girl picked at her food. 'You look a little pale. Did you have a nightmare again?'

'No . . . I'm quite well, thank you,' Flora answered as Margaret glared at her. 'But I think I might go out and get a little fresh air this morning.' She needed to visit the bank to withdraw the money that Toby had demanded, otherwise one word from him and it would all be over. Part of her half hoped that he would say something and just get it over with because the strain of having to watch every word she uttered was becoming too much. The other part of her was terrified of the consequences and so for now she had decided to just give him the money and try to placate him.

The rest of the meal passed in silence. Margaret never attempted to make any conversation with her or Alex and so Flora was relieved when she could excuse herself and escape to her room. She found Patsy there making her bed and the girl gave her a cheery grin. For a moment Flora envied her. Her life had been as simple as Patsy's was when she had been Connie's maid but now everything was so complicated.

'Off out, are you, miss?' Patsy asked as Flora took her hat and coat from the armoire. 'Just be sure not to go gettin' yourself lost.'

'I shall be fine,' Flora assured her and without another word she made for the hallway where she met Margaret just going into the drawing room with an armful of magazines.

'Off out to meet one of your beaus, are you?' she smirked nastily. 'Looking like that you'll probably get asked what you charge, especially if you flirt like you do when we have guests visit!'

Choosing to ignore her, Flora marched towards the door and let herself out into the street, but once outside tears burned at the back of her eyes. Why was Margaret always so horrible to everyone? she wondered. If it was because of Toby then she was welcome to him. In fact, Flora wished to God that it was Margaret he was paying attention to and not her.

She was so lost in thought that she found herself at the doors of the bank before she knew it. She went in and withdrew the money she needed and once it was safely tucked into her purse, she went back outside and began to wander aimlessly along the street. Now more than ever she regretted what she had done, but the problem was she had no idea how she was going to keep up the pretence.

It was some time later when she suddenly stopped to take stock of where she was that she realised she was completely lost. Looking around, she noticed with a start that almost all the people she was passing were Chinese, so she guessed she must somehow have wandered into Chinatown, a part of the city Alex had warned her to avoid. Flora's heart began to thump. The streets were narrow and dark and lined with tiny shops selling bunches of herbs and spices and the smell of curry added to the stench from the docks was overpowering. She felt as if everyone was staring at her, as if they could sense the hundred dollars she had tucked into her purse. Breathing heavily now, she looked up and down the street, unable to get her bearings. Suddenly the buildings seemed to close in on her, and she could almost sense people creeping up on her.

Turning about abruptly she began to retrace her steps, her bag suddenly feeling like it weighed a ton. She wasn't even aware that she was almost running and crying until a gentle hand on her arm startled her and she spun about to find herself face to face with a strikingly pretty Chinese girl who looked to be about her age with coal-black hair that hung down her back like a shimmering cape, and deep, dark eyes to match. She was very poorly dressed but she seemed to be kind.

'Missy is OK . . . *yes*?' The girl seemed so genuinely concerned that Flora began to cry even harder and leaning against the nearest wall she let her chin droop to her chest.

'Ah, missy is lost, yes? Do not worry, I will help you. My name is Jia Li.'

'Th-that's pretty,' Flora hiccupped.

The girl gave a smile that seemed to light up the street and placing her hands together she gave a little bow from the waist. 'Thank you, it means good and beautiful in my country. But now, how may I help you? It is not good to wander about alone around here, there are some bad people.'

'I am lost,' Flora confessed, wiping her tears and her nose on the sleeve of her dress in a most unladylike fashion. She gave Jia Li Alex's address then and gently taking her arm the girl began to lead her through a twisting labyrinth of stinking back alleys, where old women sitting on doorsteps outside rows of old terraced houses eyed them cautiously, while children played in the gutters amidst the muck and the filth.

'I think there is more upsetting you than you saying,' Jia Li told her solemnly when they at last emerged onto a city street. 'I sense something is very wrong but should you ever need help come to Yung's Laundry back there.' She pointed a thumb over her shoulder, pointing in the direction they had just come. 'You will find me there if you need friend, missy.'

'Thank you.'

The girl turned and hurried back into the alley and Flora found herself thinking that, even in her worn, shabby clothes, Jia Li resembled a rose on a dung heap. Then with a little jolt she realised that time was moving on and after taking a moment to get her bearings she set off for Alex's home. It wouldn't do to be late. If Toby were to arrive before her there was no telling what he might say and then the game would be up good and proper.

The moment she set foot through the front door she heard Toby's hateful voice talking to Margaret in the drawing room and her heart sank.

'Oh, miss.' Patsy hurried to meet her with a frown on her plump face. 'We've been real worried. There's a guest in there to see you. Miss Margaret is entertaining him at the moment.'

Flora nodded as she handed Patsy her hat and coat, then smoothing down her skirt she stuck her chin in the air and marched into the drawing room to find Toby and Margaret taking afternoon tea together.

'Ah, here you are.'

He rose to greet her with an oily smile but she ignored his

outstretched hand and asked Patsy, 'Fetch another cup in, would you, please?'

'O' course, miss.' Patsy bobbed her knee and hurried away as Flora sank onto a chair and Margaret scowled at her. She'd quite enjoyed having Toby all to herself. Trust Flora to come back and spoil everything.

'Been for a nice walk, have you?' Toby asked genially, for all the world as if he had called in purely by chance. He had turned his back on Margaret now and Flora could see the angry colour seeping up the young woman's neck, making her look even more unattractive, if that were possible.

'Yes.' Flora supposed that she should at least pretend to be civil to him in front of Margaret. She didn't want her to suspect anything.

'Right . . . well, nice as it's been talking to you I have things to attend to,' Margaret said huffily as she rose from her seat.

'Please don't let me stop you, Miss Ward.' Toby inclined his head towards her and angry that he hadn't tried to stop her leaving, Margaret stamped from the room slamming the door so loudly behind her that it danced on its hinges.

Flora meanwhile was rifling through her bag for the money, determined not to spend a second longer than she had to in his company.

'Here! I believe this is what you've come for!' She thrust the money towards him and he snatched it greedily as he gave her a slow, lazy smile and rose from his seat.

'Thank you, that will do very nicely . . . for now,' he ended threateningly and then he strode away as Flora sat staring after him with dull eyes. She was painfully aware that this could well be only the beginning of Toby's blackmail, and it wouldn't be long before he came back for more – again and again!

Her thoughts were interrupted when Patsy burst back into the room with another cup and saucer and informed her, 'The master is throwin' another dinner party tonight, miss. I forgot to mention it but I've laid your clothes out for you. Would you like to come upstairs and start to get ready when you've had your tea?'

Flora stifled a groan. The last thing she needed right then was to have to sit through yet another of Magnus's boring dinner parties. Even so, she was painfully aware that while she was a guest in his house she didn't have much choice but to fall in with his wishes, so with a sigh she followed Patsy upstairs.

'I thought you might like to wear this one tonight.' Patsy held up a green chiffon dress, and Flora nodded. She didn't really much care what she wore. 'And pardon me, but I peeked in your jewellery box and thought these pearls would look well with that outfit.'

Without stopping to think, Flora almost snatched them from her hand and threw them back into the box before slamming the lid. Patsy looked startled, and instantly repentant, Flora muttered, 'Thanks, Patsy, but I don't think that dress needs any adornment. It's one I bought when I went shopping with my aunt and I'm sure it's quite pretty enough on its own.'

'As you wish.' In a huff, Patsy sniffed before going into the bathroom to run the bath. She'd never seen Flora wear a single thing from her jewellery box since she'd arrived but she supposed it was up to her, at the end of the day. *But if they were mine I'd wear them all the time*, she thought as she tested the water with her elbow.

Back in the bedroom Flora stood at the window with the jewellery box clutched to her chest. How could she wear Connie's jewellery? It would be yet another betrayal and suddenly the need to see Jamie was overwhelming. Oh, what have I done? she asked herself miserably, but silence was her only answer.

Soon after, Flora was sitting through another boring evening when once more yet another eligible man was paraded in front of Margaret. For a second Flora almost found it amusing for it reminded her of some cows she had seen being paraded in front of prospective buyers at a cattle market. This time, the poor unsuspecting chap who accompanied his elderly parents looked to be middle-aged. He was almost as far round as he was high and completely bald, and even Margaret didn't attempt to flirt with this one. But then, even had he been handsome Flora knew he could never have compared to Jamie.

As always Magnus dominated the conversation while Alex sat silently at his side, sedately dressed as always in a plain, dove-grey dress with no adornments whatsoever apart from a strand of pearls that Flora thought looked identical to the ones in the jewellery box upstairs. The food as always was delicious but Flora was glad when she could make her excuses and slip away to her room. Once there she stood at the window for a long time, staring down at the street below and thinking of her family and Jamie as a wave of homesickness swept through her.

Connie had planned to stay here until she reached her twenty-first birthday then return to her home in London, but how could Flora ever do that? She knew Mrs Merry would guess immediately what she had done and then what would happen? The only other option was to instruct Mr Wainthrop to sell the house in London and remain in New York, but already Flora knew that she didn't wish to do this. She had an idea that now Toby was aware of her deception he would take full advantage of the fact until there was nothing left of Connie's inheritance and then what would she do? She had already taken a large sum of money out of Connie's account and should she do this too often, Mr Wainthrop was sure to become concerned.

She supposed that she could simply draw enough money from the bank to obtain a return ticket to London but then what would she do when she got there? Her family believed she was dead, so she could hardly turn up now out of the blue, and Jamie probably didn't even think of her now, which served her right. They would

Chapter Seventeen

A few days later Alex came down to breakfast sporting a black eye that would have looked more in keeping on a boxer.

She flushed as she saw Flora staring at it and after helping herself to a cup of tea from the pot she said sheepishly, 'I er . . . had a bit of a run-in with my wardrobe door last night and walked straight into it.'

Margaret smirked as Flora frowned. The whole household couldn't have failed to hear Magnus shouting at her the night before after he had returned late from his club and it was more than obvious what had happened, although Flora didn't confront her about it until Margaret had eaten her fill and left the room.

'So . . . how did you *really* hurt your eye?' she asked gently and was dismayed when Alex hung her head and began to cry.

'Magnus did that to you, didn't he?' Flora probed. She had heard the man shouting at her many times before although she had never noticed any bruises.

After a moment Alex reluctantly nodded. 'Yes . . . but he's sorry now. He has such a temper, you see? And I'm afraid I have a bad habit of speaking before I think.'

'No, I'm afraid I don't see.' Flora was furious. Alex was such a kind gentle person and as far as she was concerned, she certainly didn't deserve to be treated that way.

'A long time ago, I did something very bad,' Alex confessed

then in a small voice as she glanced nervously towards the door. 'It would have served me right if Magnus had thrown me out onto the streets but he forgave me. So you see, if every now and then I upset him I suppose I deserve it.'

'You mean to tell me that this has happened before?' Flora was horrified. 'But no one deserves to be *hit*. Why do you put up with it?'

'Because I have nowhere else to go,' Alex replied simply and after taking a deep breath she went on, 'Long ago, when your mother and I were young, I met Magnus when he was visiting England on a business trip. Your mother had recently married your father but your grandmother was very ill and she died shortly after, leaving behind a trail of debts. Magnus stepped in and offered to help if I married him and it seemed my only way out. I didn't love him then but I thought it would come with time, so we married, he settled up my mother's debts and I moved here to live with him and Margaret.

'She resented me from day one, believing that I was trying to take her late mother's place, although I swear that was never my intention. She was just a little girl then and I had dreams of us becoming friends. I knew that I would never be able to provide her with a stepbrother or sister. Magnus had quashed that dream when he informed me shortly before our marriage that following an illness he could no longer father any more children.' Her eyes had become misty as her mind drifted back in time, but she suddenly jerked as if aware that she might have said too much and hurried on, 'Oh, just ignore me, dear. This is nothing really. He didn't mean to do it and it will be healed in a day or two.'

Flora clamped her lips shut. It was clear that Alex wasn't going to say anymore but she felt desperately sorry for her and worse still for deceiving her. Alex scuttled out of the room then and left her alone with her thoughts. Flora sighed. Another boring day stretched ahead of her. She had soon discovered that being a lady of leisure could have its drawbacks, so after fetching a magazine from the morning room she decided to go outside and read in the morning sunshine.

She had no sooner settled in a chair in the rather pretty sunken rose garden when Patsy appeared. 'Mr Johnson is here to see you, miss. Shall I tell him you'll come in or shall I send him out here?'

Flora's heart sank as she clenched her hands into fists so that Patsy wouldn't see how they had started to shake, but she had no time to answer for at that moment Toby appeared.

'You may go back inside,' he told Patsy firmly and although she bobbed her knee and quickly turned about, Flora had seen the disapproving look on her face.

'He's no gentleman at all,' Flora heard the girl murmur as she retraced her steps but then she was forced to give her attention to Toby who was staring at her with an amused expression on his face.

'What do you want?' she asked abruptly, desperately trying not to let him see how terrified she was.

'Now is *that* any way to greet a visitor, my sweet Flora?' He grinned as he took a seat next to her and began to study his nails. 'You haven't even offered me tea.'

'I'm sure you're not here to drink tea,' she responded heatedly, glad that they were well out of earshot of anyone in the house. 'So why don't you just spit it out?' She could hardly wait for him to be gone.

'Very well, the long and the short of it is I'm in trouble again,' he answered with no sign of remorse. 'I must be on an unlucky streak at the moment so I need another fifty dollars.'

Flora went red in the face as she stared back at him. 'You talk about fifty dollars as if it is nothing!' she said incredulously.

'Well, it isn't to a little heiress like you, is it?' The smile was gone now and he was glaring at her, making his usually handsome

145

face look quite ugly. 'But of course . . . if you'd rather I had a little word with . . .'

'Oh, shut up!' she snapped, knowing he had her over a barrel. 'When do you need the money for?'

'Tonight as it happens.'

'Tonight!' Flora swallowed hard before bursting out, 'You do know that this can't go on, surely? I've only just given you a hundred dollars! Connie's solicitor back in England is going to start getting suspicious if I keep drawing large amounts of money out for no apparent reason.'

'That's your problem, darling, you worry too much,' he drawled as he rose from his seat. 'So, shall we say I collect it about six o'clock this evening?'

Flora so wanted to slap the silly smile off his face but she knew he had her hands tied behind her back and so she clenched her teeth as he casually strolled away stopping to pluck a delicate red rose from a bush and insert it into the buttonhole of his expensive suit on the way. She sat there seething for a time but then despair washed over her and lowering her head she began to weep.

Suddenly Margaret appeared with a smug smile on her face and Flora hastily mopped away her tears.

'So . . .' Margaret grinned maliciously. 'Entertaining gentleman callers in the garden, now, are we?'

Flora frowned at her as she rose swiftly and snatched up her magazine. She had held her tongue and not reacted to any of Margaret's sly comments up to now. She was a guest in Margaret's home after all, but today she was in no mood for her spite.

'Don't be so *ridiculous*,' she replied scathingly. 'Toby was just passing and called in to say hello.' She made to march past her but Margaret's next comment made her stop dead in her tracks as a cold finger snaked up her spine.

'Hmm, I saw him coming down the path. I was collecting some roses for the dining room.' She pointed to the half-full

146

basket on her arm. 'But why would he call you Flora? And why would he expect you to hand money over to him? I heard him quite clearly.'

The colour drained from Flora's face as she stood there trying to think of some plausible excuse. 'W-we became friends on the *Titanic*,' she faltered. 'And it seems that he's got himself into debt gambling so he called to ask if I would lend him some money to get him out of a tight spot. I don't suppose he wants his parents to know about it. And he didn't call me Flora, you must have misheard him.'

Margaret grinned. 'It didn't sound like he was asking a favour to me. It sounded like he was *demanding* money from you. And wasn't Flora the name of the maid who was supposed to be coming with Constance?'

'I *am* Constance,' Flora croaked. 'And yes, Flora was the name of my maid, either you misheard him or he got mixed up with our names. I didn't notice. He got to know both of us on board so if he did call me Flora it was just a mistake.'

'It all sounds rather fishy to me,' Margaret remarked, staring at her suspiciously.

'I really think you're reading too much into this,' Flora answered as she struggled to regain her composure. 'But now if you'll excuse me I have to go into the city.'

'I *bet* you do,' Margaret gloated as Flora hurried by without another word.

Once in the privacy of her room Flora's hand flew to her mouth as she began to pace back and forth in a panic. If Margaret were to voice her suspicions to Alex or Magnus the game would be up good and proper. Magnus had never attempted to make her feel welcome and Alex was far too afraid of him to stand up to him if he ordered her from the house. Worse still, he might choose to have her arrested for taking on Connie's identity and for theft, and could she really blame him if he did? she asked herself, for

147

she was painfully aware that every penny she drew out of Connie's account was stealing.

I've got to leave, and soon, before I get found out, she told herself. *But where shall I go?*

Margaret was spiteful and vindictive and certainly couldn't be trusted to keep her mouth shut for long. Snatching up her hat and coat, Flora hurried downstairs and slipped out of the front door unnoticed. She was quaking inside but she automatically took the route that was now familiar to her as she headed for the bank. Once there she withdrew the money that Toby had demanded and tucked it safely into her bag before going to stand on the pavement outside.

The rest of the day stretched endlessly ahead of her now. She didn't wish to see Margaret again so eventually she began to wander aimlessly until she came to a park. Slipping through the gates she headed for the nearest bench where she sat watching nannies pushing babies in prams and young couples strolling arm in arm. The sight of the babies made her think again of the tiny girl she had held in her arms aboard the lifeboat, the poor little mite who hadn't survived. The couples made her think of Jamie and she blinked away tears. *I've been such a fool,* she thought miserably. But there was no time for moping now and so after a while she pulled herself together with an enormous effort and, angrily dashing away her tears, she rose and set off again.

It was late that afternoon before she dared venture back to the house where she found, to her relief, that Margaret had gone out.

'Ah, here you are, dear,' Alex greeted her as she came out of the drawing room with a book under her arm. 'A letter from Mr Wainthrop came for you while you were out and one for me too enquiring after your health and asking me how you were settling in. I must say he does sound like a very caring man.'

'He is.' Flora lifted the letter that had been left for her from

148

the silver tray in the hall table. At the thought of his kindness, Flora's insides shrivelled with guilt. She was sick of having to watch every word she said and the longer it went on the more difficult it became. But at least it was clear that Margaret hadn't carried out her threat as yet, because if she had, there was no way Alex would have greeted her as she had. Even so, Flora knew deep down that it was only a matter of time now. Margaret had made it more than clear that Flora wasn't welcome there and now she would surely use the information she had gained to her advantage. She gave Alex a smile then hurried upstairs to read Mr Wainthrop's letter in the privacy of her room.

My dear Constance,

I thought I would just drop you a quick line to check that all is well and that you have recovered from your dreadful ordeal. I visited Flora's parents and siblings again last week just to see how they were coping and to try to persuade them again to accept the money you have offered but they are still flatly refusing what they think of as charity. They are understandably still deeply upset about Flora's death, as I'm sure you are. I know that you were very fond of each other so I hope that you are coping.

Mrs Merry sends her love as always but she too is deeply upset at Flora's loss. She is doing a sterling job of looking after the house. Have you made a decision yet as to whether you wish to keep it to return to eventually or have it sold? There is of course no rush. Just inform me what you want to do when you have reached a decision and I will carry out your wishes. Meantime I am always here if there is anything at all I can do for you.

With very best wishes
Victor Wainthrop.

Tears slid down Flora's cheeks again as she carefully folded the letter and returned it to the envelope. She thought of the pain her family must be enduring, and in that moment, she knew that enough was enough. She couldn't go on living a lie for a moment longer. Before she could change her mind, she locked the door – it wouldn't do if Patsy were to walk in and catch her packing – and hurried to the wardrobe where she withdrew one of the bags that some of her new clothes had been delivered in. She was determined that she wouldn't take much, so she packed only one change of clothes, a nightshirt and some underwear. The rest was left hanging in the wardrobe, for everything had never really been hers anyway.

Then she sat down to write a note to Alex and it was one of the most difficult things she had ever had to do. She sat for some time staring at the paper and eventually, with shaking hands, she began.

Dear Alex,

I know after you read this note you will never forgive me and I don't blame you for I have done something quite unforgivable. What I am about to tell you will be very painful for you and I can only apologise but I cannot live a lie any longer, for you see it wasn't Flora, the maid, who died on the dreadful evening the Titanic *sank, it was your niece, Connie. I am Flora. When I was rescued I was wearing a belt about my waist containing Connie's name and her jewellery and so the doctors and nurses aboard the* Carpathia *assumed that I was her. I was so terrified of arriving in a strange city with no one I knew waiting for me that I went along with the deception, but I find that I can't live with myself anymore. I know now that what I did was foolish and I also know that what I am telling you will cause you great pain and I can only apologise. If I could go back in time I*

150

*would never have done it but it is too late now and so I
must finally tell you the truth and leave your home to make
my own way.*

*Thank you for all the kindness you have shown me since I
have been in your home and once again I apologise for my
deception.*

Flora xxx

With tears flowing thick and fast down her cheeks, she slid the
note into an envelope, addressed it to Alex and propped it up
against the jewellery box, which still contained Connie's jewellery
that had been in the bag that Mrs Merry had made for her. At
least that was all still intact. Strangely enough she had always
envied Connie her jewels yet never once since her arrival had she
been able to bring herself to wear any of them.

She rose and glanced about the room, and the enormity of
what she was about to do hit her. Once she set foot out of the
door and Alex had read her letter there could be no coming
back. She would be completely alone in a foreign country with
nowhere to go and no one to turn to. But even that was preferable to continuing to live a lie, and at least she had the money
that she had withdrawn for Toby. She would borrow it for now
but once she had managed to get a job she would return it.
She put the equivalent of forty English pounds in dollars into
the belt that Mrs Merry had made for her and fastened it
around her waist. The rest of the money she tucked deep into
her bag.

She smiled through her tears as she thought how angry Toby
would be when he discovered that she had run away. He would
have to find some other poor soul to blackmail and it would serve
him right. That was the only good thing to come out of this whole
sorry mess. Then, quiet as a mouse, she tiptoed out onto the
landing. There was no one to be seen thankfully so she crept

151

downstairs and hurried towards the front door. Once outside she breathed a sigh of relief, then, lifting her skirts, she scooted along the pavement in a most unladylike manner determined to put as much distance as she could between herself and the lie she had been living.

Chapter Eighteen

By the time Flora slowed down to ease the stitch in her side, she had no idea where she was. She had never ventured this way before and she found herself amongst strangers of every nationality. She wandered aimlessly on through a maze of alleys, each one seeming to get dirtier and dingier than the one before. Rows of houses stood one after the other, their roofs almost touching overhead and blocking out the fast-fading light, and Flora began to feel nervous. Hungry dogs were scavenging in the gutters and rheumy-eyed old men stood in the doorways of the houses, smoking their pipes and watching her suspiciously. Flora had chosen to wear the plainest outfit she possessed but suddenly even that felt out of place in the warren of streets she found herself in. Clutching her bag tightly to her she scuttled along but she could feel curious eyes burning into her back.

The air was echoing with the sounds of couples fighting and swearing and children crying, and once again she felt as if she had stepped into a nightmare. She remembered many such places like this back home in London and had always been warned by her parents to stay well away from them, especially at night. And now here she was with nowhere to go and no idea where she was going to spend the night. Admittedly, she consoled herself, she had money but should she choose to stay in one of the grander hotels it would be gone in the blink of an eye and if she were to stay somewhere less salubrious there was every chance she could be set upon and have her money stolen. Silently she cursed herself. Why hadn't she thought things through before running away? She didn't even have anyone she knew to ask advice of. She quickened her steps, praying that she would be able to find her way back to the city centre.

As she passed through a particularly dark alley, she became aware of footsteps behind her and, trembling, she quickened her pace. Perhaps it was just someone walking in the same direction as her, she tried to tell herself, but the faster she went the faster the person or persons behind her went too.

Suddenly her mouth was dry and her heart was pounding painfully as she broke into a run. The hairs on the back of her neck were standing to attention and she could hear whoever it was behind her panting now as they raced to keep up with her. Then a hand snaked across her shoulder and fastened across her mouth effectively blocking the scream that was building in her throat. She could tell by the sheer size of him that it was a man. It was too dark to see his face but she could feel his fetid breath on her cheek as he slammed her against the wall so hard that for a moment she was winded. Then before she could even begin to fight back he tried to wrestle her bag from her hand and she struggled with all her might to hang on to it as muttered curses echoed down the alley. All of a sudden the man brought his hand back and slapped her hard across the cheek, making her head bounce on her shoulders, and she fell sideways as her bag was yanked from her hand.

'Pretty little filly, ain't yer,' a voice said. 'Per'aps yer'd like to be nice to me, eh?' His hand snaked out once more and tweaked her breast painfully as she tried to struggle to her feet. Sheer terror was coursing through her veins now as she realised what he intended to do but thankfully at that moment she heard yet more footsteps and suddenly the man fled taking her bag with him. Seconds later two tiny Chinese women appeared.

'A . . . a man, took my bag,' she gasped as she dragged herself to her knees but they merely glanced down at her and hurried on their way, chuntering away in their own language. Petrified that the man would come back, Flora stumbled after them sobbing quietly and eventually she emerged into a slightly wider street that was dotted with shops and run-down houses. But at least there were street lights here and she sobbed with relief. She had lost everything she possessed now apart from the money that she had thought to put in the belt about her waist, but she knew that things could have been far worse had the Chinese women not come along when they had, and she cursed herself for a fool.

Tentatively she raised her hand to her face and was surprised when it came away wet. Her nose was bleeding profusely and already she could feel her eye closing. The pins had escaped from her hair and was hanging about her shoulders and she realised that she must look a dreadful sight, yet no one looked at her twice. They merely turned their heads and hurried on their way completely ignoring her. Flora staggered a little further along the street until she came to the doorway of a shop that was closed, so she slipped into it and dropped to a sitting position.

The door was set well back from the road so unless anyone looked hopefully they wouldn't see her there. She realised with a little shock that she hadn't eaten since breakfast and her stomach began to growl ominously but she was too afraid to venture out onto the street again and so she sat on as people passed by as if she was invisible. Eventually it became quiet apart from the sounds of drunks, mainly sailors, tipping out of various pubs and finally she slept from pure exhaustion, hugging her knees and wishing with all her heart and soul that she was once more tucked up in her little bed in her home in London.

A harsh voice brought her eyes springing open early the next morning and blinking up she found herself confronting a small, stooped Chinese man who she assumed was the shop owner and who looked none too pleased to find her there. He was jabbering away at her in his own tongue and although Flora couldn't understand a word he said it was clear from his gesticulations that he wanted her gone.

'I'm going, I'm going,' she groaned as she painfully dragged herself to her feet. Every bone in her body ached, the blood from her nose had dried on her face and when she tried to open the eye that her attacker had hit the pain was excruciating. The shop owner continued to rant at her and wave his arms angrily as she staggered off down the street but she ignored him. She hadn't done anything to harm his precious shop after all, she reasoned. Further along the street she came to a café but after a glimpse inside she hurried straight past it. It was full of burly-looking sailors of every nationality and she was too afraid to venture inside.

The city was coming to life and the sound of traffic, trams and horses' hooves hung on the air. Soon the Hudson River came in sight and she stopped for a second to stare at it. There were boats of every shape and size anchored on it. Some of them would be cargo ships, others fishing vessels and some would be passenger ships. It reminded her for a moment of the River Thames and once again a wave of homesickness swept over her and her heart was crying, *Jamie, where are you?*

Sailors were rolling barrels and carrying sacks up some of the gangplanks while others were leading livestock aboard, but after a time she turned away and went in search of somewhere she might get something to eat. Her first night alone had not gone at all well and she wondered if things could possibly get any worse. She had nothing but the clothes she was wearing and the money in the belt and she cursed herself again for her foolishness. Still, it was too late to cry over spilled milk so she walked on and soon after was rewarded when she came to yet another café. Now that the majority of the sailors were busy at work this one was almost empty so she ventured inside and cautiously approached the counter. A middle-aged, blowsy-looking woman with bleached-blonde hair and wearing a shockingly low-cut blouse and a plastering of make-up on her face was lounging against the counter smoking a cigarette. To Flora's surprise she barely gave her a second look although Flora knew she must look a terrible sight.

'Could I have a pot of tea and some toast please?' she asked self-consciously.

'Yes, sit yourself down an' I'll bring it over,' the woman answered, waving her hand vaguely in the direction of the tables as she dropped fag ash all over the counter. Flora was painfully aware that the place was none too clean. The woman clearly didn't exert herself doing much cleaning but right then she was just grateful to have somewhere to sit and rest for a while and something to eat. Flora went to the furthest corner nearest to the window and sat with her back to the rest of the customers and soon the woman plodded over to her and slopped a cracked mug full of tea and a plate of buttered toast onto the table in front of her.

Flora smiled as best she could and hastily paid her. After hovering for a while the woman remarked, 'Looks like you've been in the wars.'

Flora's hand rose to her face and she flushed. 'Yes . . . I was attacked last night and a man took my bag. When I tried to stop him he . . . he hit me.'

'Hmm, well you can think yourself lucky that's all he did,' the woman commented. 'It ain't safe for a man let alone a woman to walk about round here alone at night.' Then narrowing her eyes, she asked, 'Run away from home, have you?'

Flora squirmed in her seat. 'Sort of. I'm er . . . looking for a job and somewhere to stay. You wouldn't happen to know of anywhere, I don't suppose?'

157

The woman shrugged, setting her ample bosoms jiggling. 'There's any number o' doss houses round here where yer can stay for a coupla dollars so long as you don't mind sharing with the cockroaches and the rats. But if you don't mind me saying, you don't look the sort to rough it. If I was you I'd get off home as fast as me feet would take me.'

Flora shook her head. 'I can't do that,' she said dully as she lifted the mug and took a sip of the tepid tea. It instantly opened up the split on her lip and it began to bleed again, much to her embarrassment.

'Then all I can tell you is there's always work to be found in the curry shops but be prepared to work like a dog for a pittance, an' they'll work you long hours. There's the Chinese laundry an' all. They don't tend to be able to keep staff for long. It's three streets away if that helps. Meantime get that inside you an' then you can clean up a bit in the toilet out the back if you want.'

It appeared that the woman did have a heart after all and Flora smiled at her gratefully as she started to eat the food in front of her. The toilet the woman directed her to some minutes later was out in the back yard and she had to walk through the filthy kitchen to reach it. It was just as dirty as the inside of the café, if not worse. But even so there was a sink in there at least, so Flora tore the bottom off her underskirt, soaked it in water and cleaned her face as best she could. There was a cracked mirror hanging above the sink and she was horrified when she caught a glimpse of her face. It was so swollen that she hardly recognised herself but there was nothing she could do about it and she supposed that she should just be grateful that things hadn't been worse. At least it had taught her a valuable lesson and now she was determined to find somewhere to stay before darkness fell again.

Once back in the café, she thanked the woman and set off in the direction of the laundry she had mentioned. She had done plenty of laundry when she had first gone to work for Connie, as well as helping her mother in the washhouse, so she had no doubt that she could handle the work and then she would concentrate on finding somewhere to stay. On the way she passed many shops selling everything from buckets and bowls to exotic fruits. There was also a cobbler, a bakery, a Jewish tailor and a great number of eating houses catering to the many nationalities of the people she passed. Many were Chinese, as well as people with coal-black hair and skin as dark as midnight and it occurred to her once more that the place wasn't really so very different to the docks she had lived close to in London.

As she passed the many curry houses the smell of hot spices that wafted through their doors almost took her breath away, while the smell of the fresh-baked bread in the baker made her stomach rumble again. But there was no time to stop or dawdle, she was determined that before nightfall she would have found herself somewhere to stay and a job; there was no way she wanted to spend another night on the streets like some homeless vagrant, which, she begrudgingly had to admit, she was, for now at least.

At last, after taking a few wrong turns, she found herself outside the laundry. The windows were so steamed up that it was impossible to see through them and she suddenly remembered the little Chinese girl who had helped her a few days before and she hoped that this might be the one that the girl had said she worked in.

After taking a deep breath she squared her shoulders and rang the bell on the door. Seconds later it was opened by a small Chinese woman with grey hair and oval eyes which squinted at her suspiciously.

'We no want to buy anyt'ing,' she said waspishly and Flora was relieved that the woman spoke English. That was something at least.

'I'm not selling anything,' Flora assured her as the woman looked at the state of her face and scowled. 'I'm actually looking for a job and wondered if you might have any vacancies?'

'A job? You wish to work in de laundry? Come in, come in.'
As the woman opened the door a little wider Flora stepped inside.
Instantly the heavy steam almost enveloped her and she broke
out in a sweat. Everywhere she looked there were great steaming
coppers and deep stone sinks with young girls hanging over them
scrubbing at sheets, and the heat was almost unbearable.

'We launder sheets mainly,' the woman told her, spreading
her hands. 'From hospitals and hotels. In here they are washed
and then taken t'rough there to be put t'rough the mangles and
dried.' She gestured towards a door . 'You t'ink you can do this
work?'

'Oh yes,' Flora assured her hastily. 'I was a laundry maid back
in England for a time.'

The woman still didn't seem convinced. 'We work from six in
the morning until seven at night every day but Sunday. You off
ill and you not come to work you not get paid, you understand?'

'Perfectly,' Flora said. The woman then mentioned a wage which
was ridiculously low for the hours she would be working but she
supposed that beggars couldn't be choosers and it would do until
something better came up.

'You agree to t'ese?'

Flora nodded a little too vigorously causing her swollen eyelid
to throb. 'Yes,' she squeaked and, apparently satisfied, the woman
asked, 'You start straight away? We have order to get out.'

'Yes.' Flora supposed she may as well work as wander about
the streets.

'And have you somewhere to stay?'

Flora's sigh was her answer and the woman sniffed. 'There also
I may help you. Many girls rent rooms from me. Rent is taken
from wages. Two or three girls in each room and kitchen to share.
You want this?'

Heartened, Flora nodded again. Anything was better than
nothing and at least she would have somewhere to lay her head.

'Good . . . come. But I warn, this a trial. You no good – you out!'

Flora followed the tiny woman into the back room which was as hot and uncomfortable as the first room, and approaching a young, flame-haired girl who was in the process of putting a sheet through an enormous mangle, the woman barked, 'Mahoney, this girl share your room. She start work immediately so show her what to do then take her back to your room wit' you after.'

'Yes, Mrs Yung,' the girl said subserviently, and without another word the woman turned and strode away. *She might be tiny in stature but she's certainly strong in spirit*, Flora thought.

Once Mrs Yung had gone the girl, who Flora noticed had eyes the colour of emeralds, smiled at Flora and told her, 'I'm Colleen.'

'Flora.' She held her hand out but saw immediately that the girl's eyes strayed to Mrs Yung and that she didn't dare stop what she was doing.

'I'll show you how to go on an' then we'll talk tonight, so we will,' the girl told her in a strong Irish accent and with a nod Flora rolled her sleeves up and set to work. She really didn't have much choice.

161

Chapter Nineteen

By the time seven o'clock rolled around that evening Flora was so exhausted that she could barely stand. Her face was throbbing painfully and her hands were so sore that she didn't know what to do with them. Every item of clothing she wore was sticking to her with sweat and she wondered how she was going to bear it. Mrs Yung was a hard taskmaster who would not allow any of her staff to slack for a minute and Flora was forced to question if she had been right to run away. Surely anything that Alex could have done to her when she discovered the truth would have been better than this?

Seeing her exhaustion, Colleen smiled at her reassuringly. 'It does get easier,' she promised, taking Flora's hand and leading her to the door. 'I remember my first day, so I do. I was so tired I didn't know if I could ever come back and face another day here, but needs must. Come on, I'll get you back to our room now. Our other roommate will no doubt already be cooking for us, so she will.'

They stepped outside and the cool air after the heat in the laundry hit Flora like a smack in the face and she felt dizzy. Even so she tried to keep up with Colleen as she strode purposefully along. The girl was tiny and yet Flora had noted that the amount of work she had got through that day would have done justice to someone twice her size.

Once again Flora entered the gloomy alleys and her heart began to pound with fear as she thought back to the night before but Colleen seemed confident enough.

'Nearly there now,' she told her encouragingly. 'But don't be expectin' too much, mind. Mrs Yung doesn't provide the best workin' nor livin' environment but 'tis better than sleepin' on the streets, to be sure.'

As Flora eyed the dismal houses they were passing she could well believe it and she began to shiver as she thought back to what had almost happened to her the night before. It seemed that all the nationalities of the world were gathered in these back alleys and they eyed her suspiciously as she and Colleen moved on.

Eventually Colleen stopped in front of a tiny, terraced house and opened the front door. They stepped into a narrow hallway and a multitude of smells assaulted them: curry, boiled cabbage, stale urine and other smells that Flora didn't dare to try and imagine what they might be. The walls were running with damp and ahead of them a steep, narrow, wooden stair-case rose up to the first floor. A number of dull-eyed children were playing with some glass marbles on the floor and Flora's heart ached for them as she saw how thin and lethargic they looked – as if they hadn't had a decent meal for weeks. The clothes they wore were little more than rags and were so faded that it was difficult to distinguish what colour they might once have been.

Colleen beckoned Flora to follow her up the stairs. A baby was wailing loudly somewhere and as they reached the first floor landing they were just in time to see a thick tail and a pair of red eyes disappear into a hole in the skirting board.

'Ugh, was that a rat?' Flora squeaked and Colleen giggled.

'It was so, but don't be worryin', he's more afraid o' you than you are of him, so he is.' They climbed up yet another flight of stairs and at the top Colleen took a key from her pocket and unlocked a door.

'Well, this is it,' she announced as they stepped into a small, musty-smelling room. 'It might not be much but it's home for now.'

Flora stared about in disbelief. A number of straw mattresses were scattered along one wall with blankets neatly folded at the end of them and by the only cracked window was a small table with two mismatched chairs, one of which was leaning drunkenly to one side. A pair of faded curtains hung at the window and there was an old washstand with a chipped jug and ewer standing on it. The only other furniture the room boasted was two battered chests of drawers, but what did strike her was that although the room was dismal, Colleen and her roommate had done their best to make it as clean as they possibly could. The bare floorboards had been scrubbed and she was heartened to see a small fire glowing in a tiny fireplace.

'Ah, my roommate is back,' Colleen commented when she saw the fire. 'She'll be downstairs in the kitchen cooking a meal, no doubt. We take it in turns,' she explained and the words had barely left her lips when the door opened and Flora blinked in surprise when the pretty Chinese girl who had helped her when she got lost was standing there.

'It's Jia Li, isn't it?' Flora croaked and with a wide smile the girl carried a heavy pot to the table and placed it down before nodding.

Colleen looked surprised. 'So, do you two know each other?'

Flora nodded. 'We met once when I lost my way and Jia Li was kind enough to give me directions.'

'How do you do, missy.' Jia Li again placed her hands together and gave the curious little bow that Flora remembered. 'It is nice to meet again . . . but what are you doing here?'

Flora's face became solemn. 'It's a long story but perhaps I'll tell you one day.'

164

'Well, whatever it is it won't be good.' Colleen shook her head sadly as she approached the pot Jia Li had carried in and lifted the lid, sniffing appreciatively. 'None of us end up here if we have anywhere better to go, but never mind that for now. Jia Li makes the most wonderful curries you'll ever eat. Come on, let's have it while it's still nice and hot.' She crossed to some shelves that Flora hadn't noticed before where a selection of mismatched pots and pans were placed and lifted down three chipped dishes which she proceeded to fill. Then, handing round some spoons, they all sat down on the mattresses and began to eat. Just as Colleen had said, the curry was like nothing Flora had ever tried before and was quite delicious.

'We share the kitchen downstairs with the other residents for making our main meals,' Colleen informed her. 'But we have a kettle up here so we can make tea and coffee in our room. We have a toasting fork as well, so sometimes we make our own toast too.' She smiled at Jia Li then and Flora saw that the two girls were close.

'And how do you er . . . have a bath?' Flora asked.

Both the girls chuckled. 'There's a tin bath hanging on the wall outside so once a week we cart it up here between us and boil kettles to fill it, usually on a Sunday. We're too tired to be bothered on the days we work so we just make do with a good wash down, but we get by one way or another.'

'And how long have you both shared a room for?' Flora questioned curiously.

Colleen shrugged. 'Oh, for a few months now. Mrs Yung doesn't tend to keep staff for long so the workers come and go.'

If what she had seen of the woman that day was anything to go by Flora could well understand why no one ever stayed long. She was like a mini sergeant major barking out orders with never a word of praise. Flora had even seen her cuff one young girl round the ear earlier in the day because the poor little thing had

165

slipped on the wet floor and dropped a basket of freshly washed sheets.

'I can quite understand why no one stays,' Flora commented, at which both girls giggled.

'Huh! If you t'ink she's bad just wait until you meet her son!' Colleen whistled through her teeth and frowned. 'He's a *real* tyrant! He t'inks because we all work for his mother that he has licence to do what he wants with us, so he does! He's started hassling Jia Li, here, and I've heard whispers that more than one lass has been sent packing without a penny piece with his baby growing in her belly, yet his mother won't hear a word said against him. She worships the very ground he walks on, so she does, so beware if you meet him and try to keep out of his way. His name is Huan.'

'I'll remember that,' Flora said, horrified, and they all fell silent as they enjoyed the rest of their meal. When it was done, Jia Li carried the pots down to the kitchen to wash them and returned with a jug of cold water from the tap in the yard.

'It is to bathe your face,' she told Flora gently. 'It must be very sore, yes?'

'It is rather,' Flora admitted as she tentatively raised her hand to touch her swollen face.

Jia Li gently began to bathe it for her and Flora had to grit her teeth to stop herself crying out.

'Who do this to you?' the Chinese girl questioned softly and instantly tears began to spill down Flora's cheeks. She had intended to keep what had happened to herself but somehow, she sensed that she could trust the two girls, so it all came pouring out.

'I did something unforgivable,' she told them in a wobbly voice. 'It started on the night the *Titanic* went down. I was travelling here with my young mistress but . . .' By the time she had finished the sorry tale she was drained.

166

'So, you see . . . I deserve what happened to me last night, I'm a very bad person,' she ended.

Colleen and Jia Li shook their heads in unison.

'No, you're not bad,' Colleen soothed. 'You were about to arrive in a strange country and you were scared, so you did what you had to to survive.'

Jia Li nodded in agreement. 'Yes, everyone knows of the disaster on the *Titanic*. It must have been . . . how do you say . . . trum . . . traumatic?'

'It was.' Flora closed her good eye and again in her head she could hear the screams of the poor souls in the icy water and see Connie pitching to her death. 'But what about you two? What brought you to this?'

Jia Li and Colleen glanced at each other but it was Jia Li who spoke first.

'I came here some long months ago aboard a cargo ship from my home town in China. My father, he a very rich man, he a banker. As child I was very spoiled but then my father, he arrange a marriage for me but . . .' She paused here and took a deep breath. 'The man he wish me to marry is very old and rich but I not love him. I love Bai, but he only a poor chef and my father forbade me to see him. And so just days before my wedding, Bai arrange a place on a ship coming here for me, and soon he will join me. Until then I have to work for Mrs Yung to live for I ran away with nothing but what I stood up in.'

'How very sad.'

'And what about you?' Flora looked at Colleen now and the girl lowered her eyes and shrugged.

'Oh, my story is about as opposite to Jia Li's as you could get,' she said quietly. 'Back in Ireland I was one of fourteen children, though not all of them survived. We lived on a little smallholding just outside of Kilkenny, packed in like sardines, we were, in the farmhouse, but the fields and the countryside

167

are glorious. We had pigs and sheep, as well as a cow for milk and hens for fresh eggs but me mammy was downtrodden, God love her, and me daddy was a boozer. Many the day we had not a crust on the table but me daddy never went without his ale. Then as the girls reached a certain age he decided that they could earn their keep on the streets, if you get me drift? Some of them agreed, some of them did a runner, so they did, and then it came to my turn and I couldn't stand the thought of it, so much like Jia Li I sneaked aboard a boat and ended up here, and though it's not much of a life, sure it's better than the one I had, so it is. At least I don't have to lie awake now waitin' for me daddy to come in drunk an' use one or another of us as a punchbag.'

Flora's eyes filled with tears as she gazed at them silently. They had been through so much in different ways and she felt ashamed.

'But what about you?' Colleen asked then. 'Will you be going back to London?'

Flora sighed. 'How can I now? I've no doubt Alex will inform my parents of what I've done and though they'll be relieved to know I'm alive after all, they'll be so ashamed of me. I don't think I can ever face them again now. Sometimes I even wish it had been me that had died instead of Connie . . .'

'That's a *terrible* t'ing to say,' Colleen scolded while Jai Li looked on with her beautiful dark eyes. 'Sure, life is precious an' to be lived an' though we may not have much at the minute there's many worse off than us, so there are. An' I wouldn't mind bettin' that your mammy an' daddy would be thrilled to have you home, no matter what you've done.'

'Well, we'll see.' Flora wiped her nose on the sleeve of her dress. 'But it won't be for a while. I need to save enough up for the fare for a start off, even if I do ever decide to go home.'

The three girls stared at each other silently for a moment and Flora felt a little comfort for the first time since the *Titanic* had sunk. At least with these two girls there were no lies between them and she would no longer have to watch every single word she said. They had bared their souls to each other and she had the feeling that they would become good friends.

Chapter Twenty

'Come on, sleepyhead, it's time to be gettin' up, so it is.'

Flora groaned as Colleen gently shook her arm. The straw mattress she had slept on was prickly and she'd spent half the night scratching before eventually managing to drift off to sleep. Jia Li had boiled the kettle over the low fire and made them all a pot of tea and now she carried a mug over to Flora with a wide grin on her face.

'You not sleep well,' she stated matter-of-factly, and before Flora could answer she went on with a twinkle in her eye, 'You talk in your sleep of someone called Jamie. He is your boyfriend, yes?'

'He was.' Flora pulled herself up into a sitting position and took the mug of tea gratefully. It was very weak but better than nothing. 'I was seeing him before I agreed to go to New York with Connie. He didn't want me to go and we argued and . . .'

'Ah! I see. You part on bad terms, yes?'

Flora nodded miserably. 'Yes, I don't think I realised how much he meant to me till I was on the way to New York and it was too late by then.'

'But it's never too late to put things right if you love someone,' Colleen said practically, then jumping up she urged, 'But hurry with that tea now, woudya? Sure, Mrs Yung will have us workin' all night if we're late.'

Flora did as she was told but all she had time to do was borrow

Jia Li's hairbrush, tug it through her hair and have a quick swill in the cold water in the bowl before they set off. The rest of the day passed much the same as the one before and by home time, Flora was once again exhausted and depressed as she thought of doing this day after day, yet Jia Li and Colleen seemed cheerful enough.

Flora was beginning to thoroughly dislike Mrs Yung, for her small size was deceptive and she was a bully. Each sheet that arrived at the laundry had to be boiled and scrubbed till it was as white as snow before being taken to the next room where it would be rinsed and fed through the huge mangles. Mrs Yung checked each one and it was woe betide anyone who left so much as a tiny stain on one. Flora had witnessed her shouting at one small girl who looked to be no older than twelve or thirteen until she had reduced the poor little mite to tears. She had then smacked her hard about her ear and told her that she must stay behind for an extra hour that night because of one tiny, pea-sized stain that the girl had missed.

At one stage, Flora had dropped a sheet and Mrs Yung had turned on her. 'You useless!' she had cried, shaking her small fist at her, although thankfully she hadn't raised her hand to her, and it had been all Flora could do to stop herself from walking out there and then.

'*Why* do people put up with the way she treats them?' Flora questioned as she wearily trudged back to their room that evening. Once again, she ached in every single limb and wondered how she was going to bear it.

'Any job is better than no job at all,' Colleen pointed out. 'That's why me an' Jia Li stick it.'

'But there *must* be an easier way to earn a living.'

'Oh aye, an' what is it you're suggestin'?' Colleen asked as she winked at Jia Li.

'Well . . .' Flora's mind was working overtime. 'Perhaps we could start up our own little business.'

171

'Doin' what? An' more to the point, where?'

'There are loads of places to rent. Admittedly they're all a little run down but I'm sure three of us could do one up and make it liveable.'

'Eeh, you're off wi' the fairies, to be sure,' Colleen chuckled with a shake of her head.

Flora fell silent but an idea was growing in her head and on the first day off she had, she intended to look into it.

By Friday, when she had been working in the laundry for three days that felt like years, Flora's arms were covered in small burns and she was convinced that the huge coppers would wait especially for her to walk past before they spat hot water out, which was why when she arrived at work that morning and Mrs Yung informed her that she would be working the mangles that day, she felt relieved. But the relief didn't last long and within an hour of turning the heavy handles she felt as if her arms were being torn out of their sockets.

'I'll have muscles like an all-in wrestler at this rate,' she grumbled to Colleen who was working on the mangle next to her and the girl chuckled.

'If you t'ink this is bad just wait till they set you on the ironing,' she warned and Flora groaned aloud. Surely nothing could be worse than this?

The very next day she discovered that it could when she found herself faced with a mountain of sheets that all had to be ironed till there wasn't a single crease left in them, then folded into a perfect square.

'I don't think I can do this,' she gasped as they all made their way back to their room that evening.

Colleen chuckled. 'Sure you can, you'll get used to it,' she assured her but Flora wasn't so sure. Her face was slightly better now: the purple bruises were fading to a dull yellowish grey and she could see out of her eye again now that the swelling had gone down but muscles that she'd never known she had ached and all she wanted to do was fall onto the thin mattress and sleep.

The next day was Sunday but even that proved to be hard work as the morning was spent hefting the tin bath upstairs and filling it with boiling water from the kettle so that they could all have a bath. Then when the bathing was over the water had to be carried downstairs again and emptied into the squalid back yard. Flora's clothes stank by then but between them Colleen and Jia Li had managed to sort her out another outfit so that she could at least wash the ones she had been wearing.

'There is rag stall on the market,' Jia Li informed her as they munched on toast they had cooked at the open fire. 'You want me to take you?'

'Please.' Flora was guarding the money she had left with her life and was reluctant to break into it but she knew that she would have to buy essentials. As she had discovered, the low pay meant that there was little left after Mrs Yung had taken out the rent for the room and they had bought food, but she was still determined to save every dollar she could.

The girls set off for the market and once again Flora was reminded of London as she stared at the assortment of stalls. Some were selling kosher Jewish food, others Chinese and Indian, and the smell of curry and spices was heady in the air. At the rag stall Flora was able to find a suitable skirt and blouse that although faded were of decent quality, along with items of underwear and a nightshirt. She had been grateful to borrow clothes from Colleen and Jia Li up until then, but they didn't have much themselves and she knew they needed them back. After they'd made their purchases, they set off to explore the area and although Flora didn't make comment she watched out for the properties that were for rent.

When they finally returned to their room they lay down for a well-earned rest and before she knew it Flora was fast asleep and didn't stir again until Colleen woke her the next morning for work. Slowly her life was falling into some sort of a pattern and although she didn't like it she was grateful for Colleen and Jia Li's friendship and counted herself lucky that they had befriended her. She shuddered to think what might have happened if they hadn't.

One evening the following week, when they were on their way back from work, Flora said suddenly, 'I just have to pop somewhere. Go on without me, I shan't be long.'

Both girls eyed her curiously although they didn't question her. Sometime later Flora paused in front of a run-down café close to the docks and, taking a deep breath, she went in. It was the same one that she had been to the previous week, the morning after she had run away, and the same blowsy woman who had allowed her to clean up a little in the toilet was still standing behind the counter puffing away on a cigarette.

'Ah, so you're back,' the woman said as she recognised her. 'An' lookin' a bit better than you did the last time I saw you.'

'Yes, I am, thank you.' Flora glanced around at the gloomy interior and for the first time she wondered if she was doing the right thing. The place would need an awful lot of work to make it smart again, although she thought most of it was mainly cosmetic. It would greatly benefit from a lick of paint for a start-off.

'So, what can I do for you today?'

The woman's voice brought Flora's thoughts back to her and she swallowed before saying, 'Actually, I saw from the sign in the window that this place is for rent?'

'It is,' the woman agreed. 'It's too much for me now. Me old man ain't in the best of health, but why do you ask?'

'Well . . . I was thinking I might like to rent it.' There, it was said and she watched as the woman blinked with surprise.

'You? But ain't you a little young to be thinkin' o' takin' on a business? An' could you afford the rent?' She mentioned a sum that seemed reasonable and Flora nodded vigorously.

'Oh yes,' she assured her as she shoved her hand down her skirt to withdraw some money from the belt that Mrs Merry had made for her. 'I have money, look. And I wouldn't be attempting it on my own, there are three of us. But who is the landlord?'

'Actually, I am,' the woman said as she stared at her thoughtfully, then, holding her hand out, she formally introduced herself, 'I'm Dora Casey. Me an' me old man own the place an' to be honest we'd rather sell it an' be done wi' it but there ain't much chance o' that happenin' round here, so we decided that we'd rent it out. At least that way we'd still have a bit of an income.'

'And are there any living quarters that come with it?' Flora asked.

'Well, there's a fair-sized kitchen out the back where I do the cookin', an' there's two fair-sized rooms upstairs but seein' as we don't live here we've always just used 'em for storage. I dare say you could live in 'em, though, if you were to clear 'em out,' the woman informed her. Then seeing that Flora was serious she asked, 'Would you like to see 'em?'

Flora nodded again as the woman opened the flap on the counter, and followed her through to the kitchen. Her first sight of it made her sigh with dismay. It was worse than she remembered. The range was heavy with grease and the floor so filthy that she couldn't see what colour the tiles should be. There was a window but it was so thick with grime that it let hardly any light in and the walls were heavily stained with tobacco and grease. She opened the door into the small, enclosed back yard, although she knew already that there was an outside toilet, which was a plus in Flora's books, and the two rooms upstairs were a generous size, although it was difficult to see them properly because they were full of boxes, odd bits of mismatched furniture and rubbish.

'So, what do you think?' the woman asked as she watched Flora taking everything in. The girl certainly seemed genuine enough and if truth be told she just wanted shot of the place.

'I think it could work,' Flora mused.

'But I must point out the majority o' people who use this place are sailors.' The woman's conscience suddenly pricked her. Flora was so young. 'Do you think you could handle 'em? Some of 'em are looking for a bit more than a bite to eat, if you get me drift?'

Flora blushed. 'I understand what you're saying but as I said, I wouldn't be here on my own. My two friends would be helping me to run the place and I'm sure we could manage between us.'

'Ah, then in that case why don't you go away an' have a think about it? But bear in mind, if you couldn't pay the rent you'd be out on your ear, an' I'd want a month's rent up front.'

'I quite understand,' Flora answered. 'And I will think about it. Thank you for your time.'

She left and hurried back to the room, eager to put her idea to Colleen and Jia Li who gazed at her in open-mouthed amazement.

'*Us* set up in business!' Colleen was shocked. 'Doing *what*?'

'Running a café, of course,' Flora said, her eyes sparkling with excitement. 'At the moment the place is nothing more than a greasy mess selling only the most basic food but I'm sure we could soon clean it up and improve on the menu and do a selection of more interesting dishes. For a start-off my mother taught me to make stew and dumplings, just the sort of filling food that would appeal to the type of people we'd get in there and Jia Li makes wonderful curries. Then there are your cakes, they're delicious, so between us we could cater for most tastes. I'm sure we could make a go of it and it would be so much better working for ourselves than in the laundry. Admittedly there's a lot of work to be done there and we'd have to lay some money out on new tables and chairs and other stuff, but I know we could do it.'

'And just *where* are we supposed to get the money for these things from?' Colleen asked practically.

Flora pulled the money from the belt with a flourish and flashed it at them. 'The man who robbed me didn't manage to get this, look, and it would be more than enough to get what we need. So, what do you say? Are you prepared to give it a try?'

Both girls just sat there stunned.

'I be glad to get away from laundry,' Jia Li admitted eventually with a worried frown. 'Mrs Yung's son, Huan, has been bothering me and he scares me. But this is something we must give much thought to. It is big step.'

Flora had noticed how Huan had been hassling the girl over the last few of days, and Colleen had confided to her that it had been going on for a few weeks. Tall and handsome, sadly he did not have a personality to match his looks but was vain and selfish and it was God help any poor girl he chose to target, for his mother would turn a blind eye to it.

'I understand that,' Flora told her. 'But *please*, both of you, don't dismiss it.'

'We won't,' they both promised and for then the subject was dropped, although Flora could think of nothing else.

Chapter Twenty-One

A couple of days later when they arrived at work Mrs Yung told Jia Li, 'You go work in yard today.'

Jia Li visibly paled. Normally she liked working out in the yard. Whoever was out there had to peg the sheets to the line, then fetch them in and fold them before they were sent to be ironed. It was a chance to feel the sunshine on her face but it would mean that she was alone out there and after the way Huan had been harassing her she was suddenly nervous. Should he happen by and come out to her she dreaded to think what he might be capable of. Even so, she knew better than to argue so she quietly made her way through to the yard. Soon the first lot of clean sheets were flapping on the line and she was beginning to feel a little better. Perhaps Huan wouldn't call in that day after all, in which case she could start to relax. But then mid-morning, shortly before the girls were allowed to take a fifteen-minute break, she glanced up to see him standing in the doorway with a wicked grin on his face. Her mouth was full of wooden clothes pegs and she spat them out and nervously wiped her hands down the front of her apron as she said politely, 'Good morning, Mr Yung.'

Up until then she had been able to ward off his advances while in the company of the other women and girls but she knew that out here it would be much more difficult.

'No need for formalities,' he said, licking his lips as he stared at her dainty figure. 'It is Huan to you, Jia Li.' He began to advance on her and she automatically backed away from him until she found her back against the brick wall. Rows of sheets now stood between her and the entrance to the laundry and she began to panic. In seconds he was directly in front of her with an arm resting on the wall either side of her.

'You know, you are very beautiful.'

As she stared fearfully up into his handsome face her heart began to pound painfully.

'If you were to be *nice* to me I could be very generous,' he crooned and without thinking she put her hands on his broad chest and pushed with all her might, sending him toppling backwards.

'I no wish to be nice to you. I just work here,' she whimpered as she tried to skirt around him but already he was up on his feet again and his face had turned ugly now as he brought his hand back and slapped her viciously across the mouth.

'You do *not* talk to me this way,' he ground out through gritted teeth as blood spurted from her mouth. 'I your boss's son and if I say you be nice to me you be nice!' He grabbed her arm and swung her round as if she weighed no more than a feather. Her back connected with the wall again so hard this time that the scream that had been building in her throat died away as the wind was knocked out of her.

'You nothing but a little whore *bitch*!' he screeched and then he threw her onto her back on the hard ground.

She began to cry as she tried to fight him off, but within seconds she knew that her strength was no match for his and despair and terror in equal measure coursed through her. She started to scream even though she knew there was no chance of her being heard with all the noise that was coming from the laundry. And then she heard a ripping sound as he caught the front of her blouse and buttons rolled across the floor.

'Ah!' He eyed her pert young breasts with glee as she began to

179

sob then he fastened his mouth to one of her tender nipples and began to bite it, making her yelp with pain. But that was nothing to what happened minutes later when he managed to rip her underwear to one side and he pushed himself into her. The pain of it took her breath away for a moment and she prayed for death to take her, for surely that would be preferable to the terrible agony that was ripping her apart. She felt as if she was being rent in two but he was oblivious as he took his pleasure bucking away on top of her. And then, just as she thought she could bear it no more, he took a deep shuddering breath and collapsed on top of her panting wildly. She just lay there too terrified to move in case he started again until he rolled away and began to right his clothes, then standing he stared down at her with contempt.

'Do not try to tell my mother I forced you,' he said threateningly. 'I shall tell her that you have been tempting me for weeks and who do you think she will believe, little whore! Just think yourself lucky that boss's son like you.' And then he strolled casually away as Jia Li rolled herself into a tight ball and sobbed broken-heartedly. As far as she was concerned her life was over. She was spoiled and her beloved Bai, or indeed any other man, would never want her now.

As break time approached, Colleen commented to Flora, 'Jia Li is late coming t'rough from the yard, isn't she? We'd agreed we'd go outside and sit in the fresh air for our break.'

She and Flora were working side by side that day feeding the sheets into the massive coppers and they were both running with sweat.

'She's probably lost track of time being out the back on her own,' Flora puffed as she dried her hands and slipped off her apron. 'I'll run through and fetch her.'

She walked through the rinsing room and the ironing room and looked into the yard but all she could see at first glance was rows upon rows of snow-white sheets dancing on the lines.

'Jia Li.' When there was no answer she began to duck beneath the sheets, her eyes going this way and that and it was then that she heard a low keening sound that might have been made by an animal in pain and it struck terror into her soul.

'*Jia Li!*' Her voice was louder and more urgent now and as she approached the far side of the yard she spotted a figure lying on the floor shaking uncontrollably, and her heart missed a beat.

'Oh no!' Flora dropped to her knees and gathered the shaking girl into her arms.

For a moment Jia Li thought it was Huan come back to violate her again and she struggled violently. Then when she saw that it was Flora she gave a great gasping sob and sagged against her chest. Blood was trickling down her chin and when she opened her mouth to try to speak she spat out one of her back teeth.

'Dear God, who's done this to you?' Flora asked, horrified.

Jia Li was trying to pull the front of her ruined blouse together but before she could manage it Flora could see the bruises already beginning to appear across the girl's naked breasts.

'I-It w-was Yung Huan . . . he . . .' Unable to go on, Jia Li began to sob again.

Flora rocked her back and forth and now anger took the place of her distress. 'Did he . . .?' She found that she couldn't form the question but Jia Li knew what she had been trying to say and nodded miserably.

'He . . . he *rape* me,' she gulped. 'And now my Bai no longer want me. *No* man will want me. I am ruined goods.'

'Don't be so silly. This wasn't your fault,' Flora told her but Jia Li was inconsolable as she tried to pull her skirt down to cover the blood stains on her thighs. It was then that they heard someone approaching and seconds later Mrs Yung appeared from beneath the sheets, her mouth set in a straight, grim line.

181

'What go on here?' she demanded as Flora glared up at her.

'What does it look like? She's been attacked . . . by *your* son! *He* did this to her.'

'You *lie*!' Mrs Yung was furious and her small hands clenched into fists. 'My Huan not do this unless girl ask for it! She cheap *whore*!'

'Does she really *look* like she asked for it?' Flora snapped as her eyes flashed angrily. 'Just *look* at the state of her.'

'She get out!' Mrs Yung pointed towards the rear door. 'I no longer give her job! She big troublemaker.'

'Then I go too!' Flora retorted. 'Your son is a rapist and he needs reporting to the police!'

Mrs Yung trembled with fury and began to wave her arms frantically. 'You bring trouble on my Huan and I make big trouble for you too,' she warned. 'Now go and do not come back!' She began to gesticulate wildly and chunter away in her own language.

'Don't worry, we shall. I wouldn't work for you now if I was starving,' Flora retaliated as she bodily hoisted Jia Li to her feet and pushed her way past her employer.

Jia Li was almost a dead weight and was clearly in shock but somehow Flora managed to get her through the laundry and out into the street where Colleen was waiting for them.

'Sweet Holy Mother! Whatever happened to the poor wee girl?' she gasped and when Flora told her, Colleen's brilliant green eyes seemed to flash fire.

'Why, the *filthy* scum!' she spat. 'But what happens now?'

'Me and Jia Li have got the sack,' Flora told her.

'Fine, and I'll leave too, so I will,' Colleen declared. 'I wouldn't work for that witch now if she paid me in gold, to be sure. Come away, let's get the poor lassie home.'

Between them they somehow managed to get Jia Li back to their meagre room and it was only then it occurred to them that they would lose this too along with their job, for there was no way Mrs Yung would allow them to stay there now.

'So, what do we do now?' Colleen asked despondently when they had cleaned Jia Li up as best they could and settled her down for a rest on one of the straw mattresses.

'We'd best let her have a rest then we'll clear out,' Flora sighed. 'Better we go ourselves than have Mrs Yung have someone come and throw us out.'

'But *where* will we go? I have a little tucked away and I know Jia Li has too but it's not a lot.'

'Don't worry, we'll manage,' Flora assured her with a confidence that she was far from feeling. 'We'll rent another room somewhere for tonight while we figure out what to do. In fact, if you don't mind staying here to watch over Jia Li I'll go and have a scout round for somewhere right now.'

When Colleen nodded in agreement, Flora set off on her quest. She trudged the streets for an hour getting more disheartened by the minute. The cheaper rooms that were available were so filthy that she wouldn't have felt happy putting a dog in them and the dearer ones meant that they would eat into her savings in no time at all. And then it occurred to her, Mrs Casey seemed keen to offload the business as soon as possible. Perhaps it was time for her to make the decision for the other two girls. At least then they were assured of having a roof over their heads. She set off again and soon arrived at Mrs Casey's café.

A glance through the window showed that it was almost empty as usual apart from a few burly sailors who were drinking tea and coffee from cracked mugs. Dora Casey was in her usual position at the counter, leafing through a magazine with a cigarette dangling from her lips, so after taking a deep breath, Flora entered, setting the little bell above the café door jangling.

The woman smiled when she saw her and asked, 'Come for a cuppa, have you, or have you made a decision?'

'We've made a decision,' Flora answered, crossing her fingers behind her back. 'But there's one slight problem.'

'Oh yes, an' what would that be?'

'Well . . . the thing is, one of my friends . . .' Flora lowered her voice and glanced over her shoulder to make sure that she wouldn't be overheard before going on in a hushed voice, 'One of my friends was involved in a very traumatic incident today . . . The son of the woman who owns the laundry where we work, er . . .'

Dora Casey raised a carefully plucked eyebrow. 'You wouldn't be talking about Yung Huan by any chance would yer?'

When Flora looked shocked and nodded the woman sighed. 'Then you've no need to say anymore. I can guess what he did. He's well known around these parts for takin' advantage of young women. Needs lockin' up, if you were to ask me, but how does this affect your decision to rent the café?'

Flora nervously licked her lips. 'The thing is . . . we paid Mrs Yung for the room we stay in and now that we've all left . . .'

'She'll kick your asses out onto the street!' Dora Casey sighed again as she finished Flora's sentence for her.

'Yes, so I was wondering – could we move in . . . today?'

'*Today!*' Dora Casey looked shocked. 'But, honey, that gives me no time to have a proper contract drawn up.'

'I know,' Flora agreed. 'But I'm more than happy to pay you a month's money up front and you can trust me, I promise. Then I'll sign the contract as soon as it's ready.'

The woman eyed her thoughtfully as she tapped at her lip with her forefinger, then making a hasty decision she nodded.

'All right. But I warn you, you'll all find yourselves out on the street if I have any funny business off you, contract or not.'

Flora sighed with relief as Mrs Casey shook her hand. 'Looks like you just got yourself a little business, girl,' she said with an amused gleam in her eye.

Chapter Twenty-Two

'You've done *what*?' Colleen choked when Flora arrived back at their room and told her the news.

Flora gave her a nervous smile. 'I've just paid the first four weeks' rent on the café. We can move in this afternoon.'

'Holy sweet Mother, you don't let the grass grow under your feet, do you?' Colleen gasped.

'Well, it's better than being out on the streets,' Flora retorted defensively. 'And it will be up to us all now whether or not we make a go of it.'

They both looked towards Jia Li who was still lying curled into a tight ball on the straw mattress.

'How is she?' Flora whispered.

Colleen shrugged. 'Same as she was when you left. I t'ink the poor girl is in shock, so I do, and is it any wonder after what's happened to her? To be honest, I don't t'ink she's fit to be moved anywhere just yet.'

'I agree but unfortunately we don't have a choice.' Flora looked around the room. 'Let's pack up whatever belongs to you then we can start carting it to the café.'

'Well, the pots an' pans, such as they are, are mine, an' the blankets,' Colleen told her. 'But if the rooms above the shop are as bad as you say what are we going to sleep on?'

'We'll worry about that when we get there.' Flora had already fetched a pillowcase to start packing their things into and Colleen pitched in to help.

'I'll take this first lot round there while you stay with Jia Li,' Flora told her when they were done. 'We'll take her with us on the next trip and hopefully be able to carry the rest of the stuff between us. You can pack whatever else you want to bring while I'm gone.'

Soon after she arrived back at the café to find the closed sign on the door and inside Dora Casey was busily packing a few personal possessions. She let Flora in and told her kindly, 'There's some food left in the cold store which you're welcome to, an' here's the key. You can keep the pots an' pans an' all, I won't be needin' 'em . . . but just remember this is only a little backstreet café. I doubt you'll make a fortune wi' the sort we get in here.' She suddenly felt sorry for this young girl who was taking on such a big responsibility.

'Thank you.' Flora carried her things through to the kitchen and dumped them on the floor, by which time Dora Casey was ready to leave.

'Right, I'll be off now then, an' I'll see you later in the week when I've got the contracts drawn up and . . . good luck, lovie.'

'Thank you.' Flora smiled at her and once she had gone she glanced around her new little empire. 'I *will* make it pay . . . I *will*,' she whispered to the empty room, then she left, locking the door behind her to go and fetch Jia Li and Colleen back to their new home.

'By all that's holy, you weren't jokin' when you said there were t'ings to be done, were you?' Colleen said when they arrived back at the shop sometime later. They had practically had to carry Jia Li between them and the poor girl seemed oblivious to everything that was going on.

'It's mostly elbow grease and a lick of paint that's needed,' Flora answered as she gently helped Jia Li onto a chair. 'But before we do anything perhaps we should get a doctor out to take a look at Jia Li?'

Colleen shook her head. 'No point in wasting money. There's nothing they can give her for shock. Time will be the healer,' she pointed out sensibly. 'Perhaps if she's no better tomorrow we should t'ink about it then.'

Flora supposed she was right and as she looked about her her shoulders sagged. Suddenly she was feeling overwhelmed at the amount of work that needed doing and didn't quite know where they should start, but thankfully Colleen took charge when she said, 'Show me the rooms where we'll be living then. I reckon we should get them straight and comfortable before we start down here, so I do.'

Seeing the sense in what she said, Flora led her upstairs expecting Colleen to find fault but instead she was quite taken with their new living quarters.

'Well, both t'ese rooms are bigger than the one we were all sharing,' she mused as she stared around her. 'We could perhaps make one into a sitting room and sleep in the other, and with the use of the kitchen as well we'll be snug as bugs in rugs. I reckon the first t'ing we should do is get all the rubbish out into the yard then go t'rough the furniture an' see what we can salvage.'

And so the two girls set to dragging out the empty boxes sending dust and cobwebs swirling into the air. Within an hour all the rubbish was piled in the yard and Colleen rubbed her hands together. 'There,' she said with a satisfied smile. 'We'll be able to see where we're going now, but first I t'ink we should have a hot drink and somet'ing to eat. It's been hours since breakfast.' Her red hair was coated in dust but her green eyes were bright as stars as she began to think of their new venture. After making a hasty meal of sandwiches and tea between them they managed to

187

persuade Jia Li to eat and drink a little and slowly the colour began to return to her cheeks, although she was prone to bursting into tears every few minutes.

'Just imagine how angry the old witch will be when she turns up to our old room to throw us out and finds us already gone,' Colleen chuckled. Some of Flora's enthusiasm was rubbing off on her now, despite her earlier reservations, Flora noticed with relief, and she grinned back at her. They trooped back upstairs then and threw all the windows open as they sorted through what was left in the two rooms.

'There's a double bedstead here,' Colleen whooped as if she had uncovered hidden treasure. 'It's iron and a bit knocked about admittedly but it'll do when it's cleaned up and we'll only have to get a mattress for it.'

'Mrs Casey told me about a second-hand shop not far away that sells respectable things,' Flora agreed. 'We might get one there and a single bed too, then we can all sleep comfortably.' Their search also revealed two mismatched fireside chairs which were in desperate need of recovering and a table and two chairs.

'If we buy some material I can recover the chairs and perhaps make some curtains to match,' Flora mused. 'I'm a dab hand at needlework. Connie taught me, it was one of the things they had to learn at the posh school she attended. But I think I should start to make a list now of the other things we'll need. I reckon there's just time to go there and get everything before it shuts.'

She set off for the second-hand shop armed with a list of essentials, leaving Colleen to sweep the rooms out and clean the windows. They had settled Jia Li into one of the old chairs upstairs by then and she had fallen into a deep sleep, which Colleen was happy about. 'Sleep is the best medicine of all,' she whispered to Flora, who nodded in agreement.

The shop turned out to be an Aladdin's cave of every sort of furniture imaginable and Flora wasn't quite sure where to look first. It was owned by an elderly, stooped Jewish man who was wearing a small black kippah on his straggly grey hair and had a long white beard. Although he appeared very old, Flora soon discovered that his brain was as bright as a button.

'Many bedsteads to choose from,' he told her, spreading his hands and Flora was surprised to hear that he had a broad American accent. 'This one is very beautiful.' He led her to a fine solid brass one, looking at her eagerly in anticipation of a sale, but Flora shook her head.

'No, thank you, it is lovely but I need something cheaper,' she explained.

Hiding his disappointment, he led her to another plain iron one and this time she nodded. 'That looks more like it, how much?'

He named a price and she shook her head. 'Too much,' she told him and began to barter until they finally came to a price that was agreeable to both of them. They moved on to the wash stands then, and Flora haggled until she got one that she considered was a fair price. The old man knew by then that despite her youth she was not one to be messed with and even threw in a jug and bowl in the price.

'You sure know what you want to pay, missy,' he remarked with a grin as he led her further into the shop to find some more items that were on her list.

She grinned back at him. 'Yes I do,' she said boldly. 'So how come you don't sound like a Jewish gentleman?' she dared to ask eventually and he chuckled.

'My parents came here when I was just a tiny baby,' he answered. 'So I suppose you could say I have Jewish blood flowing through American veins, although I still practise the Jewish faith.'

Flora laughed as she pointed to some oil lamps, for there was no electricity in the café as far as she knew, and in no time they were haggling once more. Gradually she worked through the list until the things she had bought were piled high by the door. As she paid old Mr Schwartz she smiled with satisfaction, until it suddenly occurred to her – how was she to get all these things back to the shop? There was far too much for her to carry.

'Never fear, my dear.' The old man stroked his beard. 'For just a small fee I can have my young Efrayim deliver them all to your door, yes?'

Flora sighed and handed over yet more money, already beginning to wonder if what she had left would cover the cost of everything else they needed to do. The four weeks rent and what she had just purchased had already made a large dent in the money and there was still paint and cleaning materials to be bought. Still, she thought, as a young boy appeared and began to load her things onto a large handcart, it was all necessary so she may as well just get on with it and shame the devil. It was far too late to back out now.

It took young Efrayim two journeys with the handcart to deliver everything and by then Flora had already visited a hardware shop and bought buckets, bowls, a mop, and anything else she thought they might possibly need.

When she got home, Jia Li was still sitting in the chair, staring vacantly into space. Her heart sank at the sight of her devastated expression, but at least she wasn't still curled up into a little ball. As for Colleen, she had made a wonderful start on the two rooms. They were now swept clean and she had even managed to scrub the windows so the place looked a lot brighter.

'Right!' She rolled her sleeves up enthusiastically as she examined what Flora had bought and pounced on the whitewash. 'I'm going to paint the walls before we put the furniture in place then when the bedroom's done we'll have a go at getting the beds up.'

So, for the rest of what was left of the late afternoon the two girls worked side by side painting the walls in what was to become their bedroom and finally, just as darkness began to fall, the first room was finished. The walls were cleaned and the floors had been mopped and mopped again.

'It's goin' to look grand when you've made the curtains, so it is,' Colleen said as she stood, hands on hips, surveying the results of all their hard work.

'It is,' Flora agreed. 'Unfortunately, I doubt I'll have time for sewing for a while. We need to get cracking on the downstairs as soon as we've finished up here. We can't afford to stay closed for a day longer than we need to.'

'Sure, and don't I know that,' Colleen agreed. 'But don't forget, it won't always be this hard. When Jia Li has got over what happened today and is feeling better we'll have three pairs of hands to get t'rough the work.'

The two girls looked over to where the pretty Chinese girl sat, fast asleep again, and smiled at each other. They were both exhausted and knew that there was still a lot of work ahead but they were confident that together they could make a go of things, or, as Flora jokingly told her friend, 'We'll die in the attempt!'

Chapter Twenty-Three

By the beginning of June the place had been totally transformed and was almost ready to be opened. Colleen had spent a whole day scraping the grease from the range and black-leading it while Flora tackled whitewashing the walls in the café. Every single window in the place gleamed, allowing the light to stream in and although they hadn't been able to afford to replace the rather tatty tables and chairs, even they had been given a new lease of life. Jia Li had painted the chairs white and stitched some pretty red-and-white gingham fabric, which Flora had bought at the market for a snip, into tablecloths that gave the room a cosy feel. Flora and Colleen were pleased to see her up and about again doing what she could to help, but it was clear that she had lost some of her sparkle and they could only hope that it would return in time. She was quiet and lethargic but then they supposed they should have expected that after the ordeal Huan had put her through.

'I swear I'd put a knife t'rough him without giving it a second thought, so I would!' Colleen stated angrily one day as her fiery Irish temper came to the fore.

'And then you'd wind up in prison,' Flora pointed out. 'Far better to let nature take its course. My ma was a great believer that what goes around comes around. He'll get his comeuppance one of these days.'

They had worked tirelessly to get the place ready for opening and had even had a new sign painted above the door which stated it was now 'The Little Tea Shop' in red letters to match the décor inside. Both Colleen and Jia Li had wanted it to be called 'Flora's Tea Shop', after all, as they'd pointed out, it was almost all of her money that had gone into it, but Flora wouldn't hear of it, insisting that this was a joint venture.

Now they were so close to being ready, the girls sat discussing when exactly the best day to open would be.

'How about we aim for next Monday as the opening day?' Flora suggested. 'That would give us time to do all the odd jobs that are left to do and buy the food in.'

'I reckon we could manage that,' Colleen agreed, wiping a stray red curl from her forehead, while Jia Li simply nodded. She didn't show much interest in anything anymore.

'Excellent, then we'll need to make a list of what food we need to buy in and we can start preparing some things on Sunday, like the curry for instance. It will keep overnight in the larder on the cold slab and then on Monday, if anyone wants it we can just warm it up. We need to talk about menus too and then it will be just trial and error until we can get an idea of what sells the best. The good thing is that anything that doesn't sell we can eat ourselves so it won't go to waste.'

'Well, I could do a batch of muffins and another of scones, they usually go down well, and of course we'll need to supply bacon and sausage sandwiches and such. I've an inkling that's the sort of grub the sailors'll be after. An' perhaps you could do a big pan of your delicious stew an' dumplings. I'm t'inking it'll be best not to do too much till we know what the demand is.'

'I suppose you're right,' Flora agreed, suddenly nervous. 'That's if we *have* any customers!'

'Goodness me will you just listen to her!' Colleen said with a shake of her head. 'Sure, this place will be a little gold mine by

193

the time we've finished, but I was t'inking perhaps we ought to do something to encourage people in on the first day.'

'Such as what?'

'Hmm.' Colleen stared thoughtfully up at the freshly painted ceiling for a moment before suggesting, 'How about we offer a free cup of tea or coffee with every meal that's bought? People like to t'ink they're getting somet'ing for not'ing, but if they like us they'll come back and hopefully tell their friends about us, wit' a bit o' luck!'

'That's a really good idea.' Flora clapped her hands and smiled as she surveyed their little empire just as a tap came on the door. It was Dora Casey and Flora hurried over to let the woman in. Once inside she stood there as if she could hardly believe her eyes before declaring, 'Why, if I hadn't seen it meself I'd never have believed it. You've done wonders with the place, girls, fair credit to you all.'

'Come and see the upstairs rooms,' Flora invited and Dora was only too happy to oblige.

As she moved towards the stairs, Dora noted the shining range in the kitchen, the freshly mopped floors and sparkling windows. Even the large oak table in the centre of the room had been scrubbed until it was almost white. The best of the pans they had salvaged had been scoured until they shone and now hung gleaming above the range, and on the shelves was displayed a range of cheap but cheerful mugs, plates and dishes for the customers use. The yard outside had also undergone a transformation and was as neat and clean as a new pin.

She puffed her way up the stairs, which were now cobweb-free and scrubbed clean, to the rooms above. 'Why, you've done *wonders*, girl,' she said in amazement as they entered what was now the sitting room. The old chairs, which Flora had painstakingly recovered, stood at either side of the fireplace and now that the chimney had been swept there was a cheery fire in the grate. The old table boasted a pretty chenille-fringed tablecloth and Jai Li had painted the wooden chairs so that they looked almost brand new. In fact, every piece of the old furniture they had found up there had either been painted or polished to a high shine.

'Actually, I was thinking you look rather dapper yourself,' Flora told Dora and the woman blushed prettily as she self-consciously patted her new mauve hat which sported a rather fine peacock feather that wafted about with every turn of her head. She was wearing a fitted mauve jacket to match and beneath it a deep-purple day dress which flattered her ample figure. Flora had never seen her look so nice.

'Well, the thing is I've got a bit o' time to make the best of meself now, ain't I?' Dora giggled like a schoolgirl. 'I'm on me way into the city to treat meself to a few more new togs. Me an me old man are off on holiday for a month then. It'll be the first we've had for over ten years so I'm feeling like all me birthdays an' Christmases have come at once. I feel like I've been given a new lease o' life but while I was passing I thought I'd just pop in and see how you were getting on.'

'We're hoping to be ready for opening on Monday,' Flora confided. 'But while you're here, Dora, I wonder if I could pick your brain? It's about pricing, actually. You see, I've no idea what I should be charging for what.'

'Why, bless your soul, that's easily fixed. Give me a pad an' pen an' I'll jot some prices down for you. Now what are you thinking of serving?'

Flora quickly told her and Dora nodded her approval. 'Right,' she said, licking the end of the pencil. 'You need to charge just enough to encourage the customers in but still make a profit. You can always raise the prices a bit when business starts to pick up and you've got a regular clientele.' She quickly wrote down some suggested prices and handed them to Flora and sighed as she glanced around again and admitted, 'I feel ashamed when I see what you've done to the place but to be honest I'd just lost heart in it and let it go. Meself too, if it comes to that, but I intend to change that now and make the most of what's left of me life.'

Flora smiled her approval and hurried away to fetch her purse. 'If you're going to be away for a bit, will you be needing the next rent payment before you go?'

'You ain't even earned anything yet so let's wait till I get back off me holidays and you can settle up then, eh?'

'Thank you.' Flora was touched at the woman's kindness and offered her a cup of tea but Dora was keen to be off to start her shopping spree. Flora followed her back downstairs and once she was gone she showed Jia Li and Colleen the prices Dora had suggested they should charge.

'Sounds good to me,' Colleen said approvingly and Jia Li nodded. 'So tonight I'll put a sign in the window saying we're opening on Monday and then we can set to and write the menus up, eh?' And so it was agreed.

All three girls were up at the crack of dawn the following Monday morning even though they hadn't gone to bed until late the night before as they were cooking and preparing everything.

'Now, are you sure everywhere looks all right?' Flora asked nervously for at least the tenth time in as many minutes. It was almost seven o'clock in the morning.

'Quite sure!' Colleen gave her a nervous grin then stood back to let Flora unlock the door and turn the sign hanging on it to 'Open'. Then all they could do was stand about and wait for their first customer and pray that the café would do well.

By eight o'clock not a single person had entered and Flora began to panic. *What if we've done all this hard work for nothing?*

she asked herself but suddenly the bell above the door tinkled and a sailor stepped inside sniffing at the air appreciatively.

'Mmm, is that bacon I can smell?' he asked and Flora grinned. He was clearly English.

'It certainly is and I can do you eggs to go with it, if you'd like some?'

'I certainly would and a nice cup o' tea would go down a treat as well,' he told her.

'Well, there's free tea with every meal served today as an opening offer.'

Jia Li had already disappeared into the kitchen. After what had happened with Huan she was still nervous around men and had stated that she preferred to stay out of sight doing the cooking. Colleen had joined her to make another batch of muffins for the afternoon trade and it was agreed that Flora would man the counter and wait on tables when the meals came through.

Minutes later the sailor, a friendly enough sort who introduced himself as Dan, was tucking into a hearty breakfast and when he was done he patted his stomach appreciatively. 'By, that certainly filled me up nicely, love.' He grinned as he placed his money on the counter. 'It needs somewhere nice and clean like this round here. Most of the places you go in ain't fit to take a dog in so I'll be tellin' me shipmates about you, you can be sure. Our ship, the *Celeste*, docks here often so you'll be seein' me an' some o' me mates again. Would I be right in thinkin' you're English?'

When Flora nodded he smiled. 'Thought so. I'm from Worcestershire but you're a Londoner from your accent, if I ain't very much mistaken?'

Flora nodded enthusiastically. It was lovely to speak to someone who came from the same country as herself.

'Thought as much.' He doffed his cap again, giving her another friendly smile. 'But I'd best be off. The ship will be loaded by now an' I don't want 'em sailin' without me. Bye and thank you very much.'

Flora beamed as she opened the old brass till that Dora had kindly left for them and dropped the money in. She had just served their very first customer and he had gone away happy, she couldn't have asked for more. For a moment she wished Jamie could see her and wondered if he would be proud of her, she hoped he would. But then she quickly pushed thoughts of him from her mind. She had to stop thinking about him. He might have been proud of her once, but if he ever found out what she'd done, she doubted he'd even want to talk to her.

The next hour was quiet again and Flora began to panic a little as she stood watching the door, praying for someone to walk in.

'Eeh, will you relax now,' Colleen scolded. 'You're making me nervous, so you are.' And then at last the customers began to drift in in dribs and drabs. Most of them were American women who were out shopping and wanted nothing more than a slice of buttery toast and a free cup of tea, but as Colleen pointed out, it was a start, and she added, 'If they enjoyed what they had they'll come again.'

Lunchtime saw the arrival of yet more sailors of many nationalities who happily tried Jia Li's excellent curry and Flora's delicious stew and dumplings. Then mid-afternoon, yet more women shoppers arrived to sample Colleen's cakes and scones.

From five o'clock onwards they found that they were serving meals to people on their way home from work who didn't want to cook, and finally, at seven o'clock they turned the sign on the door to 'Closed' and Flora counted the money in the till.

'I reckon we've just about broken even after we've taken out the cost of the food we've cooked and all the free drinks we've given away.' She sighed but Colleen wasn't disheartened at all.

'You know the old saying, "Rome wasn't built in a day",' she said wisely. 'And those who *have* been in all seemed to enjoy what

198

they had so no doubt they'll be back along with others as word spreads.'

Flora nodded, 'I hope you're right,' she said doubtfully, as they went back into the kitchen to have their own meals from what was left over and prepare fresh for the customers for the next day.

Chapter Twenty-Four

The same pattern continued for the first few days, with people drifting in and out but Flora was forced to admit that they weren't what could be termed busy. And then one evening a woman who worked in one of the packing factories on the docks called in and asked, 'How much would you charge if I were to bring me own dish in to be filled with either stew or curry? It would save me no end o' time if I didn't have to cook for the old man and the kids when I got in from work.'

'It would all depend how big the dish was,' Flora answered, reluctant to turn trade away.

'Well, enough for four.'

Flora gave the woman a price, adding, 'And we're going to start doing meat and potato pies and cottage pies as well next week.'

'Sounds good to me.' The woman smiled. 'I'll drop the dish into you on the way to work in the morning and then you can have it ready for me to pick up about this time tomorrow.'

'Why didn't *we* t'ink of that!' Colleen said when the woman had gone. 'Just t'ink how many women work in the factories, if word gets out that we can have a meal ready for them to take home at the end of the day we could sell no end.'

Flora nodded in agreement but then a clatter came from the kitchen and they both rushed to see what it was only to find Jia Li lying flat out on the kitchen floor.

'Oh, sweet Jesus,' Colleen whimpered as she dropped to her knees beside her friend. 'The poor lass is as white as a sheet, so she is, and I heard her being terrible sick in the closet outside again this morning.'

Her eyes popped then and as she glanced at Flora they exchanged a meaningful look as an idea occurred to them both. They had both come from large families so were no strangers to pregnancy and its symptoms.

'Y-you don't t'ink she might be having a baby, do you?' Colleen croaked fearfully.

'I have a terrible feeling she could be.' Flora wiped her hand around her face. Jia Li had not been herself since the rape some weeks before and if what they both feared was true she dreaded to think how the poor girl would feel about it.

'Fetch me some water,' Flora ordered as she lifted Jia Li's head and cradled her in her arms. 'We'd best bring her round and have a talk to her. One thing's for certain, she'll have to see a doctor now, whether she likes it or not. In fact, I'll drag her there myself, kicking and screaming, if I have to.'

When Colleen handed her a glass of cold water, Flora tenderly held it to Jia Li's lips and as it trickled between her teeth the girl began to cough and blinked her eyes open.

'Wh-what happen to me?'

'You fainted,' Flora said as her friend struggled into a sitting position.

'I perhaps not eating enough,' Jia Li whispered. 'But I feel so sick and ill all the time.'

'Yes and Colleen and me think we might know why,' Flora told her gently.

Jia Li stared at her blankly, she clearly had no idea whatsoever what her friend was inferring so Flora asked her gently, 'Does anything feel different? Your breasts for example.'

'Oh yes,' the girl replied with no hesitation. 'They are sore and

201

tender. Do you think I might have some bad disease?' she asked fearfully.

'No, I don't think you're ill at all,' Flora whispered. 'But . . . well, I think you might be with child.'

Jia Li's eyes opened even wider and the look of horror on her face almost broke Flora's heart.

'But . . . I . . . I *can't* be,' Jia Li gabbled, clearly in a panic. 'It is big sin in my culture to have baby unless you are married. I be outcast from my own kind forever!'

'If you are,' Flora said, hoping to calm her. 'And I say *if* because we could be wrong, you have to remember that this wasn't your fault. Huan forced himself on you so who could blame you?'

But Jia Li was inconsolable. The fact that Huan's baby could be growing inside her filled her with horror and she shuddered at the thought of it.

'Look, first thing tomorrow we'll go to a doctor and find out one way or another,' Colleen soothed as she reached out to comfort her but Jia Li slapped her hands away, her beautiful dark eyes flashing fire.

'*No* . . . no doctor. I not go!'

Flora and Colleen could see that the girl was far too shocked and upset to think rationally at the moment so Flora told her gently, 'All right then. We won't go for now. It will give you a little time to get used to the idea.'

'I *never* get used to it,' Jia Li spat. 'If baby is here then it means I am no better than the women who walk by shop at night selling their bodies to sailors!' The women she was referring to appeared as if by magic out in the street as soon as it got dark every evening, approaching any man that passed them. Jia Li pulled herself to her feet and before the girls could say another word she fled up the stairs, sobbing uncontrollably.

Colleen chewed on her lip, feeling her friend's pain as she watched her go, but Flora was more matter-of-fact.

'She'll have to come to terms with it if she is pregnant.'

'But what will happen to her?' Colleen asked fearfully.

'She'll stay here with us, of course, and we'll do all we can to support her through it. What's happened to her is awful but she'll survive and it won't be so bad having a baby here. We'll manage between us.'

'But what if Jia Li doesn't take to the poor little soul?' Colleen said worriedly and Flora smiled.

'I've never met a mother yet who didn't love her child when it arrived. Some of the women back in the courts where I lived bred like flies. Each time they found out they were having another one they went on as if the end of the world had come but it was a whole different matter when they were born. I think babies must have some sort of a magic spell that they cast over their mothers that makes them love them whether they were planned or not, and I've no doubt it will be just the same for Jia Li.'

'That's all very well but what about Bai?' Colleen said. 'Jai Li obviously loves him but will he still love her if and when he ever gets here if she is a mother to another man's child?'

'If he truly loves her he will when he realises how the child came about. But that's enough about that for now. If we don't get a move on and get everything prepared for morning we're never going to get to bed.' And so, side by side, the two girls set about the chores although both of their minds were firmly on Jai Li's predicament.

The next morning it was as if the night before had never happened for Jai Li went about her jobs with no mention of it and Colleen and Flora decided that they wouldn't mention it either. Slowly more people were visiting the café. Although the majority of the customers were still American women who called in for tea and cakes, other people were also starting to come in. There were Chinese men and others with skin as black as night and thick, frizzy hair. There were Jews, Germans and Arabs and people seemingly from every corner of the globe. Many were sailors but men from the nearby warehouses were also starting to come in, and by the end of that week they were cooking slightly more food to satisfy the customers' needs.

Flora liked nothing more than to listen to the women gossip. The American women seemed so much more open and loud than the ones back in London and now she understood why the English had a reputation for being somewhat reserved. But most of all, she loved chatting to the English sailors who found their way to the café as it made her feel like she had a link with home. One particular morning when Colleen was serving on the counter and Flora was in the kitchen with Jai Li, Colleen came into them looking concerned.

'There's a hooker just come in,' she whispered, nodding over her shoulder. 'What should I do?'

Flora paused to frown at her. 'What do you mean? You serve her, of course.'

Colleen squirmed uncomfortably. 'But do we *really* want to attract that type of customer?'

'Her money is just as good as anyone else's,' Flora snapped, uncharacteristically sharply. 'And just remember there but for the grace of God go you or I. Didn't you tell me that your daddy tried to get you out on the game? Why, most of those women who walk the streets at night walk by here in the day with a horde of little children clinging to their skirts. It's probably the only way the poor devils can put food in their mouths.'

Colleen hung her head in shame. 'I hadn't thought of it like that,' she admitted and scuttled away to serve the woman with a smile.

'It seems we've more than paid for the food we've used this

week, although we still need to earn a little more to cover the rent as well,' Flora told the other two girls on the following Sunday as she checked the books.

'It'll come,' Colleen said confidently. 'It's spreading by word of mouth now that we sell simple, wholesome food at a competitive price. In no time at all we'll be having to think of setting on more staff to cope with demand, so we will.'

Flora smiled at her. She loved Colleen's enthusiasm and confidence in what they were doing and prayed that she was right.

It was the last week in June when a letter with a foreign postmark arrived for Jai Li and Colleen and Flora stared at each other speculatively.

'I wonder who it could be off?' Colleen said curiously. 'Do you think it might be from Bai?'

'There's only one way to find out.' The breakfast rush was over now and they were having a lull in customers before they started to arrive again for tea and home-made biscuits mid-morning. 'I'll take it through to her.'

Instead of looking pleased about it as Flora had expected her to be she noted that Jai Li frowned and took it gingerly from her as if it might bite her.

'Do you think it might be from Bai?' Flora asked excitedly.

Jai Li shrugged. 'It might be. I have friend in China who passes on my letters to him. I write when we first came here to tell him new address so he know where I am.'

'Well, open it then!'

Jia Li sighed as she did as she was told and began to read the letter which was written in her own language and looked like a load of scribbles to Flora.

'It is from Bai,' she said quietly. 'He say he come very soon now.'

'Why . . . that's *wonderful*.'

Tears glistened on Jia Li's dark lashes as she shook her head.

'Not now, not if baby in here.' She gestured towards her stomach. 'It time soon to go and see doctor and find out for sure, then if I am with child I must make plans.'

'What sort of plans?' A cold finger of fear slid down Flora's spine as she saw the look on the girl's face.

'Back in my country there are women girls can go to if this happen to them,' Jai Li said solemnly. 'She make the problem go away. There must be women like this here too. I find one.'

'If you're talking about a backstreet abortionist you most certainly will *not*!' Flora snapped furiously. 'Back in London there was a girl I knew who went to one of them. The woman used a dirty knitting needle on her to get rid of the baby and the very next day she bled to death in agony. She was only the same age as me, do you really *want* to let that happen to you?'

Jia Li hung her head. 'Better that than bear the shame or have a baby I cannot love.'

Flora took her by the shoulders and gently shook her. 'What you're forgetting is that this baby didn't ask to be born, the baby is the innocent in all this and it's *your* blood as well as Huan's that will be flowing through its veins. If it's there then it must stay there and we'll see how you feel when it's born. Then if you really can't feel anything for it we could always look into having it adopted. There are always childless couples who want babies. *Please*, Jia Li, think about it. Don't do anything silly, I *beg* you.'

'Very well,' Jia Li agreed, seeing how upset Flora was becoming. 'I go see doctor very soon and then we decide what we to do.'

Flora and Colleen exchanged a worried glance and once Jia Li had left the room, Colleen whispered, 'I don't trust her not to go and do something silly, so I don't. For now, I think one of us should be with her at all times in case she slips out to do what she threatened.'

'Trouble is that's easier said than done. We're usually in the café while she's out in the kitchen. She could easily slip away. Or she could even go at night when we're asleep. I think for now we just have to believe her when she says that she won't go.'

Colleen sighed. 'I suppose you're right,' she agreed reluctantly. 'But I don't mind telling you I'm worried sick, so I am.'

Chapter Twenty-Five

On a balmy night in mid-July when the café had closed and everything was prepared for the next day, Colleen began to prowl about the upstairs sitting room like a caged animal.

'Phew, it's close, so it is,' she complained as she yanked at the collar of her dress and brushed a damp red curl from her forehead. 'I think I'll go out for a stroll to try and cool down.'

Flora looked up from the curtains she was sewing with concern. 'Is that a good idea? You know it isn't safe for a woman to be out on the streets on her own around here.'

Colleen airily waved her concerns aside. 'It's still light,' she pointed out, gesturing towards the window. 'I wouldn't go if it was dark.'

Flora felt torn, Jia Li had already retired to bed and she didn't want to leave her alone but she wanted to go with Colleen too.

Colleen chuckled as if she could read her mind. 'I'll be fine,' she promised. 'You just stay here and keep an ear out for Jia Li. I shan't be long, I promise.'

Once outside she let the cool breeze wash over her and sighed with relief before beginning to amble along. The girls were painfully aware that the café was in a far from salubrious area, but as Flora had sensibly pointed out, had it not been they would never have been able to afford the rent on it. The labyrinth of backstreets contained rows and rows of back-to-back tenements where whole families were crowded into a single room. Dotted amongst them were shops that catered to all nationalities as well as a large number of warehouses where women and men worked alongside each other packing and unpacking anything and everything that was either being imported into the country or exported out of it. There were also a number of pubs, which guaranteed that the noise of drunken seamen staggering back to their lodgings could be heard echoing along the streets well into the early hours of each morning.

That evening was no different and there were still quite a few people about, including hollow-eyed, lice-ridden children playing in the gutters, so she headed for the docks. She loved to see the ships coming and going and it always relaxed her. As usual when she arrived there was a lot going on. Ships of all shapes and sizes were being loaded and unloaded and there were sailors of every race wherever she looked. Many of them whistled at her and stared admiringly as she passed them but Colleen ignored them all and picked her way around the huge coils of ropes and cargo waiting to be loaded. At one point, she was so intent on watching what was going on that she failed to notice a thick rope trailing along the dock and before she knew it she had gone head first over it and fallen heavily, knocking the wind from her. Before she could even attempt to get up strong arms were lifting her and once she was on her feet she found herself staring into a pair of deep-brown eyes. Her heart gave a little flutter and she felt colour climb up her neck and seep into her cheeks as she tried to smooth her skirt. Her rescuer was tall with curly brown hair and his skin was tanned from the many hours he'd spent out in the open air. But it was his smile that she noticed above everything. It lit up his whole face.

'Are you all right?' the young man asked and she nodded, feeling a complete fool. What must he think of her?

'Aye, I'm fine . . . thank you. I . . . I just wasn't looking where I was going.'

'Have you hurt anything?' he asked and she found herself smiling at him, although she was usually cautious with strangers.

'Only me pride,' she assured him. He was still holding onto her elbow and the heat of his hand through her thin blouse was making her heart flutter.

What's wrong wit' me? she wondered. She couldn't remember ever feeling like this in a young man's presence before.

'Just take a few steps to make sure you haven't sprained anything,' he suggested kindly, pushing an unruly lock of his thick, dark hair from his eyes.

Colleen took a tentative few steps along the quay before nodding. 'There look. I'm right as rain, so I am.'

'Even so I think I'd better see you home. This isn't the place for a young lady like you.'

She was touched at his concern and shocked that she quite liked the thought of him walking with her. They had gone only a few paces when he nodded towards two women who were leaning with their backs against a warehouse wall eyeing the seamen and calling suggestive comments to them.

'There are always a few of those sorts around here,' he told her. 'And it's rare that they go short of customers with the sailors that have been aboard for some time. If I were you I'd keep away from this place in future. It's no place for a girl like you. Oh, and I'm Will by the way.' He held his hand out and she shook it.

'I'm Colleen,' she introduced herself.

'And do you live around here?'

She nodded. 'Yes, me and two of me friends run a little café a few streets away. We've not been open that long but it's doing right well, to be sure.'

He looked mildly surprised. 'Really? Well done then. You don't look old enough to be running a business.'

'Ah well, we didn't have a lot of choice,' she confided. 'We were all thrown out of us jobs and so we had to do somet'ing. But what

210

about you? Are you from hereabouts? You don't sound as if you come from these parts.'

'I don't, I just arrived here.'

'Oh, and will you be staying?' She didn't know why she cared, but suddenly she did. There was something about this tall, handsome young man that appealed to her. Most of the sailors she had encountered were coarse, callous individuals but Will seemed to be very kind and caring.

'Probably for a time,' he answered and when he said no more she didn't press him. The café was in sight by then and she felt almost sorry. She'd enjoyed the short time they'd spent together.

'This is it,' she told him, suddenly feeling self-conscious when they came to the door.

His eyes swept over the frontage approvingly. 'It looks like you have it nice.'

'Thank you, and yes we do. We worked hard on it, so we did, and I had blisters to prove it when we first started to rent it, but it's starting to pay off now,' she told him, suddenly feeling shy. 'And er . . . t'anks for walking me home.'

'It was my pleasure.' His eyes were tight on her face now and she felt as if she could have drowned in them. He hesitated as if he wanted to say something before suddenly blurting out, 'I don't suppose you'd fancy taking a stroll with me one evening, would you? At least if I came along of you I'd know you were safe.'

The colour was back in her cheeks again and her eyes were twinkling as she answered, 'I'd like that but the trouble is I'm not usually finished me chores afore nine at night. We have to prepare the food for the next day when we close up, see? We er . . . do have Sundays off though, if you happened to be free.'

'I certainly can be,' he agreed with a broad smile. 'How about I meet you at about one o'clock in the afternoon on Sunday? We could go and have a walk in the park if you like. I might even buy you an ice cream,' he teased.

211

'I'll look forward to it,' she told him shyly. 'And I'll meet you at the end of the road, shall I?'

He nodded and with a grin he turned about and strode away with his kitbag slung across his shoulder. Colleen watched until he was out of sight then with a little spring in her step she let herself into the café and sped upstairs.

'Crikey, you've perked up, haven't you?' Flora teased when Colleen burst into the room. 'If that's the effect the air out there has on you I might just go out for a stroll myself.' Flora stared at her friend curiously. Colleen's eyes were shining and the sun had brought out an attractive little spattering of freckles across her nose. She had looked tired when she left but now she was full of beans and beaming like a Cheshire cat.

'Well, actually . . .' Colleen suddenly felt embarrassed. 'I was down at the docks, not looking where I was going as I watched the ships come and go when I went sprawling full length over a coil of rope and this er . . . this young man helped me up and insisted he saw me home. He was the kindest man I've ever met.'

'*Ah!*' Flora grinned with amusement. 'So, it's like that, is it? You're well and truly smitten.'

'I am not so!' Colleen protested, but then, 'Well, I suppose he *was* very handsome, and *so* kind.'

'And will we be seeing this paragon of virtue again?' Flora teased, pleased to see her friend looking so happy.

Embarrassed, Colleen flushed as she made a great show of smoothing her skirt and keeping her eyes lowered. 'I, er . . . did say that I might meet him on Sunday afternoon and take a walk in the park with him. Do you t'ink I should go?'

'Why, of course,' Flora said encouragingly. 'That's a very sensible time to meet until you get to know him a little better. There'll be lots of people about at that time.'

Colleen hurried down to the kitchen to make them a last drink and found that she couldn't stop smiling. But then something occurred to her and some of the brightness left her eyes. What if he had only been being nice and he didn't show up? She supposed all she could do now was wait and see but Sunday suddenly seemed a very long way away, and what was she to wear? None of her clothes were really good enough for a stroll in the park on a Sunday afternoon when all the toffs would be taking an airing. *I'll talk to Flora and ask her advice*, she thought as she made them a cup of cocoa.

'But you must have a new outfit,' Flora insisted when Colleen mentioned her dilemma. 'The café is making a little profit now even after we've bought the food and paid the rent so I can afford to pay you and Jia Li a little wage each week.'

Colleen shook her head vigorously. 'No, we all agreed that we'd save every penny we could. After all, Dora said she would sell the café to you for what she paid for it if you can save enough. Just t'ink of that, owning your very own place!' They had all agreed that the tenancy should be in Flora's name as she had put the most money into it.

Flora shrugged. 'Let's not try to run before we can walk, eh? How do we know that trade will continue to pick up? Even so, there's definitely enough for you to treat yourself to a new dress and by the look of those you're wearing, a new pair of shoes too, so long as you don't go madly expensive.'

'Oh, I wouldn't,' Colleen assured her. 'I pass a little shop when I go to get the food shopping not far away where they sell good second-hand clothes. I'm sure I could get somet'ing there.'

'Then just as soon as the breakfast rush is over in the morning you must slip away and see if they have anything you like.' Flora grinned. 'You never know, you might just have met your Mr Right.' The words stabbed at her heart as a picture of Jamie suddenly flashed in front of her eyes but she forced herself to remain cheerful. She had never seen Colleen look so happy and she didn't want to do or say anything that might spoil it for her. She had grown to

213

love both Colleen and Jia Li like sisters and if this young man who had made Colleen smile was the one for her, then she was all for it.

The next morning when the stream of customers into the café began to slow, Flora pressed a sum of money into Colleen's hand. 'Go on, get yourself away to the dress shop and see if they have anything that takes your fancy.'

Colleen gave her a quick hug and throwing her apron over the back of a chair she tried to pat her unruly curls into some sort of order before she rushed out, shouting over her shoulder, 'I shan't be long, I promise.'

Flora and Jia Li smiled at each other like parents watching their child go off to their first ball. Colleen had told Jia Li all about her new admirer first thing that morning and like Flora, Jia Li was pleased for her.

'She not have a happy life in Ireland,' she commented. 'So, if this young man make her smile it is good, yes?'

'Oh yes. It is *very* good!'

'And I also have to ask if I may have a little time off this afternoon,' Jia Li said cautiously. 'I have decided that it time I see a doctor. It can be put off no longer.'

Flora heaved a sigh of relief, although deep down she had no doubt what the outcome would be. Jia Li was still being violently sick in the mornings and already Flora thought she could detect just the very tiny beginnings of a bulge in her stomach.

'Good,' she said approvingly and they set about preparing for the lunchtime rush.

True to her word, Colleen was gone for no more than an hour and returned with a big grin on her face, toting a large paper bag.

'You'll not believe the bargain I found,' she gushed excitedly.

''Tis the dress o' me dreams. It needs taking in a little admittedly but I t'ought perhaps you'd help me with that, Flora? You've a rare flair for sewin', so you have. And I found the most dinky pair o' shoes too.'

'Well, come on, don't keep us in suspense. Let's see them,' Flora urged, following her through to the kitchen where Jia Li was preparing a huge bowl of chicken salad. Now that the weather was so hot they were selling quite a lot of it.

Colleen dropped the bag onto the table and took out a very pretty day dress in a lovely shade of green that exactly matched her eyes. It was the fashionable new ankle length and Flora could see at a glance that it was good quality. Colleen then withdrew a pair of shoes with a tiny heel and a strap and again both girls cooed over them.

'The dress needs takin' in at the sides,' Colleen told them as she held it against her for inspection. 'But as I said, I don't t'ink it'll be too much of a job.'

'Easy as pie,' Flora assured her after a quick examination of the seams.

'I just hope the weather holds now so's I don't have to be wearin' me old coat and coverin' it up,' Colleen said gloomily and everyone chuckled. Just then the bell above the door in the café tinkled heralding a customer so the dress was hastily pushed back into the bag and they all got to work again.

As promised, Jia Li set off for the doctor immediately after the lunchtime rush and Colleen and Flora watched anxiously for her return from the café window. However, one glance at her face when she did come back confirmed their worst fears without her saying a word.

'Doctor he say baby due about mid-February,' Jia Li told them as tears trickled down her cheeks.

'Aw well, it's not the end of the world,' Flora consoled her. 'You're not the first and you won't be the last to have a baby out of wedlock. If you do, that is, Bai could be here before then and you could be already married.'

Jai Li shook her head. 'No, if he come now I send him away,' she said with conviction. 'I no let him bring up another man's child. *If* I keep it.' She looked around at them, her expression bleak. 'You want me to leave now?'

'*Leave!*' Both girls looked horrified then angry. 'You're not going *anywhere*. We'll all get through this together,' Flora told her sternly. 'So, let's have no more silly talk of leaving, eh?'

Jia Li nodded miserably, and as Colleen and Flora put their arms about her, she thought how very lucky she was to at least have two such good friends.

Chapter Twenty-Six

By the time Saturday night came around, Colleen was almost bursting with excitement. Flora had sat up late into the night altering her dress for her and on Sunday morning she happily dragged the tin bath in from the yard and placed it in the corner of the kitchen that they had curtained off. Colleen washed her hair then brushed it till it shone and slipped into her new finery.

'Why you look *absolutely* beautiful,' Flora told her and she meant every word of it. The green dress made Colleen's lovely eyes look even greener and complemented her flame-red hair perfectly.

Jia Li nodded in agreement. 'You do so. Very beautiful.' She gave one of her rare smiles and Flora's heart went out to her. But for now, their focus was on Colleen and they both told her, 'Get yourself away then. You don't want to keep him waiting, do you?'

Colleen needed no second telling and slipped away into the sunshine with a smile on her face. 'I shan't be late home,' she shouted over her shoulder and Jia Li and Colleen grinned at each other, leaving Flora to think wistfully back to those Sundays when she had gone to meet Jamie. It seemed so long ago now, yet it had only been a year since she'd met him. She'd changed so much from the happy girl with plans of making something of herself before she settled down. Oh, how she longed to have those sweet, simple days back again.

As Colleen made for the place they had agreed to meet, her heart was in her mouth. What if Will didn't come? What if he'd just been being gentlemanly? But as she rounded the corner, there he was, looking so handsome he almost took her breath away. He had clearly just washed his hair and although it was still damp it was already beginning to spring up into unruly curls despite his attempts at flattening it, and he was dressed in a clean white shirt and dark breeches. His shoes were shining too and she felt flattered that he had gone to such trouble for her.

'By God, you look grand,' he said admiringly as she walked towards him. 'I was afraid you wouldn't come.'

'I was afraid you wouldn't,' she told him shyly and the ice was broken between them and they both began to laugh.

'So, me lady, I believe I promised you a walk in the park and an ice cream,' he said teasingly. 'Would you like to take my arm? I'd like to say I have a carriage waiting to whisk you away but I'm afraid our legs will have to do today.'

'That sounds good enough to me.' Colleen grinned, linking her arm through his as they set off with eyes for no one but each other, chattering away merrily as if they had known each other forever.

Back at the café, Jia Li and Flora barely had time to settle down for lunch when the sound of someone knocking on the café front door echoed through to them.

'Who can that be?'

As Flora made to rise, Jia Li told her, 'No, you stay there. I go.' She pottered away as Flora strained to try and hear who it was as the minutes ticked away. She was still afraid that Alex or Magnus would track her down, and after a time she rose, intent on going to see who was there. She found Jia Li and a handsome young Chinese man sitting at one of the tables and was disturbed to see that Jia Li was crying. 'What's going on here?' she demanded protectively as Jia Li turned to look at her.

Jia Li shook her head. 'Not'ing is wrong,' she assured her. 'This is Bai. He arrive on boat this morning and come to find me.'

'Why, that's wonderful.' Flora's face lit up as she hurried across to shake his hand. 'Hello, Bai, I'm Flora. Jia Li has told me so much about you. But, Jia Li, why are you just sitting there? Run through to the kitchen to get Bai something to eat and drink. He's come a very long way to find you and he must be hungry.'

Jia Li silently rose and slunk away to do as she was asked as Flora joined the young man at the table. He was every bit as handsome as Jia Li had told her and she noticed that his eyes were kindly although they looked deeply troubled.

'I no understand, Jia Li not look happy to see me,' he told her miserably.

Flora chewed on her lip as she wondered how she should reply. She had no idea if Jia Li had told him about the baby and what had happened so she knew she would have to be very careful what she said. It really wasn't her place to tell him.

'Oh, I'm sure she is,' she said eventually. 'She's probably just surprised to see you. Let me go and help her, I shan't be a minute.' Once in the kitchen she hissed to Jia Li, 'Why don't you just tell him about what Huan has done to you and get it out of the way, Jia Li? Then at least he can make his own mind up about it. Now that he's here it's bound to come out sooner or later. You can't hide it for much longer.'

'I know,' Jia Li muttered miserably, 'but I feel so ashamed.'

219

Flora's nostrils flared with indignation. '*Why*, for goodness sake? None of this was your fault and you have me and Colleen to back you up on that. Go on, take that tray in to him and get it out of the way otherwise he'll think you just don't love him anymore.'

Jia Li sighed as, with her heart beating wildly, she turned and went back into the café.

Meanwhile Flora headed into the yard intent on giving them some privacy but every minute felt like an hour as she waited to find out how Bai would react to the news. Eventually she could stand it no more and she went back inside. They were still sitting at the table jabbering away in their own language but they stopped talking the instant that Flora appeared.

'Bai was just leaving. He have to find room for tonight,' Jia Li informed her.

Flora was tempted to tell him that he could stay there if he didn't mind sleeping on the settee but she didn't know how Jia Li would feel about that so she remained silent as Bai rose and hoisted his heavy kitbag onto his shoulder, looking as if he had all the worries of the world on his broad shoulders.

For a moment he stared at Jai Li solemnly and then with a curt nod at Flora he let himself out quietly and strode away as Jia Li began to sob.

'I tell him that I am having a baby,' she whimpered. 'I not tell him who did this to me though. If he know he might go to laundry and cause trouble.'

'You probably did right,' Flora agreed, coming to place her arm about her friend's heaving shoulders. 'But how did he take it? Is he willing to stand by you?'

'He not say yet. He say he need time to think.' Jia Li looked so sad that it broke Flora's heart.

'Well, at least he knows. That's the worst bit out of the way. Now he just needs to decide if he wants to stand by you, but somehow, I'm sure he will. He loves you. He wouldn't leave everything and everyone he knows behind and come all this way if he didn't. Come on now, all this crying isn't any good for the baby.' Then as a thought occurred to her she asked worriedly, 'You *did* tell him that Huan *forced* himself on you, didn't you?'

'No, I did *not*! Better for Bai to think that I betrayed him than let him take on the care of another man's child and be shamed! I *hate* baby! It baby's fault that Bai and I cannot to be together!'

'Oh, Jia Li, you little fool!' Flora scolded. 'Why weren't you honest with him? You were raped and it isn't the baby's fault. If you want to blame anyone blame Huan.'

Jia Li's shoulders sagged and after a second or two she got up and fled upstairs, sobbing wildly. Bai would come back surely? She had seen the love he felt for her friend shining in his eyes. All she could do was hope that he would return and meanwhile she would persuade Jia Li to tell him the whole truth next time.

Colleen returned late that afternoon, her cheeks glowing and her lovely green eyes sparkling. 'Eeh, I've had a lovely time,' she told Flora who was kneading the dough to make bread for the next day. 'We walked and walked and then we went into a little tea shop an' Will bought us an iced bun each an' a cup of tea.'

Flora smiled as she placed the dough into trays and covered them to let it rise. 'And will you be seeing him again?'

'Oh yes. Next Sunday.' Colleen had a dreamy look on her face and Flora was pleased to see that one of her friends at least looked happy. She went on to tell her about Bai's visit and Colleen frowned.

'You mean to tell me that the silly girl didn't tell the poor chap that Huan *forced* himself on her?' She was incredulous. 'But he will t'ink that she betrayed him!'

'I know.' Flora sighed and shook her head. 'He looked broken-hearted when he left and who knows if he will even come back again?'

'We must find him,' Colleen declared. 'An' when we explain what happened he's sure to stand by her if he really loves her.'

'But it's not as simple as that,' Flora pointed out. 'We have no way of knowing where he is or even if he'll stay now.'

The two girls stared glumly at each other for a moment then Colleen went to get changed out of her best clothes as Flora continued with what she had been doing.

Across town, a tall young man stood gazing at the façade of Alex's house. Ben had no idea why he had gone there but this was the address where his sister should have been living had she not perished on the *Titanic*. Connie would still be living there though and he had suddenly had the urge to speak to her and hear of Flora's last moments. His thoughts flew back to London where his family were still mourning Flora's loss and his heart ached. Now his mother would be dealing with his leaving too and shame washed over him as he thought back to the fateful night when he had burgled a house and left a woman for dead. Even now he could be being hunted as a murderer if she had not survived, which meant he would never be able to go home again. He had only intended to dock in New York and then get straight on to another ship but now he was considering staying for a while and seeing something of the city. If he saw Connie then at least he could write to his mother and let her know that he was safe, which was something.

After attempting to smooth his hair he approached the door of the smart town house and rang the bell, his heart in his mouth. It was opened by a young maid who gave him a friendly smile.

'Good evening . . .' Suddenly nervous, Ben coughed to clear his throat. 'I was wondering if I might see Miss Constance please?'

The girl's mouth gaped as she stared at him in confusion. 'I, er . . . think you'd best see the mistress,' she squeaked, and after ushering him into the hallway she shot off to find her.

Alex had been reading but as Patsy burst into the room she glanced up at her, concerned to see the perplexed look on her face.

'Is anything wrong, Patsy?' she enquired gently.

'Well, ma'am . . .' Patsy shifted from one foot to another, looking very uncomfortable. 'Th-there's a young man here askin' to see Miss Constance.'

Alex visibly paled as her hand rose to cover her mouth. 'I see.' But then pulling herself together with an effort she told the girl, 'You had better show him in.'

Chapter Twenty-Seven

Twisting his cap in his hands, Ben stared at the gentle-faced, fair-haired woman in front of him before saying, 'Excuse me for bothering you, ma'am, but I was hoping to see Miss Constance. My sister, Flora, was the maid that set out on the voyage on the *Titanic* with her and perished when it sank.'

'I think you had better sit down,' Alex told him with a calmness she was far from feeling. Then turning to Patsy, she asked, 'Would you bring a tray of tea in please, dear?'

'Yes, ma'am.' Patsy bobbed her knee and with a last glance at the handsome young stranger she disappeared back through the door.

'I'm afraid there has been a terrible misunderstanding,' she told him gently. 'You see, it transpires that your sister *didn't* perish aboard the *Titanic*. It was my niece that died.'

'*What!*' Ben's mouth gaped. 'Y-you mean that Flora is *alive*?'

Alex nodded and gave him a small smile. 'She certainly is and we asked Mr Wainthrop, Constance's solicitor in England, to inform your family of the fact.'

'Oh, I see. I'm a sailor and I've been at sea, so I didn't know,' Ben explained as he tried to take in the news. 'So . . . may I see her then?'

'I'm afraid not, you see . . .' Alex then went on to explain what had happened and when she had finished Ben shook his head.

'So, do you have no idea where she might have gone?'

'I'm afraid not, although I assure you we have tried very hard to find her.' Alex sighed. 'I don't really believe that your sister tried to deceive us. She was terribly ill and in shock when she came here and quite possibly very scared. Perhaps the mere thought of telling us that Constance did not survive was too much for her. Or maybe she was worried that we'd turn her away and she'd be alone in a strange place. Poor girl, I think her deception got the better of her. She must have thought that she would be in trouble but I assure you she wasn't,' she said kindly.

Margaret entered the room just then and looked at Ben curiously.

'So, who's this?' she asked rudely, eyeing Ben's clothes dubiously. He looked to be working class although he was rather handsome.

'This is Ben, Flora's brother. He didn't even know that she was still alive,' Alex explained.

'Huh!' Margaret sneered. 'Well, she's gone now and good riddance to bad rubbish that's what I say. She was a good little liar, I'll say that for her, but she couldn't keep up the pretence forever.'

'My sister is *not* a liar,' Ben retaliated, angry colour burning his cheeks.

'Now please, let's not let things get unpleasant,' Alex urged and with a sneer Margaret turned on her heel and left the room.

'I apologise for my stepdaughter,' Alex told him hastily. 'I'm afraid that she and Flora didn't get on all that well during the time that Flora was here.' She could have added that Margaret didn't get on very well with anyone and was thoroughly spoiled by her father but thought better of it.

Ben's back was as straight as a broom handle as he nodded. 'I apologise for taking up your time,' he said stiffly, although his heart was racing. Flora was alive! It was wonderful . . . incredible! Now all he had to do was find her.

'It was no trouble at all,' Alex assured him as Patsy reappeared with a tea tray. 'Won't you please stay for a cup of tea?'

'Thank you but no. Now that I know Flora is here somewhere I must find her.'

'When and if you do, please ask her to come and see me and let her know that she isn't in any sort of trouble at all,' Alex urged. 'In fact, it will be my pleasure to pay her passage back to London if that's what she wants.' Her eyes strayed to the window and she looked concerned. 'I do so hope you find her. It isn't safe for a young girl to be out on the streets all alone. Good luck, Ben.'

'Thank you.' As Ben shook the proffered hand warmly he thought what a lovely, gentle lady she was. This was a right turn-up for the books and he was thrilled to learn that his sister hadn't perished after all. Now there was yet one more reason to stay in New York; he had to find her. Even so, his elation was slightly marred by the fact that he hadn't got a clue where to start looking. New York was a big city and he feared it might be like looking for a needle in a haystack.

With his head in a whirl he made his way back to the little room he was renting in one of the backstreets that ran alongside the docks. At least work would be easy to come by here. There was always a need for men to load and unload the boats and when he wasn't working he could search for Flora. Meanwhile he could only pray that she was safe.

The next morning Jia Li appeared in the kitchen with reddened eyes but she found no sympathy from Colleen. She had made them all a pot of tea to share as she did each morning before they opened the café and now she asked, 'Why ever did you send the poor laddie away wit'out tellin' him the truth, girl? Sure, he must have t'ought you'd had your head turned by some other chap, so he must!'

226

'I'm spoiled for any man now,' Jia Li answered in a wobbly voice.

'Why, I never heard such a lot of codswallop! What happened was none of your fault and Bai would have understood that if you'd only told him so. Now the poor lad must t'ink you don't love him at all, so he must!' Colleen said angrily.

Seeing how upset Jai Li was becoming again, Flora glanced at Colleen imploringly. 'Go gentle on her now. She only did what she thought was for the best.'

'Gentle *indeed*! Why she needs her head examining to let a good man walk away from her like that!' Colleen shook her head as she slammed three mugs onto the scrubbed table, but all the same she did shut up as they all took a seat, although the atmosphere was so thick, Flora was sure she could have cut it with a knife.

They drank their tea in silence and as Jia Li began to prepare the pans for frying bacon and sausages, Colleen and Flora went into the café to open up. Within minutes of turning the sign on the door they were too busy to think of anything but serving the customers that flooded in. It was mid-morning by the time they had a lull and the sink was piled high with dirty pots and pans.

'I shall be able to buy this place in no time if trade continues as it is,' Flora told them optimistically that evening as they sat together eating their supper. The till had been ringing all day and now at last she was making a very healthy sum. They were opening an hour later each night now to cope with the factory women who called in to have their dishes filled on their way home from work, and it was proving to be very profitable indeed. Such a workload didn't give any of them much time for a social life, although that suited Flora, who preferred to keep her mind distracted. 'I reckon I ought to be thinking of applying for some more workers to relieve the pair of you,' she suggested.

227

'And why would you be t'inking o' doing that?' Colleen raised her eyebrow.

'So that you and Jia Li could have a little more time to yourselves, of course.'

'Huh! I'm quite happy with t'ings as they are, thank you very much,' Colleen told her abruptly. 'Though as Jia Li gets a bit bigger she might need to cut her hours down a little. Till then let's just leave t'ings as they are, shall we?'

When Jia Li nodded in agreement, Flora shrugged. If they were happy then so was she, or at least as happy as she could be. More and more, recently, her thoughts returned to home and her family, and Jamie, which was why she needed to be on the go all the time. While she was busy she didn't have much time to think. It was only as she lay in bed each night before sleep claimed her that she cursed herself for a fool. When Constance had first suggested that she should go to New York with her, Flora had thought it was going to be some big, glamorous adventure but look how it had turned out. Still, she supposed she was lucky that she hadn't perished with her young mistress and now she would just have to make the best of things, so whenever she got homesick or wondered what Jamie might be doing she found herself something to do.

By mid-August the heat was almost unbearable. Outside the tar on the roads began to melt and Flora had to leave the café door open otherwise the place was too hot to work in. Jia Li was finding it particularly uncomfortable as she was finding these early months of pregnancy exhausting and she was still being sick, but she battled on bravely despite the fact that Flora and Colleen repeatedly asked her to take a rest. Most days, by the time they turned the sign on the door to 'Closed', she was dead on her feet, but she never complained. However, the girls did insist that she keep her doctor's appointments to ensure that all was well, although as yet she hadn't bought a single thing in readiness for when the baby came. She just wanted to get the birth over with and she hadn't allowed herself to think beyond that.

Dora Casey still called in to see them when she collected the rent and was shocked at how well the place was doing, and it was during one of these visits that she informed Flora, 'The place next door is up for rent. Did you know? It'd make a fine extension to this place if you could afford to take it on.'

Flora's ears pricked up. She was still saving every penny she could but perhaps it would be worth investing in the property next door if she could afford the rent on it. For a start, it would give them all more living space, which would be very welcome, especially after the baby had been born.

'Do you know who owns it?' she asked.

Dora nodded as she lifted the glass of home-made lemonade and took a sip. 'It's Barker and Dodds Lettin' Agency in Manhattan.' She wiped her mouth on the back of her hand and adjusted the little hat that sat at a coquettish angle on her hair. 'I ain't got a clue what rent they'll be askin' but don't let 'em take advantage of you if you decide to go ahead. The place is even worse than this one was when you took it on so theys should just be grateful to get anything for it.'

Flora nodded thoughtfully as she glanced around the crowded little café. 'I might just pay them a visit and make a few enquiries,' she said musingly but then another customer approached the counter and she was busy serving again.

'So, what do you think of the idea?' she asked Colleen and Jia Li that evening as they sat out in the back yard. They'd taken to eating their supper out there as it was far too clammy to sit in the kitchen.

'Hmm.' Colleen pursed her lips. 'I dare say it's worth a visit to the agents but goodness knows what state it'll be in if the outside is anything to go by. All the windows are boarded up so you can't even glimpse inside it an' the paint's all but peeled away from the door.'

Even so they all agreed it might be worth looking into so for the first time in months, the following day during a lull in customers, Flora set off for Manhattan. It felt strange to be out in the busy streets again and she kept glancing nervously about. The last thing she needed was to bump into Alex or Margaret, or worse still, Toby. She often wondered how he had reacted when she ran away without paying him the money he had demanded and dreaded ever having to see him again.

At last she found the building she was looking for and stood for a moment studying the properties they had for rent in their window. This street was a far cry from the one they lived in with smart shops and well-dressed women bustling up and down the busy pavements and Flora suddenly felt very dowdy. The properties in the window were all far beyond what she could afford and there was no sign of the one she had come to enquire about. But then she supposed that now she was here she had nothing to lose, so after taking a deep breath and smoothing down the smart skirt she had borrowed from Colleen she entered the shop, setting the little bell above the door tinkling merrily.

Chapter Twenty-Eight

'So how did you get on?' Colleen asked eagerly the second Flora set foot through the door.

The café was already beginning to fill with the lunchtime customers so Flora flashed a smile and hissed, 'I'll tell you later,' and with that Colleen had to be content.

It was mid-afternoon before the girls got a breather again and as Jia Li poured them all a cold drink and they took a well-earned ten-minute break, Flora told them, 'The letting agent has trusted me with a key so that we can go around there and have a look inside this evening when we close. I've promised to get it back to him first thing in the morning. But I'll tell you now, I got the distinct impression that the property had been on his books for some time and I have a feeling that the owner just wants shot of it, which is good news for us.'

'Hmm, well we'll see when we get inside, shall we?' Colleen said cautiously. From what she could see of the state of the outside she dreaded to think what it might be like inside. Still, she supposed they had nothing to lose by taking a look and they all could think of little else as they worked for the rest of the day.

'Right, that's it.' Colleen rubbed her hands together and sighed with relief as she turned the sign on the door to closed that evening. They were all wet through with sweat and there was nothing Colleen would have liked more than to take a nice cool bath but curiosity was getting the better of her. They hastily did the dishes and wiped the tables between them then Flora fetched the key and they trailed out to stand outside the property next door as Flora struggled to get the key into the lock and turn it.

'The lock is rusty,' she told them. 'It needs a bit of oil in it.'

'A new door more like,' Colleen scoffed, but at last it was open and they all moved forward and peered cautiously into the gloomy interior.

'Phew, what a smell!' Colleen wafted her hand up and down past her nose. 'It smells as if something has died in here!'

Flora giggled. 'Oh, stop moaning. Where's your spirit of adventure? Come on, I'm going in whether you are or not.' And with that she stepped inside, followed closely by a reluctant Jia Li and an even more reluctant Colleen, who was pinching the end of her nose shut. They found themselves in a decent-sized room that seemed to be crammed with rubbish and as they set off across the bare floorboards a rat the size of a small cat disappeared into an empty cardboard box.

'Ugh! Did you see the size of that t'ing!' Colleen looked horrified as she peered around cautiously. 'I bet the place is runnin' wit' the t'ings.'

Flora giggled again. 'Scaredy cat, come on, let's see where this door leads.' She tugged at another door on the far side of the room and after some pulling managed to get it open. It led into a room with a small kitchen leading off it in one corner and another open door through which they could see a staircase. Flora was off like a shot, stepping across the rubbish fearlessly but Colleen and Jia Li were a little more cautious as they slowly followed her. Every step they took sent a whirl of dust flying into the air and Colleen began to cough and grumble.

'Sure, you take your life in your hands venturin' into this place, so you do,' she muttered irritably as she batted a hanging cobweb out of the way. 'Just be careful on them stairs now. They may be rotten,' she warned but by then Flora was already at the top of them and peering into three good-sized bedrooms.

'Why, this is a house,' she declared with some surprise as Jia Li struggled up the narrow staircase to join her. 'I'm not sure that it would be suitable for extending the café but it would be a great place to live right next door. Just look at all the space we'd have.'

'Mmm, I suppose you're right,' Colleen admitted as she screwed her nose up at the state of the place. 'But to be sure it would take some putting to rights!'

Flora nodded in agreement. 'It would but it wouldn't have to be done all at once, would it?' she answered. 'I could always come round here on Sundays and start to clear it.'

'You could *not!*' Colleen was indignant. 'Not on your own at least. I could help you and I've no doubt Jia Li will too when the baby's arrived.'

But on this Flora was firm and she shook her head. 'You two do too much as it is. If I take it on then I'll get it ready to live in,' she insisted.

Colleen grinned at her. 'We'll see,' she said, tongue in cheek, and they all trooped back downstairs. Through the small kitchen they entered a little back yard with a rickety fence dividing it from the café next door.

'That could come down for a start off and double the outside space,' Colleen pointed out practically. She was getting a little more enthusiastic now. 'And we could turn the outside toilet in the yard of the café into one for the customers use. There's another one here, look, that we could use, though it smells rank, so it does! I shan't be volunteerin' to clean that, that's for sure.'

They turned to Jia Li, who had said little up to then, to ask her opinion and she shrugged. She never got animated about anything anymore and sometimes both Flora and Colleen found it hard to remember how happy she had once been. Bai had never returned to the café since the day she had told him about the baby and they both knew that she still pined for him, although she steadfastly maintained that she had done the right thing in not telling him the truth about the baby's conception.

'It make very nice home when work done to it,' she told them quietly and they glanced at each other, wondering just what it would take to make Jia Li show any feelings whatsoever. They locked the property up and went back to the café discussing what would need to be done should Flora decide to take the place.

The next morning Flora made her way back to the letting agent and Colleen waited impatiently for her return.

'Well?' she asked when Flora entered the café again. She had been busily wiping down tables but she stopped with the cloth in mid-air as she stared at Flora questioningly.

'So . . .' Flora smiled slyly. 'As I told you yesterday I got the impression that they just wanted shot of the place which put me in rather a good bargaining position.'

Colleen grinned. 'To be sure, I doubt anyone else would be daft enough to take the place on,' she commented. 'The whole place needs gutting and redoing before it's fit to live in.'

'Quite, which is why I told them I wouldn't be prepared to rent it,' Flora told her. 'Instead . . . I've bought it!'

'You've done *what*!' Colleen's eyes almost popped out of her head.

'I've bought it,' Flora repeated with a grin. 'Or I should say I've *part* bought it. They're letting it go for a ridiculously low price so I've agreed to pay what I have up front and get the rest to them in three months' time. I should be able to manage it with what we're making in the café now.'

'But what if you can't?' Colleen queried worriedly.

Flora shrugged. 'Then I'll have lost all my savings. Obviously, it won't be properly mine and signed over to me till I've paid for it in full but I'm confident I can do it.'

Colleen looked concerned. 'But I thought you wanted to buy the café off Dora first?'

'I did and I still do,' Flora agreed. 'But I'd be a fool to let next door go. Once I've paid for that I shall start to save to buy this place next.'

Colleen shook her head. 'I dare say it's your decision but I do hope you're not making a grave mistake,' she said worriedly.

'I'm not, I'm sure of it,' Flora told her confidently.

'But next door needs a lot of money spending on it before it'll be fit to live in,' Colleen pointed out.

'I know, but there's no one saying it all has to be done at once, is there?' Flora smiled at her reassuringly. 'I shan't do anything to it apart from give it a good clear out till it's properly mine. I won't be able to afford to do too much, if truth be told. I'll just take it one step at a time.'

'Hmm, well I dare say you know what you're doing,' Colleen answered, although her voice was still heavy with doubt. She went back to wiping the tables while Flora went through to the kitchen to check on Jia Li. Walking into the kitchen was like walking into an oven, despite the back door being wide open, and she wondered how Jia Li could bear it. The girl had tied her lovely long, black hair into a ponytail and her sleeves were rolled up as far as they would go. Flora told her what she had just told Colleen.

'You make it into good home,' Jia Li said simply. She had every faith in Flora and blessed the day she had met her. Goodness knew what might have happened to her if she hadn't. Today she was once more wet through with sweat but as always, she didn't grumble as she prepared the meals for lunchtime. 'I shall help you,' she told her but Flora shook her head.

'No, you won't. I appreciate the offer but you're already doing too much as it is. I think you should start to have a rest in the afternoons now. I don't like the way your ankles are swelling. You should be keeping off your feet a bit more now.'

Jia Li shook her head. 'Swollen ankles is usual when having baby,' she said quietly.

'Speaking of which . . . shouldn't we be starting to get the things ready for when the baby arrives?' Flora suggested tentatively. She and Colleen were almost afraid to mention the baby for fear of having their heads snapped off.

'There still be plenty of time for that,' the girl replied with a frown. She tried not to even think about it but her stomach had started to get bigger and it was getting harder to ignore. Seeing that she had said all that was to be said on the matter for now, Flora changed the subject and soon the lunchtime customers began to arrive and they were rushed off their feet as usual.

That evening when the café was closed and Jia Li had retired for an early night, Flora and Colleen went round to look at the house once more. If anything it was in an even worse state than they had remembered and once again, Colleen was concerned.

'Sweet Holy Mother!' Colleen grumbled as she clipped her ankle on an empty wooden orange crate. 'It'll take a month o' Sundays just to clear the rubbish out, so it will.'

'And there's no time like the present to start,' Flora said with a grin as she flung the creaking back door open and began to throw rubbish out into the yard. 'You get back next door and put your feet up for a time. I'll be fine round here.'

'I'll do no such thing. I'm going to help,' Colleen insisted as she rolled her sleeves up. 'Though heaven knows what we're likely to come across nestling amongst this lot!' Warily she lifted a crate and following Flora's example threw it out into the yard and soon they were so busy that all conversation ceased as they concentrated on what they were doing.

By the end of the week, the house was finally empty of rubbish although the yard was full.

'You're going to need new plaster on most of t'e walls,' Colleen

236

pointed out. 'And some of these floorboards are rotten, they'll need replacin'.'

'That's all right.' Flora was determined not to get downhearted. 'But Rome wasn't built in a day, as the old saying goes. It'll all get done eventually.'

Knowing Flora as she now did, Colleen had no doubt that it would.

'I wish Bai would come back,' she commented to Flora the next evening as, armed with buckets and mops, they attacked the worst of the filth on the floor. 'If only one of us could see him and explain about the baby, I'm sure he'd stand by her.'

Flora nodded in agreement. 'I think you're right but if he doesn't come back we've little chance of finding him here. New York is an enormous place and I wouldn't even know where to begin looking.'

'I suppose you're right.' Colleen sighed. She was still seeing her Will every Sunday and was smitten with him. In fact, she knew deep down that she loved him now although she wasn't sure how he felt about her. Oh, he was attentive and kind, admittedly, but she always felt that there was something he was holding back from her. Whenever she questioned him about his family or his past he closed up like a clam or hastily changed the subject and she wasn't even sure what part of London he had come from.

'Eeh, we're a right lot to be sure,' she commented drily. 'There's me givin' me heart to a chap that seems to be holdin' back from me. Jia Li pinin' for Bai an' you still carryin' a torch for your Jamie.'

'I am *not*!' Flora denied hotly but the rush of colour that rose in her cheeks belied her words.

Colleen's voice gentled as she paused to suggest, 'Why don't you write to your mammy. Sure you've been sayin' you were goin' to for months now. What harm could it do? She will know you survived the *Titanic* by now an' whatever you've done since, I'm

237

willin' to bet she'd be t'rilled to hear from you. It wouldn't hurt to write to your Jamie neither. I bet he'd love to hear from you too.'

Flora chewed on her lips thoughtfully for a moment before admitting, 'I suppose you're right. I owe her that at least, though whether she'll bother to reply is another thing. But I'm not so sure about writing to Jamie. He . . . he might have found someone else by now.'

Flora's answer told Colleen all she needed to know. Flora still loved him. 'Well, you won't know unless you try, will you?'

'True, but then I could say this is the pot calling the kettle black.'

Colleen scowled. 'And just what is *that* supposed to mean?'

'Just that you mope about worrying about how your mother and brothers and sisters are coping but you don't try to find out. I know you daren't write home because of your father finding the letter but surely there's someone back in Ireland who you could trust to pass a letter on to her?'

Colleen thought about it for a minute before slowly nodding. 'I suppose I *could* send the letter to Niamh, me mammy's friend,' she reflected. 'I t'ink she could be trusted not to let me down.'

'So let's *both* write home then, eh?'

Colleen grinned, her mind made up. It would be lovely to hear from her mammy, so it would.

'You're on. We'll both write to our mammies this very night when we've finished here, shall we?'

They smiled and got on with what they were doing, their minds already thinking about what they would write.

Chapter Twenty-Nine

Two months later, Flora paid the rest of the money she owed for the house and came back to the café proudly waving the deeds. It had been ridiculously cheap, which Flora knew was just as well, otherwise she would never have been able to afford it. It was mid-October and they were all thankful that the weather was now cooler, although the heat of the summer had taken its toll. Outside the leaves of the sparse trees that were scattered here and there were withered and drooping, the rare patches of grass were brown and brittle and even the river levels were low and in desperate need of rain, which never seemed to come, but they all lived in hope that now it soon would. Jia Li's stomach was growing by the day and it now looked incongruous on her slight frame.

The morning after she'd bought the house, Colleen came into the kitchen waving an envelope at Flora. 'This came for you an' it's got an English postcode,' she told her excitedly.

The second Flora took it from her and looked at the handwriting her heart began to beat with joy.

'It's from my ma.' Her eyes were shining as she looked at Colleen, but the café was beginning to get busy so there was no time to read it right away. Instead she quickly put her apron on and pushed the letter safely into the pocket. She would open it just as soon as the lunchtime rush was over and she could hardly wait.

At last, by mid-afternoon, the stream of customers slowed down and Flora eagerly took the letter from her pocket and began to read it.

My dear Flora,

You cannot even begin to imagine the heartache we have suffered since you left. When word reached us that you had gone down with the Titanic *the whole family went into mourning. Then we had the wonderful visit from Mr Wainthrop informing us that it was Constance who had died and not you. Of course, we were sad to hear of her death but so relieved to hear that we had not lost you, my dear child.*

Sadly, soon after we heard of your death, Ben left too. I'm ashamed to say that he got in with a bad crowd and during a burglary a woman was badly injured. Thanks be to God she survived but Ben had already fled fearing he might be being hunted for murder. The problem is I have no idea where he is so I can't inform him that he is free to return home as the police caught the chap responsible for the attack on the woman. But enough of Ben. Please come home, Flora. We all miss you so much. Whatever has happened since that fateful crossing is over now and I'm sure Constance's aunt holds no grudge against you so there is nothing to stop you returning.

And what of your young man? I often wonder about him. You didn't say what happened between you two, but I sensed that it didn't end well. But now you have the chance to make amends with him too. Oh, please come home, my darling. We all love you so much, and I am sure your Jamie does too.

Sending you all my love, my darling girl.

Your loving mother.

When Flora finally folded the letter there were tears in her eyes. Her mother could have no way of knowing that she had indeed already written to Jamie on several occasions but up to now had failed to find the courage to post them so they were all tucked away tied with a ribbon in her drawers.

'See, Flora, didn't I tell you that things would work out?' Colleen said gently as she squeezed Flora's arm, but deep inside she was fearful of what would become of herself and Jia Li if Flora did decide to go back to London.

As if she could read her thoughts, Flora smiled sadly. 'I won't be going anywhere, at least not for a long time,' she assured her. 'I'd love to see my family again, but Jamie won't be there so I may as well stay where I am. Ma might not be right anyway. What if Constance's aunt *is* still angry with me? I took on her niece's identity and she's not going to let that go lightly, is she?'

Colleen pursed her lips. She supposed that Flora could be right, but it hurt her to see her friend so sad. 'But I still think you should have written to Jamie too,' she said and Flora shook her head as she placed the letter back in her pocket to be read again later.

'There would be no point,' she said dully. 'I must have hurt him so badly when I made the decision to come here because he never even tried to see me, and even though he said he'd wait for me at our meeting place, he didn't come. I doubt he'd ever forgive me. But come on now, we have work to do. We'll have them all pouring in for afternoon tea soon.'

Two days later it was Colleen's turn to get excited when a letter addressed to her arrived with the morning post.

'I t'ink it's from me mammy!' She tore the envelope open excitedly and began to read aloud, although the letter took some interpreting as her mother had never really mastered the art of reading and writing.

Dear Colleen,

Sure I coud ave died wit pleasure when Niamh smuggled yur letter round to me. My darlin girl I have so much to tel yu. Firstly I must inform yu that yur daddy passed away two munths ago. He just droped down ded wit a heart attack so he did! I know that we shud be sad but I would be a liar to say it. Yu know only too wel that he ruled the family wit a rod of iron so we can only feel relief at his passing. Peraps now yu might consider comin home? We miss you so much an the little ones speek of yu all the time. We was shocked to find that he had left a wad o muny beneath the floor boards. Litle Patrick found it so wit what I am able to earn takin' in washin' an iroin' an' what we make on the small holdin we is managin quite well for now. I hope that yu are safe an keepin well. Do consider comin' home me darlin. I apologis for this letter, yu know ful wel I ain't never been much of a one for leter writin.

May the holy mother keep you safe me darlin.

Luv always,

Yur luvin mammy xxxx

'Me daddy's *dead*!' Colleen stated as she stared up at Jia Li and Flora. She could hardly take it in as she thought back to all the thrashings he had given her and the rest of the family. They had all lived in dread of him rolling home drunk but he could never hurt any of them again now.

Jia Li and Flora exchanged a glance not at all sure what they should say. If it had been anyone else discovering this news they would have offered condolences but it seemed inappropriate after what Colleen had told them of her brutal father.

'He can't ever hurt none of us ever again,' Colleen muttered as she stared off into space. Then she smiled, a slow, sad smile. 'It's good to know that me mammy an' the kids are safe now, so it is. I've had nightmares wonderin' what might have become of 'em .'

242

'W-will you return to home now?' Jia Li asked anxiously. Colleen and Flora had been so good to her. She really didn't know what she would have done without them these past months and now the thought of her losing either of them terrified her.

Colleen shook her head. 'Not yet awhile.' She knew that had it not been for Will she might have felt otherwise. New York was a huge sprawling city but the concrete jungle could never replace the lush, emerald green fields of her homeland. She had only to close her eyes and she could see them still, along with the tinkling streams that ran down the hillsides like silver ribbons and the wealth of wild flowers in all the colours of the rainbow that spangled the hillsides. Sometimes the need to see them and her family again was like a physical pain and she would have returned home in a shot . . . but now there was Will and the thought of leaving him was unbearable. She had a feeling that deep down his feelings for her were perhaps not as deep as hers were for him, but even so she couldn't begin to contemplate never seeing him again. And so for now at least she would stay where she was, but one day perhaps . . .

That evening when the other two girls were in bed and fast asleep, Flora opened a drawer and added a nightgown she had stitched to the little pile of tiny clothes she had hidden in there. Both she and Colleen had secretly been squirrelling them away for months. They felt that they had no choice for Jia Li had shown no interest whatsoever in preparing for the baby's birth.

The letters she had been writing to Jamie for the past few months sat alongside them, and she stroked them briefly, wondering how he was and whether he had found someone else to love. The thought sent a shaft of pain through her, but she couldn't blame him if he had. Sometimes she was furious with him when she thought of how he had just disappeared from her life. Then at others, she remembered the look of pain on his face when she told him about leaving for America. She wished with all her heart he could see her now, with her own business and a property. Would he be proud of her? Would he forgive her? A lone tear slid down her cheek and she wiped it away angrily. She'd made her bed and she must lie in it. She had no one to blame but herself for her heartbreak.

Sniffing, she sat down at the desk. Although she knew she would never send it, writing letters to Jamie made her feel close to him, and right now, she really needed to talk to him. The responsibility she had taken on in buying the house weighed heavily on her and she worried about how they would cope when Jai Li had her baby. And what if Colleen succumbed to her homesickness and returned home now that her father was dead? Sometimes she felt as if she was carrying the weight of the world on her shoulders.

My dearest Jamie,

How can I even begin to tell you how much I love and miss you? Jai Li is growing bigger by the day and I am beginning to feel nervous about the impending birth now. She is so tiny that I can't help but worry. Colleen and I are trying to get her to rest more now and because we are so busy from when we open the café until we close I have been thinking of taking on extra help to take her place. I can only hope that the right person will show up eventually.

What are you doing now? I wonder. Are you still in London or did you go back to the Midlands to be with your family? I so miss the talks we used to have and think of you every day. I think Colleen is unsettled too. She is back in touch with her mother and her family in Ireland and I have a feeling that she would go home on the next boat if it weren't for Will, the

*young man I told you about in my last letter. I have an idea
she still might if things don't work out between them and then
I will really struggle on my own.*

*If only you were here to give me advice. I have Jai Li and
Colleen, who I love dearly, but no one can replace you, my
love. One day I shall find the courage to post all the letters I
have written to you since we have been apart and then you'll
see how much I have regretted leaving you. My only consolation
is that from morning until night I am so busy that I don't have
time to think of you during the day. It is at night that I cry
into my pillow and pray that wherever you are and whatever
you are doing you are happy and safe.*

With all my love
Flora xxxxxxx

They were in the middle of what they now called the mad hour
rush at lunchtime the next day when suddenly there was a loud
clatter in the kitchen and both Colleen and Flora dropped what
they were doing to run and see what had happened. They found
Jia Li sprawled on the floor lying amidst a mess of salad from the
large bowl she had been carrying when she fell.

'I . . . so sorry . . . I slip,' she gasped as she tried to get up.

Colleen and Flora each took one of her arms and on the count
of three gently lifted her and sat her down at the table. She seemed
shaken but thankfully unhurt they noted with sighs of relief.

'I be all right in a minute,' Jia Li insisted but now Flora put
her foot down.

'Oh no you *won't*!' She waggled her finger sternly in Jia Li's
face. 'This is a sign that you're doing too much, young lady, so
you're going to go upstairs and lie down for a while even if I have
to carry you up there myself!'

'But I not *need* lie down,' Jia Li argued. She knew how hard it
would be for them to manage with just the two of them.

''Scuse me, me dears, but can I help in any way?'

All eyes turned to the kitchen door. A woman who looked to be about sixty years old was standing there. She was short and round, with grey hair on which was perched a hat sporting a display of peacock feathers. Her periwinkle-blue eyes sparkled with warmth and kindness, and Flora immediately warmed to her. Although, how she could help, she wasn't sure.

'Hattie Lomax is the name,' she introduced herself. 'And I repeat, can I help?'

'Not unless you know how to cook curry and bake bread,' Colleen replied gloomily, keeping her arm tight about Jia Li's shoulders. 'Our friend here has had a tumble and we still have to prepare the meals for the evening customers.'

'Then I'm your woman,' Hattie told them with a grin that made her kindly face look years younger. 'Now, pass me an apron an' tell me what you want doin'. I've been looking for a job, as it happens, but your friend here has saved me the hassle.'

Flora and Colleen glanced at each other and as Colleen gave an imperceptible shrug, Hattie rolled up her sleeves. What did they have to lose, after all? And the woman did look very clean and respectable. In fact she was like the answer to a prayer.

'But we haven't discussed hours, wages or anything yet,' Flora blustered.

The woman chuckled. 'That can be done later, me dear. For now I think it's more important we feed those customers out there, don't you?'

Seeing the sense in what she said Flora hurried back out to the café and left Hattie to it. Jai Li could advise her if she needed it. For some reason, though, Flora wouldn't be at all surprised if the woman could manage perfectly well without her. She grinned to herself, it was as if someone had sent them a fairy godmother just when they needed one most.

Chapter Thirty

It was a long day, and when they finally closed, Colleen hurried into the kitchen to make them all a well-deserved pot of tea. She found Hattie up to her elbows in soap suds washing the dirty pots and couldn't help but be impressed. After her fall, Jia Li had stayed downstairs for a time until she was sure that Hattie knew what she had to do, before going upstairs to rest, and since then Hattie had done a sterling job of keeping the meals supplied and the kitchen running smoothly. The large table that dominated the room was scrubbed clean and the floor had been mopped too.

'You've done really well seeing as you were thrown in at the deep end, so you have,' Colleen told her approvingly and the woman gave her a warm smile.

'That's sometimes the best way,' she answered.

Flora joined them and stared round at the tidy kitchen, impressed. 'Thank you so much for stepping in to help, Hattie,' she told the woman. 'But do stop for a drink now. You've been on your feet ever since you got here and you must be tired. I know I am.'

Hattie chuckled as she dried her hands on a towel. 'That's the trouble wi' you young 'uns, you've got no stamina,' she teased.

They sat together at the table and as Colleen poured out their tea she asked, 'So, do you live around here, Hattie?' The woman sounded very English to her.

'Yes, not far as the crow flies.' The woman stirred sugar into her tea and sipped at it appreciatively. 'I came to live here forty years ago as a bride with my new husband who was a sailor and I've been here ever since. I brought my family up here, three strapping sons I have. Two of 'em have flown the nest and they're scattered far and wide now. I've still got the youngest, my Ernie, at home with me though. My husband, Percy, died two years ago and that's when I decided to start work again. I've been working in the match factory and I can tell you now this is a doddle compared to that.'

'Well, it was our good fortune that you happened to be here just when we needed you,' Flora told her. 'I didn't think anyone could make a curry like Jia Li but the customers have all said how delicious it was this evening.'

'Oh, I can turn me hand to most things when it comes to cookin',' Hattie assured her. 'My sons were like bottomless pits. I used to tease 'em an' say they'd got hollow legs. But tell me, have I got the job or what?'

'You most certainly have and we'll count ourselves lucky to have you,' Flora assured her. She went on to tell her what the hours and the wages would be. Hattie was quite happy with them and so before she left for home that evening she had agreed to return at eight o'clock the next morning.

'I really like her,' Colleen said when the bubbly little woman had departed. 'And she's certainly not afraid of hard work. I reckon we've dropped on our feet finding her. It was like a miracle her turning up like that.'

'I think it was more a case of her finding *us*.' Flora grinned. 'But now I'm going to make a tray up for Jai Li and check how she is.'

She found Jia Li curled into a ball on the bed but thankfully she seemed none the worse for her tumble.

'I so sorry,' she said as she pulled herself up onto the pillows and accepted the tray Flora had carried up for her. 'I be able to work properly again tomorrow.'

'You most certainly will not.' Flora wagged a stern finger at her. 'You're going to take it much easier from now on, miss! That doesn't mean to say that you can't come down and help out for short periods if you feel up to it, but your days of being on your feet all day are over, at least until well after the baby's arrived. Do you hear me? As it happens, Hattie has turned out to be a little treasure so we'll manage perfectly well.'

Jia Li sighed. She knew when she was beaten so she merely nodded in agreement.

Within two weeks Hattie had proved herself to be invaluable and all three girls had become very fond of her. She didn't seem to find it strange that three young women were running the place and didn't pry at all, for which they were all grateful. Hattie had taken a particular liking to Jia Li and fussed over her like a mother hen, insisting that she ate well, which neither Flora nor Colleen had been able to do.

'You're feeding that baby as well as yourself now,' she would tell Jia Li as she tempted her with tasty titbits and surprisingly Jia Li did as she was told.

One evening as Flora was helping her with the washing-up, she told her about the house next door that she had bought.

'Of course, it's going to be a long time before it's fit to be lived in,' Flora confided. 'Me and Colleen have scrubbed every inch of it from top to bottom but there are jobs that need doing that are beyond us, such as plastering and replacing the floorboards and I can't afford to get tradesmen in just yet. I was hoping to have it ready for when Jia Li has the baby but I can't see it happening now.'

'Then why don't you let me get my Ernie round to take a look

249

at it for you?' Hattie suggested. 'He can turn his hand to most things and I know he'd be a lot cheaper than bringing in tradesmen. He could only work at weekends when he wasn't busy at his regular job though.'

'Oh, would you? That would be so helpful. I'd be grateful for any little help he can give me.'

So the following evening as they were all preparing the café for breakfast the next morning, Ernie arrived. He was in his mid-twenties and looked very much like his mother with twinkling blue eyes, dark curly hair and a jolly smile, although unlike his mother, he spoke with a broad New York accent. Both Colleen and Flora took to him immediately and they wondered why some young lady hadn't snapped him up.

Flora fetched the key to the house next door then she, Ernie and Hattie went round there. Now that they had emptied all the rubbish out of it and given it a thorough clean it looked better already.

'Say, this ain't too bad at all,' Ernie assured her as he prodded the walls. 'I can soon patch up the walls where the plaster's come off and replacing the floorboards shouldn't take too much doing.'

'Really?' Flora gave a sigh of relief. Buying the place had taken almost every penny of the money she had managed to save and while she was still paying the rent on the café she couldn't afford to spend a lot on it.

'I'll tell you what I'll do,' he said. 'I'll order the stuff I need to be delivered and me and the guys will come round on Saturday to make a start on it. How does that sound?'

'It sounds wonderful,' Flora said tentatively with a grateful smile. 'But how much is all this going to cost?'

'Hey, don't worry,' he told her airily. 'Me an' the guys will work for next to nothin' so long as you feed us, and the stuff we'll need to do it will be real cheap, I promise. I've a buddy in the buildin' trade who'll let me have whatever I need cut price.'

Flora looked perplexed. 'But why would you do all that for us?'

He grinned. 'Cos my mom loves workin' with you an' you're good to her.'

'Then all I can say is thank you very much indeed,' Flora said.

Over the next few days bags of sand, cement, plaster, floorboards and everything else they might need were delivered and as promised Ernie and two of his friends – Jimmy and Sam – turned up bright and early on Saturday morning to start work. They could hear them banging and hammering through the wall of the café all day and the girls could hardly wait to see the end results. By Sunday evening, every inch of plaster throughout the house that needed replacing had been done.

'We'll get those floorboards done next weekend,' Ernie told them as he tucked in to a dish of Jia Li's curry. She was still spending a couple of hours a day in the kitchen to help Hattie out and looked much better now that she wasn't on her feet so much, although her belly was starting to look enormous. 'Then we'll fix up the windows an' doors if you get some paint. You'll be surprised how different they'll look when they're done.'

'Thank you all so much,' Flora told him and his friends. A mere thank you seemed so inadequate for all they'd done but they seemed happy enough with the arrangement.

'Ernie is such a lovely chap,' Flora commented to Hattie when they had gone. 'I'm shocked some young woman hasn't snapped him up by now.'

Hattie's face clouded. 'As it happens he *did* have a young lady and they were due to be married. Childhood sweethearts, they were. She was a nanny to the child of a posh family in Manhattan. They all went on holiday to London earlier in the year so they took her with 'em, but they were aboard the *Titanic* on the return voyage and none of them survived. Between you an' me, I don't know how our Ernie got through it. He was heartbroken. He loved the bones o' that girl, but there you are. These things happen.'

Flora's heart started to pound and beads of sweat stood out on her forehead but she didn't tell Hattie that she too had been aboard the ship. It was one of the things she was coming to love about Hattie, she never pried into any of their pasts and as yet none of them had confided in her.

'All I can say is he's been a star,' Flora told her sincerely. 'And we all appreciate so much what he and his friends are doing for us.'

'To tell the truth I think he's glad of somethin' to keep him occupied,' Hattie said sadly. 'Since he lost his girl he's never still for a minute apart from when he's sleepin'. I think he likes to keep himself occupied so he don't have too much time to dwell on things. But there you are. Folks deal wi' grief in their own way, I dare say. Bless him, he might put on a brave face but I reckon there ain't a minute goes by when he don't still think of her.'

Flora sighed. It just went to show, almost everyone had a cross to bear.

During the next weekend, Ernie and his friends between them replaced or repaired all the floors and the weekend after one of them set to whitewashing the walls while the other two began to repair the window frames and the doors and prepare them for painting.

'We should have it all ready for you to move into next weekend,' Ernie told them late on Sunday night as he and his team of helpers tucked into the supper Jia Li had prepared for them. She had been the one who frequently took them trays of tea and snacks while they were working and they had a soft spot for her now, not that Jia Li noticed. Her heart still belonged to Bai and always would.

Now that she wasn't working all the time she had finally started to venture out for a little fresh air, although she never went far. And then one afternoon her worst nightmare came true. She had

252

taken a stroll and was making her way back to the café when she saw a face that she had prayed she would never see again. Yung Huan was sauntering along the street towards her and her heart began to thud painfully as panic gripped her. For a second she froze but then spinning about so quickly that she almost lost her balance she hurried as fast as she could back the way she had come and slipped into the first alley she came to where she flattened herself against the wall and screwed her eyes tight shut, praying that he hadn't seen her. Her prayers went unanswered when a shadow fell across her.

'Well, well, so we meet again.'

Her eyes blinked open and she stared up into his sneering face.

'Why you run away?' He reached out and twisted a strand of her thick, silky hair around his hand and she flinched away from him. It was then that his eyes fell to her belly and the sneer was replaced by a look of absolute horror. He was due to marry a girl from a very wealthy Chinese family soon and if the child Jia Li was carrying was his it could scupper everything. Admittedly he didn't love his fiancée but Huan was bone idle and spoiled. Once the marriage had taken place he would be rich beyond his wildest dreams and never have to worry about working again. He stepped away from her as if she had the plague and stabbed a finger towards her belly. 'I hope you not try to say that *bastard* had anything to do with me!'

Jia Li stared at him fearfully. 'J-just go away.' Her mouth was suddenly so dry that she could barely get the words out.

But Huan didn't budge. His mind was working overtime. If she should take it into her head to speak to his mother he would be finished. She would have to be silenced. He drew himself to his full height and, grabbing her arm roughly, he began to shake her as a dog might shake a rat. He had just lifted his fist in order to punch her in the face when some men came into the alley. Jai Li turned her stricken, tear-stained face towards them and relief swept through her. It was Jimmy and Sam on their way home from work and they seemed to take in the situation at a glance.

'So what's goin' on here?' This was from Jimmy, the bigger of the two.

Huan silently cursed and stepped away from her as the two men approached.

'Nothing at all. Me and Jia Li just talking . . . we old friends.'

But Jimmy wasn't fooled. One look at Jia Li's terrified face told a different story. She was crying softly and now it was he who looked menacing.

'*Are* you now? Well, it so happens she's our friend too so let me tell you now if I so much as see you *look* at her again, let alone go near her, you'll be goin' for an underwater fuckin' swim in the Hudson? You *got* that?'

He was so close now that Huan could feel his breath on his cheek and, coward that he was, he paled as he backed away. Then he was running like the wind as Jimmy turned his attention back to Jia Li.

'Are you all right? Did he hurt you?' he asked gently but before she could answer Jia Li felt a warm surge between her legs and glancing down she saw that there was a puddle of water on the ground.

'I . . . I think the baby coming and it too soon.'

Jimmy quickly took one arm while Sam got the other. 'We'd best get you home,' he told her. 'I can turn me hands to most things but I don't reckon I'd be any good as a midwife.'

Jia Li was too terrified to even try to reply as they carefully began to walk her home.

Chapter Thirty-One

They had almost reached the café door when the first pain struck Jia Li. It was so unexpected and sharp that it took her breath away and she doubled over.

Panicking now, Jimmy sprinted ahead. 'Come quick,' he gasped as he flung the café door open.

Colleen was just serving a customer and looked up in surprise.

'It's Jia Li,' he told her, his face ashen. 'I think she's havin' the baby.'

His words echoed through to the kitchen and seconds later, Hattie, Flora and Colleen were all racing outside. Jia Li and Sam were almost at the door by then and Hattie took control of the situation immediately.

'Get her straight upstairs,' she barked at Jimmy. 'And you, Colleen – go and put some water on to boil. We'll need lots of it and towels.'

Then her voice gentled as she helped Jia Li inside, saying, 'Now, don't worry, dearie, everything will be fine.'

'Shall I run for a doctor?' Jimmy asked, as nervous as a father-to-be.

'Let me have a look at her and see how far on she is first,' Hattie answered. 'First babies usually take their time so she'll probably be hours yet.'

All the time she was talking she was leading Jia Li amongst the tables where customers were staring curiously.

'I'm going to close the café as soon as the last customer has gone then I'll be up to help you,' Flora promised. 'Meanwhile, Colleen will make sure you have everything you need.'

Jimmy and Sam hung about in case they were needed and Sam told Colleen what had happened. 'We found her trapped in an alley with a Chinese chap shoving her about. She seemed terrified and lord knows what he might have done to her if we hadn't happened by. I reckon it must be the shock of that that started the baby coming.' He was nervously puffing away on a cigarette as he spoke and Colleen's temper flared.

'I wouldn't mind betting it was Huan, the chap that raped her and got her into this situation,' she ground out as she placed a large kettle of water on the range to boil.

'*Raped* her?' Both Jimmy and Sam looked horrified.

Colleen nodded. 'Yes, he was the son of the owner of the laundry where we all worked at the time. He was always harassing one or other of the girls but his mother could see no wrong in him. After he'd raped Jia Li his mother sacked her so me and Flora left too and then we all came here. It would have been useless complaining to his mother, she would never have believed he was capable of doing any wrong.'

Jimmy and Sam exchanged a sly glance. 'Tell us where this laundry is. I reckon it's time we had a nice little chat with this guy. He needs teaching a lesson or two,' Sam said quietly.

'Oh *please*, don't go doing anything that will get you into trouble,' Colleen beseeched.

Sam winked at her. 'Don't worry about us, just tell us where we might find him.'

Colleen reluctantly gave them directions and after a brief low-voiced exchange, the two men hurried out of the door, leaving her staring anxiously after them. But for now, she needed to concentrate on helping Jia Li.

'How is she?' she asked Hattie as she carried the first bowl of hot water into the bedroom.

Hattie frowned. 'Let's just say this baby is impatient to put in an appearance.'

'But it's far too early,' Colleen fretted. 'Should I run for the doctor?'

'There won't be no time for that,' Hattie said gravely as she rolled her sleeves up and washed her hands in the water. Poor Jia Li was lying on the bed chewing on her lip in a valiant attempt to stop herself from screaming. 'Thankfully, I've delivered dozens of babies in me time so hopefully all will be well.'

Colleen let out a breath of relief. She dreaded to think what would have happened if Hattie hadn't been there.

Flora came scurrying in then having seen the last of the customers out of the café. Colleen quickly told her what had brought on the premature birth and Flora scowled. But then she and Colleen placed themselves at either side of the bed and let Jia Li cling to their hands as the contractions wracked her small frame.

'That's it,' Hattie encouraged as she wiped the sweat from the girl's brow. 'Just pant now then breathe through the next pain. Good girl . . . that's it, you're bein' so brave!'

At some point Colleen went back downstairs to fetch more hot water and when she came back she saw at a glance that things had rapidly moved on. Jia Li's chin was on her chest now and she was pushing with all her might.

'That's it, have a rest now,' Hattie soothed as the pain passed. 'And when the next pain comes don't push until I tell you.'

Tears of despair were rolling down Jia Li's face now as she panted and prayed for death to come and claim her. She felt as if she was being rent in two and didn't know how much more she could bear. She was also feeling unbearably guilty for hadn't she prayed every single day that she would lose this child? There was every chance she would do just that now. It was far too soon for it to be born and if it died it would be all her fault. She had never wanted it yet now that she knew it might die she finally realised

257

that it wasn't the baby's fault. The poor little soul had never asked to be born, all the fault lay with its father but she had no chance to dwell on these thoughts for as another contraction built, Jia Li could hold back the screams no longer and her anguished cries echoed around the little bedroom.

Flora was openly crying as she watched her friend's agony but all she could do was whisper soothing words of encouragement as Jia Li's face turned purple with effort as she struggled to push the child into the world.

'That's it, easy now,' Hattie told her as the pain subsided again. 'Do exactly as I tell you on the next one. I think I can see the baby's head.'

Flora quickly sponged Jia Li's forehead with cool water and smoothed the luxuriant, damp black hair from her brow but then another pain hit her and Jia Li's back arched from the bed.

'Come on now . . . *push* . . . *harder* . . . you can do it!' Hattie told her and with what little strength she had left, Jia Li gave one last tremendous effort and Hattie crowed triumphantly.

'That's it . . . I can *see* it . . . come on now, you're so close.'

From her place at Jia Li's side Flora watched a tiny head covered in thick black hair appear between Jia Li's legs and seconds later the rest of the child was delivered with a whoosh.

'It's a little girl,' Hattie shouted with delight but Jia Li was beyond hearing. She had fainted right away.

The baby was so tiny and beautiful that she took Flora's breath away but her delight turned to fear when she realised that she wasn't crying.

Hattie quickly cut the umbilical cord then lifting the infant she smacked its backside soundly as Flora anxiously looked on, secretly glad that Jia Li was unaware of what was going on. Still the child remained silent so now Hattie laid her on the end of the bed and after pinching the baby's nostrils together began to gently blow into her mouth. She seemed to go on forever as Flora held her

258

breath but finally, with tears in her eyes, Hattie rose and shook her head. She could do no more.

'Stillborn,' she said softly.

Tears sprang to Flora's eyes as she stared at the little form. She looked so perfect. Perhaps she had been too perfect to live?

'What shall we tell Jia Li?' Flora whimpered as Hattie turned to deal with the girl.

Hattie shrugged. 'The truth. It was just too soon for the baby to be born, the poor little mite.' She frowned as she noticed the bloodstains on the sheets.

'You'd best get Colleen to run for the doctor,' she ordered as she pressed a towel between Jia Li's legs to try and stop the flow of blood. 'Tell him the mother is haemorrhaging and to get here as fast as he knows how!'

Flora was gone like a shot just as Colleen came back into the room. Her breath caught in her throat as she saw what was going on but after taking a deep breath she said calmly, 'Oh sweet Holy Mother! What can I do to help?'

'Pray,' Hattie muttered. 'For there's only Him that can help her now!'

It was late that evening when Jia Li finally opened her eyes and the doctor declared that the worst was over.

'Oh, t'anks be to God!' Colleen muttered as she crossed herself. 'I t'ought we were goin' lose her for sure back there.'

Jia Li blinked and asked groggily, 'Have I had the baby?'

'Yes, love.' Flora squeezed her hand as tears sprang to her eyes. She just couldn't bring herself to tell Jia Li that the baby had not survived.

'Wh-what is it . . . a boy or a girl?'

Hattie stepped forward and told her gently, 'You had a little girl, but sadly she was born too soon and didn't survive. I'm so sorry, dearie. The poor little mite never even drew breath but at least she's in a better place now and she didn't suffer.'

Tears began to spill down the girl's face and soak into the pillow as she croaked, 'Where is she? I want to see her.'

Hattie crossed to the drawer where the baby lay, washed and dressed in the tiny clothes Flora had bought for her.

'She's right here,' Hattie said as she carried the babe to her mother and placed her in her arms. 'I wouldn't let the undertaker take her away until you'd seen her.'

Jia Li stared down into the face of her tiny daughter as a pain far worse than any she had endured during the birth stabbed at her like a knife.

'I'm so sorry, leetle one,' she said brokenly. 'I never wanted you and so this is my punishment.'

'Now that's quite enough o' that sort o' talk, miss,' Hattie scolded. 'If anyone's to blame it's the bloke that accosted you in the alley an' brought the birth on too soon.'

'It was Huan,' Jia Li said dully and Colleen and Flora glanced anxiously at each other. They hadn't had time to think of anything but Jia Li all afternoon but now they worried what might have happened if Jimmy and Sam had managed to find him.

'Right, now me an' the girls are goin' to go down an' make a nice cuppa while you say goodbye to your little one,' Hattie informed her and she ushered them all from the room. Both Colleen and Flora were softly crying and in that moment, Hattie realised just how very close the three girls were.

Once downstairs the doctor gave them a tired smile. 'She'll need lots of rest,' he told them, 'and good, nourishing food, as much as you can get down her, chicken soup and that sort of thing.'

'I'll see she gets it,' Hattie informed him. 'Thank you, doctor.'

He left then but soon after the undertaker arrived and Hattie went upstairs to fetch the tiny baby down to him. Gently prising her from her mother's arms was one of the worst things she had ever had to do and Hattie knew she would never forget the moan of agony that escaped from Jia Li's lips for the rest of her days.

Chapter Thirty-Two

It was a few nights after Jia Li had given birth to her stillborn daughter and Jimmy and Sam's patience was rewarded when they spotted Yung Huan sauntering along the road with his hands in his pockets, whistling merrily as if he didn't have a care in the world. They had been devastated when they heard that the little Chinese girl had lost her baby and ever since they had been out for revenge and had kept watch outside the laundry every night after work hoping for sight of him.

'That's him!' Jimmy said and Sam nodded.

'It certainly is an' I'm thinking it's time we taught him a lesson he won't forget in a hurry, what d'you say?'

Keeping close to the shadows they silently followed him, and soon he turned into a dark alleyway that led down to the docks.

'I bet he's headin' for the opium den,' Sam muttered.

'Then it's up to us to make sure the low-life bastard don't get there,' Jimmy muttered through gritted teeth.

They quickened their pace and when a heavy hand landed on Huan's shoulder and spun him about he almost jumped out of his skin and began to babble in Chinese.

'Not so brave when you're up against someone your own size, are you?' Sam growled as he landed the first punch. Huan fell heavily to the ground as they set about him, showing him no mercy. As far as they were concerned anyone who could harm a helpless woman deserved none. Huan cowered on the ground as kicks and punches rained down on him, and at one stage, he spat out a tooth. Suddenly, there was a sharp crack and Huan screamed in agony.

'That's enough,' Sam said breathlessly. 'We only want to teach him a lesson.' He took Jimmy's arm and both men faded into the shadows, leaving a whimpering Huan curled into a bloody ball on the cold ground.

Chapter Thirty-Three

'Brr, it's freezin' out, so it is,' Colleen groaned on a Sunday afternoon at the end of November as she pulled her gloves on. She was about to go and meet Will and wasn't looking forward to walking about in the cold at all.

'Why don't you bring him back here then?' Flora suggested for the umpteenth time.

'Haven't I tried to do just that a dozen times or more but he won't come near the place,' Colleen grumbled. She loved Will with all her heart and soul now but was a little concerned that their relationship was no further forward than it had been when she first met him back in July. She had told him from the start that she worked in a café with her two friends and all about her family back in Ireland but as yet he had still not told her anything about his own background whatsoever, which she was beginning to find a little worrying. Could it be that he was hiding something from her? she wondered.

Jia Li was still recovering from the birth of her baby, although at last she was growing a little stronger and appeared to be on the road to recovery. The doctor had told them that it would take some time because of all the blood she had lost and ten days on, Jai Li was still spending most of her time in bed.

Hattie had turned out to be a godsend to all of them and had helped to nurse Jia Li through the first terrible days as well as still

264

doing the lion's share of the cooking in the café. On top of that she had been helping Flora get the house next door ready to move into. Flora had bought some material which Hattie had sewn into curtains and they looked grand hanging at the newly painted windows. Ernie, Jimmy and Sam had done them proud and Flora couldn't wait to move in there.

'I wouldn't be surprised if it didn't snow soon,' Hattie grumbled once Colleen had gone to meet Will. She'd taken to going round and relaxing with them on a Sunday. As she pointed out to Flora, it was better than being in her own place all alone if Ernie had gone out and Jia Li was always glad of her company. She had become almost like a second mother to all of them now.

While Hattie and Flora sat contentedly sewing cushion covers for the chairs with the material that was left over from the curtains, Jia Li slipped into a doze.

'She's looking a bit better now, isn't she?' Flora commented, glancing at her sleeping friend.

Hattie nodded in agreement. 'She is so but she's still got a long way to go, I fear.'

Flora gave her a sly little look before lowering her voice and saying, 'None of the lads would tell us exactly what Sam and Jimmy did to Huan. Did Ernie say anything to you about it?'

Hattie sniffed before saying in a low voice, 'Let's just say, Jimmy and Sam don't think he'll be so keen to go about bullying innocent girls in the future. He got what was coming to him and that's all you need to know.'

Flora looked anxious. 'But what if he tells the police that Jimmy and Sam hurt him?'

'He doesn't know them from Adam and anyway, you don't think they'd have been daft enough to do anything in broad daylight do you? It was a few nights after he hurt Jia Li before he got his comeuppance. They followed him down a dark alley one night on his way to an opium den and taught him a lesson I doubt he'll forget.'

'I see.' Flora had little time to say more when the back door suddenly banged open so quickly that it slammed back against the wall and Colleen appeared all of a fluster. 'You'll never guess who I just bumped into,' she said gleefully, waving her hand behind her. 'I t'ought it was him, I never forget a face, so I took it upon meself to go an' have a talk to him an' here he is.'

A tall, dark young man appeared behind her and Flora too gasped. She hadn't forgotten him either even though they had only ever met the once.

'*Bai!*' Flora rushed across the room and hauled him inside as if she was afraid he might disappear again. 'Jia Li will be *so* thrilled to see you . . . we *all* are. Has Colleen told you what's happened?'

'She tell me everything,' he answered regretfully. 'But why Jai Li not tell me when I come see her before?'

'I don't know, we told her after you'd gone that she should have been honest with you. But anyway, she'll be awake soon. In fact, I'll go and wake her right now. I know she'd want me to. You can sit down here with her then and you can have a good talk. We can all go and sit upstairs so you can have some privacy.'

'Not me, I'm late for Will,' Colleen said with a twinkle in her eye. And then she was off again, she'd done her good deed for the day.

Flora meantime shot away up the stairs and appeared a few minutes later with Jia Li, who was looking very nervous.

Flora beckoned to Hattie and they discreetly left the room as Bai took a seat next to Jia Li and gently took her hand.

'Who is that?' Hattie whispered as Flora led her upstairs to the little sitting room there.

'It's Jia Li's young man, or at least he was.' Flora quickly told her all about why Jia Li had come to New York. She knew that

266

she could trust her now and when she'd finished the story, Hattie nodded.

'Eeh, let's hope it all works out for 'em this time then, eh? Did you see the way the lad looked at her? He still loves her, it was written all across his face.'

With broad smiles on their faces they were only too happy to make themselves scarce. It was time to give the two lovebirds downstairs some privacy.

Although Colleen was a little late she found Will standing on the dock where they always met patiently waiting for her. His hands were blue with cold and his nose was glowing red as she hurried up to him full of apologies.

'I'm so sorry I'm late,' she gushed breathlessly. 'But somethin' wonderful has happened, so it has! I was on my way to meet you when I bumped straight into Bai. He's Jia Li's – one of my friends – young man . . . or at least he was . . .' She hurried on to tell him all that had gone on and when she was done he shook his head.

'Do you know that's the first time you've ever mentioned either of your friends' names? You've talked about your family at home and why you left but you never told me anything about either of the girls you live with. I didn't know one of them was Chinese, or are they both Chinese?'

Colleen shook her head as she linked her arm through his and they began to amble along, trying to find somewhere they could get out of the wind. 'Not at all, the other one comes from England, and you could have met them be now had you taken up their invitation to come to tea.' Colleen had always been very discreet about both Jia Li and Flora because she knew they both wanted as few people as possible to know their whereabouts.

267

'Anyway. Let's just hope that Jia Li and Bai can sort themselves out.' She quickly drew him away from making any more enquiries about Flora. 'I told her from the start she should have been straight with him, so I did. I mean if she'd only been honest and told him the way the baby came about I've no doubt he'd have stood by her even if the poor little soul had lived. It's terrible sad, to be sure.'

Will nodded in agreement. It was a sad story, the sort his mother would have read about in one of the romance books she had been so fond of. He could only hope that Jia Li and Bai would find their happy ending now. He felt sad then as he peeped at Colleen out of the corner of his eye. The wind was whipping her glorious red hair into a tangle of curls and with her sparkling emerald eyes and her cheeks rosy he knew that he could never love another girl as he loved her. But what future lay ahead for them? How could he stay with her when he was nursing such a dark secret? And yet, on the other hand, how could he ever bring himself to leave her?

'Look, there's a tea shop open. Shall we go in out of the cold?'

Colleen's words brought his thoughts sharply back to the present and squeezing her hand he led her inside. It was there that she dropped her bombshell as she sat spooning sugar into the coffee he had bought for her and staring thoughtfully off into space.

'I've been t'inking . . .' She licked her lips, obviously nervous. 'That in the not too distant future I might go home to me mammy in Ireland.'

He was so shocked that he choked, causing some of the coffee from the cup he had been raising to his lips to slop all over the table.

'You've been thinking *what*?'

A guilty flush stained her cheeks. 'Well, the t'ing is, me mammy will find it hard to cope now me daddy has passed, so she will. Me little brothers will do what they can but I've no doubts the main o' the work will fall on her shoulders an' now me friends are doin' OK in the café an' they have Hattie to help 'em I could be a tremendous help to her.' She stared at him, silently willing him to tell her that he loved her and would come with her, but all he did was stare down at the coffee stain spreading across the table.

'I see,' he said eventually and disappointment spread through her veins like iced water as she was forced to admit to herself that perhaps she had been right. He wasn't as committed to her as she was to him. Yet still she clung to the hope that he might just be waiting for her to ask him, so taking a deep breath she went on tentatively, 'The ideal solution would be for me to take a good strappin' husband home w'it me who could do some o' the heavier jobs on the smallholdin'.'

When he continued to simply stare at the table she knew that all was lost and she felt as if her heart was breaking. 'Anyway.' She forced herself to go on. 'It's been nice knowin' you, but if I'm to be leavin' for Ireland soon there's no point in us meetin' again, is there?'

'I suppose not.' She was confused as he looked up and she saw what she thought was pain in his eyes but then her pride kicked in and she slowly rose.

'Goodbye then, Will. Have a good life. I shall t'ink of you often.' And with that she walked out of the tea shop without once looking back so she didn't see the tears on his cheeks as the door closed behind her.

Chapter Thirty-Four

As Colleen entered the kitchen shortly afterwards she found Bai and Jia Li sitting together at the kitchen table with their hands clasped, deep in conversation. They were so absorbed in each other that they didn't even notice her entrance as they jabbered away in their own language. Colleen smiled ruefully as she hurried on tiptoe towards the stairs. It seemed ironic that Jia Li's future was about to improve while her own dreams had just fallen apart, but she was happy for her all the same. After the hell she'd been put through over the last few months, no one deserved happiness more than Jai Li.

'Why, whatever is wrong, dear?' Hattie asked when Colleen entered the little upstairs sitting room a short time later. The girl's eyes were red and she looked as if she had the weight of the world on her shoulders.

Colleen sniffed and shook her head. 'Let's just say I forced Will's hand to see what his intentions towards me were and it didn't work out as I hoped, so I've finished it.'

Flora frowned. She knew how much Colleen thought of Will and realised that she must be hurting.

'I'm so sorry,' she said inadequately, but what more could she say?

'You come an' sit by the fire an' get warm while I go an' make you a nice cuppa, dear. Everythin' always looks better when you have a hot drink inside of you.' Hattie patted the seat beside her and went downstairs, leaving Colleen to stare miserably into the fire.

'So what will you do now?' Flora asked and the girl shrugged. She couldn't really think coherently of anything apart from the heartache she was suffering at the moment.

'I dare say I'll go back to Ireland to help me mammy on the smallholdin', but not until Jia Li is properly better, o' course,' she added quickly. 'Once she is, now you have Hattie I've no doubt you'll all rub along together a treat.'

Flora felt tears well in her own eyes. The three of them had become as close as sisters in the last months and she knew that she would miss her.

'But is there no chance that you and Will might patch things up?' she queried hopefully. 'Things seemed to be going so well between you. What went wrong?'

'I told him that I was t'inking o' going home to Ireland and more or less said that he'd be welcome to come w'it me, but he never even answered me. He just sat there starin' down at the table as if the cat had got his tongue.'

'Aw, I'm so sorry.' Flora quickly joined her on the settee and gave her a loving cuddle. 'I know how much you thought of him.'

Colleen shrugged. 'That's life, ain't it? But there's plenty more fish in the sea.'

Despite her brave words, Flora could read her like a book and knew how much she was hurting, but sadly she had no idea how she could make things better so she wisely remained silent. Soon after Hattie puffed her way up the stairs with the loaded tea tray.

'At least those two down there seem to be back on the right track,' she said, placing the tray down on the table. 'But now what are we going to do about you and your young man, eh, miss?' She raised an eyebrow at Colleen, who sniffed.

271

'There's not'ing to be done so let's not talk about it anymore, eh?'

'If you say so, dearie.' Hattie exchanged a glance with Flora and for the next little while they all studiously avoiding mentioning Will as they drank their tea and spoke of other things. After a while Hattie took the newspaper she had fetched from home and started reading while Flora sat sewing some pillowcases for the new house, giving Colleen a good excuse to escape to the bedroom.

'Poor love,' Hattie sighed when she'd gone. 'We'd best go gently with her for the next few days. I think she's taken this really badly an' she's just puttin' a brave face on things.'

Flora nodded in agreement but just then something in the paper caught Hattie's eye and she drew it closer, peering at it through the little steel-rimmed spectacles perched on the end of her nose.

'Well, I'll be . . . Looks like that terror of a boy's got engaged.'

Flora looked at her questioningly. 'What boy?'

'Oh, years ago I worked in the kitchens for a rich family, the Johnsons, when the boys were little and times was hard. Their boy, Tobias, was always causin' trouble to the mistress and playin' tricks on us as worked there. Needed a good hidin', I always thought. Anyway, says here he's got engaged. I heard on the grapevine that young Toby hadn't improved with age, what with gambling and what not. Still, I dare say the love of a good woman will put him back on track.'

Flora swallowed painfully. Was this a coincidence or was Hattie speaking of the Toby she had met aboard the *Titanic*?

'So who has he got engaged to?' she asked innocently as Hattie continued to read.

'Hmm, she's a Miss Margaret Ward, the daughter of Mr Magnus and Mrs Alexandra Ward of Manhattan.'

Flora was so shocked that she almost dropped her sewing, although she managed to remain outwardly calm. *Margaret and Toby!* They were the most mismatched couple that Flora could

272

ever have dreamed of and she knew for sure that Margaret was nothing like the women Toby favoured. She could only imagine that he was marrying Margaret for her money. It was just the sort of thing he would do as he had no morals whatsoever. She could almost have felt sorry for Margaret in that moment but as she thought of the despicable way the young woman had treated her and Alex, she felt a little spiteful thrill. Toby and Margaret deserved each other, so let them get on with it. It was hardly going to be a marriage made in heaven that was for sure!

Hattie went down to the kitchen soon after, saying she wanted to prepare some stew for the following day, but Flora sat on alone. Seeing Jai Li reunited with her Bai made her wonder what might happen if she ever saw Jamie again. Would he be as happy to see her as Bai had been to see Jai Li? What would he be doing now? she wondered, and a wave of homesickness swept over her. She almost envied Colleen who would soon be returning to the fold of her own family and suddenly the future stretched ahead of her cold and empty. *Stop feeling so sorry for yourself!* she scolded herself and then tried to concentrate on her sewing again but it was useless. Her concentration was gone so she did what she always did when she was feeling stressed, and sat down to write another letter to Jamie. It would probably never be posted but it made her feel a little closer to him.

Dear Jamie,

Once again my life is about to change as Colleen has just informed me that she will now be going home to her family in Ireland. I am pleased for her but I will miss her so much, we have grown close during the time we have lived and worked together. Sadly her young man has just let her down and I think that is why she has reached the decision to go.

On a happier note, Bai is back in Jai Li's life and I hope it will stay that way, they clearly love each other very much and

273

she is due some happiness after the heartbreak of losing the baby. Hattie, our new employee, has turned out to be a godsend and we wonder what we would do without her now. She came into our lives at a time when we really needed her and so that was a blessing.

I am feeling very lonely at the moment, Jamie. It's funny, isn't it, how you can be surrounded by people but if the person you really want most is not amongst them you still feel alone. I wonder what you are doing now? Do you ever think of me? Whatever you do and wherever you are, I pray that you are safe and well,

With my love always

Flora xxx

With a sigh she rose and hid the letter beneath a plant pot on the shelf. She couldn't go into the bedroom yet because she didn't want to disturb Colleen who obviously needed some time to herself, and she couldn't go down to the kitchen because she didn't want to play gooseberry to Jia Li and Bai, so she sat on in the glow of the fire as the shadows in the room lengthened and the afternoon turned to early evening, and she thought of her family and Jamie so very far away.

It was Jia Li gently shaking her arm some time later that brought Flora's eyes blinking open. She yawned and stretched her arms above her head before saying, 'Sorry, I must have dozed off.' Then she looked at her friend and smiled. The girl's eyes were shining like stars and the haunted look that had been in them since Huan had attacked her was finally gone.

'Me and Bai, we going to get married,' Jia Li shyly informed her and Flora couldn't have been more thrilled at the news. The way she saw it, it was long overdue. Jia Li had gone through so much over the last months but now hopefully things were starting to go right for her.

'Why, that's wonderful news!' She beamed. 'How lucky it was

that Colleen bumped into him like that! It was obviously meant to be.'

Jia Li nodded enthusiastically. 'This time I be very honest with him about what happened with baby,' she told Flora solemnly. 'And Bai say I bad for not telling him the truth before . . . but he forgive me. So now we save and when we have enough money for somewhere to live we get married.'

An idea occurred to Flora and she grinned. 'Why don't you and Bai have these two rooms? Me and Colleen will be moving in next door any day now and these will be standing empty. Think about it, it would save you having to rent somewhere and if three of us have managed up here I'm sure you two could.'

Jia Li looked around the room with new eyes as she tried to imagine living there with Bai then she nodded enthusiastically. 'You right, we be very happy here and you and Colleen only be next door.'

'Hmm, well we will be for a short time.' Flora told her about what had happened with Will.

'Ah, my poor friend. That very bad,' she said regretfully. 'I think she love him very much. He a fool. But we miss her so much when she go back to Ireland – yes?'

'Yes, we will,' Flora agreed. 'But I can understand her wanting to go. She misses her family and the place she was born. I do too.'

Seeing the faraway look in Flora's eyes, Jia Li was shocked. Flora was usually so determined and strong, it was rarely she saw this vulnerable side of her.

'You miss young man back home too, yes?'

Flora nodded. 'Yes, but that's all in the past. He probably has another girl now. Hopefully one who appreciates him and deserves him. I certainly didn't and I didn't even think about how unreasonable I was being when I decided to come to New York. I just expected him to wait for me without question. How vain is that, eh? Serves me right that he dropped me like a hot potato.'

Jia Li stared at her curiously for a moment before suggesting, 'But you *could* go back and find him. Even if he not want you anymore, at least you try.'

'We'll see. For now, I'm just going to concentrate on moving into next door and then by the sounds of it we have a wedding to plan.' Flora hoisted herself out of the chair and grinned. There was no point wallowing in self-pity. 'Wait till we tell Hattie your good news! She'll be tickled pink.' And arm in arm they went back down to the kitchen together.

Hattie was indeed delighted when Jia Li told her about the forthcoming wedding and instantly went into a tizzy. 'We shall have to get you a new dress . . . and of course some flowers. Oh, and we could perhaps have a little party here for you afterwards, what do you think, girls?'

'I think that fine idea but there not be many guests. I mean apart from you, Ernie, Jimmy and Sam,' Jia Li pointed out.

'It doesn't mean to say we can't make a bit of an occasion of it,' Hattie insisted but Jia Li shook her head.

'We just want very quiet wedding at town hall. We no want any fuss.'

'Whether you want it or not, my girl, I intend to make the day special,' Hattie told her with determination. 'And we'll start by going and getting some material and looking at patterns for your dress.'

'I shall have blue dress,' Jia Li said thoughtfully. 'Blue the colour of the sea, but not too much money.'

'And I shall make it. As you know I'm quite a dab hand with a needle and cotton,' Hattie told her.

Colleen, who had come downstairs at the sound of Hattie's loud excitement, smiled. Even though her own heart felt as if it was breaking in two she was so pleased that Jia Li and Bai had finally come together, it was clear they were made for each other.

Over the following days, Bai called into the café each day and they had all taken to him, especially as he had told them that he would still have married Jia Li even if the baby had lived. He endeared himself even further when they realised that, thanks to his days working as a chef, he was a dab hand at cooking too, and now each night he was happy to help Jia Li prepare the food for the next day, so all in all things were working out beautifully.

Chapter Thirty-Five

Not bad, even if I do say so myself, Flora thought the following Sunday as she stared around the living room in the new house. Jimmy, Sam and Ernie had been carrying the furniture from the rooms above the café into the new abode all day and now that everything was in place it was beginning to look like home. The curtains that Hattie had stitched were hanging at the gleaming little windows and a cosy fire was burning in the grate after one of Sam's friends had kindly come round to sweep the chimneys for them. A brightly coloured rag rug lay in front of the hearth and the brass fire irons gleamed in the glow from the flames. The second-hand sideboard had been polished till Flora could see her face in it and upstairs, Colleen and Jia Li were busily making the beds up. They would have a bedroom each now, luxury indeed after being used to being crammed into one room. Hattie and Bai were there too sorting out the kitchen as Flora plumped up the cushions on the sofa. At last everything was done and all their things were put away so Hattie pottered off to the kitchen to make them all a nice hot drink and some sandwiches as they hadn't had time to cook that day.

'I don't know how I shall ever be able to thank you,' Flora told Ernie, Jimmy and Sam sincerely. 'You've all worked so hard. We could never have done this without you.'

'Hey, no problem, we've had a blast. Just give us a free meal whenever we come by and we'll be happy,' Ernie told her with a grin. In actual fact he'd quite enjoyed transforming the little house. It now sported a newly painted red front door that boasted a shiny brass knocker and all the window frames had been painted white, giving the house a whole new appearance.

'That goes without saying,' Flora promised him and wondered why she wasn't feeling more thrilled. After all, she owned her own house now, albeit a very cheap one, and she ran a very successful café, yet as Christmas approached the yearning to see her family again grew stronger by the day.

'So why don't you just go home for a visit?' Hattie had suggested a few days before when Flora had admitted to her that she was feeling homesick. 'Me an' the others are more than capable of keepin' the café going.'

As tempting as the thought was, Flora shook her head, although she didn't tell Hattie why. *How could I ever go home now after what I've done?* she asked herself daily and the answer was always the same. *You can't! You've let everyone down and there could be repercussions even now.* And then, of course, going home would involve a sea voyage and she wasn't sure she'd ever be able to set foot aboard another ship as long as she lived. Every moment of that terrible night on the *Titanic* was etched into her memory and she still had recurring nightmares about it.

Hattie appeared from the kitchen then carrying a huge tray and everyone found a seat, some of them on the floor because there weren't enough chairs.

'I reckon you'll be really comfy in here,' Hattie said as she glanced around at all their hard work. 'I could quite happily live here meself now, though I'd never have said that when you first bought the place. I was worried that you'd bought a pig in a poke but everything's turned out fine and dandy.'

Jia Li and Bai didn't even hear her. They were sitting in the

279

corner jabbering away to each other, oblivious of everyone else in the room, which was just as Hattie thought it should be.

Colleen was sitting with her legs curled under her in one of the old wing chairs, staring off into space, and as Hattie glanced at her the smile slid from her face. Poor girl, she was clearly still heartbroken over her Will, and Hattie just wished she could get her hands on him for two minutes. She'd show him what for, all right, for breaking the poor girl's heart. And then there was Flora. Oh, she always put a brave face on, and almost worked herself into the ground on a daily basis. But why? Hattie wondered. What was it she was hiding or running away from that made her push herself to the limits? She actually knew very little about how Flora had ended up in New York, but she hoped that one day Flora would trust her enough to confide in her. There was obviously something niggling away at her. Meantime Jia Li's wedding was drawing dangerously close so, looking towards the girl, she said, 'I hate to interrupt you lovebirds but I was thinking that now we've got you all safely moved into here we should be going into town tomorrow, Jia Li, to get the material for your wedding dress. We've less than two weeks to go to the wedding so if you want me to make it we have to get our skates on.'

Jia Li blushed prettily as Bai took some money from his trouser pocket and pressed it into her hand. 'Buy what you need,' he urged but Jia Li shook her head.

'You not need give me money. Flora pay me wage each week and I have my own.'

'No matter, we use what money we have between us to furnish rooms above the café,' Bai insisted kindly so the girl reluctantly slid the little wad of dollars into her pocket.

'How about we slip off after the dinnertime rush?' Hattie suggested.

Flora nodded. 'That will be fine and take as long as you need to, don't rush. Me and Colleen will manage.'

280

When Hattie and the men finally departed, Colleen went up to sleep in her new bedroom for the first time while Flora slipped round to the café to make sure that everywhere was securely locked up. Jia Li and Bai were still snuggling on the sofa and chattering quietly to each other when she got back so after wishing them both goodnight she too retired to bed and fell asleep almost as soon as her head hit the pillow. For the last few weeks she had barely had a second to herself. If she hadn't been working in the café she had been working on the house but now, hopefully, things would slow down a little and she'd have a bit more time to herself.

As planned, Hattie and Jia Li left after lunch the next day and set off for the shops. Once there Jia Li looked through bolts of material until she found just what she was looking for.

'This perfect!' She held the soft, sea-blue satin out for Hattie's inspection and when she nodded, Jia Li sighed with pleasure as she stroked the silky folds.

'So what sort o' pattern were you thinkin' of?' Hattie enquired as they stood waiting while the material was carefully cut and wrapped.

'Very plain.'

Hattie sighed with disappointment but didn't argue. It was Jia Li's special day after all and not hers.

'To my ankle, split in one side to knee, small mandarin collar and short sleeves.'

'But you'll freeze to death!' Hattie objected, ever practical. Jia Li giggled, all her former sparkle restored. Admittedly she still had times when she thought of the poor, innocent baby who had come too soon, but having Bai back in her life had gone a long way to helping her recover from the ordeal. 'I wear shawl,' she

281

said, and Hattie sighed as Jia Li paid the shop assistant for the material.

Just two weeks before Christmas, Jia Li and Bai were married at a small ceremony in the register office. There were few guests, just Flora, Colleen, Hattie, Ernie, Jimmy and Sam but they all agreed that the bride looked radiant and the groom was so proud, he looked as if he might burst with happiness. The dress that Hattie had painstakingly stitched for Jia Li, working long into the night by the light of an oil lamp, was a triumph, despite Hattie's former reservations. The simple shape moulded itself to Jia Li's slim figure and with a white rose behind her ear that matched the tiny posy she carried, she looked simply stunning.

When the short service was over they all stood outside on the steps and the small congregation showered the happy couple with rice and rose petals, then it was back to the café for the sumptuous feast that Flora had laid on for them. There was even a wedding cake that Colleen had iced and decorated with sugar flowers and the café rang with laughter. Even Colleen seemed to come out of the melancholy mood she had slipped into since her break-up with Will.

'Eeh, isn't she just the *most* beautiful bride you ever did see?' she whispered dreamily to Flora as she sipped at some champagne that Flora had bought as a special treat.

Ernie made a toast to the happy couple and wished them well for the future, which brought a tear to Jia Li's eyes as she stared at her handsome new husband.

Looking at her friend's radiant face, Flora had to swallow down her tears as she pictured Jamie as he had looked on the day she had told him of her decision to go to New York with Connie. It all seemed so long ago now and so much had happened since then but she still only had to close her eyes and she could picture every inch of his face as if she had seen him only the day before. *I've been such a fool*, she silently chided herself, *perhaps we could have been married by now too if I hadn't been so foolish*. Then she plastered a smile back on her face. Today was Jia Li's special day and she was determined that nothing should spoil it.

Over the last two weeks, since they had all moved into their new home next door, Bai had been busily buying bits and pieces of furniture for their rooms above the café, which he had carted there on a barrow each night after work, and tonight they would sleep up there as man and wife for the first time.

'Wow! What a day,' Ernie commented cheerily later in the afternoon when he and his friends spilled out into the yard to have a cigarette. Flora had gone to join them to get a breath of fresh air and she nodded.

'It's been lovely.'

The young men glanced at each other then as if there was something they wanted to say and it was Ernie who finally broke the silence when he lowered his voice to tell her, 'Hey, Flora, I thought you might like to know that Huan got his comeuppance in more than one way.'

Flora frowned as she wrapped her arms about herself. 'What do you mean?'

'Well, after we gave him a bit of a lesson our sources' – he tapped his nose – 'tell us that he's off to China as soon as he gets married. Seems his mom thinks he'll be safer over there. So it's a great outcome, wouldn't you say? Jia Li will never have to worry about bumping into him again, although word is he ain't very happy about it.' He chuckled as he dropped his cigarette butt and ground it out with the heel of his shoe. 'He won't be able to get up to his tricks over there with his in-laws breathing down his neck, will he? All the bad things he's done to Jia Li and other innocent girls have come back to bite him on the ass. And about time.'

Flora's face creased into a smile. It was good news indeed. Now Jia Li wouldn't have to be afraid every time she stepped out of the door.

'I'll tell her, but not today,' she told the men. 'Today is one that she'll hopefully remember for the rest of her life and I don't want Huan's name tainting it. But thank you all again for looking out for her, and for me and Colleen.'

The men brushed aside her thanks with cheery grins and then went back inside to continue with the celebrations. Flora stayed outside a moment longer. Mention of Huan had for some reason brought back thoughts of Toby. The date of his wedding in January had been announced in the newspaper the week before, so it seemed within a matter of weeks, he and Margaret would be married. She smiled to herself. It was fairly safe to think that he was about to get his just deserts too. As was Margaret.

It was quite late by the time Hattie and the men left, and once the door had shut behind them, Colleen turned to Jia Li and Bai and said, 'You two lovebirds get yourself away to your rooms. Sure, me an' Flora can clear up down here.'

Jia Li looked uncertain. There were plates and glasses every-where but neither Flora nor Colleen would hear of her helping them.

'Go on now, get off with the pair of you.' Flora shooed them towards the staircase. 'You can both have a nice lie-in tomorrow with it being Sunday. I know I certainly will. In fact, I think I might get myself round home now. This lot will wait till morning. Come on, Colleen.' She gave Colleen a sly wink and they quickly headed for the door.

'You're quite right, the dirty pots can wait,' she said chirpily. 'Night both!'

At the door she and Flora glanced back to see Bai sweep his new bride into his arms as if she weighed no more than a feather and disappear up the stairs with her. They had eyes for no one but each other and Colleen and Flora smiled wistfully at each other.

'I don't think we'll have to worry about her anymore,' Flora remarked as she unlocked the door to their new home. With an envious sigh, Colleen agreed. At least one of them had ended up with the man she loved!

Chapter Thirty-Six

Just before Christmas it was decided that Hattie and Ernie would join the girls for Christmas dinner at the café. It would be easier for them all to eat in there because of the seating and soon Colleen was busily baking mince pies. She also had a Christmas pudding soaking in brandy and was determined to do them all a traditional Christmas dinner.

'I've ordered us a nice fat goose from t'e butchers,' she told them the day before Christmas Eve. 'And I've to pick it up tomorrow. But I'll not be volunteering to pluck it though, ugh!'

Hattie frowned. 'But what can I bring? I don't want to leave everything to you girls.'

'Just bring yourselves,' Flora told her with a warm smile. 'We don't know what we would have done without you and Ernie these last months. Giving you Christmas dinner is the least we can do.'

But Hattie wasn't happy. 'In that case if you don't want me to cook anything I'll bring us a couple of nice bottles of wine.'

Later that evening as Flora cleaned the café, she couldn't help but feel sad. This would be the first Christmas she had ever spent away from her family and her thoughts flew back to Christmas Eve the year before when Jamie had presented her with a little silver locket before leaving London on Christmas Eve to spend Christmas Day with his family back in Nuneaton. Sadly, it had been lost when the *Titanic* went down and now she bitterly regretted that she hadn't worn it all the time. She pictured her little brother Timmy, creeping downstairs in the early hours of the morning to peep beneath the tree and into the stocking his mother would have hung on the mantelshelf to see what Santa had left for him and her eyes welled with tears. She wondered who would find the shiny silver sixpence her mother always hid in the Christmas pudding. Her hands became still as she leaned on the table she had been wiping and let her thoughts drift further back to Christmases gone by.

She started when a voice suddenly asked, 'Why you so sad, Flora?'

'Oh! . . . Jia Li, I didn't see you there.' Flora smiled apologetically. 'I was just thinking about my family. I've never been away from them at Christmas before and I suppose I'm feeling a little homesick.'

Jia Li frowned as she sat down and stared at her friend thoughtfully.

'Perhaps it time you go to see them?' she suggested but Flora shook her head. Despite what her mother had told her in her letter she was still afraid of what repercussions she might face for impersonating Connie.

'No.' Her voice was weighed with sadness. 'I have to make my life here now.'

'And if that what you decide it will be good life,' Jia Li pointed out as she spread her hands to encompass the thriving little business that Flora had created. Only that week Flora had put a large amount of money away towards buying the café . . . and yet she found no joy in her achievement. Her biggest concern had been that once the bad weather set in her customers might dwindle but it had been quite the opposite.

It seemed that the inclement weather made people more determined than ever to come in for a warm drink and every night now it was all they could all do to keep up with the demands for Hattie's delicious chicken casseroles and stews and Jia Li's mouth-watering curries. Women from the surrounding factories and warehouses poured in each evening with dishes big enough to feed their families, to the point that Flora was seriously considering taking on yet another member of staff to help them keep up with demand.

Flora looked over at Jia Li. Her friend's eyes were sparkling and it pushed the gloomy thoughts from her mind. It was good to see her looking so content and she had a feeling that things would go well for her now, she certainly deserved them to. She just wished she could say the same for Colleen who was clearly still smarting over her break with her boyfriend. She put a brave face on things, but Flora had come upon her softly crying the other day and she wished she could take her pain away. But only time would do that and for now, they had Christmas to look forward to and she was determined that she would make the best of it.

The following day was Christmas Eve and Flora had decided that the café would not open again until the day after Boxing Day. Colleen went out to collect the goose and she also brought home a Christmas tree that Bai planted in a sturdy bucket of earth for them. It was given pride of place in the corner of the café and when they weren't preparing the Christmas dinner Colleen and Jia Li spent every spare minute cutting out colourful crepe paper so they could adorn it with little streamers. In the meantime, Bai plucked the fat goose while Hattie set to making her secret stuffing recipe and Colleen cooked yet another batch of mince pies and prepared the vegetables.

They had all bought each other small gifts and before they went to bed on Christmas Eve they placed them beneath the tree ready for opening on Christmas morning. It had started to snow heavily during the afternoon and that evening as Flora peeped out of the window she was shocked to see how deep it already was.

Everywhere looked sparkling clean as if some great unseen hand had painted the world white. The dusty, dirty streets were transformed but despite how pretty it looked Flora just hoped that Hattie and Ernie would be able to get there the next day.

She woke up the next morning to an eerie grey light and crossing to the window she drew aside the curtains to find the inside of the window frosted over with a lacy pattern. Breathing on a small corner of the glass she rubbed at it with the sleeve of her nightgown until a small part of it had melted, then she peered through it to the street below. The snow was still falling with no sign of stopping and lay crisp and deep on the strangely quiet streets. Usually the sounds that echoed from the docks and the tramp of people's feet as they made their way to work woke her each morning but today she could have been the only person left on the earth.

A little bubble of excitement began to grow in her stomach as she dragged her dressing gown on and went to bang on Colleen's bedroom door.

'Come on, sleepyhead. It's Christmas Day and if you don't get up now you won't have time for a cup of tea before you have to go to church.'

Colleen had told her the evening before that she wanted to attend mass the following morning but she was concerned about leaving everyone else to cook the Christmas dinner.

'Don't be silly,' Flora had told her with a broad grin. 'Everything's prepared so we've only got to pop it into the oven. You go, we'll be fine.'

Colleen and Flora made their way downstairs and Flora put the kettle on the hob.

'Do you think you'll be able to get to church through this lot?' Flora asked dubiously as she peered through the window.

Colleen laughed. 'Sure I will.' The kettle began to sing on the hob then and she hurried over to warm the stout brown earthenware teapot before she made the tea. Soon after, all done up in her Sunday best, Colleen set off, leaving Flora to get ready at her leisure.

By the time Hattie and Ernie arrived and Colleen had returned from church, Jai Li and Flora had the meal cooking and the café was filled with the delicious smell of roasting goose, so they all sat down to open their gifts. Outside the snow continued to fall but inside all was warm and cosy and the room was filled with laughter. And if Colleen and Flora were thinking of their families far away they hid it well. Christmas dinner was a jovial affair, and when they'd all eaten as much as they could, they sat back, happy and replete.

'Oh, I think I not eat again for a hundred years,' Bai groaned as he clutched his full stomach.

Jia Li giggled as she stared at her husband adoringly. 'It serve you right, you eat too much,' she teased and Bai couldn't argue with that, but it had been so tasty that he'd had second helpings of almost everything.

At that point, Ernie brought out his mouth organ and played Christmas carols while they all sang along.

'I'd like to raish a toast,' Hattie slurred some time later. She'd had rather too many glasses of wine and was feeling quite merry. 'To the newlywedsh! May this be the firsht of many happy Chrishmashes they spend together.'

Everyone raised their glasses and as Flora looked around at their smiling faces she thought how lucky she was that fate had brought them all together. Part of her was still far away with those she loved in England but the people gathered in this room had come to mean a great deal to her too.

'What shall we do for the New Year?' Colleen asked the next day. She and Flora were curled up at either end of their sofa in front of a roaring fire. Outside the snow was still falling but they felt safe and warm. 'I thought we might go to see a show or something?'

Flora instantly felt nervous. She still never liked to venture far for fear of bumping into Alex or Toby.

'Oh, I shall be quite happy to just spend it quietly here, but you could go out,' she answered.

'But that wouldn't be much fun on me own, now, would it? You know what they say, Flora, all work and no play makes Jack a dull boy!' But then seeing the nervous look on her face, she said quickly, 'But I dare say there are t'ings we could do here. We could have a game o' cards, if you like. I promised to teach you how to play patience, did I not?'

'You did,' Flora agreed.

And so, once the last of the customers had left the café on New Year's Eve, Flora and Colleen stayed safely within their own four walls to see the New Year in, each hoping that it would be a good one for all of them.

As the clock chimed midnight, Flora closed her eyes tight and wished that sometime soon she might be reunited with Jamie and her family, although she feared deep down that there was very little chance of the wish ever coming true. But still, it didn't hurt to dream!

Chapter Thirty-Seven

The bad weather continued into January but both Colleen and Flora received letters from home which cheered them considerably.

The first to arrive was one from Flora's mother and when she recognised the handwriting she tore the envelope open eagerly and read it immediately.

My dear Flora,

How can I even begin to tell you how much we all missed you at Christmas? We set your place at the table as if that would somehow make you magically appear but of course it didn't. Even so I hope it was a happy time for you. The weather here is appalling, I dare say it is the same where you are? We have had thick snow and everyone is feeling the cold. Timmy's school has been closed for the time being because they can't get it warm and he is miserable not being able to see his friends but then I suppose I shouldn't complain, there are always those so much worse off than us.

When are you coming home, sweetheart? We all miss you so much! Not a day goes by when we don't think of you so please give it some serious thought. I would like to wish you a Happy New Year and tell you that my dearest wish is to see you back home again.

Flora was sorely tempted to just hop on the first boat bound for England and do what her mother begged, for although she had now built a very thriving business she still missed her family terribly and lived in fear of what might happen to her if Margaret or Toby were to discover her whereabouts and report her to the police. In truth, she didn't really think the mild-mannered Alex would ever do that. The woman was kind and forgiving but she knew that Margaret, Magnus, and Toby were all more than capable of doing it so she continued to keep a low profile.

Colleen's letter informed her that her mother had been unwell and her younger brother Patrick was now having to manage most of the jobs on and around their little smallholding by himself. Initially, Colleen was just thrilled to hear from her family again but then she began to worry once more about how they would be coping and Flora had the feeling that it wouldn't be long before her dear friend decided to return home for good. Now that she no longer had Will in her life and her father wasn't a threat to her there was nothing to really hold her there. Flora knew that she would miss her desperately should she go, but she also wanted what was best for her. Even so they all continued to work diligently and as the trade continued to grow Hattie recommended Tilly, a young girl she knew, to come in each day to do the more mundane jobs such as washing up and clearing the tables so that they could concentrate on the cooking and serving the customers.

'She's a little godsend,' Flora whispered to Hattie the day after they had set Tilly on. As fast as she cleared the sink of dirty pots, it filled up again but she never complained and always had a smile on her face.

'Between you an' me I reckon her mom is just glad that we've

293

found her a job,' Hattie whispered back. 'You may have noticed that the poor girl is . . . what can I say? . . . a little bit slow? An' it's doubtful anyone else would have given her a chance.'

'Well, slow or not she's not afraid of hard work,' Flora said as she smiled at the girl. In actual fact Tilly reminded her a lot in looks of Jia Li. Her skin was much lighter, admittedly, but she had the same long, thick, silky curtain of black hair as Jia Li did and they were of a very similar petite build. On a couple of occasions, she had actually called her Jia Li and not realised her mistake until the girl had turned around.

Now Flora watched her as she diligently wiped down the table that someone had just vacated. Whenever she wasn't busy at the sink she simply found herself something else to do. Sometimes she would mop the floors, which seemed to be continually dirty during the winter months, or she would wash out the tea towels and drape them across the lines suspended from the kitchen ceiling to dry. It was always hot in there so they tended to dry in no time. All in all, Flora suspected the girl would prove to be worth every penny of the wages she would pay her and couldn't thank Hattie enough for recommending her.

After being there for a week Tilly became useful in other ways too. They soon discovered she was very good at running errands providing they gave her the correct money and wrote down exactly what they wanted her to get. She followed the instructions to the letter, and always came back with the right change.

'Her mom was tellin' me how much young Tilly loves workin' here,' Hattie told Flora one morning when the breakfast rush was over and they were preparing for the customers who called in for mid-morning coffee and home-made cookies – one of the first things she'd discovered when she opened the café was that the Americans were big coffee drinkers. 'Her parents are lovely people, at one time they were encouraged to put her in a home because she's . . . well, not quite all there up top, if you know what I mean?

But they wouldn't hear of it. I bet they're glad they didn't now. She's grown into a lovely young lady, ain't she?'

'Exactly how old is she?' Flora queried.

Hattie screwed up her nose as she tried to think. 'She'd be about eighteen or nineteen now, I reckon.' The door to the café opened just then and another customer came in so Hattie hurried away to serve her as Flora went through to the kitchen to see what needed doing there. Between them they had the café running like clockwork and Flora prided herself on what a good team they made.

Later that day, Flora sent Colleen home early. She had been coming down with a bad cough and cold for days but today she looked particularly poorly so Flora told her sternly, 'Get yourself round home now and into bed with a hot water bottle. You're no good here coughing and spluttering all over the customers, are you?'

It went some way to showing just how poorly Colleen felt when she didn't put up an argument. 'All right then, if you're sure you can manage,' she croaked, mopping at her streaming eyes.

'Go on, get away with you now.' Hattie shooed her towards the door. 'I'll get young Tilly to fetch you round a nice warm glass of honey and lemon in a while. There's nothing like it for a cold but see as you drink it while it's still hot mind.'

Colleen shuffled away feeling mortally sorry for herself and for a while they were run off their feet again as customers wanting to get out of the bitter cold for a warming drink streamed in.

Over the next couple of days, Colleen's cold turned to bronchitis so Flora confined her to bed indefinitely.

'But who'll do all the chasin' about?' Colleen mithered.

'Don't you worry about that. You're not indispensable you know,' Flora teased. She had popped round to the house during a lull with a tray of tea for the patient. 'As it happens, right at this minute Hattie is writing a list of things we need and Tilly will be going to get them. She does very well so long as we explain exactly where she's to go, so you just concentrate on getting better, eh?'

With a sigh, Colleen settled back against the pillows as Flora placed the tray in her lap and hurried back to work.

'Has Tilly gone?' she asked as she entered the café and Hattie nodded.

'Yes, but she shouldn't be long. I've sent her to the butcher's to get some bacon and sausages for the morning. We seem to be using more and more with every day that passes, but then I dare say that's a good thing, it shows our clientele is growing.'

Flora glanced at the window. Outside a bitterly cold wind was howling and icy rain was lashing against the glass. It was only four thirty in the afternoon but already it was pitch-dark.

'Poor thing will be frozen through when she gets back,' she commented and went on with the jobs waiting to be done.

After visiting the butcher Tilly happily tucked her purchases down into her basket and set off back towards the café. Having been brought up in the area she knew every alley and short cut like the back of her hand and although the alleys were dark they held no fear for her. Humming softly to herself she set off down one particularly dark alley that ran between two old warehouses that had long been out of use. The alley was narrow and stank of the river and stale urine but Tilly barely noticed it as she walked along.

She had gone no more than a few yards when she sensed someone behind her and turning quickly she narrowed her eyes and peered into the gloom. After a few seconds of silence, she was sure that she had imagined it and set off again, but no sooner had she gone a few more steps than the footsteps behind her started up again.

'H-hello . . . is anyone there?' Her voice echoed off the walls of the alley but no one answered, so turning abruptly she set off again, moving much faster this time. Suddenly an arm came about her throat and she was yanked backwards off her feet, causing her to drop the basket containing the precious items she had been entrusted to buy.

The hand squeezed tighter and a voice she didn't recognise muttered, 'So, Jia Li, you've had the bastard then!'

Confusion flitted across her face. Why was this man calling her Jia Li?

'You caused me some trouble,' the voice continued menacingly. It was a man she realised and he sounded Chinese. 'Because of you I being sent away to live with new bride in China! *Pah!* But your friends not here to help you this time. So now I leave you something to remember me by!' He threw her onto the ground where she landed so heavily that the air rushed out of her lungs and for a moment she couldn't breathe. Despite her age, Tilly was innocent and had no idea what was about to happen to her, but she sensed it was something bad and tears began to run down her cold cheeks as she lay there whimpering. She could feel the man tugging at the skirt she was wearing but was powerless to stop him. It was obvious to her that her strength would be no match for his. She wished that she could see his face but it was so dark that she could see nothing at all. He was swearing and calling her horrible names and then he hit her hard across the mouth and she tasted blood. The next blow came to the side of her head and she saw stars explode in front of her eyes.

'You have ruined my life, you *bitch whore*!' The man was panting now as he yanked her skirt above her waist. Every few seconds he gave her another glancing blow with his clenched fist and all Tilly could do was lie there, unable to fight back. One punch landed on her chest and she felt something crack followed by a searing pain. From then on as she struggled to remain conscious it even hurt to breathe and she was sure that she was going to die. But why was this man doing this to her and why had he called her Jia Li?

Minutes later he had ripped aside her drawers, but then, he stopped and growled, 'You not worth it, bitch whore!'

Tilly was beyond crying by then, all she could do was lie there and pray for it to end. But he hadn't done with her yet, not by a long shot. He stood for a moment, panting, as he stared down at her helpless form with contempt and then he started to kick her again and again. Instinctively, Tilly rolled herself into a fetal position until a comforting darkness wrapped itself around her and the pain was gone and she knew no more.

Chapter Thirty-Eight

It was almost half past five and they were beginning to get very busy again when Flora suddenly realised that Tilly hadn't returned.

'She should have been back ages ago,' she commented to Hattie as she glanced towards the door.

'Happen she got held up. There was probably a queue at the butcher's or perhaps she had to go elsewhere for something. Don't you worry, young Tilly is as honest as the day is long, she'll be back.' Hattie smiled reassuringly at Flora as she handed a customer their change but Flora was beginning to feel distinctly uneasy. It was so unlike Tilly to take long over an errand. She usually almost ran all the way there and back, keen to get the praise she would receive when she got back . . . and it was very dark outside and Tilly was so vulnerable.

Half an hour later Jimmy, Sam and Ernie sauntered in for their evening meal as they often did after they'd finished work and they saw at a glance that something was troubling Flora.

'It's Tilly, she's been gone for over two hours now but the butcher's is no more than ten minutes away and she's never late,' she explained when they asked her what was wrong.

'Hmm.' Like Hattie, Jimmy didn't seem overly concerned as yet. 'How about if she ain't back by the time we've finished eating, we go out an' have a scout round for her.'

Flora smiled at them. 'Would you? Thank you.' She hurried

to get them their meal, and when Tilly still hadn't returned when the three young men had finished eating, they too began to feel uneasy.

'The butcher's was it you said she went?' asked Sam and at Flora's nod they turned up the collars of their thick coats and headed for the door. 'Right, we'll go an' have a look-see and let you know.'

The butcher was closing up when they got there but a quick enquiry established that yes, Tilly had been there but had left some two hours or so ago.

Back outside the shop they stood looking up and down the street.

'I bet she took a short cut through one o' the alleys,' Sam suggested.

Jimmy nodded in agreement. 'Yes, but which one? There's three or four from here that could take her back to the café.'

The only way to find out was to walk along each one but the first one showed them nothing unusual so they set off for the next. The alleys were acting like wind tunnels and the bitter cold was threatening to slice them in two as it whistled along them. There was nothing down the second alley either and now they were gravely concerned. It was fast approaching seven o'clock at night. Tilly would never have willingly wandered the streets for so long.

'Let's just nip back to the café to make sure she ain't gone back there yet,' Ernie suggested and heads bent against the wind they hurried on their way.

'There's not been a sniff of her,' Hattie told them, drawing them away from the customers. 'Do you think we should call the police? Tilly is so vulnerable. Perhaps someone persuaded her to go away with them?'

'No, don't do that just yet, there's two more short cuts that she might have taken that we need to check first,' Ernie told her, then with Sam and Jimmy close on his heels they set off again. They hastily made their way back to the butcher's then took the third alley. They hadn't gone far along it, feeling their way along the cold damp walls, when Sam hissed, 'Hey, look there, against the wall.' Even as he spoke his foot kicked the basket that Tilly had dropped and he recognised it immediately.

'This is Tilly's basket,' he breathed as a feeling of dread coursed down his spine like iced water. Seconds later they were leaning over the prone figure and Sam asked shakily, 'Is it Tilly?'

Ernie shook his head. 'I don't know, it's too dark to see but whoever it is they're in a bad way.' He felt for a pulse in their wrist and his hand came away sticky with blood. 'Run and find a cop quick an' tell 'em we're goin' to need an ambulance. This girl is in a real bad way,' he said urgently.

Sam sprinted away but Jimmy stayed close to Ernie's side just in case the attacker came back. The police soon arrived and Tilly was stretchered out to the ambulance waiting in the road. When the men caught sight of her, they gasped with shock.

'My dear God!' Ernie breathed. 'What have they done to the poor girl?'

Tilly's face was so swollen and bloody that she was hardly recognisable and she was barely conscious. And that was only the part of her that they could see. They all dreaded to think what her other injuries might be.

It was over an hour later when Jimmy and Sam returned to the café. Hattie, Jia Li and Flora were busily cleaning in readiness for the next morning but one glance at the young men's faces told them that something was gravely wrong.

'Did you find her?' Flora asked fearfully.

Sam nodded solemnly. 'Yes, we did, she was lyin' in an alley an' . . .' He gulped deep in his throat, setting his Adam's apple bobbing up and down. He was badly shaken by what he had seen. 'She's been badly beaten by the look o' things. We fetched a cop an' she's been taken to the city hospital, but from what the

301

ambulance men were sayin' it looks touch an' go whether she'll make it.'

'Oh, dear God!' Hattie sat down on the nearest chair with a thump. 'An' where is Ernie?'

'He went in the ambulance with her.'

'Does anyone have any idea who might have done this?' Flora croaked. Tilly was such a sweet, innocent girl that it was inconceivable that anyone would want to hurt her.

Jimmy shook his head as he twisted his cap in his hand. 'She was unconscious when they took her away.'

'I'd best get to inform her parents what's happened,' Hattie said, but Sam shook his head.

'There's no need, Ernie gave the police Tilly's address an' they'll have done it.'

Hattie began to cry, great wracking sobs that shook her body. 'I've known that girl since the day she drew breath,' she gasped. 'An' she wouldn't hurt a fly. Why, when she were growin' up an' the other kids started to make fun of her cos she was a bit slow my Ernie always stood up for her. She used to follow him about like a little puppy dog. He'll take it hard if she don't make it.'

'She *will* make it!' Flora declared past the lump in her throat. 'She has to! But come on now, we should get to the hospital in case there's anything we can do.'

When they arrived at the hospital Tilly's parents were already there talking to a policeman, looking distraught.

'The doctor is examining her now,' Tilly's mother told Hattie as she wrung her hands in despair. Tilly was only just clinging to her life.

'And has she managed to say anything?' Hattie queried.

'Yes . . .' The woman rubbed her forehead as she tried to remember. She was so upset that everything was a jumble in her head. 'She only came round very briefly but I think she said something about the man who did this calling her Jia Li . . . I think she said he sounded like a Chinese.'

They all gazed at each other but it was Flora who ground out, '*Yung Huan!* He must have thought from behind that Tilly was Jia Li with her long black hair!'

'Who is this man?' The policeman was already standing with his pencil poised over his notebook and as Flora haltingly told him Huan's address and what Huan had done to Jia Li and the grudge that he bore her, the policeman nodded at his colleague.

'We'll get off and check this out right away.'

Once the policemen had gone all they could do was wait for the doctor who was examining Tilly to come and tell them what was happening.

'She has multiple fractures,' the grey-haired doctor told them tiredly when he eventually appeared. 'All of her fingers on one hand are broken. It looks like someone has stamped on them. She also has a broken leg, a broken arm and two fractured ribs. We also suspect that she may have internal bleeding so she will have to go to theatre for us to have a look at what's happening inside.'

'But she will survive?'

The doctor wearily glanced at the hope in the girl's mother's eyes and wished he could give better news.

'It's too soon to tell at this stage.' He prided himself on never giving false hope. 'We'll know more once we've had her in theatre. So now, if you'll excuse me, I have to go and scrub up. There's no time to lose.'

It was the early hours of the morning before the doctor appeared again, still wearing the gown he had worn to theatre, and looking, if that were possible, even more tired, but then he had been on duty since six o'clock the morning before.

'Well, we've set all her broken bones,' he told them. 'And in actual fact she's been a very lucky girl. One of the broken ribs was just a fraction away from piercing her heart. Had that have happened there would have been nothing we could do. We've managed to stop the internal bleeding and the rest of her injuries are cuts and bruises which will heal themselves given time.'

'So she will live?'

He looked at the sea of hopeful faces and gave them the slightest glimmer of hope. 'She's managed to survive the surgery so things are looking slightly better but the next twenty-four hours will be critical. I suggest you all go home and try to get some sleep now. There's nothing more you can do here. She's in God's hands now.'

'Thank you so much, doctor.' Tilly's mother was sobbing and he gently patted her arm before he turned and walked away.

The following morning, just as they had opened the café for the breakfast rush, the girls had a visit from the same policeman they had spoken to at the hospital the night before. None of them had slept very well, and they could only hope that Tilly had made it through the night.

'We went to the laundry and were told by some of the women and girls that work there that Yung Huan had indeed been there shortly before. He was in a very agitated state and covered in blood, which leads us to believe that he was the one responsible for the attack,' the policeman informed them gravely. 'Unfortunately, he then disappeared and we haven't been able to trace him.'

'So what will happen now?' Flora questioned.

'We have an alert out for his arrest. Every police officer in New York is scouring the streets looking for him and furthermore two other girls from the laundry have now come forward to say that he has raped them too so it's looking very worrying. He's clearly a very dangerous man.'

'He didn't rape Tilly, did he?' Flora asked fearfully. Knowing what an innocent Tilly was she dreaded to think how she would cope with it if he had.

'Her underclothes were pushed aside but it looks like he had second thoughts because the doctors found no evidence of rape,' the officer informed her and Flora sighed with relief.

'I wonder if I might have a word with Jia Li about Yung's attack on her.'

Jia Li licked her lips as she glanced around at all of them, then she nodded and holding tight to Flora's hand, they went into the kitchen away from the customers. Once there, Jia Li told him the full story of what had happened, all the while clinging to Flora's hand. Flora knew how hard it still was for her to talk about it and throughout her explanation, she could feel Jia Li trembling, but she was proud of her friend for managing to speak so calmly.

When he left the policeman was grim-faced after taking Jia Li's statement and assured them all that everything that could be done to apprehend Yung Huan was being done. 'If Tilly should die we'll be looking for a murderer,' he told them gravely. 'But even if she doesn't I can guarantee with the evidence we've got against him he'll be put away for a very long time when we do catch him.'

All they could do now was pray that he was right, and that Tilly would survive.

Chapter Thirty-Nine

For the next three days, Tilly hovered between life and death but finally on the fourth day, as her mother sat at the side of her hospital bed, she opened her eyes and gave her mother a weak smile. It was a good sign and they all began to breathe a little easier, although as yet Yung Huan had still not been apprehended.

'I hope they lock the bugger up and throw away the key when they do catch him!' Hattie raged. Since the attack both she and Ernie had been to sit by Tilly's bed every single day, although they knew she was probably unaware they were even there.

'I could be wrong o' course but I've got a feelin' our Ernie is more than a little fond o' the girl,' Hattie told Flora and Colleen one morning as they were preparing to open the café.

Flora raised an eyebrow. 'And what makes you think that?'

'Well, I reckon he's just realised she's no longer the little girl as used to follow him about. She's turned into a pretty young woman an' though she's a little slow she's got a heart o' gold.'

'You wouldn't mind, then, if something were to develop between them?'

'Oh lordy, no, quite the contrary, I'd be tickled pink. Our Ernie's had a bad time of it since his girl went down with the *Titanic* an' if he can find happiness wi' someone else, then so be it.'

'Hmm, we'll just have to see what happens then, won't we?' Flora said thoughtfully. 'But the main thing is that Tilly gets well.'

Two days later they were all sitting in the kitchen on a cold, frosty evening enjoying a well-earned break when they had another visit from the police that shocked them all to the core.

'A body was pulled out of the Hudson this morning that we have reason to believe might be the body of Yung Huan.'

They all gasped as the policeman went on. 'Mrs Yung was taken to the mortuary where she was able to formally identify it as the body of her son, Huan. He'd been badly beaten before being thrown into the river to drown so it appears that this is the end of the case.'

'It's good riddance to bad rubbish, that's what I say,' Hattie said unsympathetically. 'But who do you think did it?'

'Probably a relative of one of the girls he raped from the laundry,' the officer answered.

'Then I just hope as they get away with it,' Hattie said heatedly. 'The dirty little sod got what was comin' to him, as far as I'm concerned. At least he won't be able to bring no more young girls down!'

Of course, the officer was in no position to agree with her but being the father of two teenage girls himself he couldn't have agreed with her more. 'It seems that Jia Li wasn't the only girl who he got in the family way,' he informed them. 'One of the girls who worked at the laundry told us that he got her friend pregnant too. The poor girl was so terrified of what her folks would say that she went to a backstreet abortionist and ended up dying from loss of blood. She was just sixteen.'

He took his leave of them then, promising to inform them if there were any more developments and the second he had gone, Colleen, who was up and about again after her illness and who had remained silent up to then, looked at Jimmy and Sam, who had joined them earlier for dinner, and asked shakily, 'It wasn't *you* two who did for him, was it?'

'*Whoa* there!' Appalled, Jimmy put his hand palm up as if to

307

shield himself from her. 'I *swear* on my mom's life that this had nothing to do wi' me nor Sam. We roughed him up before, sure, but that's it!'

Colleen visibly relaxed. 'I thank the Holy Mother for that at least, so I do. Now all we have to worry about is gettin' young Tilly well again. I reckon I'll take her a can o' me home-made chicken soup in tomorrow to build her up a bit, bless her. It certainly did me a power o' good while I were ill.'

Not one of them had an ounce of sympathy for Yung Huan; he had got what he deserved in their eyes and they were sure the only one who would grieve for him was his own mother.

Over the next week, Tilly made steady progress although she still had a long way to go. She had been almost unrecognisable immediately after the attack and Ernie had openly cried at his first sight of her, and had visited her devotedly every day since while she lay in hospital, her pretty face covered in cuts and bruises. She had lost some back teeth during the vicious attack and when he first saw her, her eyes had been so swollen that she couldn't open them, and even when she did manage to, she could barely see. Her broken ribs were tightly bound and still caused her tremendous pain if she so much as moved and her broken limbs were in plaster casts. Even so every day now saw a slight improvement in her. The swelling on her face had gone down and the bruises had faded from bright blues and purples to dull greys and yellows. There was nothing that could be done for her missing teeth but the doctors were optimistic that her face would not be scarred once she had healed and because the missing teeth were at one side of the back of her mouth, hopefully being without them wouldn't spoil her lovely smile. They had warned that her broken fingers might always be a little stiff and because the two fractures in her leg had been very severe it was possible she would always walk with a limp, but even all these things could not detract from the joy they all felt that she had survived.

Jia Li sobbed uncontrollably the first time she plucked up the courage to go and see her.

'I'm so sorry, Tilly,' she croaked. 'Huan must have thought you were me from the back. It all my fault.'

But Tilly had been so gracious and it was suddenly clear to them all that she was actually a lot more intelligent than people had given her credit for. 'It wasn't your fault,' she assured Jia Li, gently stroking her hair with her good hand. '*Please* don't think that. Huan was a bad man. If it hadn't been me it would have been some other girl sooner or later so stop blaming yourself.'

Ernie, who had just witnessed the tender scene between the two girls, felt a lump form in his throat. Tilly was truly beautiful both inside and out and suddenly feeling guilty for thinking that, he hurried out into the corridor to light a cigarette.

What the hell am I thinkin'? he scolded himself as he blew a smoke ring towards the ceiling. *The girl I loved an' was goin' to marry met her end in a watery grave an' now here I am lookin' at Tilly in a different light.* It was all very confusing.

He admitted as much to his mother that evening when they were both back in their little house and Hattie smiled sadly as she gently stroked his cheek.

'You shouldn't turn your back on somethin' wonderful,' she told him softly. 'Your Carol was a lovely girl an' I've no doubt that had she survived you'd have lived happily ever after. But you have to accept she's gone now an' what do you think she would have wanted for you? I think the answer is, she'd have wanted you to be happy. She wouldn't have wanted you to spend the rest of your life mourning her.'

Hattie went off to bed then, leaving Ernie staring thoughtfully into the dying flames of the fire.

Chapter Forty

Much to everyone's relief, Tilly was discharged from hospital three weeks later, although it would be some time before she was well enough to return to work in the café. Ernie spent most evenings sitting with her at her parents' home and by then everyone had an inkling that Ernie was fast developing romantic feelings for her.

'I think it would be lovely if they got together,' Flora told Hattie one morning as they were serving in the café.

Hattie nodded in agreement and confided, 'I think her mom an' dad wrapped her in cotton wool and were a bit overprotective of her because she's a bit slow. They never let her out alone and watched over her all the time, but look how she blossomed in the short time she worked here. I think she's capable of a lot more than they gave her credit for, not that I'm blamin' 'em mind. I'd be delighted if she and Ernie do get together and I think she'd make him a lovely little wife.'

'Only time will tell,' Flora replied wisely.

Now that the fear of losing Tilly was past, Flora was more concerned about Colleen. She'd grown increasingly quiet since Christmas so it came as no surprise when, once they were home that evening, Colleen told her, 'I, er . . . I've been t'inking that it's time I went home . . . Could you manage here wit'out me?'

'Of course I could, although I'll miss you.' Just the thought of Colleen leaving made tears spring to Flora's eyes, although she

310

had been half-expecting the announcement. She had sensed how restless Colleen was and could completely understand her wanting to go home to her family again. After all, didn't she feel the same way deep down? Not a day went by when she didn't wonder what they would all be doing back in London or think of Jamie. Would he still be working in the city or would he have returned to his home in the Midlands?

'You must do what feels right for you,' she told her, reaching out to gently squeeze her hand.

Colleen nodded. 'I t'ink I have enough saved for my fare back to Ireland so I'll go to the shipping office an' make some enquiries this weekend, if you're sure?'

'Of course I'm sure.' Flora hastily turned away and busied herself with filling the kettle then so that Colleen wouldn't see her tears.

For the rest of the week they were both subdued but never once did Flora try to persuade her friend to change her mind. She sensed that New York no longer held any attraction for Colleen and she shared her thoughts with Jamie.

My dear Jamie,

Colleen has told me that she intends to return to her family in Ireland, so once more I will be losing someone I care about. Aside from knowing how much I will miss her, it has made me even more restless and envious. How I wish that it was me coming home to all the people I love. I thought that the longer I was away the easier it would become, and yet I find it is quite the opposite as I think back to the happy times you and I shared. If only I could turn back the clock, things would be so different and I would never even have contemplated leaving you, but it is too late for regrets now and the longer I am here the harder it is. I have been fortunate to have Colleen and Jai Li but Colleen will soon be gone now and Jai Li is making a life with her new husband so when Colleen leaves I will feel even more lonely.

Oh my love, I miss you so much and wonder, do you ever give me a thought or am I a part of your past now?

I will end now but know that when I close my eyes tonight yours will be the last face I see, and you will be the first person I think of when I open them again in the morning.

With all my love
Flora xxx

She folded the letter in half and prayed to God that she might find the strength to post it one day.

After mass on Sunday morning, Colleen set off for the shipping office with her savings tucked deep in her pocket to book the first part of her passage home. The next boat would not be sailing until early in May, which at least would give Flora time to find someone to take her place, she decided. As she handed over her money, she felt sad at the realisation that she would be leaving Flora, Hattie and Jia Li behind, but her stomach fluttered with excitement at the thought of seeing her beloved family again.

Three nights later as she and Flora were finishing at the café Colleen noticed a figure hovering in the shadows on the other side of the street but thought little of it. Many sailors passed that way on their route to the pub so she carried on with her work.

Jia Li and Bai had already retired to the rooms above the café, which they had now transformed into a very comfortable home, and seemed so happy that both Flora and Colleen never tired of seeing them together.

'That's about it then.' Colleen wiped her hands down the front of her apron as she glanced around at the newly cleaned tables.

The floors had been swept, the salt and pepper pots filled and they were all ready for the breakfast trade the next morning. Flora went to turn off the lamps in the kitchen and once they had let themselves out to go next door Colleen glanced across the road but the shadowy figure was gone and she thought no more about it.

The next day was busy as usual. 'I think we ought to start lookin' around for someone to take Tilly's place, love. Even if she comes back there'll still be plenty for her to do even with an extra pair of hands, especially when Colleen is gone,' Hattie suggested.

Flora supposed she was right so once more she wrote out a notice for a waitress and placed it in the window.

They were all tired when they finished that evening and as Colleen was just wiping the windows down in the café she again noticed the shadowy figure standing across the street. She frowned. That was two nights in a row the person had stood there now and Colleen was beginning to feel slightly uneasy. Could it be that someone was watching them? Or worse still, was it Yung Huan? The police only had his mother's word that it was his body they'd found, after all.

She was just about to call out to Flora when the figure emerged from the shadows and strode towards the café, and before she could move they were knocking loudly on the door.

Pulling herself up to her full height Colleen crossed the room and flung the door open ready to give whoever was standing there a piece of her mind, but when she saw who it was her mouth gaped and for a moment she was sure she must be seeing things.

'*Will!*' His name escaped her lips before she could stop it just as Flora came hurrying from the kitchen and at sight of the handsome young man she too looked shocked.

'*Ben!*'

'*Flora?*'

It would have been hard to say who was the most confused as

313

they all stared at each other, but eventually it was Colleen who broke the silence when she muttered, 'How do you know Flora, Will? And why are you calling him Ben, Flora? This is Will, the young man I was walking out with until . . .'

'Oh no it *isn't*,' Flora retorted heatedly. 'This is Ben, my *brother*!'

'B-but I don't understand!'

'I think I owe you both an explanation,' Ben said shame-faced and clearly in shock. 'I had no idea you worked here, Flora, I swear it.'

'I don't exactly work here, this is *my* café,' Flora told him indignantly. 'And yes, I do think you owe us both an explanation.'

And so they sat down at a table and Ben very hesitantly began to tell them both of his flight from England following the break-in and why he had lied to Colleen about his name when he had first met her.

'I thought the police might be looking for me for murder, you see,' he told Colleen. 'So I didn't dare tell you my real name. And, Flora, shortly after I got here I went to Constance's aunt's address and she told me that it was actually Connie who had died on the *Titanic* and that you were still here somewhere. I've been looking for you ever since not realising that you were here all the time right under my nose. And you . . .' His eyes became soft as he turned his attention to Colleen. 'The longer I knew you the harder it was to go on with the lie but I was scared that if I told you the truth about me being on the run you'd want nothing more to do with me. And then when you told me that you were thinking of going home to Ireland . . . Well, I knew that was the end. I couldn't marry you when I was using a false name, could I? So I had to let you walk away. But as God's my witness I've not known a moment's peace since so I decided the only thing I could do was come and tell you the truth. I was terrified that if I didn't you'd go back to Ireland and I'd never see you again because . . .' He blushed furiously. 'Because I love you, you see!'

314

'Oh, you stupid, *stupid* man,' Colleen scolded as she wrapped her arms around him. 'I would still have loved you too, no matter *what* you had done, so I would!'

'As it happens you're not a wanted man,' Flora was able to tell him when the two finally drew apart. 'Ma wrote to tell me that the woman who fell down the stairs survived but she didn't know where you were so she had no way of letting you know and the police caught whoever was responsible so there's no reason that you can't go home now if that's what you want.'

A look of relief flashed across his face but then he slowly shook his head. 'In future my home will be wherever Colleen is, if you're still interested in me, that is.' He gave her a smile that melted her heart before looking back at his sister. 'And I don't know how I'll ever be able to apologise enough to you, Flora. You must be so ashamed of me.'

Flora shook her head. 'You know one of the old sayings our ma was always fond of, *People who live in glass houses shouldn't throw stones*. How can what *you* did be any worse than what *I* did when I pretended to be Connie? Her Aunt Alexandra was so kind to me when I first came. I'm so ashamed of what I did and I live in constant fear of being found. I've no doubt she must hate me now.'

'But she doesn't,' Ben told her. 'When I went to see her, she was more concerned about your whereabouts than angry with you.'

'Really?' A little weight seemed to lift from Flora's shoulders. If the police hadn't been informed of what she'd done perhaps one day she could go home too? And maybe, just maybe, Jamie would give her a second chance.

Ben reached for her hand across the table. 'Oh, Flora, we've both made mistakes, and God knows, I've been a fool, but I could never hate you. When I found out you were alive, I wanted to dance down the streets.'

Flora looked into his sincere brown eyes and her own filled with tears. Standing up she went around and, as Ben stood too, brother and sister embraced for the first time in nearly a year. But considering all that had happened during that time, it seemed more like a lifetime. Then Flora pulled gently away and left him and Colleen to be alone. Jia Li had just come downstairs after hearing the voices in the café and now she asked anxiously, 'Is everything all right? I hear voices . . .'

'Everything is *very* all right,' Flora told her with a broad smile. 'In fact, they're even *better* than all right. Colleen is in there with her Will who it turns out is actually my brother Ben!'

'I am not understanding this,' Jia Li answered, bemused. 'You must be explaining it more to me.' And so slowly Flora did just that and by the time she had finished Jia Li was smiling.

'This very good, yes?'

Flora nodded. '*Very* good. Now bring that plate of cakes through would you, while I make the tea.'

Jia Li obligingly did as she was asked and when Bai joined them shortly after, wondering where his wife had got to, the meeting took on a party atmosphere. Eventually, Jia Li and Bai returned to their room and Flora went next door so that Colleen and Ben could have a little more time together.

Sitting at one of the tables in the café, their hands clasped on the table, Ben and Colleen couldn't stop talking as Ben finally felt able to be truly open with her. After a while, Colleen said, 'There is just one thing you should know, Ben.' The name felt strange on her lips. He had always been Will to her. 'You see, I t'ought I would never see you again so . . . so I've booked a passage back to Ireland. I did explain to you, didn't I, that me mammy was in need of some help now that me daddy's gone? I sail early in May.' Her eyes filled with tears at the unfairness of it all. She had thought she would never see him again and now, just when he had come back into her life, she would have to leave him.

'But that's just a few weeks away.'

'I know,' she muttered miserably as he stroked her hands. 'But there's not'ing I can do about it now. I've already writ to tell me mammy I'm comin' an' I can't go lettin' her down now, can I?'

Ben stared off into space for a while then a smile slowly formed at the corners of his lips. 'Of course you can't let her down,' he agreed. 'But there's nothing to stop me coming with you, is there? . . . As your husband of course.' He grinned at her shocked expression and dropped to one knee. 'Look, I'm not making a very good job of this, am I? What I'm trying to say is, Colleen, will you make me the happiest man on earth and marry me, *please*?'

'Is t'is some sort of a joke?' Colleen frowned.

Ben shook his head. 'It most certainly is *not*! So . . . I ask again – will you *please* say you'll marry me? This hard floor is making me knee ache something chronic!'

Colleen grinned from ear to ear as she playfully cuffed his ear. 'O' course I'll marry you. Why, I t'ought you'd never ask,' she giggled, and as she bent her head to his and their lips met she felt as if she were the luckiest girl in the world.

Chapter Forty-One

'Lordy . . . you mean to tell me I have *another* weddin' to organise?' Hattie said the next morning when she arrived at work to be met by a bright-eyed Colleen who quickly explained what had happened the night before. 'And just *fancy* your Will turnin' out to be Flora's brother. They do say it's a small world, don't they?' In actual fact she was tickled pink and thought how beautifully things had turned out for Colleen. Tilly was getting better by the day, Jia Li and Bai were happy and finally things were working out for everyone . . . apart from Flora that was, and Hattie couldn't help but notice the faraway look that came into her eyes more and more of late.

'And now we've got the rest of 'em sorted out why don't you think about writin' to that young man you left behind? I've heard you mention him from time to time and I've a notion you think a lot more of him than you let on,' Hattie said, during a lull in customers. Flora was just about to interview yet another applicant for the job of cook-cum-waitress because up to now the ones she had seen had been totally unsuitable for one reason or another.

'Why would I want to do that? We weren't that close,' Flora lied defensively as she thought of all the unposted letters tucked away in her drawer.

'Oh, come on now, pull the other one, it's got bells on,' Hattie chuckled. 'You can't kid a kidder, you know, girl. Why, there's times when you walk about the place with a face like a wet weekend on you so perhaps it's time to do something about it!'

'You don't understand!' Flora sniffed. 'I was more interested in an adventure on the *Titanic* and seeing New York than staying with Jamie. He's hardly going to forget that easily, is he now?'

Hattie shrugged. 'That all depends on how much he thought of you.'

The shop door opened then and there was no more time for discussion as Flora hurried away to interview the latest applicant but Hattie had certainly got her thinking.

As Flora and the middle-aged woman took a seat she thought she looked faintly familiar and then she realised where she had seen her before. She had worked in the laundry with her. It seemed like a very long time ago now.

'It's Hilda Nelmes, isn't it?' Flora held her hand out and the woman shook it. She was tall and thin with dark hair that was tinged with grey here and there but from what Flora could remember of her she'd been a very hard worker. 'I recognised you from the laundry.'

'Why, of course.' She raised her eyebrow. 'My, that was some to-do with Yung Huan, wasn't it?' She shook her head. 'To tell the truth none of us were sorry when we heard what had happened to him. He was a bad lot. Taken down more than enough young girls, he had. It's broken his mother though. Did you know she'd closed the laundry and gone back off to China? Best place for her, if you were to ask me. It was slave labour working at that place and I never heard her say a kind word to anyone. But anyway, that's why I'm here. It was a job at the end of the day and now that's finished I need another one.'

'Have you ever worked in a café before?' Flora questioned and the woman shook her head. 'No, I won't lie, I haven't, but I'm a quick learner and I'm not afraid of hard work. And I'm a pretty

319

'mean cook, even if I do say so meself.' She winked at Flora in a friendly fashion. 'I had to be with five growin' boys to feed.'

'So you wouldn't mind helping out in the kitchen and serving in here?'

Hilda shook her head. 'I'll do whatever is needed and gladly.'

Flora smiled. The woman was just what she was looking for. Clean and tidy and friendly too. She quickly told the woman what hours she would work and what the wages would be and when Hilda smiled in agreement they shook hands on it.

'I can start right away, if you need me to,' Hilda offered helpfully. 'All me lads have grown an' flown the nest now so time is heavy on me hands since Mrs Yung closed the laundry. It'll be nice to have somethin' to do again an' a bit o' money comin' in.'

'In that case go straight through to the kitchen.' Flora pointed her in the right direction. 'Jia Li and Hattie will show you the ropes and you'll meet Colleen shortly. She's just popped out food shopping.'

By the end of the day it was obvious that Hilda was going to fit in perfectly and she and Hattie were getting on like a house on fire.

'It's nice to have someone nearer to me own age to chinwag to,' Hattie said happily as she collected her hat and coat. 'Not that I don't enjoy workin' wi' you young 'uns,' she added hastily. 'But now I'd better get home an' get our Ernie somethin' to eat before he goes off to see Tilly.'

She went on her way humming merrily just as Ben arrived, and suddenly Flora felt like the odd one out. Colleen had Ben now, Jia Li had Bai and it made her feel lonelier than ever, although she was thrilled to see them all so happy.

'I'm going next door. Can I leave you to lock up?' she tactfully asked Colleen, guessing that it would give her and Ben some time alone. They had a lot to talk about and lots of plans to make for their future. Colleen had told her earlier in the day that they were going to set the date for the wedding for just before they sailed to Ireland and Ben had said that he would be going to the booking office to change the single berth that Colleen had booked aboard the ship for a double and buy a ticket. They would be husband and wife by then after all.

Suddenly they were all immersed in wedding plans again and Colleen had a permanent smile on her face. Like Jia Li she had opted to have a quiet wedding and she and Hattie happily went off to buy the material for her dress one cold and windy morning.

When they arrived back at the café Colleen's cheeks were rosy and her eyes sparkling as she showed them all what she had chosen. It was a heavy white satin and Hattie could hardly wait to get started on it.

'It'll be straight and ankle length with a chiffon overlay but we've bought lots of pearls and sequins to sew on it so it should look wonderful with Colleen's red hair,' Hattie told them excitedly. 'She's agreed to wear a little veil an' all,' she went on approvingly. 'We thought perhaps she could wear a little halo of spring flowers on her head to match those in her bouquet. I'm tellin' you, she's goin' to look the bee's knees by the time I'm done wi' her. But, Flora, it's down to you to sort Ben out with a new suit. You know what men are like. They'd get married in their work clothes if it was left up to them.'

'I could do the flowers,' Hilda suggested. 'I used to work in a florist for a time so I'm pretty good at flower arrangin'.'

Colleen beamed. Everything was quickly falling into place and she had never felt so happy.

Later in the week Flora took Ben off to the little Jewish tailor in the next street where he was fitted for a suit. It would be the first one he had ever owned and he seemed quite pleased about it.

'I can wear it when I first meet your mammy,' he told Colleen fondly. 'I want to make a good first impression.'

Colleen gurgled with glee. 'Then happen it'll be the only time you do wear it for a while once we're there,' she warned. 'There'll not be much call for smart clothes when you're workin' on a smallholdin', though you could wear it to church on a Sunday o' course. I just hope you'll not find the work too hard, so I do.'

Ben kissed her tenderly. 'I can't think of anything I'd rather do,' he assured her genuinely. 'Flora will tell you it's been my dream to live in the country and do that sort of job since I was knee high to a grasshopper.'

Hattie, who was watching them, grinned. 'Will you just look at that pair, why what wi' them an' Jia Li and Bai moonin' over each other I don't know which way to look!' She glanced over at Flora and once again noted the sadness in her eyes. She knew the girl was hiding her own troubles and her heart went out to her.

The wedding was set for two days before the young couple were set to sail for Ireland. Colleen had already decided that once she was home she and Ben would have another wedding at the Catholic church her family attended and so she would be able to wear the dress again. With this and the fast-approaching date in mind, Hattie was frantically sewing into the early hours to make sure that Colleen's dress was finished on time and as good as she could possibly make it.

As the big day drew closer, Colleen got a bad attack of pre-wedding nerves.

'What if Ben doesn't adapt to life in the country? He's always lived in cities, so he has,' she fretted to Flora.

Flora chuckled. 'He'll love it,' she assured her friend. 'He'll not only be getting the woman he loves but the lifestyle he's always craved, so stop worrying.'

At last the day of the wedding dawned, and it was a bright and clear May morning with the promise of sunshine to come. As they all helped Colleen get ready Hattie nodded towards the window.

'Would you just look at that sky now.' She sighed happily. 'Don't they always say the sun shines on the righteous?'

Colleen turned then to survey herself in the cheval mirror in her bedroom. Hattie had done a wonderful job with her dress and it shimmered and sparkled with every move she made.

'Come on then,' Hilda ordered bossily. 'Let's get this crown and the veil on you now. I don't want it wilting.' She had been up since the early hours of the morning fashioning the crown from tiny rosebuds, sweet-smelling freesias and baby's breath, and it was truly beautiful. Almost as beautiful as the bride whose head it nestled on.

Colleen had chosen to wear her long, luxuriant hair loose, as Ben liked it, and it curled down her back and sat on her shoulders in shimmering waves, a perfect foil for the snow-white dress and veil. Hilda had also made her a small posy of flowers to match those in her headdress and when she was completely ready she hardly recognised herself in the looking glass.

'You look absolutely *stunning*,' Flora told her with a catch in her voice. 'But come on now, Ernie is downstairs waiting for you in his best bib and tucker all ready to give you away and I don't want you keeping my brother waiting.'

The others had drifted off downstairs by then and now Colleen's eyes filled with tears as she looked at the girl she had come to love like a sister.

'I'm so happy I feel like I could fly,' she said solemnly as she took Flora's hands in her own. 'But I'm going to miss you *so* much! We've been t'rough a lot together since we've known each other, haven't we?'

'We certainly have,' Flora agreed, her own voice gruff. 'But you and my brother were written in the stars. You're perfect for each

323

other and I know you're going to be really happy together. And it's not as if we won't keep in touch, is it? I shall write to you every single week . . . well, perhaps every single month. I've never been much of a letter writer.' She hugged Colleen warmly, careful not to crease her dress, then, her voice firm again, she ordered, 'Now downstairs with you else we're going to be late and I don't want my brother thinking you've stood him up.' And so, arm in arm, they left the room.

Downstairs everyone was dressed up in their Sunday best, smiling and happy and they all agreed that Colleen looked absolutely beautiful, causing Hattie to puff out her chest with pride. Suddenly every minute she had spent labouring over Colleen's dress was worth it. Jia Li had chosen to wear her own wedding dress again for the special occasion too and would act as Colleen's bridesmaid.

It was a happy group that piled into the two cars that Flora had ordered to take them to the register office and they were happier still when they saw Ben's face. At the first glimpse of his bride-to-be he looked so proud that they thought he might burst.

The service was simple but sweet and Colleen and Ben had eyes only for each other. It was as if they were the only two people left in the world and by the time the registrar pronounced them husband and wife there was not a dry eye in the house.

There followed the customary throwing of rose petals and rice on the steps outside and then it was back to the café for a good old knees-up.

'Eeh, it's been a good day, hasn't it?' Hattie said happily that evening as she looked across at the young couple. She was keeping an eye on her Ernie too who had fetched Tilly to join in the celebrations. She was looking much better now, much to everyone's relief, although she was still walking with quite a severe limp and possibly always would. Lowering her voice, she leaned over to Flora and nodded over at her son as she whispered. 'An' between you, me an' the gate post I shouldn't be surprised if there wasn't *another* weddin' in the offin' before too much longer. Look at the way my Ernie is lookin' at Tilly. I reckon he's smitten, all right.'

Flora nodded in agreement. Tilly and Ernie did look very suited to one another and she hoped it would work out for them. Now she just had to think seriously about what she intended to do with the rest of her life.

Chapter Forty-Two

Just two days later, the mood had turned sombre as the day of Colleen and Ben's departure arrived. The ship was due to sail with the tide that morning and Flora had closed the café so she could go and wave them off.

Colleen was a complete bundle of nerves and fluttering about like a butterfly as she checked and checked again that she and Ben had got everything. And then it was time to make their way to the docks. There was quite a little crowd of them; Flora, Hattie, Hilda, Jia Li and Tilly. Sadly, Ernie and Bai, Jimmy and Sam had had to go to work and so had said their goodbyes earlier that morning.

At her first sight of the enormous ship that would take Colleen and Ben far away across the seas panic seized Flora and sweat broke out on her forehead as everything that had happened on the *Titanic* rushed back to her. In her head she heard again Connie's scream as she plummeted into the sea and she shivered as she remembered the biting cold. Colleen looked a little nervous too but thankfully Ben was in control of the situation.

'Now, don't look so scared,' he told his young wife tenderly. 'You don't think I'd let anything happen to you, do you? We'll treat this as our honeymoon and you'll be home before you know it.'

Colleen gave him a faltering smile as she glanced towards the gangplank where passengers were already embarking after passing their luggage to a row of porters who stood waiting on the dock.

'W-we ought to get on board,' she squeaked. It was time to say goodbye to the people she had come to love and it was proving to be much more difficult than she had thought it would be. Hattie and Hilda fell on her, giving her tips to stop her being seasick before turning their attentions to Ben while Tilly stepped forward and gave her a shy little kiss on the cheek. They had all seen the girl blossom with the attention Ernie was bestowing on her and were convinced that before too much longer she and Ernie would also start a new life together.

'So . . . this is it then.' Colleen took both of Flora's hands in hers and they stared into each other's eyes both crying unashamedly.

Flora nodded. 'Yes, this is it. You just take care now and make sure you keep in touch.' Then suddenly they were clinging together until Ben gently took his wife's elbow and told her, 'It's time to go, sweetheart.' She nodded as she stepped away from Flora, mopping at her eyes with one of Ben's large white handkerchiefs and then it was Ben's turn to give Flora a hug.

'You look after yourself, now,' he told her in a throaty voice. 'And just remember you could always go home if you decide that's what you want to do. Bye, sis, I love you.'

'I love you too,' she gulped as he led Colleen away and soon they were standing at the rail aboard the ship waving furiously. Eventually the anchors and the gangplanks were lifted and the two pilot boats that had come to steer the ship from the harbour into open sea appeared.

'Goodbye . . . I love you all!' Colleen was leaning across the rail furiously waving a hankie and they all stood there watching until the ship became just a speck in the distance.

'That's it then, they've gone,' Hattie said, feeling suddenly deflated. 'Come on, let's get back to the café, we have a living to earn.'

Strangely silent now they all turned as one and followed her along the quay.

The next few evenings proved to be very lonely ones for Flora. During the day she was so busy in the café that she didn't have much time to think. But the nights were a different matter altogether. She would return to the empty house next door and without Colleen's cheerful chatter she began to feel as if she was rattling around in it like a pea in a pod. And so at the end of one day as they were closing the café, she asked Jia Li, 'How would you like to move in to the house next door? It's far too big for me alone now that you and Colleen aren't there and I could move back into the rooms upstairs here.'

Jia Li frowned. 'But it your house. You have worked hard for it.'

Flora shrugged. 'What difference does it make if I'm here or next door? The house would suit you and Bai far better than it does me now that I'm alone. Have a word to Bai and ask him what he thinks of the idea.'

The next day she told Flora, 'Bai think it a great idea. We shall need a little more room soon because . . .' She blushed as her hands fell to her belly and a smile broke out on Flora's face.

'You're having a baby!'

Jia Li smiled. 'It not definite yet but I think so. Bai is very happy about it.'

'And how do *you* feel?' Flora remembered all too well what an ordeal Jia Li had been through with the last child.

'I feel also very happy . . . and blessed. This time I make sure baby is born safely.'

'I couldn't be more pleased for you,' Flora said, genuinely thrilled for her friend. 'But does this mean you won't be able to work anymore?'

'Oh no.' Jia Li shook her head. 'I intend to work till close to baby comes, then when he is here I bring him into kitchen with me, if you and Hattie and Hilda don't mind?'

'Mind!' Flora chuckled. 'Why, we'll all love it, though I fear the baby will get very spoiled!'

'All babies should be spoiled,' Jia Li declared and Flora saw how happy she was, quite unlike the last time when the child had been forced upon her.

They spent the following Sunday transferring Jia Li's and Bai's things into the house and Flora's back into the rooms above the café. They were more than adequate for Flora and yet she couldn't help but feel that she had come full circle. Jia Li and Bai had each other, Hattie and Hilda, both widows, had taken to spending their Sundays together and now her one day off a week became a day to dread.

On the following Sunday, after spending the morning reading the newspapers from cover to cover, she became restless and so she decided to venture out for a walk. Apart from the time she had seen Colleen and Ben off at the docks and the two weddings she had attended, Flora rarely set foot out of the door but today she felt that if she didn't get away for a time she would go mad, so she hurriedly got changed and stepped out into the fresh air. She doubted that too many people would be out and about on a Sunday apart from courting couples so decided to do a little window shopping and headed for the city centre.

She spent a pleasant hour staring into the shop windows, viewing the latest fashions, then finding an open coffee shop she slipped inside and ordered a coffee before finding a vacant table. It would be nice to be waited on for a change, she decided. She was sitting enjoying her drink when the door opened and as she glanced up the breath caught in her throat. It was Patsy, the maid from Connie's aunt's house. She spotted Flora almost immediately and hurried over to her with a wide smile on her face, looking very pretty in an up-to-the-minute dress and a smart hat. In that moment Flora realised just how outdated she had allowed herself to become. She had spent little on clothes since moving into the café apart from necessary work clothes and the nice, but rather plain, two-piece suit she was wearing that she had bought for the weddings, and now beside Patsy she felt positively dowdy.

'Well, I'll be.' Patsy flashed Flora a dazzling smile. 'I never thought to see you again, miss. How are you keepin'? I'm meetin' me young man but seein' as I'm a bit early I thought I'd pop in 'ere an' treat meself to a coffee.'

Flora's mouth was suddenly dry but she managed to raise a smile. 'I'm very well Patsy. And you?'

'Ooh, I'm fine and dandy thanks, miss.'

'And, er . . . everyone at the house?'

'Huh! I wouldn't know.' Patsy plonked herself down next to Flora. 'It were never particularly a nice place to work what wi' the master and Miss Margaret barkin' their orders at me all the time, but after Miss Margaret married Toby Johnson an' he moved in an' all, it became like a war zone so I put me notice in an' scarpered. I miss the mistress though, poor sod. I'm workin' in the soap factory now. Less hours, more money an' I love it,' she ended breathlessly.

'It wasn't a marriage made in heaven then?' Flora said with a little smile and Patsy chuckled.

'Hardly! They were at it like cat an' dog even before the honeymoon were properly over. He made no secret o' the fact that he only married her for her money cos his parents were ready to disown him, an' she . . . Well, I reckon she'd have married anybody just so's she got a ring on her finger. She's payin' for it now, though, he leads her a merry dance, what with his gamblin' and his women, an' serves her right, that's what I say. But what have you been doing with yourself? I thought you might have gone back home to London.'

Flora shook her head afraid to say too much. 'Oh, this and that, you know! I get by.'

'Right, well it's been lovely to see you. The mistress were right upset when you upped and left I don't mind tellin' you. Not that I blamed you. But now I suppose I'd better go an' see if that young man o' mine is there yet. I just glanced at the clock an' realised it's later than I thought. Bye, miss. Take care o' yourself.'

'And you, goodbye, Patsy.'

As the girl bustled away Flora couldn't help but smile. It seemed that both Margaret and Toby had met their match in each other but she found it very hard to have any sympathy for them. As Patsy had pointed out, they deserved each other.

Once she had drunk her coffee, Flora set off for home again in a thoughtful mood. Patsy hadn't mentioned that anyone was looking for her so perhaps she could begin to think of going home again. There was nothing to keep her in New York anymore after all, apart from the business and the house.

Later that week she received a letter from her mother. Flora had written to her a couple of months before to let her know about Ben and his impending wedding to Colleen. Her mother was thrilled for them, although slightly sad that Ben had gone to live in Ireland.

Still, she had written. *He may well come home to see us all again one day and at least he's happy. But when are you coming home, Flora? We all miss you so much!*

Flora looked around at the little business she had built up and thought of the house next door. If she *did* go home, and it was a big *if*, what would she do with them? Jia Li and Bai had made the house their home, and Hattie and Hilda depended on the business for their livelihoods now so selling them on was out of

331

the question. And what would she do when she was home? Would she look for Jamie and try to win him back? Did she even dare?

Later that night, as she lay in bed pondering over everything yet again, the answer came to her in a flash and suddenly she saw a way of going home without hurting anyone that set her heart pounding.

Chapter Forty-Three

It was late the following afternoon when they finally had a quiet spell that Flora was able to assemble everyone in the kitchen so she could have a word with them, and her solemn face immediately began to make them feel nervous.

'Is something wrong, dearie?' Hattie asked nervously.

Flora shook her head. 'No, not wrong exactly, but I do need to talk to you . . .' She looked around at their anxious faces and went on, 'The thing is, as I'm sure you're all probably aware, I miss my family terribly and so . . . Well, the long and the short of it is I've decided to go home.'

'Oh, I see,' Hattie said dully. She had come to look upon Flora almost as a daughter and she admired her tremendously. How many other young women her age had managed to achieve what she had, after all? And of course, she would miss working at the café so much but . . .

'Why I wanted to talk to you all was to tell you what I intend to do with the house and the business,' Flora went on, knowing that she had their full attention. Then turning to Jia Li she told her, 'I really don't want to sell the house, it's all bought and paid for now and I was saving again to buy the café instead of renting it off Dora, so I thought, how would you and Bai feel about buying the café if I signed the house over to you?'

'*What?*' Jia Li looked shocked. 'But you worked so hard to do all this.' She spread her hands to add emphasis to what she was saying. 'And me and Bai not have money to pay for it all.'

'No, no you misunderstood me,' Flora told her patiently. 'I'm not *asking* you to buy it straight away. What I thought was you could take the business over and once you've managed to save enough to buy the café, you could then pay me a little at a time what the house cost. But not until you're comfortable and making a profit, of course. It wouldn't matter if it took a year or two. I have no doubt that you'll be able to pay for the café too in no time with what we're taking in there now. All I'll need to do is have it signed over into your names. And you, Hattie, I was wondering if perhaps you'd like to come and move into the rooms above the café? You've said that you think it's only a matter of time before Ernie and Tilly get wed so if he carried on paying the rent on your house for now they'd have a home to move into.'

They all stared at her for a moment open-mouthed but then Jia Li objected, 'But that not fair. You work so hard to build business up!'

'And so did you,' Flora pointed out. 'All I need is enough to buy my fare home then I can get another job in London.'

Jia Li's lip trembled. 'But I miss you if you go,' she said in a tearful voice and Flora put her arm about the girl's shoulders.

'And I'll miss you too. *All* of you, but I'm not really happy here and I miss my family *so* much.'

'For what it's worth I think it's a grand idea,' Hattie said, already picturing herself in the comfy rooms above the café. 'And it'd be nice not to have to turn out in all weathers to come to work. But are you quite sure this is what you want, dearie?'

Flora nodded. '*Quite* sure. So if you speak to Bai, Jai Li, and if you're all happy with the idea, I'll set the wheels in motion. I can speak to Dora for a start, but I don't see a problem there. So long as she gets her rent regularly she won't mind who pays it and I can get the papers drawn up to change the names on the deeds of the house tomorrow then it'll be yours all legal and above board and you can pay me back when you can.'

'I not know what to say,' Jia li said chokily. 'You give us a whole new future but we miss you so much.'

'I'll miss you too,' Flora told her and turning about she quickly busied herself at the stove before she broke down completely.

Over the next few days Flora had everything transferred into Jia Li and Bai's name. She also sent a note to Dora asking her to pop in when she could. Dora breezed in a few days later, done up to the nines, in a waft of perfume that almost took Flora's breath away. Her face was heavily made-up and she had a little hat perched at a jaunty angle on her bleached blonde hair.

'So you wanted to see me? What's the emergency?' she asked, settling into a chair and lighting a cigarette as she glanced around at the café approvingly. She was the first to admit that when she had owned it, it had been sadly neglected but with all her hard work Flora had transformed it into a business to be proud of.

'There's no emergency as such but I wanted to tell you what my plans are.' Flora quickly told her what she intended and when she had finished, Dora narrowed her eyes and peered at her. 'An' are you quite sure this is what you want? After all the hard work you've put into the place.'

Flora nodded decisively. 'Yes, I am, but I think I can promise things will go on just the same as they are now. Jia Li is very efficient and more than capable of doing everything that I do. She and Colleen have been running the place with me since the beginning and I could never have done it without them, so after all her hard work it would be wrong to put her out of her home and a job, so this is for the best all round.'

'Well, I ain't got a problem with it if you ain't,' Dora said in her usual forthright way. 'So I'll wish you all the best o' luck for the future, love. I must admit when you first come to me tellin' me what you wanted to do I had reservations. You were so young I didn't think you'd last a month but you proved me wrong. When are you thinkin' o' leavin?'

'I haven't got that far yet,' Flora admitted with a rueful grin. 'I've been too busy running around trying to sort out everything for Jia Li, but as soon as I know I'll let you know.'

'You do that, I'd like to come an' say goodbye.' Dora leaned forward then and in a rare affectionate moment planted a kiss on Flora's cheek. 'You're a plucky kid,' she said thickly and snatching up her gloves she swept out of the café like royalty with her head in the air, leaving Flora to swallow the huge lump in her throat. It was only now that she had decided to leave them that she was realising just how much they had all come to mean to her.

A week later Flora booked a passage on a ship back to London for early in July and suddenly it was all real. *She really was going home.* She had written to tell her mother and could hardly wait to see her family now. And, as always when she had momentous news or needed to get something off her chest, she also wrote another letter to Jamie.

My dearest Jamie,

So my passage to England is booked! I set sail on the 4th of July and I very much hope that you will want to see me when I am home. Perhaps in person I can explain to you why I behaved in the way I did. My dearest hope is that one day you might find it in your heart to forgive me and give me a second chance.

Your loving Flora xxx

And then with a heavy heart she added the letter to the others that had never been sent. Even now she couldn't quite pluck up the courage to post it.

'Before you go anywhere we need to go shoppin' for some new clothes for you,' Hattie told her one day. 'You can't go aboard a ship in them you're wearin'. They'll think you're the cleaner, my girl.'

'I suppose I could do with a few new ones,' Flora admitted doubtfully, looking down at the faded skirt and blouse she was wearing. Since opening the café clothes hadn't been high on her list of priorities. She'd always reasoned that she never went anywhere to wear them anyway. But now she supposed it wouldn't do to turn up at home looking like some down and out.

And so a few days later, after leaving the café in the capable hands of Jia Li, Hattie and Flora hit the shops. Flora had gone prepared to buy just a few basic necessities but Hattie had other ideas and dragged her from one shop to another.

'I don't need anything else,' Flora protested eventually. 'I'm loaded down with bags already.' But although she was protesting, she'd been really enjoying herself. She wasn't used to spoiling herself and had forgotten what good fun it could be.

Hattie sniffed. 'Hmm, I dare say we've got most of what you need but we'll go and have a cup o' tea and a bite to eat now, my treat. Then I can check what we've bought and see what else you might need.'

As Flora had quickly discovered, Hattie could be as stubborn as a mule when she wanted to be, so she meekly followed her into a small restaurant where they ordered sandwiches, a selection of small cakes and a pot of tea.

While they were eating, Hattie rifled through the bags and

smiled with satisfaction. 'I reckon a nice new pair of shoes an' a new coat and you'll be able to hold your own against the gentry now,' she chuckled. 'But don't think we're done yet. I'm taking you to the hairdresser's then for a good trim. How long's it been anyway since you had a decent haircut?'

'I can't remember. Probably about two years or so,' Flora admitted hesitantly.

Shortly after they were off again and Flora began to wonder where Hattie got all her energy from. She was really quite remarkable for a woman her age and showed no sign of tiring whatsoever. At the hairdressers Flora was placed in a chair while the young woman who was about to cut her hair eyed her thoughtfully through the mirror.

'Slightly shorter styles are getting very popular, you know,' she told Flora as she fingered her silky tresses. 'And I think it would really suit you. How about I trim it up to your shoulders? You could always have it cut shorter next time if you like it but for now it would still be long enough for you to put it up if you wanted to.'

'I'm not sure . . .' Flora said hesitantly but Hattie was right behind her nodding vigorously.

'Go on, what have you got to lose, you're only young once,' she urged persuasively. 'And it'll soon grow back if you don't like it.'

Flora took a great gulp and nodded. 'Go on then.'

She sat nervously watching the young hairdresser snipping away as her hair fell in sheets to the floor until she could bear to look no longer and closed her eyes.

'All right, you can look now,' the girl said eventually and Flora cautiously opened her eyes to peep in the mirror. She gasped with surprise when she saw her reflection and a smile spread across her face. Her hair felt bouncy and light and she actually loved her new look.

'It looks *wonderful*,' Hattie said approvingly. 'There's no point

338

having lovely thick hair like yours and tying it back all the while so no one can see it.'

Flora turned her head this way and that, feeling like a new woman, and then quickly paid the hairdresser and gave her a generous tip.

'They'll not recognise you when we get you home,' Hattie teased on the way back. 'Especially when we've got you into some of these new togs.'

She was quite right. When Flora entered the café laden down with bags and sporting her brand-new hairdo both Jia Li and Hilda gasped.

'Why, you look just like one o' them fashion models in a magazine.' Hilda declared doing a full turn around Flora and making the girl blush to the roots of her hair.

As her hand rose self-consciously to stroke her hair she told them, 'It was Hattie's idea.'

'And a very good idea it was too,' Hilda crowed. 'If she can make me look like that I'll let her take me shoppin' an' all.'

'Huh! I ain't no good at miracles,' Hattie snorted, which earned her a gentle whack with a tea towel.

During their next quiet few minutes Flora tipped all her new clothes out onto the table for them all to look at and they couldn't help but be impressed.

'It's about time you treated yourself,' Hilda said as she held a fine lawn blouse up to inspect the stitching. But then the bell above the café door tinkled and Flora hastily stuffed all the new clothes back into the bags and dumped them on the stairs leading to her rooms until later. The shopping spree was over and for now at least it was back to business as usual.

Chapter Forty-Four

Flora had jammed all her clothes and possessions into an old carpet bag that she had found in the market for a pittance, but three days before she was due to sail home Hattie, Hilda and Jia Li surprised her one evening when they presented her with a brand-new, brown leather suitcase.

'We club together to buy it,' Jia Li told her solemnly. 'It our going-away present to you.'

Flora was so touched that for a moment she couldn't speak. 'Thank you so much . . . it's lovely and I shall treasure it.' She sniffed at the new leather appreciatively and, laughing, she told them, 'The trouble is, it's so smart I don't want to use it.'

Tilly who had now come back to work on light duties, giggled. She'd been in the process of peeling some potatoes, a job she could do sitting at the table, but she'd stopped to see them give Flora her present. Each morning on his way to work, Ernie walked her to the café then came to collect her to take her home again when he'd finished. He watched over her constantly like a mother hen and Tilly was opening up like a flower before their very eyes thanks to his devotion. She had hero-worshipped Ernie ever since she was a little girl and could hardly believe that he now had feelings for her.

'You just mark my words, them pair will be wed before the year's out,' Hattie whispered to them later that afternoon when they all sat together having a well-earned break. Flora hoped that she was right because she'd seen a change in Ernie too. The sad, haunted look had gone from his eyes now and she had an idea that he and Tilly were going to be very happy together.

Just the day before she had received a letter from Colleen who had informed her that Ben had taken to work on the smallholding as if he'd been born to it. He never tired of working with the animals and Colleen was happy to report that he and her mammy and siblings all got on like a house on fire.

Sure, I sometimes t'ink they love him more than they love me, so I do, Colleen had written, which made them all titter when Flora read it out to them.

'Seems like love is in the air,' Hattie said as she and Flora worked side by side in the kitchen later that day. 'Now, let's just hope that some of it rubs off on you eh, miss?'

'I doubt that's very likely,' Flora answered.

'Hmm, that all depends on if you're big enough to swallow your pride and make the first move towards that young man you left behind when you get home.'

Flora pretended she hadn't heard her and got on with what she was doing.

Before they knew it the day that Flora was due to sail had rolled around and the mood in the café was subdued. Dora had come to wish her well and say a tearful farewell to her the day before and now they all got ready to go with her to the ship to wave her off. Everyone she had come to love was there: Hattie, Hilda, Jia Li and Bai, Ernie and Tilly, and even Jimmy and Sam had come along.

As they set off, with Jimmy carrying her spanking new case for her, and Flora looking lovely in one of the pretty summer dresses that Hattie had talked her into, she paused just once to stare back at the little house and café she had worked so hard on, but then she purposefully looked straight ahead. She would never forget the friends she had made in New York, but it was time to think of the future now.

Everything was hustle and bustle on the quay when they arrived as people hurried for the gangplank and yelled for porters.

'Now, are you quite sure you've got everythin'?' Hattie asked to hide her distress. She had never been blessed with a daughter but had she been she would have wanted one just like Flora. 'Tickets? Money?'

'It's all in here.' Flora patted her bag and gave her a reassuring smile as the others gathered around to say their goodbyes. There was a quick pat on the back from Sam and a peck on the cheek from Jimmy and Bai. A hug from Ernie and Tilly, tears from Hattie and Hilda, and finally it was time for her to say goodbye to Jia Li. Her pregnancy was now confirmed and she had a special glow about her.

'You take good care now,' the little Chinese girl told her. 'You very special to me, like sister. And thank you for all you do for me and Bai. We never forget you.' She patted her stomach then and told her, 'If baby is girl we going to call her Flora after you.'

Flora could only nod as they clung to each other for a moment. She was too choked to speak. And then she broke away and headed blindly for the gangplank. The goodbyes were proving to be far more difficult than she had thought they would be.

As she began to ascend the gangplank, the first flutters of panic began to set in and Connie's face flashed in front of her eyes. What if this ship sank too? Flora gripped the rail firmly as sweat broke out on her forehead and her heart began to thud painfully. By now she was amongst a rush of passengers all eager to get aboard and she felt herself being swept along with them until suddenly she was on the deck where a waiting steward asked to

342

see her boarding pass. She fumbled in her bag and handed it to him and looking at the clipboard he held he told her, 'You're in cabin 208. Your luggage will already be there, miss.'

'Thank you,' she croaked as he turned to the next passenger in the line. She stumbled to the rail and gazed down into the sea of faces on the dock, desperate for a sight of her friends. After a moment she saw them, all smiling and waving frantically and it gave her courage.

I can do this, she told herself sternly. *Lightning doesn't strike twice.*

Even so it took every ounce of courage she had to stand there and wave back at them. It seemed an age until the gangplank was hauled up and the sound of the enormous engines chugged into life. She was gripping the rail so tightly that her knuckles had turned white but still she managed to keep the smile plastered to her face until eventually New York and the faces of the people she had grown to love became just specks in the distance. Only then did she venture away from the rail and on legs that felt as if they had turned to jelly she went to locate her cabin. When she eventually found it she discovered that it was nowhere near as opulent as the ones she and Connie had had aboard the *Titanic*. It was quite small with just a single bed, a small wardrobe and a tiny bathroom leading off it. There was no balcony but it did have a porthole that looked out over the sea, and it was comfortable and adequate for her needs so she had no complaints. She stayed in her room all day reading and didn't venture out until hunger got the better of her and she went in search of the dining hall. Every second her ears were straining to listen to the engines in case they stopped abruptly as they had when she was aboard the *Titanic*. But they chugged away comfortingly and slowly she began to get over her panic and feel a little more in control of herself.

Over the next few days she kept herself very much to herself. Occasionally she went for a stroll on deck but the majority of her time was spent reading as she took full advantage of the ship's small library. And then, at last, her homeland came into sight in the distance and tears of relief sprang to her eyes.

It was late in the afternoon when the passengers finally left the ship and for a moment she stood on the quay relishing the feel of dry land beneath her feet. Tightly clutching her shiny new suitcase, she wondered if she should book herself into a small hotel for the night, but by now she was so eager to see her family again that she decided she would head for the train station, even if it meant travelling through the night on the next train bound for London.

Late the following morning she was at last walking along familiar streets. She had catnapped on the train but now she was suddenly bright-eyed at the prospect of seeing her home again. Minutes later she turned a corner and there it was. Her heart was thudding again, but with joy this time as she raced towards the door and threw it open. Her mother was standing at the sink but her face instantly broke into a smile and tears of joy began to streak down her cheeks as she ran across the room to wrap Flora in her arms.

'Oh love, you gave us a right scare, I don't mind tellin' you,' she sobbed. Then holding her daughter at arm's length, she took a long hard look at her. Somehow, during the time she had been away from home, Flora had grown from a young girl into a confident-looking young woman.

The reunion with the rest of her family later that evening was an emotional one. They had all believed her to be dead but as yet no one had broached the lie she had lived when first arriving in New York.

It was actually Flora herself who raised the subject with her mother over breakfast the next morning when she said quietly,

'I'm so sorry I put you through all that heartache, Ma. It must have been so hard for you all thinking I was dead. I'm so ashamed now of what I did.'

'Shush now!' Her mother smiled at her. 'I admit it was hard for us but we accept that it must have been even harder for you. There you were after surviving the ship going down in a strange country with no one you knew. It's no wonder you were afraid and decided to take on Connie's identity for a time.'

'I never intentionally set out to do it,' Flora explained as she fiddled nervously with the fringes on the edge of the chenille tablecloth. She went on to tell her mother about the mix-up on the boat when they had found Connie's aunt's address in the belt she was wearing. 'They thought I was Connie so I just sort of went along with it, but then once I had met Alex it got harder and I couldn't go on living a lie.' She also told her about Toby and the way he had tried to blackmail her and about the café and all the friends she had made as her mother listened, solemn-faced.

'So, you signed over everything to Jia Li before you left, did you? You must have thought a great deal of her after all your hard work. I just hope she doesn't let you down, but then I'm sure you know her well enough to trust her. But now tell me all about Colleen, Ben's new wife.'

'Oh, she's a really lovely person and she adores Ben,' Flora assured her mother. 'I just know they're going to be happy together.'

Her mother nodded. It still hurt that he had chosen to live so far away but she was coming to terms with it. 'It's perhaps as well he did decide to settle in Ireland,' she said sadly. 'He got in with a bad lot over here. It sounds like this Colleen will keep him on the straight and narrow and all I want at the end of the day is for him to be happy. That goes for you too, which leads me to ask, do you still have feelings for the young man you were seeing before you left?'

Flora glanced towards the window as colour rose in her cheeks and she slowly nodded. 'I didn't realise just how much I did think of him until I was on the way to New York,' she admitted. 'But it's too late now. I've been gone for well over a year. Jamie has probably got himself another girl by now and who could blame him? I put what I wanted to do before his feelings.'

'It's never too late if you still have feelings for him,' her mother answered gently. 'Why don't you write to him?'

Flora shook her head. She had come home with very little apart from a new suitcase, a load of new clothes and her pride. And a pile of unsent letters to Jamie tied in ribbon. Her mother secretly thought that Flora was making a grave mistake but she said nothing and for then the subject was dropped.

Over the next few days, Flora began to search for another job and eventually she found one in a busy café in the city centre. It wasn't long before the owners realised that she knew every aspect of the business so they left more and more of the running of it to her and soon it began to feel as if she had never been away as her life settled into a pattern again. And if Flora felt deep down that something was still missing from her life she gave no sign of it and threw herself into her work. It was only at night when she was curled up in her bed that she allowed herself to think of Jamie and what might have been.

Chapter Forty-Five

July 1914

'Didn't I tell you that a war was on the cards?' Flora's father said one evening as he sat reading the newspaper. 'The Archduke Franz Ferdinand and his wife have been assassinated in Sarajevo! Nothing good will come of this, you just mark my words.'

Emily didn't look over-concerned as she continued to fold the washing she had just fetched in from the line ready for ironing the next day. 'I really don't see how somethin' that hasn't even happened in our country could affect us,' she commented, but her husband shook his head.

'Let's just wait an' see then, shall we?' he answered and went back to reading the papers as Emily and Flora exchanged a worried glance.

For some reason Flora's thoughts instantly turned to Jamie, as they often still did. Many a time since she had returned home, she had been on the verge of going to see him, or at least writing to him, but her pride had always stopped her and the longer it went on the harder it got. But what if her father was right and war was declared? Would it mean that all the young men would be called up to fight? Would Jamie be one of them? The thought filled her with dread so she tried to push it to the back of her mind.

There was something else worrying her too. Ever since coming home she had intended to go and see Mrs Merry, the housekeeper she had been so fond of when she had worked for Connie. Of course, she had no way of knowing if Mrs Merry still even lived there. She could have left, or the house might even have been sold. But now at last she felt brave enough to find out, so on her very next day off she dressed carefully and set off in the direction of her late employer's house.

Once outside she stood there gazing at the façade as the memories flooded back. She could picture Connie standing on the steps laughing and happy, and then another image came to her mind: an image of Connie tripping down the frozen steps in her beautiful new gown on the night her father had died. The night, if they had only known it, that would change both their lives forever. She looked up at the bedroom window then and could almost imagine she saw Connie flitting about the room. They had shared so many happy times together there before that terrible night, but they were both gone forever now.

On the outside the house looked just the same but whether it now had new owners or not she had no idea. There was only one way to find out, so after taking a deep breath she climbed the steps and rapped on the door.

From within she heard footsteps approaching and when the door opened she saw Mrs Merry standing there. The woman stared at her for a moment as if she couldn't believe what her eyes were seeing, then with a whoop of delight she caught her in a hug that almost lifted her off her feet.

'Oh, Flora, I can't believe you're *really* here,' she cried happily. 'I thought you were an apparition for a second there. But come in, come in, the mistress will be so happy to see you.'

'The mistress?'

When Flora looked confused the smile slid from Mrs Merry's face. 'There's been a lot of changes around here,' she told Flora solemnly. 'But it ain't for me to tell you about them. Let me go an' tell the mistress you're here. I know she's been frettin' about you ever since she arrived.'

The kindly woman hurried away in the direction of the drawing room leaving Flora feeling more confused by the minute. How could there be a new mistress here? Connie's father had left the house in trust for her when she reached her coming of age but Connie was gone now, so who else could possibly have a claim on the house?

She could hear Mrs Merry excitedly jabbering away and then someone appeared in the doorway of the drawing room and Flora's heart skipped a beat.

'Flora, my dear. Thank goodness you're all right!'

Connie's Aunt Alex was hurrying towards her with her arms outstretched, but she looked nothing like the downtrodden, dowdily dressed woman that Flora remembered from New York. This woman was dressed in a pretty, flowered dress that just grazed her ankles and she now wore her lovely blonde hair in a style similar to Flora's, only slightly longer.

Seeing how confused her visitor looked, Alex smiled warmly and taking her hand she told her, 'Come with me. A lot has happened since I last saw you. We have so much catching up to do. Oh, and Merry, would you be a dear and make us some tea? You can join us then if you like.'

It was more than obvious that Alex and Mrs Merry were getting on famously and Flora was growing more confused by the minute. As they entered the drawing room she saw at a glance that it looked much as she remembered, although some of the furniture had been shifted about slightly. There was a large bowl of lilies in the middle of the table and their scent wafted about the room.

Alex noticed Flora looking at them and she giggled like a schoolgirl. 'They're lovely, aren't they? They were a present from

Victor, or Mr Wainthrop as you probably know him. He's *such* a darling.'

Now Flora's eyes were almost popping out of her head as Alex ushered her towards a chair, before sitting down opposite her.

'I . . . I think I owe you an apology,' Flora mumbled, feeling decidedly ill at ease. Never in her wildest dream had she ever expected to see Alex again, let alone here. 'For running away as I did and for pretending to be Connie in the first place . . . it was unforgivable of me.'

Alex stared at her thoughtfully for a moment as if she were deciding whether or not to say whatever was on her mind, but then taking a deep breath she said quietly, 'You don't need to apologise. You see, from almost the moment you arrived at the house in New York I knew that you weren't Constance.'

'*You did!*' Flora was truly shocked now. 'B-but how?'

Alex frowned as her small white teeth played with her bottom lip but then raising her head she looked Flora in the eye and gently lowered the sleeve of her dress to reveal a tiny heart-shaped birthmark on the top of her arm. 'Because of this. As her maid you surely must have known that Connie had one in exactly the same place?'

Flora had forgotten all about it but now she nodded. 'Yes, yes she did . . . but how could you possibly know that? You hardly ever saw her.'

'She was born with it,' Alex told her and then after taking a deep breath she went on, 'And I should know . . . because I was her mother.'

Flora gawped at her uncomprehendingly. This was all getting a little too much to take in.

Alex sighed and standing up she began to pace up and down the room. 'I know it must all sound very far-fetched.' She was clearly distressed and her voice was little more than a whisper. 'But the truth of it is, Edward, Connie's father, and I fell in love

350

and had an affair. I had already realised that marrying Marcus had been the biggest mistake of my life and Edward was unhappy with Alicia too, so somehow it just happened. We never meant it to and we ended it very quickly because we couldn't bear to think of the pain it would cause to our partners, even though we loved each other deeply. But then I found out that I was pregnant and it all came out. Marcus knew that the child couldn't be his and it didn't take long for him and Alicia to put two and two together.

'Edward wanted me to leave Marcus and live with him so that we could marry after we had both got divorced, but Alicia was my sister and I just couldn't do it to her.' Alex paused to dab at her eyes with a scrap of a lace handkerchief as the painful memories flooded back. Then, taking a deep breath, she went on, 'It was decided that once the baby was born Edward would come to New York and bring the child back here to live and he and Alicia would adopt it. And that was exactly what happened. I felt as if my heart had been ripped out of my chest on the day Edward took her, and Alicia . . . well, she never took to the child, although her father adored her. I suppose it's understandable, really. I had betrayed her in the worst possible way with her husband and poor Connie must have been a constant reminder of what we'd done. Anyway, when you arrived after the tragedy on the *Titanic* I sensed almost immediately that you weren't my daughter. You were very ill, as you may remember, and it was as I was helping Patsy change you into a clean nightgown shortly after you arrived that I noticed you had no birthmark and my fears were confirmed.'

'B-but *why* didn't you say something then?'

Alex shrugged. 'What would have been the point? Marcus was such a cold person. He hadn't wanted me to have Connie there in the first place and I have no doubt had he known that you were merely her maid he would have turfed you out on the streets without a second thought. That's the kind of man he was. I was devastated when I learned that Edward had died but I saw it as a chance to finally get to know my daughter and try to make it up to her for abandoning her. And then when I realised that she was dead, I suppose having a young person around that I could get on with helped with my grief, so I said nothing. I had to grieve for Connie in private, you see, and it was doubly hard knowing that I had missed my chance yet again of being able to show her how much I loved her. I suppose I saw you as a chance to make it up the only way I could.'

Mrs Merry came back into the room at that moment trundling a tea trolley and seeing Alex's tearful face she said, 'You've told her then – about Connie bein' your daughter?'

Alex nodded. 'Yes, I've told her.' She looked back at Flora. 'And now I suppose you're wondering what I'm doing here?'

'I . . . I am rather,' Flora answered unsteadily. She was still all of a dither.

'Shortly after you left, Toby started to be a frequent visitor to the house. He was very angry when I told him that you had left, but he quickly turned his attentions to Margaret. Of course, I've no doubt she knew that he was only after her fortune but Margaret wanted a husband at any cost so they got married and he moved in with us. Not long after that Marcus had a massive heart attack and died. On the day of the funeral when the solicitor came to the house to read the will I discovered that Marcus had left the house in New York and everything he owned to Margaret. I can't say that I really blame him. After all, I did him a grave injustice all those years ago. Anyway, Mr Wainthrop got in touch to tell me that in Edward's will he had stated that should anything happen to Constance, then *this* house would pass to me . . . So, here I am and I've never been happier in my life.'

'Neither has Victor Wainthrop,' Mrs Merry told Flora with a cheeky wink. 'He's round here most days wi' a twinkle in his eye. I ain't never seen him so happy since his dear wife passed away.'

'Merry, *really*!' Alex objected, blushing prettily. But then, turning her attention back to Flora, she said, 'There, I've bared my soul to you so now I want to hear all about what you've been up to since you ran away from us in New York.'

And so, for the next half an hour Flora told them everything. About working in the laundry, meeting Jia Li and Colleen, renting the café and buying the house until she had brought them right up to date.

'And did you manage to meet a nice young man in New York like your friends did?'

'Oh no. I've had no time for all that. Anyway . . .' She shook her head.

'Anyway?' Alex said curiously.

'Oh, well . . .' Flora paused, wondering whether to say anything. But then after everything Alex had told her, she felt that maybe she'd understand. 'Before I left for New York I was walking out with someone, Jamie, but I hurt him badly when I said I wanted to go to New York with Connie, and he disappeared. I tried to see him again, but he'd left, and as he never bothered coming to see me again or try to stop me before we left, I can only suppose he decided he'd be better off without me. But I've never managed to forget him.' She smiled sadly.

At this, Mrs Merry lowered her head looking utterly ashamed. 'Actually . . .' she muttered. 'That's not quite true . . . See, shortly before you left to get the boat he came here sayin' he needed to see you an' I . . . Well, I was afraid you'd change your mind and wind up letting Connie go alone . . . so I . . . I told him you'd already gone. I kept some letters he sent here for you as well. I'm *so* sorry, pet. If I could go back in time I wouldn't do it again, I *swear*.'

Flora stared at her numbly as the room began to swim around her. So Jamie *had* come looking for her . . . and all this time she had thought that he hadn't cared enough to try and persuade her to change her mind about going to New York. Perhaps he had really loved her after all?

'Can you ever forgive me?' Mrs Merry asked then, her voice heavy with regret and tears.

Flora was so choked that she couldn't even answer her as she thought of all the heartache that could have been avoided.

'I . . . I'll make it up to . . . I *swear* I will!' Mrs Merry babbled as she wrung her hands together. 'We'll try and find him . . . I could help you. I just couldn't bear the thought of Connie goin' all that way on her own so soon after losing her dad. Please try an' understand. I loved that girl like my own but I loved you too and it's been hard to live with meself knowing what I did!'

Flora looked at her in disbelief. For a moment she didn't know what to say, but then a rage grew within her. How could Mrs Merry expect her to forgive her? She'd ruined her chance at love, and for what? She hadn't been able to save Connie from death and she'd almost died herself. It was all too overwhelming. 'But . . . But how *could* you? How often did he come here? Where are the letters? Oh, poor Jamie. He must hate me even more than I thought if he thinks I couldn't even be bothered to reply to his letters. And all this time . . .'

Mrs Merry got up and rushed over to her and, kneeling on the floor in front of her, she grasped Flora's hands. 'I'm a foolish and stupid old woman. All I could think of was Connie on her own on that big ship.'

Flora snatched her hands away, as if she couldn't bear the woman's touch. 'Did you never think of me? Of Jamie? Of the lives you've ruined?'

'I don't know what to say.' Mrs Merry was crying now too. 'Just let me make it up to you. I'll do anythin'.'

'There's nothing you can do that will make up for this. All this time . . . All this time when we could have been happy and you snatched it away from us.' She started to sob now, unable to bear the thought of poor Jamie and his shattered heart.

Alex intervened then. 'It seems to me that we've all three done something to be ashamed of in our pasts, don't you think, Flora? But perhaps it's time to put it all behind us and move on now,' she said gently.

Flora looked at her. The soft, kind expression on Alex's face moved her more than Mrs Merry's pleas. Alex had suffered so much, and yet she had managed to forgive her for impersonating her long-lost daughter. Which seemed, when she thought of it, a much greater crime. She had pretended to be Connie because of her own fear and selfishness, whereas Mrs Merry had acted only out of love. Her shoulders sagged, and she nodded in agreement.

They had all done things they deeply regretted but maybe now they could each start to forgive themselves.

Chapter Forty-Six

It was early in August before Flora was able to book any time off work and by then it seemed from the reports in the newspapers that war was inevitable. Recruiting offices were opening up all across the country and young men were flocking to them to join up so that they could go and fight for their king and country. But war was the last thing on Flora's mind as she prepared to catch the train at Euston Station one overcast morning.

She had spent weeks visiting places she and Jamie had frequented and houses where he had lodged in the hope of finding him but up until now all her enquiries had drawn a blank and there was only one option left open to her. Mrs Merry had given her the letters that Jamie had sent and Flora knew each word off by heart now and was heartened by the fact that he had loved her. Whether things were still the same now was another matter entirely. A lot of time had passed but she had decided that there was only one way to find out.

'I'm not so sure you shouldn't have written to him first before you go rushing off like a bull in a china shop,' Emily complained as Flora slid a hat pin into the new hat she had treated herself to. 'And what if you can't find anywhere to stay, or if perhaps you can't find him?'

Flora smiled at her. 'I'll find him, never you fear,' she said with more conviction than she was feeling. 'I know he said his foster parents who brought him up lived in a place called Treetops in a village called Hartshill just outside Nuneaton. It's only a small market town, it won't be anywhere near the size of London, so how hard can it be? Someone is sure to know where it is and once I've found it, his parents will hopefully be able to tell me where he is. As for finding somewhere to stay – I shall just come straight back home if I can't find him, so stop fretting. I'm a grown woman now you know, Ma?'

'Of course you are,' Emily placated her. 'But us mas can't just stop worryin' about their kids no matter what age they are, so just think on that, my girl.'

Flora crossed the room to give her a hug and a kiss. 'I shall be all right, I promise,' she assured her.

'And what if you're goin' all that way on a fool's errand? What if Jamie's found himself someone else or moved away?'

'I'll cross that bridge when I come to it,' Flora answered, jutting out her chin, and Emily sighed. She knew that look. Flora had made her mind up she was going and nothing would sway her from it now. She handed her daughter a pack of cheese sandwiches, saying, 'These are for on the train. And just make sure you get a proper meal inside you when you get there. Now go if you're going else you'll miss the train and there ain't another till this afternoon . . . And, Flora, good luck, love.'

After giving her mother another affectionate kiss, Flora set off and an hour later she was seated in a carriage in the train bound for Nuneaton. She settled herself in a corner and now that she was alone all the misgivings she had been trying to keep at bay flooded back. What if Jamie *had* found himself another girl . . . or if he didn't live there anymore? But then she scolded herself, *Stop it, you'll never know if you don't at least make the effort to find out, will you?*

At that moment the engine gave a hiss of steam and the train chugged into life and once they were well under way Flora took the latest letters she had received from Jia Li and Colleen from her bag. They still wrote to each other regularly and Flora was always thrilled to hear how happy they sounded. The first was from Jai Li.

Dear Flora,

The café is doing so well, and we hope to be able to save enough to pay Dora for it by Christmas, then we start to send you money we owe for the house. You have made us very happy.

We very settled in our little house too. Hattie and Hilda send their love, they miss you very much as we all do and they spoil new baby Flora very much. She is lovely baby with always a smile like her namesake and we hope to have brother or sister for her in not too distant future. Tilly and Ernie are now married and settling into Hattie's old house well and Sam and Jimmy also send much love dear friend . . .

All in all Flora was thrilled that everyone in New York appeared to be thriving. And she knew that the same was true of Colleen and Ben. She opened Colleen's letter.

My dear Flora,

We hope this letter finds you well as we are. I am now the size of a house and waddling like a duck so will be very pleased when our baby decides to put in an appearance. It should be very soon. Ben can hardly wait and is treating me like an invalid not wanting me to lift anything heavier than a kettle, so he is! Ben says when the baby is strong enough to travel he is bringing us all to London to visit the family and I can hardly wait. It is lovely being back in Ireland but I do miss you and Jai Li something terrible and often think back fondly to some of the happy times we shared.

She went on to tell Flora about what was happening on the small-holding and by the time Flora had finished reading there were tears in her eyes. Everyone seemed to have found happiness, and now she just had to pray that she would too.

She tucked the letters back in her purse and as the minutes ticked away the time until she would arrive in Jamie's hometown, she settled back in her seat to stare at the fields from the window. Looking at the cows and sheep dotted over the bright green grass, she could quite understand why someone would prefer to live in the country rather than a city. It struck her then that all her life she had lived in built-up areas. London and New York had been very similar in many ways and it was lovely looking out at the peaceful views where everything looked so bright and clean. But the distraction provided by the scenery didn't last long, and the bubble of nervousness that was growing in her stomach was starting to make her feel a bit sick. Would she be catching the train home with a broken heart? Only time would tell now.

It was just after lunchtime when the train drew into Trent Valley Station and as Flora emerged from the platform she peered around with interest at the little market town before approaching a man who was leaning idly against the carriage door of his horse-drawn cab as he waited for his next fare.

'Excuse me, but would you happen to know of a place called Treetops? It's in a village called Hartshill just outside of town.'

He nodded. 'I know it, miss. It's Lady Ashley's old place, though her daughter and her son-in-law own it now. I reckon it's some sort of children's home.'

'That's it,' she said eagerly. 'Is it within walking distance?'

He stroked his chin. 'Well, I'd say it's a good five or six miles as the crow flies at least.'

'In that case would you mind taking me there?'

'O' course, miss, my pleasure. Hop in.' He politely opened the door for her and once she had climbed up into the carriage and settled against the faded leather squabs he took the nose bag from his loyal old nag and urged her into life. Soon after they passed a large market that seemed to have stalls displaying everything from buckets and bowls to buttons and bows and on the edge of it she spotted the cattle market that Jamie had often spoken of. There were crates of chickens squawking indignantly, and larger pens, where horses pawed the ground impatiently. Others contained goats, cattle and sheep and Flora wished she had more time to look around. Maybe if Jamie still felt the same, they could come here together. Then she chided herself for getting her hopes up. For all she knew, Jamie could be married by now, so she had to be prepared for heartbreak.

Finally, after passing a large, five-sail windmill and jogging through a forest, she realised she must be close as she remembered Jamie telling her about how he used to play in the forest when he was young. The cab drew to a halt before two enormous wrought-iron gates and the cabbie climbed down to inform her, 'This is Treetops, miss. Would you like me to take you down the drive to it?'

'No . . . thank you, I think I'd like to walk.' It would be nice to see the place where Jamie had grown up, plus it might give her some time to calm down. After collecting her things together and alighting the carriage she paid the driver and added a generous tip.

He doffed his cap as he politely asked, 'Will you be wantin' me to wait for you, miss?'

'No, I shall be fine from here, thank you,' she told him, although she felt sick with nerves now. Very soon she might see Jamie again but would the encounter have the outcome she was hoping for?

She stood and watched the cab pull away, then taking a deep breath she set off down the tree-lined drive. Through the trees she could hear the sound of children's laughter as they gambolled on the lush, green lawns. After walking some way, the house came into sight and she caught her breath. It was very large and much grander than she had expected. The sky was a deep, azure blue with powder puff clouds floating across it and there was the scent of new-mown grass in the air, and she thought what a lovely place it must have been to grow up in.

The closer she got to the house the more nervous she became as memories of the times she had spent with Jamie assailed her. Images of his laughing blue eyes and his wonderful smile flashed in front of her eyes. Would he still look the same? Would he still be the same? She had no way of knowing, she only knew that the next few hours could well determine the rest of her life. Would Jamie send her away with a flea in her ear, or would he be pleased to see her? Would he even still live here or would he have moved on to pastures new? She knew that one way or another she would have the answer to all these questions soon and then at last she could start to plan her future.

When she reached the imposing oak doors she smoothed her skirt and patted her hair then, after taking a deep breath, she pulled on the large brass bell that hung at the side of the door. Within minutes it was opened by a middle-aged woman with a kindly face who was enveloped in a huge white apron.

'Hello, love, can I help you?' she asked.

'Er . . . I was wondering if Jamie Branning was here?' Flora answered in a wobbly voice.

'Jamie, why yes, he's about somewhere.' The woman frowned as she tried to think where he might be then suddenly remembering her manners she smiled and said, 'I'm Cissie, I live here. Well, not in the house exactly. Me an' me husband live in a cottage in the grounds wi' our family. But do you mind me askin' who it is wants to see him?'

'I'm Flora . . . Flora Butler. Jamie and I were friends when he was working near my home in Londo—'

'*Flora!*' Cissie snorted gleefully. 'Well, I'll be. You're the one who broke 'is heart. But never mind that for now. Come in, come in. I'll just tell Sunday you're here then I'll try an' find Jamie.'

But she had no need to call Sunday for at that moment an attractive woman appeared in the hallway and after glancing at Flora asked, 'Is this the young person who's come to apply for the maid's job, Cissie?'

'No, it ain't,' Cissie told her, nothing like Flora would have expected a maid to address her mistress. 'This young lady 'ere is Flora . . . The one who stole our Jamie's heart.'

'Flora!' Sunday looked shocked then her face broke into a smile that seemed to light up the whole room. 'Why, how *wonderful*! But Jamie told us you'd gone to New York.'

Flora was heartened to learn that Jamie had spoken about her. 'I had but I came back home a while ago and . . .'

'Oh, you must come in,' Sunday urged. 'Cissie run to the kitchen and get cook to make a tray of tea, would you, please? Then ask one of the children to run and find Jamie. I think he's in the stables with Tom. Just tell them to tell him he has a visitor.'

Taking her elbow, Sunday led her into a large room where the table was covered with colouring books and crayons. There were toys scattered everywhere and it wasn't anything like Flora had expected it to be from the outside. It was spotlessly clean but looked lived in and was very comfy and cosy.

'Cissie will be in with the tea in a minute,' Sunday told her in a state of great excitement. 'It's lovely to meet you, Flora, but I'm going to leave you now. I have a feeling that you and Jamie are going to have an awful lot to talk about when he arrives and you don't want me playing gooseberry.' And before Flora could get a word in, Sunday was gone, closing the door quietly behind her.

Flora put her bag down and crossed to one of the enormous windows overlooking the gardens. They were just as lovely as Jamie had told her and she could see now why he loved the place

362

so much. Cissie came bustling in shortly after to place a tray of tea on the table but then she too scuttled away like a cat whose tail was on fire.

She stood there with her back to the door, every second seeming like an hour and then at last she heard footsteps, and as the door opened she held her breath as she slowly turned. Jamie was standing there looking completely thunderstruck, but after a moment he pulled himself together and held his hand out politely.

'Hello, Flora. I never expected to see you again. How are you?'

His formal words made her heart sink. He wasn't pleased to see her. Still, she was here now and determined to say what she had come to say.

'I . . . I'm very well, thank you, and I . . . I came to say I'm sorry,' she said quietly.

He raised his eyebrow. 'For what? Preferring to go off to New York than carry on seeing me?'

Her head wagged from side to side as she wrung her hands together. 'It wasn't like that, I promise. After we argued that first time, I went to meet you the next week to say I loved you and wasn't going to go, but you weren't there. I kept going back every Sunday, waiting to see if you'd come, but you never did. And then I went to your lodging house to try to find you, but you'd moved away, so I thought you'd changed your mind. That you didn't love me after all.'

He shrugged.

'And then when I came back . . . Mrs Merry told me that you had come to see me and she'd told you that Connie and I had already sailed. She kept your letters from me too. She was afraid that I was changing my mind, you see? She didn't want Connie to have to travel alone so soon after losing her father.'

His face gentled a little and he sighed. 'Well, it's all in the past and over and done with now, isn't it? We've both probably grown up an awful lot since then. It clearly just wasn't meant to be.'

She stared at him long and hard before saying quietly, 'Do you *really* believe that, Jamie? Because *I'm* not ashamed to admit that there has never been a single day that I haven't missed you since we've been apart. I wrote so many letters to you but never had the courage to post them. They're all here, look.' She slowly withdrew the bundle of letters tied with ribbon from her bag and placed them down on a small table. 'Perhaps when you do read them, if you want to that is, you'll see just how much I do care for you! It was only when Connie and I were on our way that I realised what a fool I'd been to even consider going in the first place, even though I thought you didn't care, I should have stayed and tried to come and find you here. But clearly your feelings have changed now, and I understand. It's been a long time, after all.' Humiliation and pain were threatening to swamp her and suddenly she just wanted to be gone. Somewhere far away where she could lick her wounds and tell herself what a fool she'd been.

'Goodbye, Jamie. I'm sorry to have troubled you,' she said in a strangled voice as she grabbed her bag and headed for the door, but just then it was flung open and Cissie and Sunday stood there side by side looking for all the world as if they were ready to do battle. They had seen how much he had pined for the girl yet now she was here he was willing to let her go again.

Over my dead body! Cissie thought. 'Just what the *hell* do you think you're doing sending this girl away when you've done nothing but moon about over her like a lovesick cow for years?' she demanded with her hands on her hips.

Jamie flushed with temper. 'You've been eavesdropping at the door the pair of you, *haven't* you?'

'Aye, an' it's a good job we did an' all, ain't it?' Cissie snapped back with no trace of shame. 'I know *exactly* why you're sendin' her away but perhaps you should tell her the reason an' then let *her* make a decision on what happens next. The poor lass clearly loves you or she wouldn't have come all this way now, would she?'

Jamie's temper drained away as he looked towards Flora who was watching him avidly.

He looked back at Cissie and the woman who had been the only mother he had ever known and told them quietly, 'All right, you win. But could you please leave us alone now and give us some privacy. I mean *properly* leave us alone!'

'With the greatest of pleasure, you daft young oaf,' Cissie replied, and taking Sunday's elbow she led her smartly from the room with a big, satisfied grin on her face.

For a moment the two young people stood facing each other, then Flora asked falteringly, 'So what did Cissie mean, Jamie?. . . That she knew why you were sending me away? Did she mean that you *do* still have feelings for me?'

'Of *course* I do!' He ran his hand through his hair distractedly in the way she remembered so well. 'I've *never* stopped loving you . . . but it's too late for us now.'

'Too late?' She looked confused. 'But *why* is it too late?'

He sighed. 'It's too late because war is going to be announced any day now and I . . . I've already signed up for the army. I'm leaving to start my training in Wiltshire in two weeks' time. Do you understand what I'm saying? I'm going to fight and there's a chance I might not come back . . . I couldn't expect you to wait for me under those circumstances.'

Flora's face darkened as she went to stand in front of him and now it was she who was angry. 'Cissie was right, you *are* a silly oaf,' she scowled. 'I love you *so* much I'd wait for you under any circumstances, *forever* if need be!'

'You *would*?'

She nodded and as his arms came around her, she said more gently, 'I would, but only on one condition. If you're not going for two weeks then we have time to get a special licence and you can make an honest woman of me before you leave.'

'Flora Butler, are you *proposing* to me?' His face was as bright as hers now as she nestled her head on his shoulder and sighed contentedly.

'I suppose I am.' She looked up at him. 'So . . . what's your answer?'

'Well, never let it be said that I didn't do the right thing.' And then his lips were on hers and suddenly all was right with the world.

Straightening up from the keyhole, Cissie smiled at Sunday who was standing anxiously behind her.

She put her thumb up. 'Seems like we have a weddin' to plan,' she told her, and arm in arm they went to the kitchen to celebrate with a good strong cup of tea and share the happy news with their husbands.

Epilogue

March 1919

Flora shifted her weight as she tried to get comfortable in the armchair and glanced out of the cottage window to where Constance, her four-year-old daughter, was playing in the garden. Spring was upon them and daffodils and primulas were peeping through the earth but it still tended to be cold in the wind so Flora had made sure the child was well wrapped up in a warm coat and bright red hat, scarf and gloves that she had knitted for her. She smiled fondly as she watched her gambolling about the garden with her puppy, a mischievous Jack Russell terrier that she and Jamie had bought the child for her last birthday. The two of them were inseparable. Patch, as Constance had named him, even slept on the child's bed at night.

She turned her attention back to the room then to make sure that everything was just right for her mother's arrival. Jamie had gone to meet her from the train and they should be home very soon now, provided the train was on time. She had planned to go to London to attend church with her mother for the Mother's Day service, which was the next day, but because she was so advanced in her pregnancy her mother had decided that it might be safer if she came to Flora instead. Now the little cottage in Mancetter that had been a wedding present from Sunday and Tom, Jamie's adoptive parents, gleamed from top to bottom and a cheery fire was burning in the grate, turning the highly polished brass fender to molten gold.

She smiled reflectively. The last four years had been full of ups and downs. She and Jamie had married in the tiny church in Mancetter – the village where they now lived – before he left for his army training, and the time they had shared before he left to fight had been all too brief. And then two months later, Flora had discovered that she was carrying his child. Little Connie was now referred to as their honeymoon baby, but she had been two years old before Jamie finally got to meet her when he was shipped home after being shot in the leg during the Battle of the Somme.

Flora had prayed that this would be the end of the fighting for him but once the leg had healed somewhat, Jamie had insisted on going back. Shortly after, his leg had become infected and gangrene had almost cost him his life. Flora had spent weeks in a hospital in Plymouth with him after he had been shipped home for the second time, as he hovered between life and death, until the surgeons finally decided that the only way to save him would be to amputate his leg below the knee.

Jamie had been devastated whereas Flora was simply relieved when at last, following the operation, he slowly started to make a recovery. However, when he finally returned home on crutches, Jamie was a changed man and had slipped into a deep depression.

'What use am I to man or beast now?' he would ask Flora as she tenderly nursed him back to health.

'You're alive, that's all that matters,' she would tell him over and over again. But Jamie had seen sights that would haunt him forever. His best friend had died in his arms on the battlefield and there had been nothing whatsoever that Jamie could do to save him. He had seen men buried still alive in thick cloying mud and lived in rat-infested trenches, and it had taken a long, long time for him finally to return to being the man she had known before he went to war. Thankfully the year after he lost his leg he was fitted with a prosthesis and although he had suffered terribly getting used to it, it made him feel like a man again and once he had learned to walk on it he had found himself a job in the post office sorting office in Nuneaton, which had given him back his pride.

There had been a difficult time again last year when she had given birth to a stillborn son, which brought back horrible memories of poor Jai Li's ordeal, as well as the little soul she had been unable to protect on the *Titanic*. She and Jamie had grieved deeply for the little boy, and though she knew she was not to blame, Flora had felt guilty; she knew how much Jamie longed for a son. On top of which, after all the tragedy of the previous years, the baby had represented hope for the future for them. But now, with this new little one about to arrive, they had managed to come to terms with their loss.

During the time Jamie had been away, Flora had grown very close to Sunday and Tom, and sometimes she wondered how she would have coped without them. Sunday was a regular visitor to the cottage and she never came without some sort of treat or sweeties for Connie, who she adored. Her love was returned and the child lovingly referred to her as Nanny Sunshine.

Leaning over to the small table beside her, Flora picked up the latest letter from Colleen in Ireland. It had come just a few days before and was already much read, as was the one that had arrived shortly before hers from Jia Li in New York. Both families were still thriving and doing well and Colleen and Ben were now the proud parents of two-year-old twin boys and two girls who were three and five. Jia Li and Bai also had a boy and a girl and in her latest letter, Jia Li told Flora that Hilda had now moved into the rooms above the café with Hattie and the two women were as thick as thieves. Happily, Ernie and Tilly were also awaiting the arrival of their first baby. She glanced impatiently at the clock again only to have her thoughts interrupted by a whoop of glee from Connie outside who had spotted her granny and her daddy walking along the lane.

'They're here, Mammy,' the child called and with a wide smile on her face Flora hauled herself out of the chair and waddled to the door.

'Why, just look at you! You're the size of a house.' Emily grinned as Flora swayed down the garden path towards her. 'That's got to be a boy or I'll eat my hat.' A shadow temporarily flitted across Flora's face as she experienced another sharp twinge, they'd been coming on and off all day, but then they were in each other's arms as Connie and the dog danced around them.

Eventually they all went inside and Emily glanced around the little cottage appreciatively.

'Well, you've got this nice, love,' she commented as she drew off her gloves and took the pin from her hat. The dresser that stood against one wall was full of Flora's best china and the table that took up the centre of the room had been scrubbed until it was almost white. Gay floral curtains hung at the windows and on the floor in front of the hearth was a large, colourful peg rug that had taken Flora many months to make out of any scraps of material that she could find. A small horsehair sofa adorned with comfy cushions stood to one side of the fire and on the other was Jamie's favourite wing chair with another identical one positioned in the window where they could sit and admire the garden.

'We like it,' Flora answered modestly as she placed the kettle on the hob to make some tea, although she could have said she actually loved it and had no idea how she would ever be able to thank Sunday and Tom enough for providing them with such a grand little home.

'But now tell me about everyone at home,' Flora urged and so for the next hour as they relaxed with a large pot of tea and a jam sponge that Flora had made especially for the occasion, Emily did just that. Eventually the afternoon darkened and Emily bathed Connie in the tin bath before the fire and slipped her into her nightdress before giving her springy damp curls a good rub with the towel.

'Will you tell me a story, Granny Ems?' Connie pleaded. 'The one you told me the last time you came about the princess and the pea?'

Emily smiled indulgently. 'I think I could manage that but let's get this hair dry first, miss. We don't want you going to bed with it wet, now, do we?'

Flora and Jamie exchanged an amused glance. Connie had clearly got her granny wrapped around her little finger but then that was no bad thing as far as they were concerned. She didn't see quite as much of Granny Ems as she did of Nanny Sunshine because of her living so far away in London, but when they did get together they certainly made up for lost time.

'Are you looking forward to the service tomorrow, pet?' Jamie asked Flora affectionately when Emily had gone off to tuck Connie into bed.

'I certainly am.' The Mother's Day service at the church was one of Flora's favourites and she never missed it, but this year it would be extra special with a new little life about to make an appearance.

Later that night as she lay in their soft, feather bed with Jamie snoring softly beside her and an owl hooting in the tree outside the bedroom window, Flora sighed with contentment as she considered how lucky she was. And then, as the child inside her became still, she took advantage of the fact and quickly fell asleep.

A niggling pain in the small of her back woke Flora in the small hours of the morning and not wanting to disturb Jamie she inched towards the edge of the bed and quietly pulled her dressing robe on before making her way downstairs as quietly as she could.

Jamie had damped the fire down with tea leaves the night before

371

but now she quickly gave the dying embers a rake and threw some logs on it before beginning to pace up and down the room.

It'll probably go off in a minute and just be a false alarm, she tried to reassure herself but the pain persisted, in fact, if anything, it was getting slightly worse. Still, Flora was determined not to disturb anyone. She had been in labour for hours and hours with Connie so she wasn't panicking as yet. At last she saw the first fingers of dawn touch the sky and soon it began to get lighter.

It was Emily who found her still pacing the kitchen when she came down shortly before seven o'clock in the morning.

'You're an early bird,' she said brightly, smothering a yawn. 'I thought I'd be the first up and about. I wanted to treat you and Jamie to breakfast in bed an' give meself plenty o' time to get ready for the Mother's Day service . . .' She stopped abruptly as she saw the way Flora was holding her back and asked, 'Is it the baby coming?'

Flora nodded. 'I think it might be, Ma. I was having pains all day yesterday on and off but they got worse in the night.' Even as she spoke she felt a warm gush between her legs and she glanced down to see a small puddle on the flagstones.

'It's coming all right,' Emily chuckled. 'Come on now, sit yourself down and have a cuppa while you can then I'll get Jamie up to go an' fetch the midwife. I've a feelin' we won't be goin' to church this mornin'.'

'Oh, but you *must* go,' Flora protested. 'Sunday is picking us up in the carriage.'

Emily grinned. 'I doubt she'll be goin' anywhere either when she knows her next gran'child is about to make an appearance.' All the time she was talking she was bustling about, preparing the cups and the teapot and soon they were sitting with steaming drinks in front of them. Flora's pain had moved around to the front by then and had grown much stronger.

Jamie found them sitting there soon after and when he realised what was happening he flew into a panic.

'Shall I run for the midwife?'

'No, not yet awhile, pet,' Emily said calmingly. 'Just sit yourself down and get this inside you. I'll tell you when it's time to go for the nurse.'

Jamie obediently did as he was told although he never once took his eyes off his wife and was as nervy as a cat on hot bricks. Amazingly little Connie was still sleeping like a top, so at least he didn't have to worry about her as well.

Just before ten o'clock, Emily told him, 'I reckon it's time to fetch her now, pet. This little 'un seems to be very keen to put in an appearance.'

Jamie was off like a shot, his face as white as chalk. While he was gone, Emily helped Flora into bed while she huffed and puffed through yet another contraction.

'I . . . I feel like I want to push,' Flora croaked as they heard a coach pull up outside.

Sunday's voice floated up the stairs soon afterwards. 'Hello, are you in?'

'We're up here, come on up,' Emily shouted and the next minute Sunday appeared in the bedroom door looking very elegant and sophisticated in an ankle-length two-piece costume and a matching hat.

'Y-you'd best go on without us,' Flora grunted through her pains. 'I, er . . . seem to be otherwise engaged.'

'What? Go and miss this, not on your nelly!' Sunday said and pulling her hat off she sent it sailing across the room before hurrying towards the bed.

'I . . . I *do* need to push,' Flora yelped then as she went red in the face and Sunday caught her hand and gripped it as Emily yanked the bed clothes back to have a look what was happening.

'Good Lord . . . I can see the baby's head,' she said in amazement as she hastily rolled her sleeves up. 'That's it, pet. Now . . . on the next pain *push* as hard as ever you can . . . That's it . . . good girl . . . and *again*!'

Unbidden Flora's mind flew back to the birth of her little boy the previous year and she began to panic. What if that happened again? It had been her biggest fear throughout this pregnancy, although she had never admitted it to anyone.

She squirmed on the bed. 'I . . . I can't do it,' she whimpered through gritted teeth. 'Where's the midwife?'

'Never mind about her for now, you've got me,' her mother told her calmly. 'An' you of all people should know how many babies I've helped into the world. Now come on, girl! Push for all you're worth, we're almost there!'

And so Flora dropped her chin to her chest and strained with all her might and suddenly, with one last push, a newborn baby's wail echoed around the room and it was surely the most beautiful sound she had ever heard.

'Wh-what is it? Is it all right?' she asked weakly as she dropped back onto the pillows.

Sunday was crying tears of joy as Emily hastily cut the cord and wrapped the baby in a towel she had laid ready before handing the babe to its mother just as Jamie and the midwife burst into the room.

'I'm afraid you're a bit late,' Emily told them with a broad smile. 'Jamie, come and say hello to your brand-new little son. He's a whopper and a little beauty into the bargain.'

Jamie stopped dead in his tracks as he looked towards the bed where Flora was cradling her new son with a look of pure delight on her face.

'Oh, Jamie, he looks just like you,' she breathed as he approached the bed. 'I thought we could call him James Thomas?'

Too full of emotion to speak, Jamie nodded his happy approval and at that moment little Connie appeared in the doorway knuckling the sleep from her eyes and demanded, 'Where's my breakfast? I'm hungry.' Then seeing what her mother held in her arms she moved to the bed and slipped her tiny hand into her father's.

'Has the stork brought our new baby, Daddy?' she asked innocently and tears of pure joy sprang to Jamie's eyes as he nodded.

'Yes, sweetheart. The stork brought you a brand-new baby brother to love.'

'Shall we go an' leave this little family to get acquainted, ladies?' Emily asked. 'I don't know about you but I could murder a cup o' tea. Me mouth's as dry as the bottom of a bird cage!'

Sunday and Emily edged towards the door with the midwife close behind. Downstairs, Emily was pouring the tea when Sunday began to giggle. 'Well, I have to say the present she's given us for Mother's Day this year is going to take some beating, isn't it? It's isn't every Mother's Day you get presented with a lovely little grandson, is it?'

Emily nodded in agreement and they all smiled and raised their mugs in a toast to the beautiful new member of the family.

'To our new little beauty, James Thomas Branning,' Sunday said and they clinked their mugs together as they thought of the new little soul they had been blessed with, nestling safe and sound in his mother's arms upstairs. It would certainly be a Mother's Day none of them would ever forget.

Acknowledgements

Once again I would like to say a very big thank you to my brilliant team at Bonnier, to Eli, Sarah, Kate, James and Nico, and each and every one of you who works so hard to make the books I write the best they can be. Special thanks too to my brilliant copy editor, Gillian Holmes, who helps me to give the books their final 'polish'. Never forgetting my wonderful agent Sheila Crowley at Curtis Brown and her lovely assistant Abbie, who are always there if I need them. I am so lucky to work with such a great team of people.

Finally, of course, a massive thank you to my readers, who make my day when they get in touch on social media to tell me how much they have enjoyed my efforts. You all make every hour I spend locked away in my office with my imaginary characters worthwhile!

·MEMORY LANE·

Welcome to the world of Rosie Goodwin!

Keep reading for more from Rosie Goodwin, to discover
a recipe that features in this novel and to read a sneak peek
of the first chapter of Rosie's next novel . . .

We'd also like to introduce you to MEMORY LANE, our special
community for the very best of saga writing from authors you
know and love, and new ones we simply can't wait for you to
meet. Read on and join our club!

·MEMORY LANE·

www.MemoryLane.club

Dear Readers,

Summer is upon us. At last! I hope you are all enjoying it.

In this, book five of the series, *A Maiden's Voyage*, you're going to meet Flora. According to the rhyme, 'Thursday's child has far to go'. As it happens, I'm a Thursday's child myself, and the rhyme got me thinking – where should I take her? And then it came to me in a flash: let's go a little further afield and visit New York. Better still, let's have a voyage on the *Titanic*.

When our children were young, a very dear friend of mine and I used to joke and say that when they were older we would go off to New York on our own. Some years ago she was diagnosed with cancer and it broke my heart that we hadn't got to go. It was then our husbands suggested, 'go now while she's well enough'. Sure enough, the very next week saw us on a flight to New York.

What a wonderful break that was. We did lots of sight-seeing, including trips to Battery Park, The Statue of Liberty, The Empire State Building and Central Park, to name but a few – although I admit we also spent an awful lot of time in Macy's. Wow! The shoe department in there is every woman's heaven.

I'm very happy to report that my friend is still with us. She has put up a valiant fight against this horrible disease and is a real inspiration.

From the second the idea for this book occurred to me, it was plain sailing all the way – excuse the pun. As always, I've put poor Flora through the mill, and this book just seemed to flow along as if it was writing itself. I must admit that whilst doing the research on the sinking of the *Titanic* I found myself in tears. It's impossible to imagine how awful and terrifying it must have been for all aboard, but I loved writing it and bringing all the characters to life. I hope that you will all love reading it too.

The hardback edition of this book, which came out in March, got wonderful reviews from you lovely readers, so I really hope those of you who have been waiting for the paperback edition will enjoy it too!

As always, I shall be eagerly waiting to hear what you think about it. Your messages always make my day and I love hearing from you all.

And so all that remains for now is to wish you all a very happy summer! I hope some of you get to read the book lying on a lovely sandy beach somewhere as you lap up the sun with a nice glass of wine in your hand. Meanwhile, I am busy putting the finishing touches to the next one, book six of the series, which will be out for Christmas, and is aptly called *A Precious Gift*!

· MEMORY LANE ·

If you enjoyed *A Maiden's Voyage*, please do share your thoughts on the Memory Lane Facebook page 🄵 MemoryLaneClub.

Take care and much love to you all,

Rosie

xx

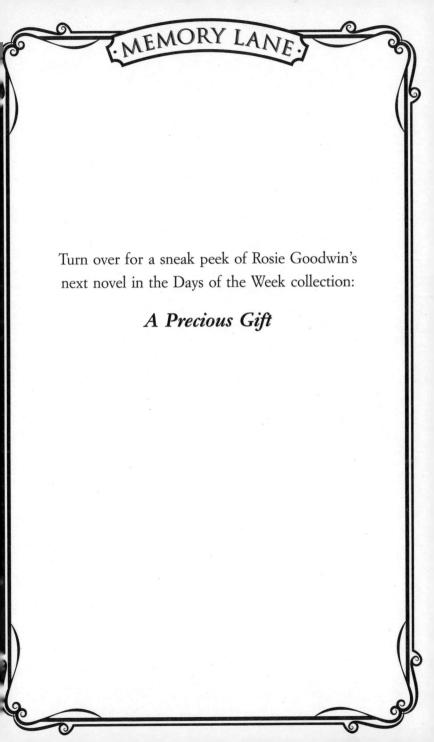

· MEMORY LANE ·

Turn over for a sneak peek of Rosie Goodwin's
next novel in the Days of the Week collection:

A Precious Gift

Prologue

Nuneaton, December 1911

'Miss Holly, the master and the mistress said I was to tell you that you're wanted in the drawing room the second you came in.'

Holly Farthing frowned as she handed her hat and coat to Ivy, the maid. She nodded. 'Thank you, Ivy.'

After quickly tidying her hair in the mirror in the hallway and smoothing her skirt, she approached the drawing room, wondering what it could be that they wanted. Her grandfather rarely sent for her and when he did it usually meant trouble, which was why she had learned to keep out of his way as much as possible.

Taking a deep breath, she entered the room to find her mother standing at the window, wringing her hands, a sure sign that something was amiss. Her grandfather was sitting in a wing chair at the side of a roaring fire and the second he set eyes on her, his lips set in a grim line. He was a tall man with a rigid posture who, although advanced in years, was still handsome, boasting a full head of steel-grey hair, a thick beard and piercing blue eyes. Holly briefly wondered why he seemed to dislike her so. She and her mother had lived with him since her mother had been widowed when Holly was just a baby and she could never remember him saying so much as one kind word to her. As a child it had troubled her greatly but now, at eighteen years old, she had become accustomed to his surly ways.

'Ivy told me you wished to see me?'

'Yes, dear. Your grandfather has something he must tell you. Won't you sit down?' Her mother gestured to a chair identical to the one her grandfather favoured on the other side of the fireplace, and Holly perched on the edge of it, folding her hands primly in her lap.

For a second the old man narrowed his piercing blue eyes and stared at her before beginning, 'The thing is, you're eighteen years old now, so I've been thinking it's high time you were married. I've kept you an' your mother for long enough.'

Holly's deep blue eyes stretched wide as she stared back at him; she was so shocked that for a moment she was speechless.

'M-married?' she stuttered eventually. 'And do you have someone in mind, Grandfather?'

'As it happens I do, an' you'll meet him tonight. He owns a big hat factory in Atherstone and he's recently widowed with three young children who need a mother. I've invited him to dinner.'

Colour flooded into Holly's cheeks as she stared steadily back at him. 'And may I know the gentleman's name?'

'Dolby, Walter Dolby. That's all you need to know for now, except that you'll be set up for life with him; he ain't short of a bob or two. So just make sure you mind your manners when he arrives and we'll take it from there.'

Holly opened her mouth to protest but clamped it shut again as her mother gave her a warning glance.

'Will that be all?' She stood up, her straight back and rigid stance an indication of how angry and upset she was. It wasn't lost on her grandfather and he leaned forward in his chair, his hands tightly gripping the arms.

'Don't look at me like that, girl,' he barked, making Holly's mother visibly start. 'There's many a man would have seen both you an' your mother out on the streets, but I've kept you fed and clothed with a roof over your head for all these years.'

Holly merely inclined her head and, turning, left the room, closing the door softly behind her. In the hallway she almost collided with Ivy, who had clearly been listening at the door. Quickly straightening her mop cap, which was askew, the girl gave her a guilty smile and stepped aside. Normally Holly would have found it funny but today she was so angry and upset that she couldn't even raise a smile. Life as she had known it was about to change forever, and it was completely out of her control. Brushing past her, she stalked to the stairs without giving Ivy so much as a second glance. She was halfway up when the drawing room door opened again and her mother chased after her.

'I'll talk to you in a minute,' she hissed up the stairs. 'He's going back to the mill shortly and then we'll be able to talk in private.'

Holly nodded and hurried on her way, too shocked to even answer. Once in the privacy of her room she let out a sigh and flopped down onto the side of her bed.

Married! Her grandfather wanted her to be married, and worse still to someone she had never even met. Rising, she began to pace the floor. As soon as she heard the front door slam, she peeped from the window and watched her grandfather climb into the coach that the groom had fetched from the stables at the back of the house and leave for the mill he owned in Attleborough. Seconds later a tap came on her bedroom door and her mother appeared looking pale and terribly upset.

'Oh, darling, I'm so sorry,' she muttered, rushing over to Holly and wrapping her arms about her slim figure. 'I had no idea he had this in mind until he told me this morning.'

Holly wriggled free of the embrace and resumed her pacing. 'Well, you know the old saying, you can lead a horse to water but you can't make it drink,' she spat, with a toss of her head.

Her mother chewed on her lip as she watched her precious girl marching up and down as if she was trying to wear a hole in the carpet.

'P-perhaps Walter will be nice?' she suggested softly, and Holly snorted in disgust.

'Nice! Is that a good enough reason to marry someone you don't know, just because they're nice? It sounds to me like this Mr Dolby is merely looking for a replacement mother for his children, but I'll tell you now, it won't be me! When and if I ever marry it will be because I love the person, not because Grandfather has ordered it!'

'Oh darling, I'm so sorry.' Her mother was openly crying now and Holly's mood softened slightly. She'd lost count of the times she'd seen her grandfather make her mother cry with his harsh words and often wondered why she allowed him to be so hard on her. It was as if he had some sort of a hold over her and she was afraid of him.

'Look . . . I'll go through with this farce and meet him for your sake,' Holly reluctantly agreed. 'But I warn you, if I don't like him, nothing will induce me to see him again, let alone marry him!'

Her mother nodded helplessly. 'In that case we must look in your wardrobe and decide what you should wear. You'll want to look your best.'

'I will not!' Holly disagreed with a glare. 'Why should I dress myself up like a dog's dinner for a stranger? He'll take me as I am or lump it!'

'All right, dear, whatever you say.' Afraid to say another word, her mother turned and quietly scuttled from the room like a frightened mouse. Crossing to the cheval mirror that stood to one side of the four-poster bed, Holly stared at her reflection. A serious young woman with unruly long, blonde curly hair and periwinkle blue eyes that were fringed with thick, fair lashes stared solemnly back at her. It was almost as if she was staring at a younger version of her mother, for they had the same fair hair and eyes. Holly was trying to see herself as Walter Dolby might see her and she supposed that she was reasonably attractive, although she would never term herself as beautiful. She was slightly too tall and slender for a girl and whilst her complexion was clear she considered her mouth to be a little too wide and her nose too snub. Yet another tap on the door interrupted her thoughts and Ivy appeared, looking worried.

'I just thought I'd pop up and check you're all right,' she said cautiously. Holly usually enjoyed her chats with Ivy, and because she had been tutored at home and so never mixed much with people her own age, the maid was the closest thing to a friend Holly had ever had. They were complete opposites in looks for Ivy was short and inclined to be skinny with mousy straight hair and grey eyes, but what she lacked in looks she more than made up for in personality. She often had Holly roaring with laughter as she spoke of her family. She came from a large family – eleven in all – and when she had first started working at the house as a maid at the age of fourteen, she declared she felt as if she had died and gone to heaven. She was paid a pittance and was often expected to work all the hours God sent, but despite that, for the first time in her life she had a room all to herself and regular meals, so she considered herself very lucky.

'We're all crammed into a tiny cottage, two up, two down in the courtyards in Abbey Street,' she had once told Holly bitterly. 'Crammed in like sardines in a bloody tin, we are.' She had flushed then and apologised for swearing, much to Holly's amusement. She usually provided a breath of fresh air in her grandfather's rather formal household, but today Holly wasn't in the mood to speak to anyone.

'Why wouldn't I be?' Holly instantly felt guilty for snapping. None of this was Ivy's fault after all. She sighed. 'Sorry, Ivy, I take it you heard what was said, then?'

Ivy nodded vigorously, setting her mop cap dancing as if it had a life of its own. 'I couldn't help it, I were polishin' the hall table an' I just want to tell yer I think it's bloody awful what yer gran'father is proposin'.'

Holly shrugged. 'Aw well, there's nothing for it but to meet the chap, I suppose, but don't get worrying. Before I've even met him I can tell you I have no intention of marrying him, whether it upsets Grandfather or not.'

Ivy gave her a smile, then, glancing at the door, she told her, 'I'd best get on. I've just been told to lay the table in the dinin' room wi' all the best silver an' china. Poor old Cook is runnin' round like a headless chicken tryin' to get everythin' ready an' the mood she's in I don't want to go upsettin' her.'

'It's all right, you get on, I'm fine,' Holly assured her, and once the girl had gone she lifted a book and tried to read. Unfortunately her head was so full of meeting Mr Dolby that all the words kept blurring into one, so eventually she gave up and went to sit by the window. It looked set to be a very long day, and an even longer night.

Early that evening the first snow began to flutter down. It was no surprise; they had been expecting it for the last week but Holly hoped that it might put Mr Dolby off.

At seven o'clock precisely she went downstairs to find her mother and grandfather in the drawing room.

'Is that the best you could find to put on?' her grandfather snapped, as he stared at the plain grey dress she was wearing. 'And couldn't you have done something a little bit more elaborate with your hair instead of scraping it back into a ribbon!'

Holly shrugged. 'I'm perfectly clean and tidy,' she answered, but she had no time to say anything else, for just then they heard the doorbell ring and Ivy hurrying along the hallway to answer it. Holly suddenly felt sick and the colour drained from her cheeks as she heard Ivy taking the man's hat and coat.

'They're waitin' for you in the drawin' room, sir,' they heard her say, and the next minute Holly's worst fears were realised when Mr Dolby appeared in the doorway and gave a polite little bow towards herself and her mother.

'Good evening, Mrs Farthing, Miss Farthing, Gilbert.'

'Come on in, Walter,' Gilbert Mason boomed in a jovial voice. 'You're just in time for a drink before we go in to dinner. Now, what will it be? Whisky, brandy or perhaps you'd like a glass of wine?'

While her grandfather was pouring the drinks, Holly had time to study Walter Dolby from the corner of her eye and her heart sank. *He must be forty at least, if he's a day*, she thought glumly; even older than her mother. And he certainly hadn't been at the front of the queue when looks were handed out, although he seemed to be kindly enough. In fact, he looked almost as uncomfortable as she felt. Mr Dolby was tall and thin with a large moustache that wobbled on his top lip. His dark hair was streaked with grey and his nose seemed to cover half his face and Holly knew instantly that she could never marry him. He was old enough to be her father at least, no matter how friendly he was.

The next twenty minutes were spent in stilted conversation, which Holly deliberately didn't participate in, unless a question was directed at her, in which case she answered to avoid appearing rude, and she breathed a sigh of relief when Ivy finally came to tell them that dinner was ready.

Mr Dolby offered her his arm, which she reluctantly took, and led her into the dining room where he pulled a chair out for her and then, to her dismay, sat down next to her.

The meal that followed was excellent. A thick, warming pea soup was followed by a beef dinner with all the trimmings that had been cooked to perfection. For dessert, Cook had made one of her special sherry trifles, and this was followed by coffee and biscuits. Normally Holly would have thoroughly enjoyed it but tonight she hardly ate a thing. The food seemed to stick in her throat and the smell of the oil on Mr Dolby's hair made her feel nauseous.

'So, Miss Farthing, or may I call you Holly? Your grandfather tells me that you'll be starting a Red Cross course after Christmas.

Holly nodded. 'Yes, I'm greatly looking forward to it. In fact my greatest ambition is to become a nurse.'

'Really?' He looked astounded. 'But surely a woman's place is at home, running the house and caring for her children?'

'I believe that tradition is becoming rather outdated now,' Holly informed him haughtily, dabbing at her mouth with a crisp, white napkin. 'More and more women are pursuing careers, and of course there are the suffragettes who believe that women should have equality and the right to vote.'

'Don't you dare talk about those hussies at my table! They're a disgrace to their sex, chaining themselves to railings and smashing shop windows,' her grandfather growled, before giving Walter Dolby an apologetic smile. 'I do apologise for my granddaughter, Walter. I'm afraid she's at that age where she is very susceptible to these silly modern ideas. But for all that, I think she'll make someone a wonderful wife. She's more than capable of running a house and she's quite a fine pianist too.'

Angry colour rose in Holly's cheeks. Her grandfather was talking about her as if she wasn't even in the room, and to make things worse she could see that her mother was becoming increasingly agitated – so much so that at that moment she tipped a glass of red wine all over the tablecloth.

'Oh dear,' Emma flustered. 'Now look what I've done.' She was dabbing ineffectively at the scarlet stain that was slowly spreading across the crisp, linen cloth.

'Leave it,' her father ordered shortly, and Holly stared at him resentfully. She had always thought that her grandfather was an attractive man, with his full beard and thatch of grey hair, but it suddenly hit her that he was aging. His back was becoming slightly stooped and for the first time she noticed the lines around his eyes. His once firm stomach had turned into a slight paunch, no doubt caused by the port he was so fond of, and suddenly she could stand it no longer.

Standing so abruptly that she almost overturned her chair, she glared at him. 'If you will excuse me, I'm afraid I have rather a bad headache so I think I'll retire.' Then, before her grandfather could object, she turned to Mr Dolby and held out her hand. 'Good evening, sir.' She swept away with her head held high, but once she had reached the safety of her room, she took a long, deep breath and flattened herself against the door as the tears finally came. Walter Dolby seemed a pleasant enough man but the thought of having to be intimate with him turned her stomach.

I shan't marry him no matter what Grandfather threatens, she silently told herself, then, throwing herself onto the bed, she sobbed.

She was still there almost an hour later when her mother tentatively tapped on the door before entering. 'Oh, Holly, your grandfather is very angry with you for charging off like that. Didn't you like Mr Dolby?'

'Like him!' Holly stared at her incredulously. 'It's nothing to do with liking – the man is old enough to be my father, older even than you, I wouldn't mind betting.'

'Even so, you were rather rude leaving so abruptly,' her mother said gently.

'Good! I hope it made him realise I'm not good wife material then,' Holly answered rebelliously.

'Unfortunately it didn't. In fact he remarked that he found you quite charming, and so your grandfather asked if he might like to call again next week to see you.'

Holly groaned aloud. 'Well in that case I shall just have to be honest with him and tell him that there's no chance of me ever marrying him.'

'B-but your grandfather . . . He's going to be very angry with you if you do that. He's even saying that if you don't go along with his wishes on this, he'll turn you out onto the streets.'

'So be it.' Holly swiped the remainder of her tears away on the sleeve of her dress. Of one thing she was sure: she would sooner be homeless and sleep in shop doorways than ever be tied to Walter Dolby!

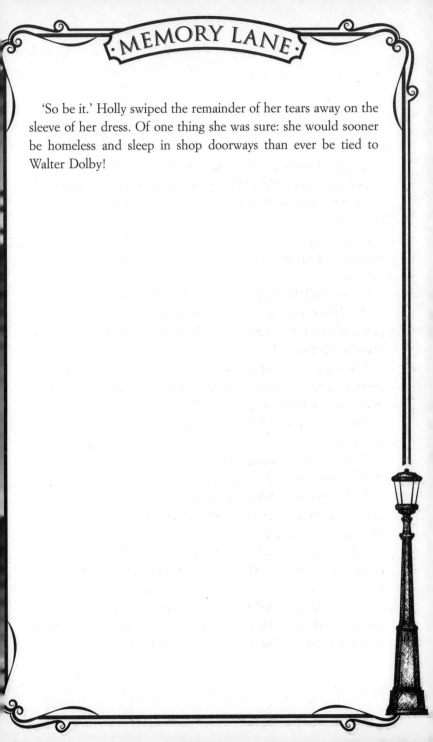

Jai Li's Chinese Curry

This delicious dish, inspired by Jai Li's famous curry which amazed Colleen and Flora, not only tastes incredible but will also bring the aromatic scents of Chinatown to your kitchen.

You will need:

2 tbsp coconut oil
1 medium onion, diced
1 garlic clove, crushed
2 tsp curry powder
1 tsp turmeric
½ tsp ground ginger
1 red chilli, sliced (optional – if you like it hot!)
Pinch of sugar
400ml chicken stock
1 tsp soy sauce
4 chicken breasts, cut into chunks
2 tsp cornflour
Handful frozen peas
Juice of 1 lemon
Rice to serve

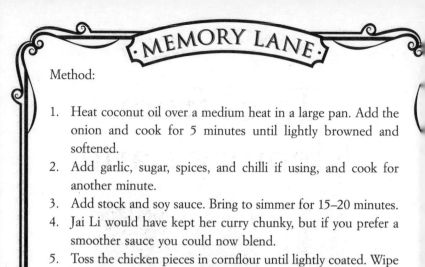

Method:

1. Heat coconut oil over a medium heat in a large pan. Add the onion and cook for 5 minutes until lightly browned and softened.

2. Add garlic, sugar, spices, and chilli if using, and cook for another minute.

3. Add stock and soy sauce. Bring to simmer for 15–20 minutes.

4. Jai Li would have kept her curry chunky, but if you prefer a smoother sauce you could now blend.

5. Toss the chicken pieces in cornflour until lightly coated. Wipe out the pan and fry the chicken in the remaining oil until brown and cooked through.

6. Tip the sauce back in and bring the whole dish to a simmer. Stir in the frozen peas and cook for 5 minutes. Squeeze over the juice of a lemon.

7. Serve with fluffy boiled rice and enjoy!

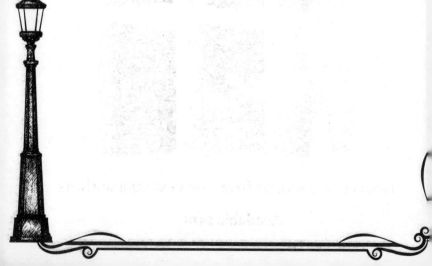

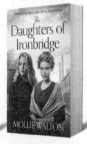